Initiation

Charnaye Conner

B.O.Y. Publications, Inc.
P.O. Box 262
Lowell, NC 28098
www.alwaysbetonyourself.com

Paperback ISBN: 978-1-955605-67-0

Cover and Interior Design: B.O.Y. Enterprises, Inc.

Printed in the United States of America

Dedication

Thank you, God, for this opportunity and for this gift. This book is dedicated to my mother Denise who always believed in me and supported me; the rest of my family, Pop, Rocky and Diamond who listened to me tell this story verbally; and to anyone out there who hasn't seen their dreams come true yet, hang in there.

~Chapter 1~

The loud music from downstairs vibrated the floor of the poker room. The red lights cast dark shadows along the floor. The cheap black plastic table vibrated from the bass. The chairs squeaked as they moved across the floor. The smell of sweat was heavy in the air and the nervousness was palpable. A small smirk played on my face as I looked down at the cards in my hand and then around the table where the five men were. The fat gray haired man looked at me over his glasses as he shakingly adjusted them. I couldn't pass up the moment to mess with him.

"Are you all right, Mr. Ito? You look nervous." I smirked. He looked at the other men around the table. The short red headed American man laughed loudly.

"I like this bitch! She's funny!" I looked over at him and chuckled. He was the only one in the room that was confident. I couldn't have that.

"You sound confident. Are you willing to raise the bet then Mr. Jankowski?"

There was fifty million yen in bets on the poker game. "You know what little one? I'll do it. I'll raise you thirty more." My grin expanded and I leaned forward crossing my arms on the table. I can leave here with eighty million yen that I wasn't expecting?! Hell yeah. I want that. I wondered if the bravado of these men would cause them to jump in as well. I looked over at the gray-haired man. He looked over at the other men to see what they would do. Ito shook his head and put his cards down. Bitch. The other men were deep in thought. The brown-haired Italian man nodded.

"Another thirty million. I'm in." he said in his thick accent. One hundred and ten million. The other two men agreed. One hundred and seventy million. Sold.

"I respect the courage, gentlemen." I put my chips in and grinned as I watched the others.

A rush of excitement filled my stomach. In US dollars, I just won a little more than 1.2 million dollars. That's a new car. Another house. Clothes. Bags. "Go ahead. New friends first." I offered. I gestured to the American first. Watching the men flip their cards, my grin widened. I won. "Royal Flush, boys. Read 'em and weep." I cackled as I flipped my cards to show them the winning hand. The men groaned in disappointment.

"You little minx! No fucking way!" the American yelled as he stood up in anger. In an instant, there were 3 men standing beside him with guns and they were pointed at me. I chuckled and crossed my legs, adjusting the black mini dress while the other men at the table tensed up. Two gunshots rang out and two of the men hit the floor. Panic crossed Jankowski's face as he jumped back and looked around.

"What the fuck!? What was that! Where did that come from?" he screamed.

From the shadows emerged a tall blue haired Japanese man. He wore a crooked smirk as he pointed his trusty Glock 17 at the foreigners. "Is there a problem, boss?" Code chuckled. I looked up at him and shrugged.

"Mr. Jankowski, you tell me. Do we have a problem? I thought we were playing poker." He remained frozen in fear. My grin widened at the sight. There was such a rush of pride and satisfaction that ran through me at his expression.

"I don't know, Code. We were having fun. I won. Next thing you know. Guns. I'm shocked honestly. I didn't see this coming." I pretended to be clueless. An evil smirk crossed my face as I watched the fear turn into terror. I laughed loudly as the other men at the table sat frozen. It's so sad that men can't take a loss. Code smirked as he looked at the foreigner again.

"She asked you if there was a problem, sir. I would answer her." Code growled.

"I-I-I... N-no... It was a misunderstanding...I-" Jankowski stammered as the color drained from his face.

"I frankly don't give a damn. There's only one way this ends. You're going to die. But I want my money first. So, let's make this shit quick." I said as I stared at him. The foreigner tapped his last bodyguard and nodded his head. The guard moved to grab a briefcase and put it on the table.

"Open it and turn it to me." I demanded. I slowly reached into Code's waistband and pulled out my gun. Once the briefcase was opened and turned, I aimed and shot Jankowski right between the eyes. Code killed the last bodyguard. I stood up and readjusted my dress.

"I hate sore losers. Shit's annoying. Why are men like that Code?" I questioned as I grabbed my purse. I suddenly remembered the other men at the table. I looked back at the remaining men at the table who were still frozen in fear and staring at me wide eyed. That aggravated me. I fired four more shots. More money for me.

"Damn Rose. Was that necessary? They were innocent bystanders." Code laughed as he put his gun away and started to collect the money.

"They were annoying. Especially the fat one. Grab the money from them too. I'm going to get the earnings from the club. Meet me at the car." I commanded as I left the room without another word.

I made my way down the stairs to the first floor where the electronic music was loudest. The bodies parted for me as I made my way through the floor. The VIP section was separated by red velvet ropes and beside one of the couches was an entrance to a hallway. Large burly guards stood in front of the ropes. They were talking with some girls in the section and upon seeing me they scrambled to stand up straight and bowed in respect. I nodded in acknowledgement. "Where's Aoi?" I asked plainly.

"In his office. I'll take you, Miss Rose," the guard on the right said as he let me through the ropes. The one on the left led me down the hall to another section of doors. The first door on the left is where he stopped. He knocked on the door and a shrill and enthusiastic voice replied with an order to enter. I slammed the door open and marched into the room as the man in the chair spun around to see me. He stumbled when he saw me.

"M-M-Miss Rose! How are you? You look beautiful tonight! How can I help?" he exclaimed as he climbed off his chair and walked up to me carefully.

I scoffed. He was short and fat with messy black hair and a cheap suit. He smelled like sweat and cheap cologne. I chose not to address the smell this time. "Aoi. I'm here for our cut. I have no time for your cheap suits or funny smells today," I replied as I looked down on him. He turned bright red and stopped in his tracks. He nodded in understanding.

"Of course! I'll get right on that! One moment, ma'am." He scurried off to another room. I walked to sit at his desk and put my feet up. I picked up one of the small statutes on his desk to examine it. It was the shape of a naked woman. I rolled my eyes and put it down. "Fucking weirdo." I whispered to myself.

I noticed the large cheetah print clock on the wall and looked at the time, I yawned. Another late night in Tokyo. Another collection night. I was running on 3 hours of sleep from the previous night. The side door opened and Aoi returned to the room with a cart. There were 15 black briefcases on the cart. I groaned loudly in annoyance.

"Damn you, Aoi. You couldn't put the money in bigger briefcases? You know what, nevermind. It's fine. You got my invoices? Did you make sure they're not fucked up this time?" I critiqued as I scowled at him.

"I did it right this time. I apologize about last time. I had all the girls count it for me. We're good." Aoi bowed in apology.

"Hopefully we don't have a repeat of last time. Take it to the car. Code's outside." I warned as I looked at him sharply. He shivered in fear and looked away to push the cart out the back door. I texted Code and told him to come to the back of the club. He responded that he was already there.

I stood up and turned to pick up the statue again. I smirked and threw it to the ground, watching it shatter. Whoops. When I walked outside, Code was standing by the car holding the back car door open for me. The trunk was open and Aoi was putting the money inside. I nodded in approval. I liked seeing sights like this. It was a reminder of how much power I held. It was addictive in the best way. "You're five hundred million yen richer, congratulations." Code chuckled. "You can have fifty million. Consider it as a bonus." I replied as I got in the car and he shut the door and he went to the driver's seat. Aoi knocked on the window and I rolled it down.

"I finished up! Here's the paperwork. Is there anything else you need?" Aoi smiled pathetically.

"No. You have a mess in the poker room though. Bastards stepped out of line." I replied as I rolled up the window before he answered. Code pulled off to begin the ride home. I pulled out my phone and started to scroll through the Chanel website.

"Are we done for the day or another stop, Rose?" I shook my head. I wanted to be in the comfort of my home. I had enough of the loud music and all of the crowds. I wanted to be in silence.

"I'm done for the night. I need you to drop the money off and have it counted. Get it to where it needs to go." I answered. Code hummed in agreement. Code had been in my life for as long as I could remember. He was a big part of my training. We did assignments and completed missions together for years. We compliment each other. He was always ready for a fight. Always ready to kill. He was fiercely loyal and charming. He stayed out of my way while I led. My position and power didn't intimidate him.

He doesn't require much direction. I liked that about him. He understands my goals and wants, and he gets it done. I gave him free reign to complete his tasks however he saw fit. He loved the freedom that I gave him. He could be as destructive as he wanted to be. When I rose through the ranks of the Yamaguchi, it made sense to bring Code with me. He became my wakashagira. And together we built a thriving and strong clan in the Yamaguchi. When there's enough money and power, getting what is wanted is easy. We didn't use any tactics that were too different from what the Yakuza is known for. We provide what people need. If someone needs money to fund a political campaign, I can arrange that. But once the money is taken, I own them. They owe the clan. If we call for a favor, it must be done or there are consequences.

That's how the Yakuza has been integrated into Japanese society. We have built institutions, businesses, government agencies that people need and want. Whether they admit it or not. Every syndicate has had its own personal role in the integration. We never had an overwhelming outward presence in the world. It was always in the background and subtle. It always makes me laugh when big company CEOs share their success stories on their websites and in magazines or whatever, about how they worked oh so hard to build their multimillion-dollar businesses. I laughed because I know the truth. The truth is the Yamaguchi or another syndicate, funded the business; we invested the money or loaned the money. I have seen it happen.

I, personally, am on the payroll of 15 businesses that I gave money to or loaned money to. I sit on 9 corporate boards where I help make decisions about the direction of the business. Help isn't really the right word to use. I'm the deciding factor. It's my decision. It always is. I have taken over 3 businesses just this year simply because I wanted to. I just wanted more money. It's a lucrative business. The world is at my feet and I loved the power it gave me. Nothing felt like it. I was proud of it.

I looked out of the window as the car drove through the Tokyo night. It's a genuinely beautiful city. I liked it here. I moved to Tokyo six years ago when I took the position of Saiko Komon. Before my official title, I was special because I was also the Yakuza's designated and most trusted assassin. It was common for other syndicates to pay for my services if they needed someone taken care of despite belonging to the Yamaguchi syndicate. Much of my training happened in Kobe, the headquarters of the Yamaguchi. It started at a very young age. I wasn't in school with other kids at 4 or 5. I was sitting in Judo classes, Jujutsu classes, any type of fighting classes available. I mastered each and every fighting style there is. I could shoot a gun before I could ride a bike. I started training with weapons at 8. It was small revolvers at first.

I was smaller in stature as a child so I didn't start working with Glocks and rifles until about 11 or 12. Even though I worked with revolvers, I still proved to be an expert marksman. It was set in stone at a young age that I was going to be active in the Yakuza. In what capacity, Code and I didn't know back then. We just knew it was going to happen. My father, Han, knew though. With him being the Kumicho, the boss of the Yamaguchi, there was no way I was avoiding this life. He made sure of it. I was homeschooled and my learning was structured around my training schedule.

As I grew up, Han never made any mention of our relationship. So, I learned to do the same. It was a secret between him, Code, and me. Han handpicked Code to help train me and that is a big deal. Han is the type of man where money and power drives him. Especially the opportunity and thought of more money and more power. Han chooses people who will help him achieve that. My training was dedicated to making sure I was the best at everything and anything. Anything that could be used to bring him power and money. In addition to the physical training, it was important for me to learn strategy, finances, and business, so I could learn how to take care of money and learn the inner workings of the Yamaguchi. It was that foundation that led me to become a ranking member of the Yamaguchi. I was built for it. I was molded for it.

"Rose. We're here." Code called as he looked up at me through the rearview mirror. I looked around and internally sighed in relief, seeing I was back home. I watched as he got out of the car and came to open my door. He handed the briefcase from the poker game and bowed. "I took the liberty of adding all the money into one briefcase from the poker room. A good night of poker I'd say, Boss," he chuckled.

"A very good night," I agreed as I sent him off and started the walk to my house. I heard the car speed off as I walked up the driveway. The driveway to my house was long. It led through a small, wooded area for 1.6 kilometers. Once the trees broke, my 914-meter squared villa stood alone. The exterior paint was licorice black, and the flat roof was slate gray. The walkway up to the house was made of gray flagstone and led to the elevated front porch with two columns that were painted the same licorice black color. The four steps up were slate gray. Black and gray are comfortable colors for me. Much of the inside is black and gray as well. The floorboards are gray throughout the villa and parts of the kitchen, living room and dining room had wooden wall panels. That's the closest to color I have.

In this profession, it doesn't leave me with room for many things. The dark and secrecy of my life became normal. In today's time, it's more convenient to present yourself as a normal member of society as opposed to saying you belong to the Yakuza. I just didn't have that luxury. I was marked in the government's system as a wanted person. The ramped-up police crackdowns on the Yakuza have had their effect on the organization as a whole. It has cost a lot of money. The blocking of accounts and laws passed have forced the organization to get smarter and work in the shadows more. In our business holdings, we have to keep surrogates in high profile positions to interact with the public. I know a couple of people who have been arrested because their surrogate betrayed them. Han's wakashigira, Kai, was recently released from prison after 5 years for that reason.

I try to tell everyone to change them out, but no one listens. I usually keep my surrogates in position for 2-3 years before I kill them and their families and replace them. It's easier to wipe out the bloodline. No one notices or suspects anything. One of the sad and heartbreaking tragedies in the city of Tokyo. Bad things happen to good people.

Walking into the living room, I placed the briefcase on the glass coffee table and unzipped my dress to remove it. Stepping out, I caught sight of the tag. Hmm. I didn't remember this dress being made by Versace. I examined the latex mini dress and shrugged before tossing it over my shoulder. I collapsed on the couch and opened the briefcase to count my earnings for the night. I grabbed my black finance book from under the table and got to work.

~Chapter 2~

My eyes flew open when I heard a branch snap outside. I snatched my gun from under the couch pillow and jumped up. The adrenaline that coursed through my body fought off the exhaustion that I felt. I tiptoed to the glass window on the left. No one should be here. I didn't send for Code, so who found my house? The blinds were closed, so I couldn't see who was on the other side. I pushed the button to roll the blinds back with my gun aimed ready to strike. I held my breath to steady my aim for the kill shot. The two bouncing black ponytails made me groan loudly. Fucking Remi. I lowered the gun and walked up to the glass, tapping on it harshly. She squealed and turned quickly to stare me down with wide brown eyes.

"What the fuck, Remi!?" I yelled. She blushed bright red and looked around. She looked like a child when she did that and I hated it. Her petite frame and baby face made it worse. She wore her hair in pigtails often and I couldn't give an explanation why. She hadn't answered me yet and that irritated me.

"Do you hear me, bitch? What are you doing creeping around my house?"

The kid was weird. She followed me everywhere when she first joined the clan. She was more of a fan than an asset, but Han took a liking to her, and he assigned her to me to train. It's been a waste of time, so I decided to make her a foot soldier doing errands for me. She was more like a secretary or personal assistant. It kept her away from anything of importance and out of my face. The three missions I took her on with me, she almost got me killed.

"I-I'm sorry, ma'am. I was told to meet Code here and I came the wrong way. He said the door was nearby." she squeaked out. She bowed as she apologized. A knock sounded at the door, and I rolled my eyes. "Door's all the way around, stupid. Go." She nodded quickly and scurried off. I walked to the door and opened it to see Code standing there.

"Morning. Hope you don't mind the interruption. We needed to speak." he nodded to my half-dressed form. I fell asleep on the couch while I was working. I waved him inside. "Refrain from messing with Remi. She almost died this morning." I suggested as he followed me inside.

"In my defense, she's gullible and it's funny. How was I supposed to know she would actually believe me when I said the front door was next to a window?" he chuckled, and I shook my head. Remi appeared at the door and stood there. I pinched my nose in annoyance.

"Come inside. Why are you standing there? We're in here." Code called as he waved her inside. He was too nice to her. She scurried inside to join us and she was smiling brightly like a puppy who did their first trick and wanted a treat. I really want to kick her sometimes. How can someone have that much innocence and be so naive? It just doesn't make sense. It made my blood boil.

I made my way into the kitchen and grabbed a bottle of vitamin water. "What's this about, Code? It's supposed to be my day off." I asked curtly. He cleared his throat and leaned against the wall. "This morning, I got a report that two arms deals were attacked last night. There were no survivors. Well technically, there was one who lived to tell us what happened, but he died from injuries earlier this morning. So we got nothing." he answered. I sighed deeply and downed the rest of the water with two painkillers. This was exhausting.

"That's five in the past two months. What the hell? You're talking about the ones in Nagoya and Kobe?" I clarified. Those areas were under different leaders, but I helped facilitate those two deals. I had just pulled some strings in the background to make sure they went through. Han controlled Kobe since that was the Yamaguchi headquarters. So, I was a little surprised to hear that his deal was attacked. I still didn't know what this had to do with me because it wasn't affecting my money. I kept listening though.

"Yes ma'am. So, of course, Han wants us in Kobe." Code confirmed. There it is. I haven't seen Han in almost 3 years face to face. However I am in the city fairly often because I have an office at headquarters, but we don't speak unless it's necessary. My title of saiko komon meant that I was Han's senior advisor and I helped handle the accounting as well. I helped manage all the Yamaguchi bank accounts and cash that we have on hand in the headquarters. The income from the legitimate businesses that we own; have stocks in or the money we smuggled in from people working inside of other corporations. The money we make from illegal trade and assassinations and other activities have their specific accounts that it goes to first and then I make sure the correct percentage gets to the main Yamaguchi account. The main Yamaguchi account funds our operation.

Every year I run the mandatory meeting with every clan head in the areas of our control. I know more about what happens in our syndicate and to us than Han does. Part of the reason why I had so much free reign and power in the ranks was because of that. It's hard to put a leash on someone or tell them no when they can ruin your life. It's an unspoken understanding between Han and I. As long as I secure our standing in the world by doing whatever it takes, I'm free to be as much of a menace to the world as I want. I can have whatever I want and do whatever I want.

I leaned on the kitchen counter and hummed in irritation at the news that he wanted to see me. "I hate seeing him…" I mumbled under my breath. I remembered a point in time when I didn't know Han was my dad. I was six years old and my surrogate mom of the month, Arisu, sat with me on the floor of my judo classroom. I was crying my eyes out because Han came to one class and watched a practice sparring session of mine and I lost. He wasn't pleased. He berated me in front of everyone and stormed out of the studio. Before he left, he made sure to threaten the teacher. He told the poor man to make me better or he'd kill everyone in the room. Class let out early that day. Arisu hugged me and told me my father just wanted the best for me. He just didn't know how to show it. She told me he loved me. I knew she was lying in the pit of my stomach, but at six years old it felt good to hear. Arisu was around for a few more years after that. Other women were too but Arisu was my favorite.

She had been there the longest, so for a while I assumed she was my mother. A small part of me chooses to believe that even still. Even though I know I'm wrong. I have no idea who she is. I've never had a conversation with him because he probably doesn't know himself. There's no need for it anyways. I'm an adult. "Rose? Are you all right?" I heard Remi's shrill voice break through my thoughts. I scowled at her. "Don't you have something you're supposed to be doing?" I snapped. She stared at me blankly.

"I'm supposed to be going to Kobe. Where's the train tickets?" Remi blushed and nodded before she ran off to do her job. Code watched in silence, and I looked over at him. "I'll wait for you to get ready and clean up for you." Code said quietly as he gestured to the money on the table. I nodded and made my way upstairs to my room.

Turning on the bathroom light, I took in my disheveled appearance. The makeup from last night was smudged, eye bags dark and heavy underneath my eyes and my maroon-colored hair was sticking up all over the place. I checked the clock in my room. It was 9:45am. I sighed heavily. At least I got almost five hours of sleep. I was getting barely enough sleep to keep my body up and moving. I was just waiting for the moment when my body would give up on me and force me to rest. Han could wait. I had to take care of this mess. I am still a twenty-five-year-old woman. I just have an unconventional job and life.

Using a wipe, I removed my makeup and washed my face. Luckily after days of wearing makeup, my skin was still clear. I gathered my hair into a high bun. In doing so I caught sight of the colorful ink in my tattoos. Turning slightly, the brightly colored red dragon circled around a red rose plant with large thorns revealed itself. It was my first tattoo and I got it at 18 to keep in line with the irezumi tradition. Then I just enjoyed getting them. It felt right to continue with the Yakuza theme in the rest of my body art. The dragon and rose tattoo was in the center of my back between my shoulder blades.

My most recent tattoo was located further down on the left side of my back near my kidney. It was a snake and oni mask in red and black ink with splashes of blue, yellow and green mixed in. The traditional meaning of enforcing codes wasn't what inspired the tattoo. Onis in Japanese mythology are demons that terrorize villages and snakes in folklore represent divine feminine attributes. It felt right for me. I'm considering more. After another quick glance at my tattoos, I turned on the shower and got in. A quick wash of my hair completed the shower. After applying lotion and blowing drying my hair, I slip on a pair of black leather pants, a black strapless corset and a cream-colored moto jacket with matching cream stiletto Jimmy Choo sandals. I grabbed a simple black Chanel bag with a chain and checked my appearance. Good to me.

It was an expectation that at headquarters you were put together and you were dressed sharp. You can't give the wrong impression to the other clans and any potential visiting families. Making my way downstairs, I found Code and Remi standing in the kitchen with onigiri sitting on a plate and they were eating. Remi almost choked when she saw me. I raised an eyebrow in confusion. "You look really pretty, Miss Rose! Sorry about that. I got food," Remi exclaimed. She blushed after the outburst.

"You're not so useless after all, kid. I'm starving," I said as I grabbed a piece. I had just realized how hungry I really was. I hadn't eaten since yesterday morning.

"The train leaves in an hour and a half so once you're done, we can go. We'll meet you in the car." Code bowed slightly as he looked over my figure once. He quickly turned away before he started staring and he dragged Remi away. I smirked. Men.

Over the years, Code and I had an on and off fling. It never led to anything. There's no time for any of that. I knew Code harbored some sort of romantic feelings for me, I just don't give a damn. I am incapable of giving him that and he knew that. Not that he had a choice. There's nothing wrong with Code. He's handsome. He's one of the tallest men I have ever met at 190 centimeters. He worked out every day, so he was physically attractive. Broad shoulders, a nice, developed chest and strong arms. He was physically perfect. He is equally cold and quick to kill just like me.

Money and power are just as important to him as they are to me. On paper anyone would say we would look good together. This life just doesn't allow for love. Especially not for me. There are members of the organization who are married and have children. But they're men.

This is a man's world, so the very few women in this life rarely have the ability to exert their power and influence. Being married or having children would just make it harder, so it was best to stay single. Societal pressures and expectations plague the organization and that makes it difficult for women to even get into the Yakuza. Even though Han was my father, I earned my status and position. I fought, manipulated, politicked and killed to get here. But of course there are rumors that suggest otherwise. I've heard that people thought I had been sleeping with Han. That's my personal favorite. It makes me laugh the hardest. It almost disgusted me the most. Most of the rumors about me say I slept around. I guess being pretty does give reasons for people to hate you.

I finished the onigiri and left the house. Code stood at the passenger door and opened it for me. He gave me a hand to help me step into the raised black SUV. He closed the door and went around to the driver's seat. Pulling out of the driveway, we started the journey to the train station. About 30 minutes into the drive, Remi started talking. "Miss Rose. Can I ask you something?" she asked. I sighed. I just wanted to nap.

"I'm sleeping." I answered.

"Just one question. Please?" I groaned and opened my eyes.

"What?"

"Can I borrow your jacket sometime?"

I scowled and looked over at Code and all he did was chuckle. I turned my head to the window and closed my eyes again.

"No. Stop talking to me. Nothing for the rest of the trip. I'm tired." I closed my eyes and began to drift off to sleep again.

I found myself sitting at a desk in an office overlooking the city in the middle of the night. I stood up and walked around the desk to see Han's body on the ground. A bullet hole in the middle of his forehead leaked fresh blood. He was wide eyed, and I could see the shock and underlying fear in his eyes. I stepped over his body and left the office. I opened the door to see the hallway on fire. I walked through the hallway watching everything burn around me. It was comforting for some reason. I felt calm and at peace. There was a strange sense of enjoyment watching everything burn this way. A door at the end of the hallway caught my eye. The fire didn't touch the door and I tilted my head intrigued. I walked towards the door and the cool air was refreshing. I reached out for the door handle, but just as I was about to open it I heard my name be called.

My eyes opened and I looked around. Code was staring at me with a strange expression on his face. "What? Why are you staring at me?" I snapped while sitting up.

"We're here. You were talking in your sleep. Are you okay?" Code asked.

"I'm fine. Let's go."

He nodded and came to the door to open it for me. I stepped out of the car. We made our way into the station to continue our journey.

~Chapter 3~

We arrived at headquarters around 4pm. I made my way up the steps and the two guards dressed in sharp black suits with black shades bowed. "Rose. Han has been expecting you." the guard on the left said. I nodded in acknowledgement. The Yamaguchi headquarters is a large business building in Kobe. It was 35 floors, and the top 7 floors were designed for us. The other floors were rented out to businesses for their usage. Another stream of income for us. The doors were opened for us, and we walked into the building. The receptionist greeted us, but I ignored her. Knowing that Han was on the top floor was causing my heart to race. My palms started to sweat, and my breath started to quicken. A nervous feeling started to settle in the pit of my stomach. I was starting to get a headache.

I could feel Code's eyes watching me and my demeanor change. I chose to ignore him. He would ask questions and I didn't want to be bothered. We entered the elevator, and I pushed the 35th button. Code pressed the 30th button. "We'll wait for you," he said quietly. I hummed. I prefer to do this alone anyways. I hated interacting with Han in front of others. It was awkward and tense constantly. It was not the image of unity that he so badly wanted to portray. The elevator ride was silent. The others left on their floor, and I continued on. The elevator doors opened on the 35th floor. I took a deep breath to try and calm my racing heart. An impending sense of danger started to come over me.

This floor looked like it belonged in an expensive hotel. Red lush carpet with gold designs lined the floor. The walls were painted a golden color with decorative red oval shaped sconce light fixtures. At the end of the hall was a lone door. There was nothing spectacular about it except for the four heavily armed bodyguards in front of it. A regular person would crumble under the tense atmosphere in the hall. Combined with the turmoil already happening internally, the tense atmosphere just added to it. There was a heaviness that sat on my chest and it was almost suffocating. I pushed my shoulders back and held my head up as I stepped off the elevator.

The guards bowed ninety degrees to me and I nodded in acknowledgement. One opened the door and announced my arrival. A gruff voice full of malice told me to enter. I stepped into the room as the door shut behind me. Han stood with his back to me. I fought to keep my face and voice neutral. He was average height but you could tell he was muscular under the long black suit coat he wore. Salt and pepper hair showed his age. I waited for him to say something. After a while he did. "Something is going on. And I don't like it." he said simply. I rolled my eyes.

"The deals being attacked? Or is something else going on?" I replied. He finally turned to face me. His face was stony. He gestured to a folder on his desk. I stepped forward to pick it up and I opened it. There were pictures of dead bodies and dates on them. Some of the men I recognized as a part of Han's inner circle. They were members and leaders of Yakuza syndicates and some were close associates of Han within the Yamaguchi. There were at least 15 bodies here. I looked up at Han waiting for more information. He gestured to another folder. I internally groaned and picked up the other folder. There were financial graphs from 2008 to January of 2022. The first graph was from 2011 to 2021. The graph was fairly stable. Slight drops here and there but nothing concerning. The second page was the graphs from 2008 to 2011 and these graphs were extremely off. There were large drops and we took a hit income wise.

"In late 2007, the global economy crashed as you probably remember. Every professional or expert that you ask will list numerous reasons why the crash happened. But none of them are completely true." Han walked to sit at his desk and sip his tea. He was dramatic. Everything he did was grandiose, and he spoke in a convoluted way. I folded my arms across my chest waiting for him to finish.

"Our financial advisors predicted the crash was coming. In order to get ahead of the crash and preserve our way of life and the country's economy. I met with the other leaders in the Yakuza," he continued. I was shocked by this. I've never heard of a time where the Yamaguchi worked with the other two largest syndicates in the Yakuza.

"We decided that stealing money would be the answer. Specifically steal from the United States banking system. That was a big task to pull off for just us. So, we reached out to the Jopok."

I raised an eyebrow confused. I was always taught that the Koreans were our sworn enemies. They had been our sworn enemies for years.

It's hard to believe that one time, we worked together. "The Jopok agreed. So by February of 2007, we had people in positions to smuggle and embezzle money from the US. Long story short, we accomplished the mission. Caused the largest investment bank in the US to file for bankruptcy. If I had to guess how much we got... Maybe 80 billion yen. Definitely enough to keep everything afloat. The money went into an account that the leaders had access to. Only the leaders knew the pins and codes. All the participants were back home by January of 2009," he paused looking down at the table.

"The agreement was 50/50. The Yamaguchi would, of course, split the 50% with the other families. Should have been easy and fair, right? Well it didn't happen that way. Those greedy bastards stole 70% of the profits and single handedly ruined any future cooperation between our ranks."

Logically, it made sense. If I missed out on thirteen billion yen. I'd never work with that person again. I'd kill them but that's neither here nor there. It would explain why the Koreans and us have so much animosity. What doesn't make sense is the relation to the dead bodies. None of this explained why I was called here. He remained quiet and we stood in the room in an awkward silence. I spoke up to break the silence. "So you think the Koreans are responsible for the dead bodies and have been attacking the deals?" I asked as I looked up from the files.

"I have a suspicion that they are." Han stated simply.

"But why? Is there something we're missing? 2008 was years ago. They got the money, why start a fight now?"

The logistics weren't making sense. The reasoning wasn't there. I wouldn't be starting trouble with the people I ripped off. He wasn't telling me something. "I need you to start being more involved in these arms deals, so that we can figure this out," he said plainly. I let out a deep breath.

"What aren't you telling me? I don't know why we're beating around the bush. You never call me to your office unless you have an assignment for me. And it's not investigating this. We have people who do detective work. That's why we have policemen on our payroll." I responded just as plainly. I'm not wasting my time with that. I'm an assassin. I have rank. I have better things to do with my time. He was silent.

"Have you ever wondered what happened to your mother?" Han asked out of nowhere. You could hear a pin drop because it was so silent. My chest constricted. I felt like I had been sucker punched. He looked up at me. I kept my face stoic. It got hot. Way too hot. Internally I felt like screaming.

"What does that have to do with anything?" I said, deadpan.

"She was killed when you were a baby. She was assassinated. By the Koreans." he answered. There was a look I had never seen before on his face. He looked sad. That's all I could equate the look to. He looked pathetic. Broken almost. I remained quiet. My thoughts were racing a thousand miles a minute. All this time, I wondered what happened to her. I had a sneaking suspicion that she was dead but I never said anything about it.

"I called you here to offer you the assignment for your revenge. Kill the man who ordered your mother's death. Kill the whole family."

He handed me the familiar black envelope. I mentally reminded myself to keep my hand steady as I took the envelope. I didn't know how to process any of this. Han and I never talked about my mother. He never offered any information. He never even told me her name. I've never seen a picture of her. I don't know who the woman is. Yet I'm being told, offered, the chance to kill the person who caused all of this. There was a part of me that leapt in excitement, but I couldn't ignore the part of me that was irritated? That wasn't the right word. I could only equate the feeling to a wound that had been aggravated and it throbbed and burned. It felt tender, as if it had been physically touched. It was a raw emotion that I was unfamiliar with.

I willed my hand to stay steady as I opened the envelope and pulled out the paperwork. There were a few pages. On the first sheet, there was a man who looked too young to be anyone of importance. Let alone a leader in the Korean mafia. He looked to be in his late thirties, early forties top. His thick black hair was combed back and he had hazel eyes. His skin was free of blemishes or wrinkles. Whoever was tracking him had a good zoom on their camera. His eyes held too much knowledge to be that young though. Given that fact, I suspected he probably was in his mid or late forties. His eyes told the story of his age. He was dressed in a long beige trench coat that was buttoned up and it was apparent that he was muscular. His broad shoulders filled out the trench coat causing it to be a little tight. From the picture angle, I could tell he was about Code's height. The name under the photo said Omega and identified him as the leader of the Jopok. Fitting name.

In the second photo, Omega's arm was there but the focus was on a short woman next to him. She was around my height, about one hundred seventy one centimeters tall. She had long blonde hair pulled into a tight bun on top of her head. She wore a white fur coat that was buttoned up and leather pants with black stiletto ankle boots. She was in the process of pulling off her sunglasses and she was looking in the direction of the camera. She was looking into the camera. She knew the picture was happening. That spy died shortly after this photo. Her brown eyes were cold and deadly. They held a wild edge to them. She was identified as Arsyn, but there was no information on what her role was. I examined the facial features. They could be father and daughter. They shared a similar round face and high bridge nose. She had this air of confidence and swagger. She could be his second in command or a close advisor. Something about her reminded me of myself. A small shiver ran down my spine at the thought. That was going to be a fight when the time came. There was a third person in the photo that couldn't be seen very well.

I flipped to the next page and there was a full blown photo. The new man was also about Code's height and was extremely muscular. Broad shoulders held muscular arms. He looked like a bodybuilder. Way too many muscles to count. His white button up shirt was too tight and tucked into black slacks that also fit too tight. His light brown eyes held a wild edge as well, but he was more on the reckless side. His hair was dyed silver and he shared a round face too, but his features were more sharp. I'm almost positive that's the son, but I couldn't be sure. He was identified as Viper. That was all the paperwork I had. These were the people who killed my mother. Dressed up and living what appeared to be a lavish lifestyle. I wondered if they had a mother. What did my mother do that was so bad? Why her? Was it out of spite? Was it retaliation? The questions ran through my mind and the fact that I had no answers infuriated me. I felt the emotions bubble up and it formed a lump in my throat as I glared at the pictures. I looked up at Han.

"Well? Say something." he asked as he stared at me expectantly. How dare he look like that when he sprung this on me? I held my tongue even though my blood was boiling.

"I want to see my mother. I want to see what they saw before she was killed." I demanded. It was hard to put my feelings into words. I was struggling trying to sort them out. It enraged me to know that my mother was killed. Of course it did. It enraged me to have that information hidden from me for twenty five years. It made me feel nauseous. I was pissed off. Would he answer all of the questions that I had? Was he ever going to tell me? Why did he choose to tell me now?

The longer I stood in front of him, the angrier I got. I could feel the anger turning into bloodlust. Visions of his head pinned against the wall and his body cut into little pieces started to fill my mind as pieces started to come together. How dare he lie to me and throw me off with this old story? He was toying with my emotions. He threw this mission at me and framed it like it was for me to get my revenge. The spineless bastard. He wanted revenge for him getting screwed over and was using my emotions to fuel it. And I fell for it. I was invested. As vexed as I was, I still understood the logic. Why not use my emotions to get his way? It wasn't like he hadn't done it before. What good would telling me have done at a young age? It would've affected my training. My childhood was already fucked up. I was already damaged from it. I endured what I went through and I survived.

25

Han reached inside of his desks' drawer and pulled out a framed photo. He slid it across the desk gently. My hands trembled as I picked it up. The woman in the photo had long brown hair. It was done up in soft, bouncy curls. The curls were neatly laid to perfection. Brown eyes looked warm and inviting. Her make-up was light and natural. Even the light eyeliner was perfectly done. Her full lips were painted in a soft pink color. She was beautiful. That couldn't be denied. Prim and proper. Was it the money that drew her in or was she one of the good girls who fell for the bad boy?

She was about my height. A long black velvet off shoulder dress adorned her slender frame and she folded her hands neatly in front of her. It looked like I got my style from her. The perfectionist streak probably came from her too. My natural hair color was black, so I wondered if she dyed her hair or was it naturally brown. Where my green eyes came from was still a mystery. Both Han and her had brown eyes. As I looked at the picture I fought back tears. I wouldn't give Han the satisfaction of knowing his sick manipulation worked.

"What's her name?" I asked.

"Nakano Sora. Gorgeous isn't she?" he answered softly. Even her name was beautiful. Way too beautiful to be with a monster like him. I nodded wordlessly.

"How much do I get for taking down the Jopok single handedly?" I asked as I looked up at him. I had to remain unaffected and cold. A small smirk crossed his lips.

"Whatever you want. Complete the mission and give me a number." he replied, sitting forward. "I'll be gone for a while, it seems then." I put the paperwork back in the envelope.

There wasn't much to go off of. Which I expected because I was dealing with high-ranking members of an underground organization. The Jopok and the Yakuza were the most powerful criminal organizations in the world. There were eyes everywhere. "You will be. To help you out, I decided to get you an undercover identity to keep your presence a secret. I figured I'd give you a little bit of a head start in your mission. You're a law student at Seoul National University. I figured getting you in the capital would give you an advantage. I have everything ready in advance. You just have to give me a name. It'll take a few days to get the documents. So I'd take the time to get your affairs in order." Han said as he passed a piece of paper to me. I wrote the name Choi Ae Ri on the paper. Han nodded.

"Good luck, Choi Ae Ri. I'll be in touch." With a final nod, I left the office.

I boarded the elevator and it was only when the doors closed and I was in solitude that I let the tears fall. It was cruel and unfair. I was Han's biggest asset in life and he found it so easy to toy with the little emotions I had left. I always knew he was a monster. That wasn't a secret but this was a different level of disrespect. I put my life on the line to protect his constantly and I don't get so much as a fucking thank you. Whenever he died, I was going to throw the biggest party. I could feel the animosity build up even the more. I quickly wiped my eyes before I met back up with Code and Remi and we got on the road to the train station.

"While I'm gone, you're in charge, Code. Keep the businesses going, my money flowing in. You're going to have to oversee all of the next coming expansion plans. I would suggest you put your second in command in charge of your gang. This is a full time job." I explained as we whispered on the train.

"Yes ma'am. I got it covered. I won't let you down." he said as he looked through the black book of plans and moves I created.

"I'll be watching. Don't fuck this up." I reminded him.

"It wouldn't be you if you weren't overbearing." He chuckled and I punched him in the chest quickly. He huffed in pain as I reached over and smacked Remi in the forehead who was leaning on his shoulder as she slept. She jumped up and looked at me wide eyed.

"My place in Seoul isn't going to find itself, stupid. Get to work." I demanded. She nodded, rubbing her eyes to adjust. She pulled out her phone and started typing. I was going to be comfortable while in foreign lands.

~Chapter 4~

"**D**amn it! Be careful with those boxes, idiot!" I screamed as I threw the knife in my hand at Remi as she struggled to carry a box of my shoes. She ducked and stared at me wide eyed. I yelled in frustration as the knife embedded in the wall behind her.

"Now I have to get that hole fixed! Fuck! Why didn't you hold you still!?" I pinched the bridge of my nose in irritation. A small laugh sounded behind me.

"A little sensitive today, Rose?" Code said as he walked up behind me with a clipboard. I turned to face him.

"Go to hell. I want to get my clothes and shoes to get to Korea in one piece. Not damaged. That stuff is expensive."

"Right. So you want to leave the furniture here while you're gone?" Code asked with confusion in his voice.

"I bought new furniture. Too much work to coordinate getting furniture overseas. Clothes and shoes are easier." I explained as I took the clipboard. Why work harder, when I can work smarter?

"Spending unnecessary money as usual. But I get it," Code laughed as he dodged a punch.

"Did you do the money conversion? Since you have time to be a dickhead." I asked as I looked over the sheets on the clipboard.

"Already done. You're a rich woman in South Korea as well. Seven hundred million yen converted into South Korean currency is 6.5 billion won. You're set. Barely made a dent in your personal account." Code answered as he handed me the conversion receipt and my card.

He followed me outside. I watched the small team move boxes of clothes, shoes and other accessories into a truck. A small shiver ran down my spine. It had been a few days since I had gotten the assignment. It was another thing that kept my mind occupied at night. I couldn't help but feel like this assignment was different. It felt different. I had been on assassination assignments before. It felt different not just with the new information I found out about my birth mother, but I was going into this with limited information. I had no leads, no contacts. No starting point. This was the first time I ever went on an assignment this blind. It was extremely dangerous. It was too late to back out now though. I couldn't even if I wanted to anyway. My emotions wouldn't let me. I checked my watch and looked at the itinerary Han sent me.

"I need to get to the airport. The plane leaves at 6." I announced. I looked over at Code and he sighed heavily but nodded. I raised an eyebrow. Whatever that was. He grabbed the bags that I was taking with me and loaded them into the car.

The car ride to the airport was silent. The atmosphere was tense. Code's body language and energy screamed that something was wrong. "What's going on Code?" I asked when we stopped at a red light.

"What're you talking about?" he answered.

"Don't make me shoot you." He chuckled and then suddenly went silent.

"It's just going to be weird. You never said when you were coming back. I'm not worried about you dying or anything. It's just weird. I'm not usually the one front and center, running the show. I usually follow you. All of this is unheard of." He paused for a moment, and I waited for him to speak again.

"I hope you get some rest, Rose. Honestly. You'll obviously be gone for a while. Try to live a little. You've earned it."

The car parked in the drop off terminal and Code looked back at me. I raised an eyebrow in confusion. "You're a sap. But okay. I hear you. Will I listen? Probably not." He laughed at the statement.

"Korea's pretty. You'll miss out." he warned as he opened my door and got my luggage out of the trunk. I stepped out and we stared at each other for a moment. This was the first major assignment I had been on without him. We've been the only constant in each other's lives. I understood what he was saying. It was going to be weird. But this was different. It was too personal. I just couldn't tell him that.

"Be safe Aria." he said as he extended a hand for a handshake. I shook it.

"Always." I grabbed the luggage and walked into the airport to start the tortuous check in process.

Sitting with my back to the window overlooking the airfield, I watched the people rushing by to get to their destinations. It's not very often that I'm among the regular people. Their lives seem so easy. Simple may be the better word. They don't have to worry about danger lurking around every corner. They have normal family units. Normal jobs. Kids were being kids. They just went about their lives. It was worthy of envy. I sighed and put my headphones in as I looked at my watch. I had 30 minutes to wait before the plane started to board. I'd land in Seoul around nine, so I started to look at hotels for the night because I couldn't get my keys until tomorrow morning. An email notification popped up on my phone and I opened it immediately. Han chose a class schedule for Choi Ae Ri. That was a nice tip. Only two classes actually interested me. One was Law301: Independent Study-Police Internship and the other was CRIM302: History of Street Gangs and the Police.

If those would be useful to track the Jopok and get information on the family. I'd actually have to go to each of the classes. Just in case I have to use this undercover personality again, I would like to keep them in good standing wherever they are. I was so immersed in my search that I didn't notice a man somewhere around my age standing in front of me. I looked up to see him fully. He was around Code's height or a couple inches taller with sharp features. His jawline was sharp and his brown hair was combed to the right and he had a beauty mark under his left eye. His nose was sharp. Full lips held a warm smile. He looked harmless. I made eye contact with him and his light brown eyes held specks of green in them. It felt like I was in a trance watching him. He was handsome. Pretty. Every adjective you could use to describe beauty, he was that.

I snapped out of staring when he laughed softly and gestured to the seat beside me. My bag was sitting there. I silently moved the bag and nodded looking away. He was something to look at for sure. I watched out of the corner of my eye as he sat down. His muscles rippled under the tight white shirt that he wore. He was way more muscular than Code. He must body build or at least lift weights. I found myself staring when the stranger laughed lightly again. It was a smooth tenor sound. Almost calming. I looked around quickly and cleared my throat. It was really hot all of a sudden. "You know it's rude to stare. Even if you are beautiful." the stranger teased. I wanted to hit him. Not in a bad way though. Strange. His presence didn't irritate me like anyone else's would have.

"I wasn't staring. I noticed that your shirt had a small tear in it." I replied quickly. There really was a tear in the left arm sleeve. Slivers of skin would show when he moved. He sat up straight and looked around.

"Left arm area." He pulled at the shirt and smirked lightly.

"So I do. Well thank you." I nodded, feeling vindicated.

The stranger was interesting. He was confident and I found it extremely amusing. He didn't shy away from me. Most men kept their distance. "So what's putting you on a plane to Seoul?" the stranger asked casually as he leaned his head on his hand and looked at me curiously. I paused for a moment before I responded.

"Returning from study abroad." I lied smoothly.

"What school do you go to?"

"Seoul National University."

"No fucking way! Me too! What year are you?" he asked.

"Graduate. Decided I should spend my last year at my home school." I shrugged. The lies were easy. He was none the wiser to who I really was. It was that easy. Fooling people.

"What department are you in?"

"Law."

"Oh, you're a smart one, huh? That's impressive." He genuinely seemed surprised by the answer.

"You sound shocked. Pretty girls can't study law? What's your department?" I asked as I turned to him and raised an eyebrow. His constant questions were starting to feel invasive. The man was clearly harmless, he was just being overly friendly but I felt different. I couldn't explain it.

"Ah, I'm not saying that. I've probably been asking you too many questions like a creep. I'm sorry. I'm a second-year graduate student in architecture. I'm Nam Jaehyun by the way. You?" he answered. He sat up fully and extended a hand. I looked at it for a second while pausing. Code's words rang in my hand. Live a little.

I shook his hand. His grip was loose but I could feel how strong he was still. That wasn't what I noticed right off the bat. It was the shiver that ran down my spine when our hands met.

"Choi Ae Ri." I answered. He looked me in my eyes and smirked lightly.

"Pretty name. And a firm handshake." he said softly. I chuckled.

"I'm a pretty girl. What did you expect?" He laughed and shrugged.

"You never know. I've had some horror stories. It's hard for someone like me."

Now that made me genuinely laugh out loud and I bit my lip to stifle it. Him having trouble dating or getting pretty girls, laughable. His looks rivaled that of those actors that you see in Korean dramas. Architecture felt like the wrong field for him. It was a shame.

"I am offended. I can't find dating difficult because I'm handsome? Is that what you're saying?" Jaehyun gestured to himself with a playful expression.

"You're fine, I'm sure. You're not struggling that bad."

At that moment, the overheard announcement said that the plane was starting to board first class. I stood up and looked back at him. "That's my cue to leave. I'll see you around." I smirked. To my surprise he stood too. He towered over me and I felt tiny. I cleared my throat quickly.

"Looks like we're walking together then. I fly first class too." he smirked back. Somehow it made sense. He was bold.

"Big money, I see." I looked down at my phone to pull up my ticket.

"You're one to talk, Miss Designer Everything. You're the one with big money. Only women with money wear heels in the airport. Red bottoms at that." He looked down at me and examined my shoes as I grinned slyly and shrugged.

"If you got it, flaunt it. Especially if you can *actually* afford it."

"True statement. But the classic red bottoms are a good look. I like it on you." Jaehyun grinned back.

"I agree with you. It is a great look for me."

We walked to the kiosk and I scanned my ticket first and went through the gate with Jaehyun following behind me. "Where's your seat?" he asked while we waited in the small line to board.

"C. Yours?"

"Damn. H. Not even close. Can I have your KaKao and maybe we can talk when we get off the plane?" Jaehyun asked almost shyly. He seemed almost disappointed. It was strange seeing as to how we just met. I didn't get it. I had made a KaKao randomly when I couldn't sleep for Ae Ri and I decided to give the information to him and we added each other. I never knew who I would meet along the way to help with my assignment. I got to my seat first and waved Jaehyun off as he went further back to his seat. I got comfortable in my seat and continued to search for hotel rooms. I settled on a nice suite with a kitchen for the night and confirmed the booking. With that done, I leaned back to take a nap until a notification pinged. I looked down to see Jaehyun's name flash across the screen. That was fast. I opened the notification and rolled my eyes at the hi meme he sent me. I replied that I needed my beauty sleep with a quiet emoji. Locking the phone again, I closed my eyes again and leaned back to go to sleep.

I found myself in a living room where everything was white. The walls, the couch, the rug on the ground, the silk nightgown I wore. The couch was facing towards the front door and I was in the back of the room. A woman with long brown hair in curls sat on the couch singing a lullaby and looking down at something. Her back was to me and I walked around the couch to see my mother holding a baby. The baby was swaddled in a pink polka dot blanket and my mother looked up at me. "Sit. Come hold the baby." she smiled warmly. I stared at her for a moment, confused. I walked over to her despite the confusion.

Sitting next to her, I awkwardly held my arms up as she placed the baby in my arms. I tensed in awkwardness. I've never held a baby. Never spoken to one. I've never hurt a child. I have traumatized them though, I'm sure. I've killed a parent in front of them before as they watched, orphaned some kids and left them alone, sometimes brought them to the Yakuza and dropped them off. Whatever happened to them was none of my business. So it was safe to say that I never had a good relationship with the little ones. My mother chuckled warmly trying to adjust my arms. "Jesus Aria. You're going to squish the baby and hurt yourself. Loosen up. Here, let me show you." She helped me reposition the baby and relax. It felt a lot better, but it was still awkward as hell to be holding it. I looked down at the baby and I felt my stomach twist. The baby was precious. Her round fat cheeks held a pink tint to them. Her nose was small and button shaped. She had full lips as her defining feature. Her eyes opened and my heart almost stopped. Green eyes stared back at me as she started cooing. My throat went dry.

"Mother…. Is this my baby?" I asked softly as I continued to stare at the baby. She chuckled. "Sometimes, it's a surreal experience. But you will get the hang of it and you have an amazing support system." she replied as she proudly stroked my hair. My heart swelled with a foreign emotion as she stroked my hair. I never felt that someone was proud of me before. It brought a genuine smile to my face. I was about to speak but then the front door opened and a stroller appeared through the opening. A baby's giggle came from the stroller and a loud joyous laugh came from behind the door.

I glanced up and my eyes widened as I saw Jaehyun walk in and lean down and pick up a second baby.

"Hey baby boy. We're home." he cooed proudly. He turned to me and smiled widely.

"Hey babe. What're you doing out of bed? You're supposed to be on bed rest." He removed his shoes and shuffled over to me and my mother. He kissed her cheek warmly and leaned over to kiss me on the forehead. I gasped lightly and looked up at him. He beamed with pride at me with the baby.

"You look so beautiful. Adjusting to motherhood so perfectly. I'm so proud of you." he proclaimed. My chest swelled again with a sense of newfound pride and confidence.

The loud beeping of the plane jolted me awake. My face felt hot and I looked around to see that the flight attendants were preparing the cabin for landing. I placed a hand over my chest and my heart was racing. I've never had a dream like that before. Most of my dreams were violent and destructive. They weren't warm and cozy. All of my dreams felt real, but that one felt almost too real. It felt too specific. I had just met Jaehyun so I couldn't understand why he would appear in my dream. I never had a desire for children, they didn't fit into my plans. Let alone any children with him. I rubbed my eyes and shook my head to erase the thought. It was a one off dream. They occasionally happened. No big deal. I checked my phone to see that Remi had texted me and asked if I was okay. I rolled my eyes and sent a period in response. I didn't need her bothering me the whole time I was gone. Why couldn't she be like Code? Normal.

The plane made its successful landing, and I stood up to grab my luggage. It shifted in the overhead compartment. I groaned in frustration. I couldn't reach it anymore. A hand reached over me and pulled it closer to my hand. "You're really short, you know?" Jaehyun laughed softly. I rolled my eyes and looked up at him.

"Not all of us can be giants, Nam. I'm a normal height." I replied as I grabbed my bag and put it on the floor. We made our way off the plane and into the airport. He checked his watch and looked over at me. "It's pretty early. Would you like to grab a drink with me?" he offered. I felt less tired with the nap I took. I shrugged. It was harmless.

"As long as you're paying. I'm there." I told him.

"I'm a gentleman. Of course, I'd pay."

He led the way through the airport and I followed so we could get our luggage. "My car's parked here. I can drive us, so you won't have to carry all of your stuff. Or we can walk. It's your choice." We stood in front of the parking garage and I nodded.

"I can handle myself if need be."

"I don't doubt that." He led the way to his car. It was a sleek all black Mercedes C-class sedan and again it made sense. He seemed like the type to like classics like that. He had good taste. I had a C-class in my personal car collection. He opened the door for me to get in and he took my bags to put them in the backseat. It was good that I didn't have to tell him to open the door for me.

The drive was about twenty minutes. It was a small building that looked unassuming. It had the name Mae's in red lights. Soft jazz music came from the building. "It's a lounge. Their drinks are epic. And good food too. It's a hole in the wall place, but it's popular." Jaehyun informed me as he looked over at me. It was a stark change from the busy clubs and loud EDM music back in Tokyo. It was soothing in a way.

"Seems relaxing. A big change from other places I've seen." I answered.

Walking inside was definitely a different vibe. The inside was bigger than it looked outside. Along the walls there were tall circular tables with high top chairs and a singular candle in the middle of the table. There was a stage in the front of the lounge and a band was playing music. There was a dance floor in front of the stage. The lights were dimmed and the purple and blue LED lights gave the building a sensual feel. A few people were dancing and swaying to the music, some people were sitting at the tables already and talking. It was really different. "Is that Jaehyun!? I haven't seen you in forever! How are you?" an elderly woman with curly black hair that was shorter than me ran up to him. She looked like a grandmother.

"MaeMae! I'm doing well. How have you been?" he chuckled as he hugged her.

"I'm good. I'm still here, of course. Where have you been?"

"I was in Japan handling some business for my dad. I was gone for a few weeks." Jaehyun answered as he smiled warmly at the woman. He did that often, I noticed. He was nice to everyone and warm to everyone.

I hummed to myself quietly. Where in Japan was he? The woman looked at me and gave me a quick look over. She smirked and nudged Jaehyun. "Ah Jaehyunnie…. She's pretty. Where did you find her? Did you bring her from Japan?" I chuckled and shook my head.

"We go to school together. I'm returning from studying abroad in Japan." I lied smoothly. She nodded slightly and gave me another look over.

"You two look good together. Come on, let me show you to your table." Mae laughed as she walked off. I glanced over at Jaehyun with a raised eyebrow. He was blushing.

"Ignore her. That's Mae, she owns the place. She used to watch my dad and his friends while they were younger. She's a staple of my childhood. She's always trying to get rid of me." he explained as we followed her.

"No, no! Not get rid of you, give you to someone who will be able to deal with you. And that's hard to do. But one day, she'll find you." Mae corrected as she sat us down at a table. She smirked at me.

"Mae, stop it. It's not like that. I'm trying to make a new friend." Jaehyun sighed.

"Fine, fine. What's your name, dear?" she asked as she turned her back to him dramatically. She's funny. I like her.

"Choi Ae Ri." I replied.

"Pretty name. Well welcome back. I hope to see you again." She smiled and turned to walk away.

Before she walked away, she swatted Jaehyun in the back of the head. "Hey! What was the reason for that?" he exclaimed.

"Be good. She's different." Mae warned. There was a slight moment of panic that settled in the pit of my stomach. She knew something or was suspicious about something. I needed to be careful of her. Maybe I needed to do a background check. I turned back to Jaehyun. He rolled his eyes lightly.

"Sorry about that. She's a lot to deal with sometimes. Hope you're not weirded out." he said.

"She's entertaining. A lot of attitude. I respect it." I chuckled. He laughed along with me, his face blushing. He was cute like that. I enjoyed the sight of it. It was quiet for a moment.

"What does your dad do? I heard you tell Mae that you were in Japan handling business for your dad. What part?" I inquired. I was genuinely curious. There was a part of me hoping he didn't say Tokyo or Kobe.

"Osaka. My dad has his hand in a lot of different things. He owns a huge corporation called Nam Industries. He's a real estate mogul by trade, but technology and science have become an area of interest for him. Osaka's hosting the World Expo in 2025 and there's a lot of opportunities for business there. Both architecture wise and real estate wise. And he's looking forward to the science and technology opportunities too." Jaehyun looked extremely proud talking about his father. I couldn't relate.

"Is that why you chose architecture? Because of your dad? You seem more like someone who is built for business." I asked. It was peculiar because I never took an interest in learning about someone else's life. I find most people boring and insignificant. Jaehyun was different though. Something about him drew me in. He was easy to talk to.

"Partly. I already have a bachelor's degree in business management. I double majored in that and architecture in undergrad. I chose architecture as my graduate degree. Business came naturally to me. My dad has been a businessman my entire life." Jaehyun explained. I hummed in understanding.

"Impressive. All of this is to prepare to take over the family business?" I asked. He laughed loudly at that and I tilted my head in confusion.

"My sister is more prone to do that. She wouldn't let me even if I tried. She's ruthless. I don't mind it though. I'd rather do my own thing. Build my own empires. Not saying anything bad about my sister, but she's the oldest. She's a good person though. She's just rough around the edges. Really rough. But she does have good qualities."

"I definitely relate. It's hard being that way." I grinned slightly.

"Rough around the edges? I can see that. So what's your story? Did you grow up with your dad?"

I was surprised that he could pick up on that. I didn't let the shock show on my face though. He was a true business man. He read people well. It was unnerving, but I didn't feel any negativity or ill intention. He wasn't fishing for information for some nefarious reason. He was just curious. It was easy to feel comfortable with him.

"I actually did. It was…something. My father worked a lot, so we weren't close. He worked around a lot of men, so the bravado made him emotionally unavailable. I was raised to take over the family business. Second best wasn't good enough. Perfection was the goal. You can't be too soft. You stay guarded. But it didn't break me. So there's that." I looked down at the table trying to shift through the words. I obviously couldn't tell him I was the daughter of a Yakuza leader, but it was freeing to be transparent for a moment. It was uncomfortable at the same time. My chest tightened. I cleared my throat. Jaehyun looked at me with sadness in his eyes. I hated that.

"Don't look at me like that. I don't need pity or sympathy. I am fine." I commanded. It wasn't supposed to come out that harshly. He didn't seem phased though. He just nodded in understanding and smiled lightly.

"Understood. My sister has said that to me before." I couldn't help the feeling of envy and bitterness. He had a sister too? Something must have flashed in my eyes because his face dropped.

"I'm guessing that look meant something?" he asked quietly.

"No siblings. It was just me and my father." I answered, the bitterness slipped out slightly. It wasn't intentional. My feelings were still raw after talking to Han and finding out about my mother. He was working hard to keep his expression neutral. I respected that.

"Well, you're a survivor and that's commendable. How about shots to celebrate?" Jaehyun cheered as he clapped. I snickered at the wording. My mood instantly lifted though as he called Mae over. She shuffled over and he ordered four shots of tequila. I laughed shortly and he looked over at me.

"What? No tequila? Want something else?" he offered.

"Why four shots? Why not six?" I grinned as his and Mae's face dropped, and they stared at me.

Suddenly Mae laughed joyously. "I like her! She handles alcohol well. You have met your match, Jaehyun," she patted my back and agreed.

"Okay then. Let's go shot for shot." Jaehyun smirked as he looked at me with a challenge in his eyes.

"A drinking competition is not something you want to do with me, Nam. This won't end well," I warned him.

"Oh, come on. You sound scared. End badly for who? You?" I wasn't one to turn down a challenge and I wasn't about to start now.

"Care to put a wager on it? 265,196 won."

"Deal. It's a bet," he agreed. Mae brought out the shots and we cheered for the first one.

~Chapter 5~

I woke up in my hotel room to the sun beating down on my face. I looked over at the clock and saw that it was 8am. My head was pounding. I pulled the blanket over my head and laid back down, settling into the soft mattress. I turned over and found myself face to face with Jaehyun. I studied his features for a moment and felt a lump form in my throat. He was really handsome. The more I looked at him, the prettier he got. His eyes slowly opened, and he blinked sleepily at me.

"Good morning…I guess I owe you some money." he chuckled and leaned up to look around. "Where are we?"

I laughed lightly and nodded. "Yeah. I definitely need my money. Because you were wasted after eight shots. But I respect your efforts. You tried to hang in there with me." I teased him.

"I underestimated your drinking prowess. All hail the queen of drinking." He smiled and then winced as the light hit his eyes.

"It's really bright out. And my head is pounding. Do you mind if I stay in bed longer? Or if you're busy, I'll head out." he questioned with a small pout on his face. I looked over at the clock and contemplated. He was pretty messed up, letting him drive like that would be messed up. I didn't want to see him get hurt. He was good company to have around. I just needed to get the keys to my place. But they could leave it under the mat or I could get it later. I was still tired anyways. A few more hours of rest couldn't hurt.

"You'll need to help me move into my place later on if I let you sleep in. Deal?" I offered. He smiled sleepily and agreed quickly.

"I can do that. It's a deal. What time?" he agreed.

"Around 1pm or so."

"That's plenty of time. I can get my shit together by then. Thank you. Also thank you for looking out for me last night too. I can tell that it was new for you, so I appreciate it. I'll have to buy you dinner to properly say it. But all I have is cuddles right now. So... Come here!" Jaehyun grinned. I stared wide eyed and tensed as he enveloped me in a crushing hug that buried my face in his chest as he pulled me close to his body. He placed his hands on my upper and lower back to softly rub the spots there.

My face felt hot suddenly and my chest tightened. I could hear my heartbeat in my ears. This was completely foreign to me. I've never been cuddled before. That wasn't something I did. Not even after sex, I usually sent men home. We didn't do anything when we got to the hotel. He was way too drunk. I'm cruel, not a monster. He passed out as soon as he hit the bed. He had enough left in him to ask if I could remove his shirt so he could sleep easier. Thinking back if I had known a cuddle was in the future, I would have disagreed. His skin was way too soft and even though his pecs were large and solid it was mildly comfy. He smelled good too.

"You can cuddle back, you know? It's okay. Here, I'll show you." he chuckled as he grabbed my hands folded in front of me and he ran them up his hip and over to his small waist. It was more comfortable like this. I admit. I looked around awkwardly trying to calm my raging heartbeat. Every nerve was firing on all cylinders, screaming at me to move away.

I've been shot at by armies of men, chased with machetes, kidnapped and beaten up. None of that had my heart racing like this. This was an entirely different feeling. I couldn't describe it. I wasn't in danger. I just had that as my base to go off of. "Are you okay? Your hearts' racing." Jaehyun tilted his head down to look at me. I looked up from his chest and blinked once. I should've said no and that I wanted him to let go but instead I nodded and looked down at his arms wrapped around me. He smiled lazily and chuckled. "Cute. Go to sleep. You need rest." he started to stroke my hair and it was soothing as he rubbed my back as well. I didn't hate the feeling of it at all. It was just unsettling. I felt comfortable with him nevertheless. The amount of affection he showed was strange to me. It was uncomfortable but I didn't want him to let go. Thinking too hard was making the pounding worse. I chose to close my eyes and let sleep take me away for the time being.

My alarm went off and my eyes opened slowly. I wasn't in his arms anymore. I looked around and he was nowhere to be found. I sat up quickly and looked around. A sense of dread and panic settled in my stomach. I was disappointed. He just left without saying goodbye. I was unsure why I cared so much because I had done it plenty of times, but I couldn't help it. I sat in bed for a moment pouting. The door handle jiggled and I tensed up as I jumped to go grab my pocket knife from my luggage. Stepping into a fighting stance, I waited for the intruder. The door opened and I quickly straightened up as the familiar brown hair came into view. I hid the knife behind my back and stared as he backed into the room with his back forward. Such a dangerous move and he didn't even know it. "What're you doing, Nam?" I asked. He turned around slowly and he held a tray of food in front of him. He frowned at me.

"You're awake? No fair. I was supposed to be back before you woke up. I bought food." he set the food down and pouted as he crossed his arms.

He shrugged and turned to me, smiling softly. "Figured you'd be hungry. So I made a run and I took the spare hotel key. Hope you don't mind." he explained. He was bold, but a gentleman. It was a nice gesture, I had to admit. I appreciated it. I noticed the bookbag on his back.

"You're a bold one, Nam. I can respect it. As long as you brought back the key that's fine." I replied as I sheathed the pocket knife in my back pocket.

"With the world at your feet, how can you not be? I always return what I borrow. One key returned." He laid the key on the desk and chuckled.

"What's with the bookbag?" I asked as I reached over to the tray and grabbed a few grapes.

"I was hoping to shower here so I can help you move, remember?"

"So did you drive home or do you keep clothes in your car normally?" I laughed as he blushed bright red.

"Don't say it like that. Makes me sound like a whore. I'm just prepared. I'm a businessman, remember?" he explained as he walked to the bathroom.

"Enjoy your breakfast. Even though you just insulted me." he teased as he closed the door.

Looking down I saw french toast, eggs, sausages and a bowl of different fruits: grapes, pineapples, and strawberries. I grinned slightly and took the knife out of my back pocket. I frowned. He had been around too long. He felt too comfortable with me. I was starting to feel comfortable. If I'm not careful here this could be disastrous. I shook my head to clear it. I'm overthinking it. This isn't that deep. It's breakfast. Code and Remi have brought me breakfast before too. They've helped me move. I've gone drinking with Code and played drinking games with him. Remi too. This was no big deal. I chose to ignore the tug in my stomach. After I ate, I opened my suitcase and pulled out a pair of leggings and a crop top hoodie with black sneakers. The door to the bathroom opened and a shirtless Jaehyun came out drying his hair. I stared as I watched the muscle in his back ripple under his skin. In the light I noticed his skin had a slight tan to it. It looked really nice on him. It fits.

"You okay, Ae Ri?" he joked as he turned around and glanced at me. I looked down quickly realizing I was caught. He snickered slightly.

"Awww… Are you shy all of a sudden? Why? We cuddled like this!"

I felt my face heat up and I grabbed my clothes to walk past him. I felt like a child. This was humiliating! As I went to move around him, he stepped in front of me and trapped me against the wall. I gazed up at him and he stared back. His eyes were extremely nice to look at. There was a sparkle of mischief and light in his eyes that was captivating. He gently lifted my chin and leaned in closer. My face felt even hotter.

"Your blushing is cute." he commented softly. His nose brushed against mine and I closed my eyes. It was hot everywhere. The room felt like it was closing in and my hands were tingling. It was terrifying. My brain couldn't process everything that was happening. A light kiss was given to my forehead and I felt him pull away. Opening my eyes, I saw him smirking cheekily as he pulled a white T-shirt over his head. I was stunned and felt like I had to avenge myself.

"I-I don't blush!" I exclaimed as I quickly ran into the bathroom and closed the door.

I looked in the mirror and I noticed the bright pink hue on my cheeks. I don't have make-up on, so why were my cheeks pink? Was my body reacting naturally? That's never happened to me before. A forehead kiss too? I couldn't describe the feeling in the pit in my stomach. It was a warmth that I had never experienced in my life. The closest thing I could relate to was when a large sum of money hit my personal account after completing a job. That wasn't a strong enough feeling to compare it to. As I scrambled to think of something, I realized I had nothing to compare this feeling to and that worried me. What was it? The unknown was killing me. It made my palms sweat and my chest started to race. My breath quickened. Everything that I knew in life was screaming to run and get him away from me, but there was something unknown screaming twice as loud saying to keep him close.

I groaned and shook my head as I turned on the shower and hopped in. The shower helped me calm down. I needed to focus. I needed to get back into my space. Time alone, I'll be back to normal. That's it. I'll be fine. I breathe a sigh of relief. The problem is fixable. I turned off the shower and dried off. Once I was done getting ready, I came out of the bathroom and saw that Jaehyun had my bags stationed by the door and he wore my purse across his shoulder.

"Hey there you are. Are you ready? I got your stuff together for you... What's the-" Jaehyun turned to face me and his words trailed off. I tilted my head. I was in leggings and a hoodie with my hair in a bun. Nothing special. No makeup. I'm pretty yeah but that seemed like an overreaction.

"Nam? You okay there, buddy?" I chuckled. He blinked once and then grinned.

"Ah yeah. Let's get you to your house, so we can get you moved in. What do you think?" He walked to grab my bags while I grabbed my phone and small bookbag that I had bought with me.

"I can take something. There's a lot of bags." I offered. Surprising.

"I'm good. Let's go. If you open it, I'll follow you." I nodded and opened the door for him.

~Chapter 6~

I unlocked the door to the penthouse allowing for Jaehyun to step inside. He whistled as he looked around. "You didn't tell me that you got a penthouse? Or that you were rich like this! This is the Asterium. Besides Seoul Forest, you can't get any richer than this," he exclaimed as he placed the bags down.

"You don't live where the rich live?" I questioned. That was strange, if you have the money why not live like you have the money? That's why I do it. I'll make the money right back.

"I do. I actually live in Seoul Forest, that's why I said that. It's about fifteen minutes away." he laughed. He looked back at me and winked. I rolled my eyes.

"It fits. I looked there. I like the quieter living areas. But I want to live in Seoul Forest at least once or twice," I said walking into the kitchen.

"Oh, you got money like that?" he inquired.

"The family business passed on early. Passive income, active income, it's all money." I shrugged. "What's your thing? Your industry?"

"We do business. International and domestic. Some banking, trade as well." It wasn't technically a lie. The Yakuza was all business, sometimes legal, a lot of times illegal.

"Ah that makes sense. Your family's based in Japan?" he asked. I could be honest here. Needed for this to work.

"Yeah. Business boomed out there." I replied.

Jaehyun was smart. Incredibly smart. He just doesn't know how smart. This conversation could've gone bad if I slipped up, but the doorbell rang and he went to open it. The furniture had arrived and the rest of my clothes and shoes came.

"All right. It's go time. Since I'm nice, Nam you can help me with my clothes and shoes. The movers can do the furniture." I checked as he looked over at me.

"This is fine. I'm not trying to actually lift anything heavy. Rearrange I can do. I can push." he agreed. I signed for my furniture, and they brought in the pieces to the L-shaped couch. I sent Jaehyun out to help with boxes while I directed everything. He listened well and made jokes and kept me laughing the whole time. He talked to the movers and made friends with them. He looked so comfortable and, in his element, walking around my place. Almost like he had been here the whole time. I fought off the crazy thoughts about how good of a team we made and how *right* this all felt. It looked like we were a couple moving in together. The movers made that comment more than once. I pinched myself roughly. I wasn't going down that rabbit hole. Too busy.

"Just wanted to ask out of curiosity. What's your deal with white and silver? You have a lot of white stuff. Are they your favorite colors?" Jaehyun asked as he leaned against me. I hummed as I thought about it. It was a stark contrast from my place in Japan.

"I don't have a favorite color. I just wear a lot of white and black. The white and silver looks better with the penthouse. I like the clean look as well." I looked around the building taking in the pure white walls and cream-colored flooring. The entirety of the space's back wall was a glass window from floor to ceiling. I could see the Seoul skyline when I looked out. I loved that my bedroom was positioned where I had that feature too. I looked at the furniture in its set position. The couch was white but had silver legs. The large rug that took up a large part of the living room floor was silver and the coffee table was made of glass and outlined with silver. It looked good. I felt comfortable. It was minimalist but expensive.

"You don't like it? I think it's very high class and elegant." I said as I put my hands on my hips. The room was cohesive, and it fit together like a puzzle piece.

"Have you gone to design or fashion school?" he looked up at me, with curiosity in his eyes. "No. I just like things that look good. I like coordination and aesthetics. Always have." I replied. That was an honest thing. I liked things that looked nice. I like luxury items. I was never short on money, so I always splurged on lavish things.

"Then why are you studying law? Because you obviously don't need the money. It seems like you'd be happy doing design or fashion. Just hearing you talk about it, it sounds like you could be really successful at it."

I hummed in thought. What would my life look like if I did something else? I never thought about it. Being a regular person. No more Han. No more isolation. I didn't hate the thought strangely. But nothing about it felt right. How was I supposed to just be normal after all I've seen? After all I've done. That was impossible. This life is all I have ever known. It's not like Han encouraged me and told me I could do whatever I wanted to do. He said the opposite as a matter of fact. I was pulled from my thoughts when I looked down at Jaehyun's tall frame and his face held a small smirk. I had to think fast.

"I'm a little too far into this, don't you think? I'm getting a graduate degree in it. That'd be insane, wouldn't it? It's familiar to me." I replied.

I knew the double meaning in my words. He would never understand. I've done this so long, I can't just go do something else. It's familiar. It's stable. The underground world will exist forever. There's always going to be criminals who need guns and drugs. Laws are always going to be broken. That's why there will always be a need for judges and law enforcement. They went hand in hand. "Sometimes stability and familiarity doesn't always mean good. It doesn't mean it's right for you. Sometimes it traps you. I think we could do good business together with me being in architecture and you being in interior design. That's a power move, if I have ever heard one." he grinned as he reached up and put his hand on my thigh reassuringly. Something about that made my heart skip a beat.

"Shouldn't you wait to get to know me more before you say that?" I told him.

"I'd say the same thing even then."

"Well then. I guess that's a tempting offer, Nam."

"Consider it. You may find some joy." he winked playfully. I lightly swatted him away.

"You're scatterbrained. You're supposed to be making sure my stuff is good. Move it."

He laughed and ran off to check on everything. Once he was out of the house, I sighed heavily and rubbed my temples. I knew it was too late. I couldn't leave him alone. I enjoyed his company and conversation. Something about Jaehyun felt safe. He was magnetic. He had the ability to make me talk and open up and it intrigued me. I groaned in slight annoyance at the warmth that appeared in my chest at the thought of him. I couldn't explain what any of these feelings were. Since I couldn't explain them, it had to mean that I was overthinking. It's not that complicated or serious. The reality is Choi Ae Ri and Nam Jaehyun couldn't do... whatever this was because she doesn't exist. Point blank. End of story. I was making all of this up in my head. He was just flirting. He wanted to sleep with me just like anyone else. It went no further than that.

I looked up when I heard Jaehyun grunt in effort. He was struggling with a heavy box. It took me a moment to realize what he was holding. Once I did, I froze slightly because those were my weapons.

"Be careful, Jaehyun! That's an important box. Just leave that there. I'll move it." I exclaimed as I watched him continue to struggle. He nodded and squatted to set it down softly. Luckily, I had Remi put all my weapons in their designated boxes, so there wasn't any metal clinking around and the risk of an accidental shooting was negated. I couldn't explain that and I would really hate seeing him hurt.

"That was heavy as hell. What was that? A rock collection?" he joked.

"Girl things. How is everything looking?" I answered.

"Few more boxes and then your mirrors. You have like three more to bring in. You're really vain."

I looked up stunned. I was unprepared for the sting that shot through me. "Oh my god! I was kidding! You look like a hurt puppy. I am so sorry. Come here!" he gasped as he quickly pulled me in for a hug. The sting lessened slightly but it didn't feel like a joke to me. And something told me that the feeling was completely on me. Not him. He pulled away and ran his thumbs along my cheeks.

"Don't look like that. I am sorry. I didn't know you'd react like that. I won't make that joke anymore. Can you forgive me?" he pleaded as he looked up at me sincerely. The sincerity in his apology made me feel better. I nodded in agreement.

"Oh, you poor thing. You looked like you were going to cry. Come sit down." he soothed as he walked me over to the couch and sat down with me. He pulled me into his lap and held me like a baby. It was comforting and I leaned into his chest. We were silent for a little while.

"When do your classes start?" Jaehyun suddenly inquired.

"Monday. Yours?"

"Monday as well. How are you getting there? I'll come pick you up." he offered as he looked down at me. I felt like a child looking up at him, but I felt completely safe.

"I'm going to buy a car but it will probably take some time to get here. I'll take you up on your offer." I shrugged.

"You have a place in mind? I know some good car dealerships. If you want I'll take you."

"I want a G-wagon. I'm not going to a regular car dealership. So don't try it." I warned him as I sat up.

"There you are. Back to normal. But of course. I wouldn't dream of it. You'd probably chew my head off." he laughed. I looked at him and grinned. I did feel better. I was impressed but also shocked that he knew a conversation about a new car would bring me back to normal. Was I easy to read or was he noticing things about me?

"Do you have everything you need? To be comfortable, I mean. I didn't see anything for your kitchen or bathroom. Or any decorations, really. Do you want to go to Deco View or Lotte?" he asked. I hummed. I don't know how long I'll be here, so I may as well get as comfortable as possible.

"I'm okay with that. Deco View is best." I replied as I stood up. He jumped up and grabbed his keys. I laughed and made my way to the door and grabbed my purse.

"You seem excited to go shopping." I noted as we made our way to the car.

"I want to make sure you're okay. Besides, you'll like the store. I'm sure of it. Your interior decorator's heart will panic." I shook my head. He was so sure of himself, and I was becoming fond of it.

"Whatever you say. I'll let you have that one." I sat back and let him drive us down the road.

~Chapter 7~

As Jaehyun promised, he appeared outside my door on Monday to pick me up for classes. He was a prompt person, he consistently showed up on time every day he promised to come over. Today when I opened the door, he offered me a cup with my name on the side. I stared at the cup confused. He chuckled. "It's coffee, not poison. I got you a hazelnut latte." I offered him a small smile as I took the drink and took a sip. I wasn't a big coffee drinker, I survived off of energy drinks the majority of the time. If I did drink coffee, it was usually black, so I was surprised by the sweetness of it.

"Pretty good. I like it." I confirmed and nodded in approval. I followed him to the car, adjusting the small backpack with an iPad in it. He opened the door for me, and I got in the car and he got in after me.

"Are you excited for the first day?" Jaehyun asked. I chuckled and turned to him. I wasn't a star student, but Ae Ri was. I was street smart and knowledgeable about real life things.

"It's nerve racking. But necessary." I answered. That was honest. This was the beginning stages of my assignment. I couldn't shake the feeling that this was going to be unlike any other assignment I have ever been on. The feeling sat in the pit of my stomach like a weight. I've done plenty of assassinations before. In the research I have done personally, the Jopok keeps a low profile. They are rarely in the news. The last headline about them was in 2019 when there was a shootout between two gangs. Anything I found came from self-proclaimed experts on the internet. It wasn't ideal but I had to work with what was available. They are active in a bunch of different cities, but nothing pinpointed to the headquarters. Seoul, Busan, Gangnam, Daegu and even Jeju. That was a lot of distance to cover. The internet forums I was reading said that the Jopok was heavily integrated into society but it was very secretive. It makes sense because Koreans are more judgmental and secretive about their mafia and gang history. Even with the current government crackdown on the Yakuza, people accept the reality of our existence.

"First days can be rough, but something tells me that you'll be okay." Jaehyun put a hand on my arm and softly rubbed it. I looked up at him and his eyes held a comforting warmth. I felt my face get hot.

"Such a cute blush. I like it." he chuckled. I rolled my eyes.

"I don't blush," I said.

"The red cheeks say you do, Choi."

He pulled into the parking lot and I looked around to see all of the school buildings and students walking around the campus. It looked just like what I saw in the movies. Everyone was in their own worlds and going about their business. The campus was peaceful and that unsettled me. It made the inner chaos of my thoughts seem louder and *that* made me uncomfortable.

"Hey. I'll walk you to your first class, how about that? That should help you calm down." Jaehyun offered. I shrugged and handed him my class schedule. He looked it over and beamed.

"Our buildings aren't too far from each other. Awesome, I can swing by and see you. That's fun."

"Don't be a creep, Nam." I teased.

"I'm checking on a friend. How is that creepy?" I shook my head, snickering.

Honestly, I wouldn't mind seeing his face during school. I don't need to see it, but it's a nice sight. He broke the comfortable silence we had settled into as we walked. I looked over at him and he was looking down at the ground. His demeanor seemed timid almost. "Do you want to grab lunch together? I'd like to ask you something. It's kind of important." he asked.

"Can it be asked now? What's up?" I answered. For some reason, his timidness made my stomach twist in knots. It wasn't in a bad way though. The change in his demeanor made me curious.

"I'm still working up the courage to ask you. I need some time." I rolled my eyes and playfully pushed him.

"Fine. I'll wait even though I hate to do that."

"You won't have to wait long. I swear." He looked up at me and gave me a wide and warm smile. Before I knew it, I returned the gesture. He stared distractedly and mumbled under his breath. "Absolutely beautiful…"

I didn't think I was supposed to hear that, so I chose to pretend that I didn't hear it for both of our sakes. I felt my cheeks heat up again and I looked away. It started to tug at my emotions the more he complimented me. Things were tense for a moment. Luckily, I saw my classroom number ahead and I pointed at it.

"I think this is my classroom, right? You're a horrible guide. I had to find it by myself." He raced ahead a little and looked inside the room. "Wow, law uses the plainest classrooms, I see," he teased as I met him at the entrance and looked in.

I playfully punched his arm. "I mean it's not the most exciting thing in the world. But I won't be here much. This is my police internship class. I'll be paired at a police station for this class." I told him.

"That sounds kind of exciting. You'll have to tell me about it at lunch." He gave me a blinding smile and I lost my train of thought for a moment. I leaned against the wall and shrugged.

"I can do that."

"Awesome. Well, I'll let you get your day started. I'll see you for lunch. I'll text you when I'm out of class."

I agreed and he fixed the stray hairs that flew out of place and my heart started to race. I didn't trust my voice so I hummed in agreement. He winked and gave me a small wave as he walked away. I let out a breath I didn't know I was holding and watched his figure disappear around the corner.

It felt like a weight was sitting on my chest. It had nothing to do with the assignment. I knew that. I was in trouble. Nam Jaehyun was definitely going to be a problem. I didn't hate it. He was kind. He was funny. Something about his presence was calming. He was confident and interesting. Whenever I said I wouldn't see him anymore, I found myself standing next to him or sitting next to him the next day. I talked to him all the time. He was becoming a part of my routine. I looked forward to seeing him.

The thought of him not being around made my chest physically ache. I shook my head to fight it off. Obviously, a part of me didn't like that idea. This feeling was new and it didn't make sense. A feeling of panic started to set in my chest and I felt nervous. Sweat broke out along my forehead and my hand started to tremble. I pinched the bridge of my nose and took a few deep breaths. This wasn't the time or place for this.

I straightened up and adjusted my clothes while I walked into the classroom. I chose a seat in the back of the room. It was a smaller lecture hall, maybe 50 students could fit inside. The room had steps and the back of the room sat higher up then the front row and it was darker. I had about ten minutes before the class started and I chose to spend that time trying to get my breathing under control by closing my eyes. "Oh. My. God! I love your outfit!" a high-pitched voice broke through the silence and I opened my eyes to see a petite Korean girl with blonde hair standing on the row below me. Her makeup was done precisely and her large brown eyes sparkled with joy. She looked at me expectantly. She wanted an answer. I looked around for a second before I spoke.

"Appreciate that." I said dryly. She beamed brightly and nodded excitedly.

"Of course! I'm a big fan of the Dolly pump Altas. They're classic. I love how you paired it with the Versace latex leggings." she complimented. Ah, she's one of those.

"Fashion snob?" I asked. She laughed loudly at the comment. She's tolerable. Not uptight, but she was loud. She was a little dramatic too.

"You're funny. I like you. I'm Miyeon. Want to be friends?" Before I could answer, she shuffled her way to the empty seat beside me. I internally sighed and listened to her tell me stories. She reminded me of Remi, except Miyeon screamed diva and she was older. She was unashamed of her pushiness. She didn't care. That had to be respected. My saving grace was the other people flowing into the room and she started to talk to them.

When the professor arrived, the classic introductions began and I suffered through them. The premise of the class was to get us hands-on experience working in the justice system in different areas and we would work in a designated police station. The professor took preferences into consideration. Han didn't tell me that. Thanks to him I was assigned to the Seoul Metropolitan Police Agency. The primary police force for Seoul and I was assigned to the High Profile Crimes division. That sounded exactly like where I needed to be. We were supposed to start within the next two weeks. Our designated stations would reach out to let us know when they were ready to bring us in. The rest of the class passed in a blur and I was on my way to the next class.

It always amazed me how easy it was for me to blend in with people my age. With my tattoos covered and dressed in designer clothing, people just assumed I was the daughter of a wealthy businessman. They didn't see me as a threat. They just knew that I had a lot of money and could feel the power that came with it. I walked through the campus with a map and the only whispers I heard were people asking who my parents were and where I came from. Some girls commented on my outfit. Pretty normal things.

This undercover persona was so plain and unassuming. There was nothing extraordinary about it. The Jopok wouldn't see me coming. It was refreshing to not have to look over my shoulder every second to make sure I wasn't being followed or chased by someone or something. Code's words replayed in my mind before I left. I did deserve a break. I am still young. Other leaders in the organization took vacations. Han took vacations at least three times a year and left me in charge. Sometimes he would disappear for months.

Bitterness and irritation coursed through my veins as the memories replayed of all the times, I escorted Han to his private jets and watched them ascend into the sky. He didn't work as hard as I did. None of them did. Life was cruel that way. I didn't get a say in becoming this. I didn't choose this life for myself. The kids I grew up with in the dorms all dropped out of the training at 16. Some parents pulled their kids out earlier than that, when they saw how cruel it was. Whenever I asked Han why he wouldn't allow me to leave the program and go to real school like the kids on television, he'd smack me around and tell me I was stupid. All I was made to do was follow orders and directions. The joke was on him. We were one in the same now.

If I planned and strategized right, I could use this as a vacation and complete the assignment. I would like to think my mother would encourage me. A lot happened over the course of a few days. My phone vibrating in my pocket broke me from my thoughts and I checked it to see that Jaehyun was messaging me. He informed me that he had one more class and he would meet me at my next class and we could go to lunch together. It was a satisfying feeling knowing that he was so giddy about this. I text him back the building and room number as I stood outside of the class. It was my luck that I had both of the useful classes on the same day and then I was free. I walked into the classroom and looked around. This lecture hall was much bigger. It could hold at least 200 students. This must be a required class for law students. I sat in the back of the classroom again and pulled out my iPad. It was imperative that I took notes and gained as much information from this class as I could. It was like a switch flipped when the professor walked in.

The professor introduced himself and he was a stern man. He pulled up a PowerPoint and started his lecture. The first day wasn't a waste of time. It was quite entertaining and informative. We started talking about the mafia right away. And the police's inadequacies. That was a first. I learned that a lot of the police databases were outdated. The head family could potentially be larger than what the police originally thought. He said the police were investigating potential leads. I thought back to the files Han gave me. Two kids and a dad. Who could be the missing members of the head mafia family? A mom, an extra kid? Who was that good to go undiscovered and unknown by the police? Even the police in Japan knew of my existence. They just could never find me.

I learned that the Jopok mainly operated out of two cities and that their headquarters could be in either place. Seoul and Busan. They had different areas under their control and conducted business in those areas. For a police force, there is a lot they don't know. Hopefully, this class was just a rumor mill and when I actually got to the police station there would be real information. I learned that the Jopok had ties in manufacturing, real estate, business and government. I guess that's a start. I could work with that. The professor let us out early since it was the first day. I could appreciate a short day. I gathered my things and left the room.

"Hey! Choi Ae Ri! Wait for me!" a familiar voice called out from behind me. I turned to see Miyeon running towards me. Was she following me or something? I watched her run up to me and she waved excitedly. "Are you a law student? What are you doing here?" I asked bewildered.

"Yes! I'm studying to be a lawyer." she exclaimed. She dramatically crossed her arms over her chest.

"A barbie doll lawyer? Who are you? The girl in that American movie?"

"Her name is Elle Woods and I love Legally Blonde. It's my favorite movie! We should watch it sometime."

"Eh, not my style really."

"You're missing out. What are you doing this weekend? It's the first weekend of the semester. You know what that means, don't you?" Miyeon grinned sneakily. I stared at her blankly. She gasped and turned away from me. "It means parties! We party to start the semester off right! So there's this party I'm having this weekend... Oh. My. God. Is that the student council president coming towards us right now?" She had the attention span of a goldfish. She pulled me closer by the arm and I turned to see Jaehyun coming towards us. Student council president? No way. I chuckled to myself. He jogged up smiling.

"President Nam! How are you?" she giggled softly as she twirled her hair. Oh she had a crush on him. I bit my lip in vexation. She's not as tolerable as before. Jaehyun bowed once in greeting. "Hey Miyeon. Hey Ae

Ri." Miyeon gasped stunned and looked back at me with wide eyes. I fought to keep my expression neutral.

"You two know each other?" she questioned.

"I know Nam Jaehyun. Now President Nam, I am unfamiliar with." I answered. He rolled his eyes and pinched the bridge of his nose.

"Ha ha, very funny. Yes, we know each other. You guys are in the same class?" he replied. Miyeon cut in before I could respond.

"Yeah! We have our internship class together. She's in the High Value Crimes unit and I'm in the Investigation unit. I think we'll be close friends. She's cool."

There was a look of concern that flashed over his face. It was gone as quickly as it came, but it was there. I chose to ignore it. I raised an eyebrow and looked at Jaehyun. He held back a laugh. Miyeon was pushy. She would be a good foot soldier with that quality. It would just be way too annoying to use her. She'd be dead in two hours.

"Well Miss Song, I think you have good taste. I think Choi Ae Ri is pretty cool as well. If you don't mind, I'd like to talk to her in private, please." Jaehyun smiled softly. She started to protest, but the look of warning he gave her told her he did not want to hear her out. She nervously chuckled and scurried off in the other direction with a rushed goodbye. That was peculiar.

"Well, Mr. Student Council President, that was somewhat intense. What was that?" I teased as I leaned against the wall.

"Ah nothing. She can just be a lot. You have to get your point across firmly without hurting her feelings. Her dad is the school's largest donor. She's the student council's social media coordinator." he answered with relief.

"So, a role to pacify her? Who gave her that?" He snickered and rolled his eyes.

"The student body voted on her. It wasn't like that."

"Sure. Why didn't you tell me about the student council thing?" I inquired.

"So, you can call me a nerd and bully me? Absolutely not." He looked at me in disbelief. I laughed and shrugged my shoulders because he had a point. I would tease. It's my thing.

"The rich chaebol son who is the student council president. Sounds like a drama. You might want to check into that. Just give me royalties once it gets popular." I playfully nudged him. He chuckled.

"Fair. I'm a businessman. I am open to negotiations. We can talk about it." A comfortable silence formed between us, and we stared at each other for a moment. Under his watchful stare, I felt a lump form in my throat, and I started to play with my fingers. There was something that lurked under the pretty color that made me feel small and nervous. It wasn't threatening per say. I just couldn't explain it and that made me nervous.

"Well since we're here. Before I forget. So, remember when I told you about Miyeon's dad being a big donor for the school?" he suddenly remembered. I nodded.

"There's another fundraising gala happening at the beginning of next month and I was wondering if you would accompany me. What do you say?" He folded his hands together and he looked extremely hopeful.

"L-Like as a date? To a gala? I don't know... That's a really elegant first date, don't you think?" I questioned. I definitely blushed this time. There was no way around it. Warmth spread throughout my body and a rush of excitement sat in the pit of my stomach.

"Yeah like a date. Or as friends. Whatever you want to call it. I just want you to come with me. You'd look beautiful in a gown. I'm sure your family's done these before. I'd really like for you to come with me." he pouted.

I have gone to big events like that before but never for fun. It was always for business. Forming business deals, to incite fear, assassinations, hostile takeovers, things like that. The thought of going to one without having to do any of that made my heart race faster and there was a churning feeling in my stomach. It was unnerving. I already felt like an outsider. I watched Jaehyun's eyes filled with sadness at my silence. "Please? I don't want to be forced to go with Miyeon again," he pleaded. A growl rumbled in my chest at the mention of her name. "Absolutely not. No. I didn't say I wouldn't go. I was thinking about what to wear. I'm going." I snapped at him. He grinned widely and cheered. He was sly. I had to give him that.

"Don't stress about what to wear. I got you. Want to grab lunch still? My treat." he invited as he made eye contact with me. His eyes sparkled too much for a normal person. It was memorizing. He looked at me like there was something worth looking at. I felt too seen and exposed. Code's words circled in my head again and combined with the leftover bitterness from the memories with Han, I made the decision to stop stressing or trying to figure out what to do with Jaehyun. Trying to figure it out was making me miserable. I didn't have to define it. It can be what it is.

"Of course. I'm starving. Where do you recommend?"

"It's a cool place a few blocks from here. Do you like sushi?"

"I've spent a lot of time in Japan. So yes." We settled on the restaurant and headed out to the car.

~Chapter 8~

We were seated at a table on the patio enjoying the weather. The restaurant was a popular spot for the students at the college since it was so close. As people were walking by they stopped to talk to Jaehyun for a moment. He knew a lot of people. I wasn't sure if it was because he was the student council president or if they were his friends, but the fact was he was sociable. He was just as charming with other people as he was with me. It was apparent that he was a good man. A rarity these days. Through conversations I learned that he was really close with his brother and sister and his parents. He really adored his family. He was passionate about architecture. He had actual hobbies. He was the polar opposite of me. There was a part of me that scoffed at myself. Despite the differences, I was drawn to him. He was magnetic and I was intrigued. It was hard to describe what it was really.

Jaehyun waved the last person off with a cheerful goodbye. He turned to me apologetically. "I'm so sorry. People like talking to me. I forgot this was a popular place. Probably not the best idea for a lunch date when you want to get to know someone." he rubbed the back of his neck sheepishly. I waved it off.

"You're the student council president. I'm sure you have a lot of friends. Popularity comes with the territory, I would think. You thrive in it."

"It's not all it's cracked up to be. Trust me. Sometimes I wish I could sit back and relax." he took a sip of his soda. I tipped my head to the right, curious.

"What do you mean? You don't like it?"

"It's not that per say. I love the student council. I love helping the school, I really do. But sometimes it's a lot. On top of doing business with my family and pursuing my master's degree. It's a lot of pressure." he admitted as he looked down at his plate. From conversations about his family's corporation, it was a heavy burden he was carrying. Nam Industries owned a ton of different companies. Several financial companies specialized in different areas, five different real estate agencies, they participated in international business, and they owned multiple businesses that operated in Korea. He helped in the business sectors and occasionally used his architecture background in the real estate portion. Any reasonable person would understand that. Even though my line of work wasn't legal, it was a lot to keep up with. Not everyone could do what I did. It took a different type of strategy, organization, and fearlessness to do what I do. It was dangerous and I constantly had to look over my shoulder. The effect it had mentally just added to the pressure.

"I read this story from Greek mythology about the guy who was punished by holding up the sky. That's what I always equated the pressure to." I commented.

"Atlas? I didn't take you as someone who read Greek mythology. Yeah it feels like that. That's the best way I've heard it described." He gave me a half smile and looked up at me.

"I'm full of surprises. I relate to the feeling. It's really fucked up. Especially when people talk so much about you and don't know anything."

"Your family specialize in anything in particular?" Jaehyun inquired.

"International trade. We do a lot of investing in other corporations and stocks. He found his market there." I lied smoothly.

"Do you like it?"

"It's lucrative. I've been helping out since I was sixteen. Before that I just typed up paperwork and did errands for him. When I turned sixteen, he let me be more involved and eventually I was running business meetings with men twice my age when I was nineteen. My roles have just changed and expanded over time."

"That doesn't answer the question. I asked if you liked it? I think it's obvious that we have a lot to do with running the show." I paused at the question. I had never thought about if I liked it. I just did what I had to do.

"I don't worry about whether I like it or not. I just do what needs to be done."

"That doesn't sound like a fun way to live. Is that how you always feel?" Jaehyun said with concern. I shrugged my shoulders. I didn't have an emotional attachment to anything I did, it was the money and power that I was addicted to. People listened to me and I was revered and feared. The sight of men, who were much larger and taller than me, cowering in fear when I walked into a room gave me a rush of exhilaration.

"I'm not sure what you're asking. Isn't that what life is? Doing what needs to be done?" I responded. His confusion baffled me.

"It shouldn't be. You should be living life too. What's the point of having all this money and you do nothing with it? It's a waste. You bought a new 2023 G-Wagon G550 right out. Before it was supposed to be released. Just collecting materialistic things isn't a life, pretty." he sighed as he leaned towards me, placing his arms on the table. I tilted my head. Materialistic things were how I lived. I never had any issues. Jaehyun shook his head and looked across the table at me, sighing sadly.

"You need to live a little. Don't worry, I'm here to teach you the ways. Starting with Miyeon's party on Saturday. We're going together." Jaehyun grinned slyly.

A house party? I had never been to one but I had seen enough movies and tv shows to know they never ended well. I didn't need a run in with the police. They were dangerous enough without the police. Crowded areas were a sure way to get killed. Someone could stab you close range. A silencer on a gun, no one would know a thing. Someone could poison you. A house party would leave me exposed. The thought of that made my palms clammy and worry spread through my chest and heart started to race. I cleared my throat and shook my head.

"A house party? I don't know about that. Too many people." I disagreed.

"You're going to let me go to Miyeon's house alone?" Damn it. I already hated when he did that. The thought of him anywhere near Miyeon alone made me sick. It aggravated me. I couldn't explain why her crush on him made me feel that way, but it did.

"Fine. I'll go. You don't have to bring her up, you know?"

"Miyeon? Why? Are you jealous?" Jaehyun teased playfully.

"Absolutely not. I barely know her." He grinned knowingly and I felt my face heat cheek up. He was so pretty.

"Instead of being a smart ass, why don't you tell me about this fundraising gala." I demanded softly as I took a sip of my drink. He snickered.

"We have fundraising galas once or twice a year. It's for our donors, sponsors and old alumni to come and see the work that the school is doing. A few programs in the school are highlighted every year for work and research that they've been doing. There's a vote across the entire student body to decide who is displayed. We try to do the galas before the next academic year begins to secure funding ahead of time. It's a big deal. Getting this right is crucial. As the student council president, this is the first big test of the year. Urban legend says it determines how successful the presidency will be. I've gotten to do a few of these and each one has been better than the last." Jaehyun beamed excitedly. It was apparent that he was proud of his position and the hard work he put into it. It was admirable. I smiled softly watching him. As I was listening to him, the overwhelming need to protect him filled my chest.

"Are you listening to me or just staring?"

"Both." I blurted out without thinking. My eyes widened and I quickly looked away.

The gorgeous laugh that came from him made my heart stop. It was so warm and welcoming. The urgent need to protect him got stronger. I was in trouble, and it felt like I was reaching a point of no return. It was becoming more and more apparent that Jaehyun was solidifying himself as a presence in my life. "That's cute. I don't mind." he chuckled softly. I cleared my throat and gathered myself together.

"Yeah, yeah. Don't let it go to your head, Nam. You told me you had me on the clothes to wear. What did you mean by that?"

"I meant just that. I got you; don't you worry about it. When do you want to go shopping?"

I raised an eyebrow at him. Was he really suggesting that he'd buy me a gown for the gala? I paused for a while. I didn't know how to respond. My brain could not understand why he would want to do that. I clearly didn't need his money. So why would he say that?

"Did you malfunction on me? Are you alright, pretty?" Jaehyun asked as he raised an eyebrow at me. The longer I stayed quiet the angrier I became.

"Just trying to understand why you want to buy me a gown for the event. I have my own money. What are you trying to get at here? I don't need your pity-" I started to berate him but his hands going up in defense stopped me.

"No, no! Oh my god… That wasn't it. That wasn't what I was saying. It wasn't like that. I just want to. That's all. No strings attached." He smiled warmly and his eyes were soft. I searched them looking for anything malicious in them. There was an uneasy silence for a while. He just sat there smiling at me softly. The anger started to slowly dissipate and I was calm again. It was my turn to rub my neck sheepishly.

"O-Oh… Then I guess in that case… If you still want to, we can go whenever you want." I whispered. His demeanor was still cheerful and warm. It was almost as if the last outburst didn't happen. He was unphased by it.

"I'll check with my stylist and see when they have openings. The gala is next month, so there's no rush to choose anything right now. I'll have them send over some catalogs and we can pick some out. Then we can go try them on. I'd like your help to choose something for me too." he smiled brightly as he pulled out his phone. He said it like it was a normal thing and I found it odd. His style looked natural and authentic.

"You have a stylist? She must be rich. She dresses you well." I commented. I looked over his light blue short sleeved button up and khaki jeans and a pair of white Gucci sneakers. He looked sophisticated. As I was looking over his outfit, I found my eyes wandering over his frame. His forearms were muscular and his hands were large with clean fingernails. Traveling up his arms to his muscular biceps and toned shoulders. Jaehyun was muscular in a way that wasn't too obvious or too obnoxious. He was probably an athlete at one point and all of his hours in the gym were beneficial. His jeans were tight and hugged his legs nicely. He probably trained legs in the gym often. Even through the jeans you could see his jeans were stretching to accommodate the thickness.

"First off, she's like the family stylist. Second of all. Hey! She only helps with big event looks. Or like super important corporate meetings. Day to day looks, I dress myself. I'm a fashion icon around here. My brother is a different story. He's a lost cause. He makes her rich." Jaehyun joked as he flexed his bicep playfully. I laughed to cover up the fact that I had been staring.

He checked his watch quickly and his face dropped. "Damn it. I have class in an hour. Are you done for the day?" he sighed.

"Yeah. I only have two classes today." I replied. He looked disappointed when I told him that.

"I'll drive you back to your place and then head back to campus." He stood up to grab his backpack and mine and he extended a hand for me to take.

"I can call a cab. It's fine. Don't worry about it." He rolled his eyes and gestured to his hand again. I sighed and took it as he helped me stand up. I blushed as his fingers intertwined with mine and he smiled softly and led me out of the restaurant without letting go.

~Chapter 9~

My phone ringing roused me from a much needed nap. It had been another few sleepless nights and I had been operating on minimum sleep. Over the course of six days, I had gotten maybe fifteen hours of sleep total. I never could sleep well. Even as a kid. I just accepted it as a part of my life. I spent the time awake trying to research and find anything on the Jopok. I was coming up empty. I had started my internship, but I was still in training. I hadn't actually gotten to my assigned unit. I grumbled and rolled over grabbing my phone. Jaehyun's name appeared on the screen. I sat up and answered with sleep heavy in my voice. "Hello?"

"Hey, pretty. Did I disturb you?" he wondered. I checked the clock to see it was 2pm. I added another two hours of sleep to my collection.

"No, no. I was waking up from a nap. What's up?"

"It's Wednesday, you know what that means. Want to go to karaoke with me and some of my friends? And my stylist has a late opening at 4. We can go see some of the clothes we picked from the catalogs. Then go to karaoke afterwards." he invited. I stood up and walked over to my closet to grab something to wear.

"I'm definitely up for going to look at the clothes with your stylist. Karaoke on a Wednesday though?" I hesitated. I've never done karaoke. I know what it is of course but I didn't get the concept.

"Come on, Ae Ri. You always say next time when I invite you. I really want to take you for your first time. You haven't come out to enjoy life yet. There's a deal on food and drinks too. Can't pass that up. But most importantly, I miss you. I haven't seen you." I could hear the pout on his face.

"You saw me this morning. We walked to get a snack together. We have seen each other everyday for the past month."

"It wasn't enough time. Pleaseeeee," he begged. I rolled my eyes and chuckled.

"Okay, okay. What time should we meet?" I answered. The joyous laugh that came from him made me smile. Jaehyun and I had been spending a lot of time together. We saw each other a few times a day and I treasured it. His presence was becoming a constant for me and I started to expect to see him everyday. The thought of seeing him again sent a rush of excitement through my body and the soft smile that graced my face was genuine.

"I'll be in class until 3:30. And your place is a little far. Do you mind driving to meet me at the store and then we can go from there? I'm sorry I can't come and get you." Jaehyun said, clearly disappointed.

"I'm an adult, you know? That's why I bought a car. To drive. It's not a big deal."

"I know. But I like driving with you. You're like the perfect passenger princess." he teased. My face heated up and I smirked. He was getting more comfortable with throwing compliments my way and it kept chipping away at my guards. I cleared my throat.

"Okay, I'll meet you at 4 then," I agreed.

"Text me when you leave out and be careful. I'm excited to see you."

"See you later."

We hung up and I put a hand over my pounding heart. I breathed deeply and sat down on the edge of my bed. My mind started to wander back to our conversation. The excitement I felt before was overshadowed by an intense feeling of impending danger. That was the first time I felt in a non-threatening situation. I sighed in annoyance. I was used to the feeling, it happened often. It just never happened when I was doing something so mundane. I looked over at the clock again. I had time to take another quick nap. It was an easy fix this time. Normally sleep didn't help, but because my body and mind were so tired it would work. I set an alarm and laid back down.

At 3:30 my phone was ringing and I answered without looking at the screen knowing it was Jaehyun. "Like clockwork, Nam." I teased him as I finished buttoning up my jean shorts. He was a prompt person. Anytime he set a time to meet or plan a phone call, he stuck to it. It was a stark contrast from my style. I learned how to operate spontaneously and handle setbacks and be adaptable. His life was more structured than mine, but it was understandable. His loud laugh filled the entire room and I watched a stupid grin spread across my face. His laugh was full of life. It was like a breath of fresh air and it helped ease my racing thoughts. "I feel like you're making fun of me. Is that what this is?" he asked with a smile in his voice.

"Isn't that the foundation of who we are?"

"Point taken. I'm just getting out of class. I'll be headed toward the store. I'm going to send you the address."

"That works for me. I'm putting clothes on and I'll be on the way soon."

"Perfect. Want something from Starbucks? There's one near the store." he offered. I sighed in relief.

"Yes! I need it. Whatever you get, I need it to have espresso in it. I am so tired." I exclaimed. I looked over the outfit in the mirror and shook my head. The white tank top and jean shorts were too plain.

"Why are you so tired, pretty? I've noticed you have been pretty tired lately." Jaehyun asked with worry evident in his voice. The concern made my heart skip a beat. I wasn't used to it. But it made me feel special in a weird way.

"I don't sleep," I answered bitterly.

"What do you mean? Why aren't you sleeping?"

"I've always had issues sleeping. It's just a part of life."

"That's not normal. You know that right? You may have insomnia."

I looked down at the phone confused. "What's insomnia?" I tilted my head. I constantly moved around at night, and I did most of my work at night. I always figured it was because my brain didn't recognize the night as a time for rest. I worked well into the morning and by the time I realized that I hadn't slept, it was too late. Sometimes I would just go and go, until my body gave me no choice but to sit down and rest. It was a part of life.

"Insomnia? It's a sleep disorder. It causes you to have trouble falling asleep and it's hard to stay asleep. It can be really serious. How long has it been happening?"

"Since I was a kid. I can't tell exactly when. If I had to tell you, I probably remember being 11 or 12 and I couldn't sleep then. Maybe earlier than that," I explained as I grabbed a black pair of high waisted shorts and a black lace bralette. I grabbed a thin see through white button up shirt and put it on over the bralette and a Gucci belt. I tucked the shirt in as I zipped the shorts and put on the belt. I looked in the mirror and nodded in approval.

"That's concerning. I'll do some research. Have you left yet?" he said. I heard wind in the background, and it sounded like he was driving.

"Okay. I'm grabbing shoes and my purse, and I'll go get in the car. I'm coming, I'm coming. I couldn't find anything to wear," I assured him. I grabbed a pair of black YSL heels and white Gucci sneakers to be on the safe side.

My keys were hooked onto my purse on the living room table, and I made my way out to the living room. "Okay. Get here safe. I'll see you soon, pretty." Jaehyun said as he gave me a goodbye. I hung up and sat on the couch putting on my heels. Afterwards, I grabbed my purse and the keys making my way down the hallway to the elevator. The elevator ride to the parking garage felt longer than usual. I looked at my reflection in the glass of the elevator and I suddenly felt self-conscious. Was I overdressed for a karaoke and fitting? Is this an excessive amount of skin showing? Would Jaehyun think it was tasteless? I felt my breath quicken. "Not again. I'm already late." I mumbled to myself. I closed my eyes and took a minute to breathe deeply. There was nothing wrong. Everything was fine. My outfit was fine. Jaehyun met me in an outfit that showed skin. If he didn't like it, he would've left me alone.

My breathing returned to normal and the voices in my head were silent again. I don't know why that happens all the time. Everything can be completely fine and all of a sudden, my brain takes a detour down some kind of twisted road. I have to fight to get it back on track. I could tell when it was happening and sometimes, I could stop it before it started but if I wasn't paying attention and I let it get away from me, the thoughts would spiral out of control. Then I was suddenly sitting in the middle of my room on the floor falling apart. Putting myself back was a lengthy process after those moments, so I tried to stay busy constantly, so I didn't have a chance to be still for too long. The elevator doors opened. I stepped out into the parking garage and found my car.

I grinned smugly taking in the Rubellite red metallic color of the truck. I got lucky when Jaehyun took me to the dealership he used. The dealership didn't get too many G-wagon SUVs shipped in since they weren't very popular. The 2025 G 550 SUVs weren't officially out but the company started to send them to gauge reaction from dealerships. They got a shipment with a silver; a metallic lunar blue; a bright cardinal red and this darker metallic red one. I was stuck between either red color, but I liked the way the slightly tinted windows looked on this one. Elation filled my chest as I ran my hand over the smooth paint. I climbed in and started the car. The smooth sound of the engine eased me back into a calm state. Material things were a sure way to level me out.

The address he sent was a large white pristine building. The large windows revealed mannequins wearing expensive brands and under the mannequins you could see the label names written in bold black letters. Inside you could see a large open area and some clothes racks scattered around. I saw Jaehyun standing next to his car in one of the first parking spots and I slowed down and rolled down my window, honking the horn loudly. I cackled when he yelled out and jumped in fear. "Choi Ae Ri! That's not fucking funny!" he yelled as he put a hand over his chest. I parked the car in the middle of the lot for a second.

"It was too tempting. You looked cute just standing there waiting for me. Did you wait long?" I teased playfully.

"No. You're not *that* late." I checked my watch. It was 4:06. I really wasn't that late.

"I got caught up trying to choose an outfit. It wasn't my intention."

"It's fine, pretty. I was teasing. Go ahead and park. Let's get inside."
I nodded and parked two spots down from him. He came up to my side
and waited for me to turn the car off and he opened my door for me. I
looked at him for a second. He smiled and offered his hand to help me
down. I took it and once I was on the ground, I could feel him staring at
me. I turned to him and he made eye contact with me smiling as he held
out an iced coffee for me.

"It's hot so I got you an iced coffee today. You liked the hazelnut
flavor last time, so I got that again and I had them add two espresso shots
for you. You can't taste it." he explained. I sighed in relief. I tilted my head
for   a   second.
"You tasted my coffee? What? Are you trying to get an indirect kiss from
me?" I mocked lightly. He paused for a second. He was contemplating
something. "I used a straw for your information, but if you ever want a kiss
let me know. I'd be happy to oblige." He winked and walked off as I stared
at his back. I was caught off guard. His duality was something that I had
never encountered before and it made my head spin. I cleared my throat
and followed after him. He led the way into the store and a man and woman
greeted us at the door.

"Good afternoon, Mr. Nam. It's nice to see you again." the woman
smiled and bowed respectfully. She was foreign. Definitely not Korean or
Japanese. Probably American or European. The man beside her was quiet
and he bowed as well. I could feel him staring at me, so I looked at him
fully. His eyes quickly looked somewhere else as I smirked. I turned to
notice Jaehyun looking at him too with an unreadable expression.

"Hey Rachel. Who's the new guy?" Jaehyun greeted cheerfully. His
demeanor switched to a lighthearted and happy one. I kept my expression
neutral to hide the shock.

"Oh, this is a new employee. His name is Sooyoon. I'm training
him." Rachel introduced him. The man bowed respectfully again and
offered a small hello. He was nervous now.

Jaehyun nodded in acknowledgement. He turned to me and smiled
warmly. "This is Choi Ae Ri. This is who we're looking at dresses for."
Jaehyun informed her. I reached out to shake her head and just to spite

Jaehyun, I shook Sooyoon's hand too. Sooyoon blushed slightly and didn't look at me.

"Sorry about him. He's really shy. It's his first day. But he'll get warmed up soon." Rachel apologized. She told him to go to the back and get the rack of clothes set out for us. He nodded and walked off quickly.

"If I can say Miss Choi, you are extremely pretty. I love your outfit." Rachel complimented me.

"I appreciate the compliment. You recognize style, so you must be good at what you do." I laughed.

"I would hope so. I've been working for the family for about 4 years. So I really appreciate their trust in me."

"Oh stop it, Rachel. You're one of the best. Don't be so humble." Jaehyun interjected. She smiled softly and blushed a little at the compliment. I had to work harder than I liked to admit to keep my expression neutral. A small spark of jealousy settled in my stomach.

"Thank you, sir. Please follow me." When she turned her back, I stared at Jaehyun incredulously.

"Payback's a bitch." he smirked as he stuck his tongue out at me before he followed her. I gasped slightly. That bastard.

She led us to the back of the store and it was a preview room. There was a curved white couch and a large mirror along the wall. In the middle of the room was an elevated platform. Must be where the viewing happens. This set up felt like it came from a TV show I saw in America once while I was doing some business over there. The name of the show escaped me. Jaehyun sat on the couch and smiled as he crossed his legs. "It's just a fitting. There's no pressure to choose a dress right now. We can keep looking if needed. Whatever you want, I got it." Jaehyun explained. He made it sound so casual. Like this was normal for him. Nothing about this was normal. But he was in his element apparently. It was glaringly obvious that I was not. When I did leave my house and go somewhere, I was always alone. I went shopping alone. I tried things on my own and bought them for myself.

75

Seeing Jaehyun being so eager to buy me expensive things was strange. Men couldn't do that for me. They always gasped and got frustrated to see the price of the things I liked. It made me laugh normally. I got a kick out of it. However, Jaehyun didn't bat an eye. He didn't sweat. He didn't stutter. He was just cool about it. It was attractive. But the kindness of the situation was starting to settle over me and it made my chest tighten slightly. No one had ever done something like this for me and I almost felt awkward. There was a part of me that felt unworthy? And it wasn't about the clothes. I felt like I was unworthy of the kindness he was showing me. I didn't really believe him when he said that he wanted me to go with him to the gala. And I certainly didn't believe him when he said he wanted to buy my dress. Especially after my outburst all that time ago.

"Is there a preferred style of dress you'd like to see first, Miss Choi?" Rachel asked politely. "Mermaid or bodycon." I replied. She nodded and turned to go to the rack of clothes that had been positioned along the back wall. I turned to see Jaehyun on his phone scrolling through something. "Checking your bank account?" I teased. He looked up and rolled his eyes.

"Don't make me laugh sweetheart. I do what I want and buy whatever I want." he laughed loudly as he grabbed a champagne bottle out of an ice bucket on the end table next to the couch.

"Want a glass? It's Dom Perignon." He poured two glasses and offered one to me. I took it and looked up at him as he stood in front of me.

"Cheers to a beautiful girl finding a lovely dress." he smirked playfully and chuckled. It was cheesy but I liked it. Something about him being cheesy and cheeky while still being suave and cool worked for him. It was a good mixture.

"Cheers." I clinked my glass to his and took a sip. We held eye contact until the attendants rolled a smaller rack of evening gowns into the room. I turned around to start looking for something. A gold beaded dress caught my eye. It was off shoulder and the top was ruffled. Upon closer inspection the design was lace and almost feather shaped. It was still gold and beaded. The dress had a long split on the left side that started at the of the thigh. The bottom half of the dress was lace and I noticed the entire thing was see through. There was a one piece under the top of the dress that was a darker gold color for modesty. I wouldn't usually wear something so decorative, but I really thought it was nice. I decided to put it aside to try it on.

The next dress was plain black and had a mermaid body shape with thin spaghetti straps. The third dress was a short silk bodycon dress and it had a matching silk cover up that dragged across the floor and it had a belt attached. I liked that one, but it didn't feel right for a gala. I would wear something like that at home. Another dress was red and made out of velvet and it was strapless and swept the floor. It was simple and elegant, but it felt a little too warm for April. The last dress was a white blazer dress that stopped above the knee. I never saw a blazer dress that long. I faced Jaehyun and he was smiling warmly watching me. His eyes held amusement and a genuine warmth that made me look away and my heart pounded in my chest.

"Having fun princess? Did you want to keep looking? Want to try on your stuff?" he asked. I could hear the snicker in his voice. My ears heated at the nickname. It wasn't a new nickname, but it felt different in this setting.

"I'll try these on." I answered as I grabbed the dresses and went to the dressing room. Catching my reflection in the long mirror, I saw my reddened cheeks and ears. I internally groaned. I'm better than this. I seriously am. I'm not some teenager. "Get it together." I mumbled to myself.

"Do you need help Miss Choi? I can hand the dresses to you." I accepted the help and closed the door to the room. I tried the blazer dress first. I was a fan of the style, but it was too business-like for a Gala. But back home I could use this. I decided to get it for myself. A hostile takeover would be a good setting for it. Or when I kill the head family of the Jopok wearing all white. The thought of me standing over the corpses of the people who killed my mother made me chuckle darkly. "Ae Ri! You got it there? We'd like to see, please?" Jaehyun called from outside. I sighed gently.

"That was a shitty thing to do, universe." I mumbled. My shoulders slumped. I was brutally reminded that Jaehyun's kindness wasn't supposed to make me smile or feel shy because I was here on actual business. None of this was actually supposed to be happening. A part of me didn't care though. I wanted to enjoy this for however long it would last. It couldn't hurt right?

I opened the door and walked out to show the dress. "You look pretty, princess. What do you think?" Jaehyun smiled. He looked like he was having fun.

"Too business for the Gala, but I like it. I may buy it for myself." I replied, twirling once. "Absolutely not. I got it. It's yours." His tone told me it wasn't up for debate. I nodded wordlessly and turned to go back and try the velvet dress on. The velvet dress was nice but too long, I didn't want it. So I put it back on the rack. The matching silk dress and cover up looked really nice on me. It was form fitting and comfortable, so I decided to show Jaehyun.

"You like it?" Jaehyun beamed as he glanced over my body. I blushed and twirled a few times to examine it in the mirror.

"Not for the gala, but I'd wear this at home lounging around or out somewhere. I do really like it." I said mindlessly as I stared at my reflection.

"I know somewhere you can wear it. It's yours." he said matter of fact. I turned to him to protest.

"It's not necessary really. I can buy this one at least." He stared at me unwavering. I went silent. He was serious about this. He was really going to buy these dresses. I felt like a doll that was being dressed up and shown off. I wasn't used to this much attention. It was slightly off putting. Rachel and Sooyoon waiting to see what dress I would choose combined with Jaehyun's intense staring and his unwavering attention made me feel exposed.

I retreated back into the dressing room and took a minute to calm my racing heart. I looked around for the next dress. I picked up the gold dress and put it on. "This is…amazing," I gasped as I turned around. The dress laid flawlessly. It was a perfect fit. It wasn't too tight or too long. The split was laid perfectly at the top of my thigh. It hugged my hips and snatched my waist in. The design up top was prim and proper. The off the shoulder gave my cleavage the respect it deserved. The gold color meshed well with my skin. This was the dress. I knew it. It made me feel like a real princess. A bright smile graced my face and it almost took me by surprise. I rushed out to the others. Jaehyun was talking to Sooyoon and Rachel and it was her who saw me first. She gasped loudly and covered her mouth. That caught his attention. He adjusted his body to see me and his jaw dropped. It was silent for a while. It made me nervous.

"Okay someone say something. Because I really like this one and I know this is the one. I will pass out if you guys say it's ugly." I demanded as I looked down. I felt extremely shy. I put my hand over my chest and willed myself to breathe. I have never felt so desperate for someone's approval.

"You look beautiful. Seriously Choi Ae Ri. You're stunning." Jaehyun beamed, staring me down again. He had a dream-like look in his eye as he stared. I blushed and my chest hurt. Like physically hurt. I was hit with a wave of emotions that I had never felt before. Hearing him say I was beautiful in the most heartfelt way set my body on fire. He looked at me like there was something worth looking at. My eyesight got blurry for a moment, and I realized I was tearing up. I turned away to save face and I caught sight of my reflection in the mirror to the left and I just looked different. I felt different.

I was never insecure in my looks. I never had trouble getting male attention, but I felt genuinely beautiful. I think for the first time ever. There was a different type of sparkle in my eyes. "I think we have a winner." Rachel applauded excitedly. I nodded and looked over at her.

"You really do look gorgeous. I've never seen him look at anyone the way he does you. There's something really special between you two." she said softly as she made a few adjustments to the dress so it fit even better. I looked at her through the mirror and she smiled. I looked away and toyed with my fingers.

"That's what I'm worried about." I admitted. I didn't want to acknowledge it. That would make it real and that would complicate things.

"It'll work itself out. But don't cheat yourself. He's a good man." she suggested.

"We'll take this one too, if it wasn't obvious Rachel." I said as I caught Jaehyun turning to look at us. I caught him gleaming with the words.

"That's my favorite. Of course, we're buying." he agreed.

"Of course, sir."

After I got dressed and met back up with him at the front, he paid for everything just like he said he would. 3,969,900 Korean won. He didn't flinch. I respected that. "Safe to say, you're officially spoiled, sweetheart. Is there anything else you need? We're already out and about. Might as well, keep shopping. We don't have to meet others until 8. I'll get your makeup or whatever you need." he offered as he rubbed the back of his neck. Was he shy? He had to be a shapeshifter in a previous life. He switched personalities quickly. I shrugged. I was having fun. I didn't care what we did next. I agreed.

"We can do that. I need some makeup and skincare. I guess I should wear some since it's for a special event." I grinned and Jaehyun smiled and nodded. Taking my bags to the car, he opened the car door for me.

"Where do you usually go? Or what do you use?" he asked as he walked me to the car.

"I've used Innisfree for skin care. I like shopping in Chicor for makeup."

"Ever been to Stylenanda? I heard that's a good place." I looked over at him inquisitively. How did he know about that brand?

"I have a sister. Don't do that." he chuckled lightly. A bright and genuine laugh escaped me. It shocked me because it just sounded different. I paused for a moment and looked at him. He was staring too. "I'm glad I was able to make you smile today." he smiled warmly. I returned my own warm smile.

It was quiet for a moment between us. Things felt a little easier between us. It was comfortable. I know the change was because something in me happened when I tried on that gold dress. I couldn't describe what happened. I just felt truly safe all of a sudden. It was a new feeling but I liked it. "Thank you." I told him suddenly. He laughed softly.

"I got a thank you. You're feeling really good today." He dramatically put a hand over his chest and gasped. I playfully punched him.

"I was trying to be nice and you ruined it, Nam." I complained as I got in the car. He grinned and leaned on the door of my car.

"I'm sorry, princess. I'm teasing. It's really no problem. I like seeing you smile. I'd do it again." he said as he gently put a stray hair back in place for me.

~Chapter 10~

Jaehyun led me down the hallway of the karaoke lounge and the laughter of people filled the building from the doors we walked by. The atmosphere of the building was upbeat, and the floor vibrated with the music. He stopped in front of a room and knocked before he opened the door slightly and peaked in. Calls of his name rang out and he opened the door fully. He waved me forward and took my hand. "Everyone's really nice. You'll like them." he promised. I took a deep breath and nodded as he let me walk ahead of him slightly.

Six new faces waved and greeted me excitedly when I walked in. "I love your outfit! It's so pretty!" a girl with blue hair exclaimed as she ran up to shake my hand. I looked at her stunned for a second before I smiled back lightly. She was kind of adorable.

"Easy Haeun. Give her a chance to settle in and feel us out first." a short man with blonde hair and a tattoo sleeve on his right arm laughed.

"I'm being nice. I'm excited to meet her. You said Jaehyun was excited to bring her out." she whined. I turned to see Jaehyun walk up behind me and he grinned.

"So, you talk about me? It better be good things." I joked. He rolled his eyes in response.

"What good things? I'm confused," he jabbed at me. I gasped and punched his arm.

"Relax Ae Ri. I was just joking. No need to look so hostile. I rolled my eyes and punched him in the arm. He laughed as he held his arm.

"You're so strong. Why?" I shrugged and let a smirk spread across my face.

The group laughed softly as they watched us interact. "Okay guys. This is Choi Ae Ri. She just came back from studying abroad in Japan. Ae Ri, these are my friends. That couple over there in the matching Hello Kitty shirts, that's Seojun and Jiwoo." Jaehyun introduced them as they waved. The girl had short brown hair cut into a bob and the boy was taller and really skinny with glasses. They really were wearing matching Hello Kitty shirts. It was kind of cute.

"The guy with the tattoo and the overly excited smurf is Minhyun and Haeun." Jaehyun told me. The girl who shook my hand was still standing in front of me and she pouted up at Jaehyun. She was tiny. She was shorter than me, but Jaehyun definitely towered over her.

"I will not tolerate this slander! I'm not a smurf," she protested.

"Yeah, you're more like Stitch from the Disney show." Jiwoo interjected. Haeun turned around shocked and stomped over to the taller girl. I snickered watching the interaction.

"Anyways. The giant in the back dressed in the orange hoodie and the girl dressed in pink in the corner is Seunghyun and Nari. The stars of the night." Jaehyun smiled warmly as the new faces saluted him. Even as he was sitting, it was apparent that Seunghyun was just as tall as Jaehyun. He looked stern and the black long haired woman beside him looked softer and had a mature aura about herself.

They were an interesting group altogether. The affection was apparent between them though. It could be seen when they all rushed to hug him and give him handshakes as he approached the couch with me in tow. I stood awkwardly behind him watching the interaction. I couldn't relate to what was happening and I felt a twinge of jealousy. No one had ever been that excited to me. It was a stinging reminder of how different I really was. And I would never be like him. I folded my hands in front of me and I could feel myself start to shrink back as my heart started to race. My breath quickened. I toyed with my fingers trying to fight the anxious feeling off. "Ae Ri? Why are you so far away? Come join the group!" Nari welcomed me as she held her arms out to make a space for me on the side of the couch with the girls. Jaehyun turned to face me quickly when she spoke to me. He looked concerned. I made eye contact with him, and instantly started to feel better.

"You okay, princess?" he checked in with me.

I nodded. "Yeah. I didn't want to interrupt you guys," I lied smoothly. He tilted his head and looked me over once. My breath started to slow down, and I felt at ease again. I walked over to join the girls on the left side of the couch.

"You are so pretty, Ae Ri. Oh my goodness. It's so great to meet you finally. Jaehyun says great things about you." Jiwoo cooed excitedly as she leaned over and put a hand on my shoulder. I blushed lightly and looked over at the other girls.

"Aw, thank you. What do you guys study?" I said as I looked over at everyone.

"Jiwoo is in the business department. I'm in the art department. Nari is in the nursing department." Haeun smiled.

"You're in the law department right? Do you like it? What made you want to do that?" Nari asked curiously. I shrugged.

"I just wanted to do something different," I said.

"I knew it! Rebelling against the family business." Jaehyun exclaimed as he looked over at me and pointed dramatically.

"I told you that when you first told us about her!" Nari corrected as she threw a napkin at him playfully. I didn't feel jealous watching them interact. Knowing that all of the girls in the room had a significant other eased me. I didn't feel the need to be protective over him. I was at peace around them. They seemed like good people, he was safe with them.

After a little bit of conversation and a few songs, Haeun suddenly gasped and tapped Nari quickly. "I just realized we never told Ae Ri what we were celebrating." she said quietly. I looked up from the beer I was drinking at the mention of my name. I suddenly remembered Jaehyun called them the stars of the night. I didn't know what we were celebrating. Nari gasped and looked over at Jaehyun.

"You didn't tell her what was going on?" Nari shook her head sadly.

"We had a lot to do today. It slipped my mind. I figured you guys would tell her." Jaehyun said defensively. We ended up talking a lot as we hung out together after the fitting, but the karaoke event was not a topic of conversation.

"Sure Jaehyun. Sorry about that, Ae Ri. Well Jaehyun went to the US a week ago and he landed an engineering job after graduation and we're all really excited for him." Nari smiled brightly as she pinched his cheek. Seunghyun blushed slightly and looked down.

"Stop it. You have to tell them your good news too." he reminded her gently. The others sat up a little straighter. I guess her announcement was new to them. Nari smiled brightly and reached into her purse and pulled out a small box and opened it revealing a diamond ring. The others gasped loudly as she put it on her left ring finger. A small smile crossed my face.

"I'm engaged!" she squealed. Everyone erupted into loud cheering for them. I clapped along with them and cheered for them.

The genuine happiness and celebration happening around me was really sweet. It was beautiful that she found her forever person. I didn't know them that well but watching them interact I could see Nari and Seunghyun were a really nice couple and there was a lot of happiness there. A feeling of resentment coursed through my veins and I fought to keep it at bay. It wasn't directed towards them. I would never have that and the realization hurt more than I thought it would. Yes, I chose to remain single because of my position, but the reality of the situation was harsher than I thought. No one would want me. I was way too cynical and I had seen too much to be someone's significant other. I found myself glancing over at Jaehyun and he was celebrating with Seunghyun over the news. A crushing wave of frustration and disappointment washed over. It was a reminder that I couldn't have Jaehyun. No matter how much I may be fond of him. This was fleeting. It wasn't going to last. I had a completely different life than him.

I caught his eye and he tilted his head. I gave him a small smile and raised my glass to him before drinking my beer. The beer definitely was not strong enough to cover up the pain that was coursing through my chest. I didn't realize just how deep Jaehyun was already ingrained in me. I hadn't changed a lot. I was still short tempered and defensive. He saw that firsthand. I was standoffish and didn't interact with people a lot. He saw that, but he was still kind to me. He wanted to be around me. He chose to be around me. It wasn't like Code who had to be around me because we worked together. Jaehyun saw something in me that made him want to be around me. I wish I knew what it was.

"This calls for soju everyone! We need to kick this celebration into high gear! It's on me!" Minhyun cheered loudly as put an order in on the tablet. That was what I needed. It would lessen the feeling. I cheered with everyone so no one would suspect a thing. Nari made eye contact with me and she smiled softly at me. I smiled back and nodded at her in congratulations. A waiter knocked on the door and Minhyun went to grab the bottles of soju. He ordered 5 bottles to start off with.

"Everyone grab a glass. We need to make a toast. Jaehyun hyung! You do it!" Seojun said as he grabbed a glass and handed one to Jaehyun. It obviously took him by surprise, but Jaehyun still stood and poured himself a shot.

"Oh man. Put me on the spot, Seojun. Okay. Um… Seunghyun hyung and Nari nuna, we are all so happy for you. It's been a long journey for you guys. And you have taught us all a lot. May one day our relationships grow into what you guys have. Congratulations and we wish you all the happiness and joy! Cheers to the happy couple!" Jaehyun cheered and we all touched glasses and downed the shots. The burn was pleasant and eased the ache.

After a couple of shots, I could see why people liked karaoke. A bunch of drunk people singing the words to popular songs out of tune and completely wrong. I had never laughed so hard. Seunghyun was fully enjoying his time. "Dude, you guys will have to come and visit us when we get settled into our place!" Seunghyun shouted as he stood in the front of the room. Nari was laughing and trying to clean up some of the mess he had made. This had turned out to be really nice and I was having fun. The girls were all strong and opinionated in their own rights. I liked them and hoped maybe I could see them again.

"J-Jaehyun! A-And you have to bring Ae Ri! Your girlfriend is awesome and fun to be around!" Seunghyun drunkenly said as he pointed at him. Nari gasped and looked over at me.

"I am so sorry. He's drunk. Jaehyun, you know how he is… Baby, they're not a couple. Stop saying that. You're embarrassing us." Nari hissed. She playfully swatted at him as he hogged the microphone.

I waved off the comment. In my buzzed state, the comment didn't hurt so much. It was more of an annoying ache. "But why not?! They look so good together and they seem like a couple. It's confusing! Whatever! Jaehyunnie! You have to promise to bring her!" Seunghyun pressed.

"Okay, Hyung. I promise I'll bring her. She will be around for a long time," Jaehyun promised.

I looked at him with a raised eyebrow. It sent a warm feeling hearing him say that, I couldn't lie. It almost eclipsed the pain I felt. He was so hopeful and he didn't care about my flaws. Maybe there was a way I could figure out how to balance it. His hopefulness was infectious. Seunghyun smiled widely and then turned to me.

"You'll come right, Ae Ri?" he asked hopefully. He was trying hard to keep his voice low and talk to me in a level tone. I chuckled at effort and nodded.

"I'll be there if you want me to be." I agreed. He cheered loudly and wobbled over to his seat to collapse next to Nari.

With the microphone free, Jaehyun took it and stood up. Everyone cheered loudly and whistled. "Finally! We were wondering when you were going to sing!" Jiwoo cheered as she sat up and leaned over to me.

"Did Jaehyun ever tell you he's the king of karaoke?" she teased. I took another shot and shook my head. He had not mentioned that.

"No. He kept that to himself." I replied as I looked over at him.

"Stop it guys. It's embarrassing." he waved it off.

"Jaehyun sings like an angel!" Minhyun teased. I smiled and nodded.

"Well, I think he should sing. What's the hold up?" I added. Jaehyun rolled his eyes and turned to choose a song.

A melody that sounded familiar started to play. It was a Korean song that I had heard before. I just couldn't remember the name. The girls all gasped and started to giggle. I looked over at them and everyone was staring at me. I didn't understand what was happening. Then he started to sing. He really had a great voice. He definitely had some training in it. The lyrics played on the screen guiding him along and I followed along reading them. I couldn't hide the blush that took over my face. The song was about telling someone that you liked them. I was the only single person in the room, so was he talking about me? Was he telling me that he liked me in front of all his friends?

I didn't want to overthink, but I couldn't help it. A lyric in the song talked about how if the other person wasn't comfortable, the singer would back off and they were willing to wait. Jaehyun sang that part as he was looking at me. It felt like it was directed towards me. If that's what he was telling me, what was I supposed to say in response? How was I supposed to respond? I had never done that before. My palms started to sweat and my chest started to feel tight with anxiousness. The idea of actually opening up and being vulnerable enough to say something like that sent more fear through me than anything else.

While trying to keep my face and body language neutral, a strange thought crossed my mind. What if I was punishing myself for something I had no control over? It wasn't my fault that this was who I was. I did what I was taught. I was a product of my environment. Could I be blamed for that? Hell Han, as much of a monster as he is, he at one point had someone who was with him. He had other women in his life too. My mother at least cared enough about him to have a child with him. Maybe she loved him. The thought sent a chill down my spine. If she did love him and he failed to protect her… He was weak. He was careless and uncoordinated. I would never let that happen. When I looked up at Jaehyun, he made eye contact with me and it broke me out of my thoughts. He got to the final chorus of the song and there was something sincere and unfamiliar in his eyes. The song ended and everyone started cheering loudly. I clapped along with them and I smiled softly. He came and sat next to me after the song.

"When were you going to tell me you could sing?" I questioned. I just wanted to keep things normal. I didn't want to question it just in case I was wrong.

"I did chorus in school when I was younger. Don't make fun of me." Jaehyun answered as he looked at the screen to see his score. A perfect 100. Of course, he did everything perfectly. Everyone cheered and congratulated him.

"Our Jaehyunnie is perfect as usual. And as always, the hopeless romantic." Seunghyun teased from his slumped over state on the couch. Jaehyun blushed slightly and leaned over to hide his face on my shoulder. I chuckled and reached up to ruffle his hair. I was more confused than before about what to do, but Jaehyun was worth it. I couldn't describe how I felt about him, but he was worth everything.

~Chapter 11~

I pulled into the parking lot of the Ivory Springs event space and parked in the closest spot available. Jaehyun had called me and asked to come to the hotel to see the set up for the gala tonight. He sounded extremely stressed out too, so I had to come and see if he was okay. He had been busy lately so I didn't see him as frequently as I had but he made sure to call me and Facetime me and he would stop by to see me at my classes. I was eager to see him. I walked up to the building and looked up the wide staircase to get to the entrance. There was a red long carpet going up the twenty steps and leading into the massive building. Jaehyun had told me this event space was fairly new, being built a year or two ago. It was two stories, and the first floor had a second set of doors that led to a lobby and lounge area. There was a bar off to the right straight ahead and the kitchen was towards the back left of the building. The event space was upstairs.

As I walked into the building, I saw the doors were open to see into the lounge area decorated in dark blue and white balloon clusters tied to two decorative boards welcoming everyone to Seoul National University's twentieth fundraising gala. Blue and white streamers hung from the ceiling and there were blue and white LED lights behind the bar lighting the bar up. I saw the long winding staircase that led upstairs and I started the journey. When I arrived at the top, there was a small hallway and then I would reach the event room. When I arrived at the space, I saw Miyeon standing in front of Jaehyun happily chirping about something. Decorators were running around and setting up round tables and decorating the walls. I grimaced as I saw them talking.

I walked up to them and he turned to me smiling. "There you are! I'm so happy to see you!" he exclaimed excitedly as he moved in to hug me. Miyeon waved and smiled at me.

"Hey Ae Ri. How are you?" Miyeon said taking a step back. I nodded in acknowledgement and gave her a forced smile.

"Good. I'm happy to see you too, Jae. It's been a while since I've seen you face to face. I've missed it." I answered.

"Aw. Missing my presence already after a few days? I've called you and still saw you in between classes. I never missed our lunch outings." he smirked. I noticed that Miyeon was gone and I smirked slyly. I liked her better when she was not around him. He snickered.

"Jealousy is cute on you." Jaehyun teased as he put an arm around my waist. I raised an eyebrow and tilted my head.

"Jealous? Absolutely not." I shook my head laughing.

"Are you sure? You barely acknowledged her and when you did it was short." He looked back at me with a mirrored expression.

"She had nothing to do with what we were discussing. She was irrelevant. That's all." I explained. He chuckled.

"If you're not jealous, then maybe I should ask Miyeon to join us. How about that?"

My face dropped as I snapped at him with a sharp no. Anger rose in my throat and it tightened at the thought and I felt annoyance rush through me. "Relax princess. I was just joking. No need to look so hostile." Jaehyun said as he pinched my cheek. I rolled my eyes and punched him in the arm lightly. He laughed and led me into the room further. We walked to the stage that was built for the night and he helped me climb up to sit on the edge. He followed beside me.

"How have you been? You look tired." I was genuinely concerned. I noticed the dark circles under his eyes and the tiredness on his face. I also didn't miss the way his jaw clenched.

"This has been a long ass ride. Honestly. I'm tired. I've been up since 6am. I had to do some business with my dad and then I had to drive over here to get the keys and let the workers in by 8am. Then tonight I have to charm the hell out of 300 donors, the press and anyone else who shows up as a plus one. It's tiring." he explained as he sighed deeply. The weight was starting to get to him. He sighed heavily.

"If you're tired of it, why not let your vice president take over for a while? At least so you can rest. They're decorating, what harm can be done?" I asked.

"What are you suggesting? I ditch?" He turned and looked at me with a conflicted expression.

"At least for now. We obviously have to come back. But it's only 11 right now. You can at least rest. We can go back to my place. I drove." I suggested.

He went wide eyed for a moment. He hadn't been back to my place since helping me move in. He paused for a moment and nodded. "I like the way you think. Could I get ready at your place? I brought my stuff just in case I got stuck here all day. My driver dropped me off." Jaehyun said as he hopped down and helped me down. I nodded. He grinned widely and kissed me on the forehead with an excited mumble of how I was the best. I giggled and folded my arms watching him run off. Having him back beside me was a relief.

I was having a hard time not seeing as much as I used to. It was lonely. I spent a lot of time by myself and in solitude but I never realized how lonely and isolating it really was until Jaehyun came along. It didn't feel the same as it did back in Japan. In Japan, being alone was a necessity. I didn't go anywhere. I had to hide because I was wanted. I moved in silence. I moved in the shadows. If I did go anywhere, I had to take great lengths to disguise myself. Here in Korea, being alone felt like a punishment. I didn't have to be alone. Not when Jaehyun and his friends were so willing to incorporate me into their lives. When I was alone, I was tormented by my own thoughts and feelings and then that made it worse. I found myself replaying the most violent and cruel moments over and over again because I could rarely sleep. I have spent hours trying to figure out why it happened or explain why it happened and I never got an answer.

Whenever I was with Jaehyun or around him, things were quiet in my head. There was peace with him. I was becoming certain of him the more time we spent together. Did it complicate things for me? Yes. I still didn't know how to describe how I felt about him. I still was trying to figure out how I could juggle my assignment and my job and keep it a secret from him. I was still struggling with trying to understand what was going on with my emotions and in my head. I blamed my possessiveness for a large part of the problems. I just wanted Jaehyun close. I wanted him with me only. I wanted his kindness for myself. The thought of him with anyone else drove me insane with murderous jealousy. And I really didn't need that type of trouble at this time.

I was pulled from my thoughts when Jaehyun jogged back up to me snickering and holding a large black clothes bag and a large duffle bag. "Come on, let's get out here before Miyeon and the secretary find out I'm leaving. The vice president has it covered." he said quickly. I laughed along with him and we made our way out of the event space quickly. We hurried to the elevator and made it downstairs in record time. "Have I ever told you, your car is really nice?" Jaehyun chuckled as he hopped into the passenger seat. I laughed as I put on my seatbelt and pulled out of the parking lot.

"It may have been mentioned once or twice, but you're welcome to say it again. It strokes my ego." I replied.

"Nevermind. You don't need any more of that."

"You're very ungrateful for someone who I just saved from a hostage situation." I teased as I looked over at him. He chuckled and looked back at me.

"Thank you. I mean it. I appreciate the ride and the escape opportunity." he told me seriously.

"Of course. I know the feeling. So, I figured I'd help. Have you eaten?"

"Only some fruit and a couple of nutrition bars. I'm starving."

"I made some onigiri at my place. You can have it."

A small smile graced his handsome face. "Aw, you're feeding me? You care about me. I feel special." he jabbed lightly. I looked ahead at the road. He just might have been right. Instead of agreeing, I resorted to sarcasm and teasing him.

"It's a privilege. Consider yourself lucky." I said breathlessly. The knowing smirk on his face made my hands tighten on the wheel. I was completely dressed but I felt bare and completely exposed. A quiet settled over us until I heard light snoring. I looked over to see he had fallen asleep and I chuckled. He looked really peaceful while he was asleep. The stress was gone from his face and he looked much younger than twenty six. He was older than me by a year but when people saw us together they swore we were twenty, twenty two at most. I pulled into the parking garage of my building and parked in my designated spot. I spent a few minutes sitting there in silence and watching him sleep.

A warmth settled in my stomach as I looked at him and I sighed softly. He didn't make this easy on me. Over the time I've known him, he's proven himself to be a genuinely good person. A good man. A damn near perfect man. He was hard working and passionate. He loved people. He cared about them and cared about them being happy. That care extended to me. He took time out of his schedule to send me a lot of information about insomnia and what could cause it. I hadn't actually read it, however. Something made me nervous about reading the information. I don't know what I would find out. What if I found out something that would make me feel worse than I already have been feeling? What would Jaehyun say if I told him I read it and then he made fun of me? The thought made me shiver uncomfortably. I couldn't take that.

"What are you thinking about? You've been staring at me for a while." he mumbled quietly as he sat up slowly. I slightly jumped back at his voice. How long had he been awake? I cleared my throat and looked out of the window quickly. I could feel my cheeks heat up.

"I-I wasn't staring. Your neck was at a weird angle, and I adjusted it. I was making sure it didn't move back," I lied. He scoffed and I could feel him roll his eyes.

"I can feel when someone is staring at me while I'm sleeping. It's not a weird thing. You've been staring at least for 5 minutes. Since we've been parked at least."

"I was making sure your neck was okay." I repeated almost defensively. I had been embarrassed enough in front of him. I didn't need anymore embarrassment. He let out a small laugh.

"Okay, Choi. I believe you. Thank you. I appreciate your concern. Are you still willing to feed me, so I can take a nap again?" I turned to him and he was grinning playfully at me. I couldn't help but soften.

"Yeah, I am. Come on. I want to show you the new stuff I've gotten since you were over last." I invited him as I started to open the door.

"I got it! When do you ever open the doors when we ride together?" he snapped as he hurried out of the car and came to open my door. I shook my head softly and stepped down as he held my hand to help me.

I sat at the bar in the lounge while Jaehyun went to check in with the student council vice president and secretary. The lounge area was beautifully decorated in the dark blue and white colors of the school. The gala was in full swing, the majority of the people were already making their way upstairs to find the places at the tables that had been set up. The upstairs was decorated extravagantly and it looked fantastic. Jaehyun and his student council had done really well. The hard work paid off and I know he was relieved. "Oh my god! I love your dress! It's so pretty, Ae Ri!" I heard Miyeon's shrill voice yell out. I looked up at her approaching figure over the rim of my glass. I fought the urge to roll my eyes. She ran up to me and embraced me in a tight hug that I stiffly returned. I offered her a small smile in politeness.

"Thanks. Jaehyun got it for me. He helped me choose it." I beamed. It was petty, I know. She audibly paused.

"O-Oh, I was just going to ask you if you've seen him. He did say you guys were coming together." she stumbled over her words and I pretended to be clueless as I smiled wider at her. The color drained from her face and she cleared her throat to regain her composure.

"He went to meet with the vice president and secretary. He should be back soon." I scanned her dress of her choice. She wore a floor length sheath dress that was made of black velvet and covered in silver glitter. It was rather plain for her. I was expecting more.

"Oh well. I'll see him later. What do you think about everything? I helped design it." she smiled brightly. She recovered from the blows quickly, I have to give her that. I fought the urge to roll my eyes again. More like she pitched a few ideas for some table centerpieces and banners. Maybe a few banners. She didn't put in any real work to do anything from what Jaehyun told me. She blew a gasket when she found out Jaehyun slipped away earlier today.

"It's nice. I give you props. Congratulations!" I told her as I sipped my champagne.

"Thank you! Where did you get your dress from? I really do love it."

"It's Prada," I replied.

"I knew I'd find you here, Ae Ri. Oh hey Miyeon. When did you get here? We missed you at the meeting." I heard Jaehyun's voice approach from the opposite direction. I turned to look at him. His hair was slicked back and his black double breasted wool jacket fit across his chest and shoulders perfectly. I smiled sneakily at the gold buttons on his jacket, he had the original buttons switched out because he wanted to match with me. His black slacks fit him very well. I came to realize he had a nice butt. I understood why Miyeon had a huge crush on him. It was something that I was constantly reminded of whenever I saw him.

"Hi Jaehyun. Yeah I was a little late. Daddy fired my driver right before the event, so he had to find me a new one. He'll be here later on. Do you like everything? We were going for something modern and classy with the blue and white." she answered brightly. I shouldn't be having thoughts of violently stabbing her and dismembering her tiny body at that moment, but I did. It took a great deal of self control. The only relief from the thoughts was watching Jaehyun try to keep his composure as she spoke like she contributed anything. He nodded in agreement.

"It looks good. You did a good job." he complimented her flatly. I covered my mouth to hold back the laugh that threatened to escape as I sipped on my champagne. He looked over at me and smirked lightly.

"How are you doing? Enjoying the champagne?" he questioned. There was a glint of mischief in his eyes. I decided to play along.

"Yes actually. It's really good. I was telling Miyeon that the gala was really fitting for our outfits you bought." I said as I caught Miyeon rubbing her arm uncomfortably. She glanced between us and her eyes widened, noticing the gold pieces among our ensembles. He wore a gold watch and a small gold chain that matched my dress and his jacket's buttons.

"You both look very nice. Well, I'll go greet some of the others. Have a good night. See you later." she waved as she hurried off. Jaehyun sat next to me and grinned smugly.

"What was that?"

"What was what?" I questioned as I looked at him. I would never say that I was jealous or annoyed by her obvious crush. That was beneath me. Making her disappear felt like a more appropriate solution. Maybe.

"Someone's a little jealous, aren't we? That was a little mean, sweetheart. What's wrong? Don't like someone flirting with me?"Jaehyun leaned over and playfully poked my sides as he teased. We stared into each other's eyes and I held my breath. The flicker of mischief was brighter than before and I was captivated. The way he made me feel timid wasn't fair. I looked death in the eyes more times than I could count, but this one man made me feel like a little schoolgirl. This was terrifying. This feeling that burned in my chest was more dangerous than anything I had ever done or felt. And I felt like I was losing control of everything. I couldn't look away but I also wouldn't. The desperation to feel like I had some power in this situation was overwhelming.

"You're blushing again. You look really innocent. I'll never understand how you pull that off." he mumbled as he reached over to place a stray hair back into place in my bun. He leaned back and smiled.

"Perfection."

"You're cheesy." I replied, releasing the breath I was holding slowly.

"But you like it. And you can't deny it." he laughed. I was going to try to.

"Don't flatter yourself, Nam." I rolled my eyes. He smirked and picked up my hand to hold for a moment before kissing the back of it. I knew what he was doing. I cleared my throat as a lump formed. His lips were soft and gentle. It didn't feel creepy like when other men did it with ulterior motives.

I think that was what scared me about Nam Jaehyun. I never felt that he had ulterior motives. He wasn't trying to get something from me. He wasn't trying to take something from me. He didn't want to hurt me. I knew that deep down. But it was hard to accept because everyone wanted to take from me. Whether it was money, sex, my abilities, my life. I was always aware of my position in the world and I acted accordingly. I gained power and status. I acquired more money. I became untouchable and solitary. It was safe for me at the time. Maybe my idea of safety was flawed though. Because safety didn't feel the same way around Jaehyun.

Safety was peaceful with Jaehyun. My version of safety never let me rest. My thoughts constantly raced without a break. My version of safety felt like a prison and I was the only prisoner. Safety was freeing with him. I could interact with people and people were nice to me and welcomed me. My version of safety made me defensive and callous. Safety with him made me want to let down my guard, at least a little. It made me hyper aware of all my issues and being reminded of them constantly was difficult. It wasn't his fault. Knowing that sometimes, I snapped at him because of my issues added an extra layer to the complicated feelings I was having. I felt Jaehyun rub his hand over my arm pulling me from my thoughts,

"Earth to Ae Ri. Are you okay?" he asked as he raised an eyebrow. He looked concerned. It was things like that? Why did he have to act like he cared? It was cruel. I gave him my best fake smile.

"Yeah. Zoned out for a second. It's a lot going on. I was never really good with these things." I lied smoothly. It wasn't a total lie. He hummed.

"Let's go upstairs. There's a balcony. Get you some air. You look stressed." he invited as he stood up and offered his hand. I agreed and we made our way upstairs. Entering the event space, I gasped as I looked at all the crystal decorations and the blue LED lights gave the room a soft blue glow. It was beautiful. "You did really a good job, Jaehyun. It looks amazing." I complimented him genuinely. He beamed proudly.

"Thank you. I appreciate the compliment. It's my favorite one." he stated as he held my hand a little tighter. He started to guide me through the room and a familiar voice called out.

"Mr. Student council president!" a lively feminine voice called out. We turned to see Haeun speed walk up to us. She held a camera in her hands as she greeted us warmly.

"Well don't you guys look so cute with the gold?" she grinned as she gestured to us both. She wore a black tailored blazer and black slacks and a white fitted button up shirt with ruffles and black heels.

"What are you doing here?" Jaehyun asked.

"Photography extra credit. They needed more hands on deck to capture your achievement. Two presidencies in a row, four straight fundraising galas. High hopes were realized." she answered as she playfully punched his arm. He grinned again.

"It looks good. But take a picture. I'm getting the first shots of the genius behind it all and his mysterious vixen, as people call you Ae Ri." she laughed. Mysterious vixen? Seriously?

Before I could interject, Jaehyun pulled me outside and waved Haeun along too. I could hear her laugh behind us. "Here seems like a good place. Against the railing with the view." she ordered. He pulled me to his side, wrapping his arm around my waist and placing his hand on my hip. I felt a shiver run down my spine when his hand rested there. I stood there awkwardly for a moment before he whispered in my ear.

"You can put your head on my shoulder if you want. Or put your hand on my chest. Whatever's comfortable for you." I cleared my throat to fight off the incoming blush. I placed my right hand on his shoulder and placed my head on it to avoid getting make up on his expensive suit. My other hand rested on my thigh as I posed with my exposed leg. She aimed her camera and did a thumbs up pose. "Smile~" she sang as she snapped a few pictures. She cooed at the pictures.

"These are so cute. Okay one more pose. Do a pose that can be put in the school paper now."

We adjusted ourselves and stood next to each other like professionals. His hand rested on my lower back out of the camera's sight. I smiled at the camera and he started to rub circles along my lower back. I put my arm around his waist to lightly pinch his side and he laughed out loud. He was ticklish, good to know. Haeun stopped taking pictures and smiled smugly.

"As to be expected. A beautiful picture for the lovely Choi Ae Ri and the handsome Nam Jaehyun. Look here." she said as she walked towards us. She showed us the second pose pictures and he looked like the perfect student and I looked... exactly how people described me. Mysterious and my small smile made me look fiercer than I intended to be in the simple photo. The gold eyeshadow and heavy eyeliner did not help either. I didn't mind honestly.

"I like this one. Can you send it to me?" he asked, smiling. I looked up at him and tilted my head.

"I'll send it to you as well." I nodded in agreement. Haeun giggled.

"I gotta get back to work. I'll see you guys later, okay? Ae Ri, I'll text you. The girls want to get brunch soon!" she called as she hurried off before waiting on my reply. I shook my head softly as I turned to lean on the balcony and take in the view over the balcony. There was a large garden with a pond in the middle of it. Some people were walking around and conversing in the garden. It was really beautiful. The night sky was clear, and you could see all the stars. Among all the chaos, it was peaceful and tranquil. I could understand why he chose this place instead of the hotel he was thinking about at first.

"Beautiful, isn't it?" Jaehyun stated as he leaned beside me. And looked up at the stars too.

"It is. You chose a good place. You should be proud of yourself, Jae." I answered as I looked over at him. The nickname felt right all of sudden. He was already looking at me when I turned. He looked conflicted and his stare was very pointed and focused on my face.

"What? Is there something on my face?" I asked as I gently wiped around the corner of my mouth. He shook his head silently and continued to stare. I felt self-conscious under the intense stare and an anxious feeling began to creep into my stomach. My breath staggered for a moment as I stared back. I couldn't read past his expression. He was a stone wall before me. I couldn't handle the silence anymore, so I made a joke.

"Are you okay? You look constipated." His serious expression broke when he let an amused grin cross his face.

"Very funny. You ruined the moment. Since you want to know so bad, I was trying to figure out how to tell you that I wanted to kiss you." he teased back. The seriousness was still clear in his voice.

~Chapter 12~

It felt like time stopped at that moment. I stared at him wordlessly. There was no way I could tell him that I wasn't blushing. I could feel the blood rush to my cheeks and my heart started to pound in my chest. A kiss? *Our* first kiss. It wasn't that I didn't want to. Quite the opposite actually. I wanted to. But I knew once I kissed him, it was final. I would be out in uncharted territory without a life vest. I was going to be in a world that I was unfamiliar with and forced to confront a lot of things that I wasn't ready to deal with. I was going to risk ruining his life. I didn't want that. Another crushing wave of unworthiness rushed over me. It felt like the weight of the world was sitting on me.

"I'm blushing..." I muttered. I had to try to buy some time. I was *terrified*. Ae Ri wasn't real, but these emotions are. They're very real. I couldn't describe them or name them, but they were intense.

"That you are. But I don't hear a no..." he chuckled. It was a harmless kiss, right? What if I was overthinking it? We had been flirting so much, it was a natural progression. I wasn't a virgin or anything, but I sure as hell felt like one. Hell, deciding to lose my virginity wasn't as monumental as this. This was going to change everything I knew. Was I ready for that? I looked up at him and he was looking at me with hopefulness and worry in his eyes. A light blush spread across his face as he watched me.

"You think a lot, you know? You should follow your gut more. What's the harm in that?" he asked as he stepped closer and tilted my head up.

"That everything may change..." I whimpered. He didn't understand the gravity of those words. Everything would change. And the thought was physically terrifying. I wouldn't be able to let him go when the time came for me to leave. He would have to come with me. By force or willingly. The possessiveness that I had tried so hard to control and contain was starting to slip out and course through my veins. I didn't need that to fuel this decision. I didn't want him to get hurt.

"It could be for the better. If you plan life too much you'll miss it…" He bent down and his lips met mine softly and the spark that ran down my spine was enough to make me shiver. The possessiveness burned brighter. I could feel him smirk slightly and… I gave up. My hands ran up his chest to hold his face in a tight grip as I kissed him back. His lips were soft and he tasted like strawberries and champagne. His hands moved from my face to grip tightly at my waist. His grip fluttered between tight and soft. He was trying to be gentle with me, but he was struggling. He wanted to be gentle with me and I felt delicate for the first time. Flames of desire blared in my stomach. It was completely different than any other kiss I ever had. It was disorienting. The need for air was an inconvenience.

He pulled away slightly catching his breath and gave me a few more innocent pecks before pulling away completely. He smiled gently and ran a thumb gently across my cheeks. "I knew your lips would be soft," he grinned.

I looked down to hide my face. "Can you stop trying to embarrass me?" I begged as I playfully hit his chest.

"If you stop being so pretty then sure. But that's impossible. So no." I looked up at him and stared at him. It was official that everything changed. I wanted him. And I was determined to do whatever it took to keep him. He could have his life and I'd never reveal myself to him if that was what it took. I'd move here and take over the Jopok after I killed the head family. I'm sure it would be easy. Moving troops in to crush any resistance. I'd have my revenge for my mother's death and more power and money. The assignment became two folded now. Easy.

"You're lucky, you're pretty Nam Jaehyun." I warned him teasingly. He grinned mischievously and leaned in to kiss me again. He pulled away and tapped my nose.

"Let's get the rest of this over with and we can go. How about that?" he offered. I nodded, giving him a small smile.

We made our way inside and out of nowhere, Miyeon ran up to us. She was out of breath. "Mr. Sung is here. You gotta say hi, Jaehyun! Come on!" she panted. Jaehyun smiled and tugged me along with them. It pleased me to watch Miyeon's face drop at him holding my hand and bringing me. I winked at her as we walked by.

"Mr. Sung is another big donor we have. Every year he's gotten close to beating Miyeon's dad in donations and this year, I'm hoping he does. Just to stop this chokehold she has on the school. How does a third year undergrad student have that much pull, you know? So every time we have the gala, the student council and the president of the school have one-on-one time with the biggest donors. This year we included Mr. Sung." he explained quietly as we made our way through the crowds of people.

"His wife has a lot of pull on where his money goes. She wants to see that we're well rounded. A girlfriend, wife, husband, partner or boyfriend. It's a thing she has. She loves love. Used to pretend it was Miyeon. And she never really got that it wasn't real." he continued.

That explains a lot about Miyeon's actions. Mr. Sung was standing in the foyer at the top of the stairs when we walked up. He turned to us when he saw us. He was the typical old man. Gray hair, short and round. His wife was visibly younger, maybe in her thirties, early forties at most. She smiled brightly. "Mr. Sung. Mrs. Park. It's nice to see you all again. How have you been?" Jaehyun smiled softly as he bowed. I followed his lead. Bowing to someone else was a foreign feeling. I didn't do it often. "Jaehyun. My favorite student council president. I thought you weren't here." The man greeted him excitedly.

"I'm sorry. My girlfriend was having a hard time with her shyness. So I wanted to make sure she was okay." he lied smoothly. I smiled softly and waved.

"Such a gentleman. She's gorgeous, this one is. I like her. You two look good together." Mrs. Park gushed at the story. I had to hide the laugh when she said I was gorgeous, because that meant Miyeon wasn't and they didn't look good together. Miyeon was somewhere behind us too, so she heard the comment too. It was petty, I know. My possessive side was overjoyed. I just knew they didn't match. Jaehyun squeezed my hand and sweetly smiled.

"Thank you, I appreciate the compliment. You're lovely as well, ma'am." I played the role well. I've had way too much practice doing things like this back in Japan. Same shit, just a different country.

"Our table is all ready. We are beginning to settle down for the presentations of this year's chosen departments. Allow us to lead you." he offered as he held an arm out to the older woman for her to hold. I did the same for the old man and he laughed boisterously.

"No, no. You hold my arm. Here." he chuckled as he held his arm out. I smiled softly and we followed Jaehyun. The table was in the front near the stage and it was decorated in expensive glass centerpieces and fine china. There were signs with their names and the school president's name. My name and Jaehyun's name were beside each other and Miyeon's name was across from us next to what I assumed was Miyeon's father and another unknown name. We had to eat with them too? I didn't know one on one time meant eating with them. This was going to be torture.

We secured another donation for the year and we got a grant on top of that from one of Mr. Sung's associates. Jaehyun led me down the stairs of the expensive event building. It was about 1 in the morning and Sung decided he had enough fun and freed us. "Thank you for hanging in there with me, princess. I know it was last minute and you had no time to prepare. I would've told you earlier but you know shit happens. You handled everything with so much grace and you were perfect at it. If I can ever repay you, tell me." He kissed my hands gratefully. I shrugged and shook my head nonchalantly.

"I've done it before. Had to charm a few old people for money for the family business. No need to thank me," I replied.

"Well, you're fucking good. Because you got us the biggest donation from Sung ever and he definitely beat Miyeon's dad. And an extra grant too. It was wild. I've never seen Sung call someone to tell them about the fundraising gala in the middle of it. He liked you a lot. So you're definitely stuck with me now. Hope you're ready for that." He pulled me in the waist and held me close to him. We stared into each other's eyes for a moment.

"Have I ever told you that you're beautiful?" he whispered.

My chest swelled in pride at the compliment. Things felt easier and lighter without me running from the feelings I had for him. I still didn't know how to describe it but being here like this made me feel amazing. I felt like I was cloud nine. It was almost too good to be true. "You may have said it once or twice." I teased as I placed my hands on his shoulders.

"I'll say it a hundred times over then. You are so beautiful." he leaned down and kissed me softly. He was dizzying and all consuming. It made my chest swell with something I couldn't describe. He pulled away and nudged his nose against mine. "Should I have the driver drop you off at home?" he asked as he pulled away to open the door to the black SUV that parked beside us. I didn't want to leave his side. I was afraid that I would wake up from this dream and it would be over.

"I'll stay with you. Stay a while." I tried to hide the desperation in my voice. I shakingly reached up to run my thumb across his cheek and he beamed in delight and shock. I offered a sign of affection, who would've thought? He agreed and helped me into the car and slid in beside me. "Rowoon, hey man. It's been a while. Home please." Jaehyun greeted the man behind the wheel. The driver looked in the rearview mirror and smiled. "Hey Jaehyun. I just got back to town. They said you needed a pick up so I decided to swing by and get you. I'll tell you about it later." the young man said as he pulled off into the road.

They spoke for a little while after he introduced me and I sat in a comfortable silence watching the city pass by. I had never been to his house before. I looked down at our hands resting between us on the seat and I reached over and hooked our pinkies together. It felt right. I couldn't explain it, but it felt like it was something I needed to do. I don't know where to go from here. I spent so long fighting this and I was unprepared to go forward. I didn't have experience in this. Were we a couple now? But I don't know what that looks like. I never did this before. How could I describe that to him without telling him what I do? Wouldn't it be weird to be a couple and not tell him what I did. Nope. That was too risky. I couldn't tell him that. Absolutely not. I had to figure out another way to tell him why I was so screwed up. That wasn't it though.

Jaehyun nudged my shoulder. "What are you thinking about? You're tense." he asked quietly. I peeked over at him and the worry in his eyes could've stopped my heart. I wasn't sure if I would ever get used to it. I wasn't sure what to say. All I could mutter out was, "I don't want this to change. I like this." He looked confused for a moment.

"Us? Because I don't think we could change this." he responded confidently. I raised an eyebrow. He chuckled.

"We've been together pretty much since we met. We've spent every day together at least once a day. Most days it was multiple times a day. I don't think that's a coincidence. You've met my friends, they adore you already. You're not good with feelings, I can see that from a mile away. You have anxiety so it makes sense. I'm not going to rush things with you. That would be cruel. So I'm going to be here. I can't explain why I'm drawn to you the way I am. I just am. You're magnetic and you pull me in. I am still figuring out why but I like the adventure I'm on with you. That's all I can call it." he explained as he smiled down at me. I felt relief fill my chest. Hearing him say how I had been feeling for so long was comforting. I wasn't alone in this. This was just as new and different for him as it was me. It made me feel good that he wouldn't try to force anything. I tugged his pinky closer to mine and he grinned.

"You're precious. It's cute to watch you figure it all out. I guess linking pinkies is your version of holding hands?" he asked.

"Don't judge me. That's not understanding." I lightly pushed him.

"I'm not. I'm asking. I want to understand. We're doing this together, I promise."

He held our connected pinkies up and kissed the back of my hand. I blushed and nodded my head. "You're a mystery to me as well, Jaehyun. I don't know why I want you as much as I do, but I do. And I only feel this way about you. With you. I can't let this go." I admitted timidly. He smiled brightly. His eyes lit up when I said it.

"Thank you for saying that. I know it was hard. You did good, princess. I knew it already, but the reassurance is always nice." He tilted my head and kissed me once softly as he put an arm around my shoulders and pulled me closer.

"Can't stop being cocky, can you Nam?" I laughed.

"I do both well. Humble and cocky. You like it. Trust me, I noticed. You're hard to understand but easy to read. Especially if you pay extremely close attention. I'm still figuring some things out though." he replied as he stretched slightly. I always felt exposed whenever I was with him, now I understand why. He was studying me and trying to figure me out. It was like being in a shootout with no cover or no back up, but instead of facing certain death, I was facing a new world that looked peaceful. It was tempting.

"I guess I should ask you out on a normal first date, huh?" he said suddenly as he looked down at me.

"It better be nice." I told him seriously.

"Only the best for you. So will you go on a date with me, Choi Ae Ri?" he chuckled as he held my hand and leaned his head on my shoulder. That was the first time I had actually been asked on a date. It brought me a lot more excitement than I expected. I felt delicate and soft again. I felt valued. He gave a soft kiss to my exposed shoulder, and I shivered once.

"I'd like that, Nam Jaehyun." I agreed.

"I have to look at my schedule, but I know you won't have to wait too long. I promise. I have some meetings tomorrow morning. And it may take my day away, so maybe tomorrow or sometime next week?" he yawned. The tiredness was catching up to him.

"You may need to sleep tomorrow after your meetings. I won't disappear." I said as I looked at him.

"I hope not." he smiled softly.

We arrived at his penthouse and made it inside finally. I collapsed onto the side of his bed and sunk into the soft mattress. He joined me into the room holding two cups of tea. I sat up and looked at him curiously. "Tea helps me sleep, so I usually have a cup before bed. It may help you with your insomnia. Here, let's get you into something comfortable." he offered as he set the cups down and sat on the floor next to me to help me untie my shoes and he gave me a pair of house slippers. I sighed in relief. My feet were killing me, and I was ready to take everything constrictive off. He stood up and gestured to his dressers.

"I have guy clothes, but you're more than welcome to grab a shirt and some shorts or whatever makes you comfortable." he offered.

"Thanks. I appreciate it. I should be able to manage with a shirt. You're tall." I stood up and reached into a dresser to grab one of his plain white tees. I gasped slightly realizing I needed to remove my makeup and needed help with my dress. "Hey. Can you help me with my dress please? And do you maybe have make-up remover wipes?" I reminded him. He chuckled and nodded. He handed me some wipes and I looked up at him confused.

"I have a sister. Don't start." he told me before I could make a joke. That is right. He unzipped the dress in the back, and he stepped away.

"Make yourself comfortable. I'm going to shower, I'll be back." he told me as he stepped into the bathroom.

~Chapter 13~

I slipped out of the dress and laid it on the dresser and then put the shirt on. It was huge on me. I used the mirror in the room to remove the stubborn makeup and picked up the cup of tea he left for me. It tasted pretty good. My eyes scanned the room finally. The room was dimly lit with a red light giving the room a red appearance. The king-sized bed had a headboard. His dresser and nightstand were black as well. The furniture looked nice with the red backlight. In the corner of his room there was a door and next to it there was a bookshelf with trophies and awards on it. I walked over to it and started looking at them. A few trophies in soccer for being player of the year, rookie of the year and most valuable player. He had his bachelor's degrees on display and other academic achievements for the highest GPAs and the highest grades in specific subjects. He was good at everything and anything, it seemed. He ran track, he was a swimmer. He was damn near perfect. I felt a little insecure looking at his accomplishments.

"Oh you saw the trophy case?" Jaehyun asked as he appeared behind me. I jumped in shock, I didn't hear him come in. "You're just good at everything, huh? The perfect son." I teased. He shrugged and laughed.

"Well, what can I say? I'm amazing. No, I'm kidding. I just work really hard. It takes dedication." he said warmly as he looked at his accolades. The pride radiated off of him.

"What's something you're proud of?" he asked, looking over at me. I hummed in concentration. I wasn't like him. I didn't have any medals or awards from sports. I didn't have school achievement awards. Everything I had to be proud of was from the Yakuza. Being the only woman in my position was an achievement. If it was to be looked at objectively that is.

"It's nothing like yours. I don't really know." I answered honestly.

"Oh come on. I'm sure you do. Even if it's small." He was encouraging me. That was really sweet. I felt like I had to give him something.

"In my dad's company, I'm the only female high ranking official." I shrugged.

"There you go! That's something to be proud of. You earned it." He smiled brightly.

"Yeah, I suppose. It was something that I was just meant to do, so it happened the way he intended. I was pushed hard and as usual, everything happens the way he intends." I tried to keep the bitterness out of my voice but even I could hear it. So I'm sure he did. I walked to sit on the bed to escape his concerned gaze.

"It's hard to talk about your dad, isn't it? May I ask why?" He kept his distance as he watched me for a moment. I sighed heavily and pinched my nose. I knew at some point I would have to at least start to open up about him. I just was dreading the day it came. I didn't think it'd be so soon but better now then later. He could still back out.

"It's complicated with him. He's a stranger pretty much. He always was. If it wasn't for all of the women in and out of my life, I wouldn't know anything about my body. They were my link to him. It was almost like they had to remind him I existed."

Talking about it out loud, probably hurt more than keeping it in. Speaking it meant I had to acknowledge it and which one is worse, I couldn't tell. It felt like my heart was tearing in two. It was almost terrifying because sometimes I forgot I had one. I didn't feel numb anymore. The walls were crumbling even the more and I fought back the tears that were threatening to fill my eyes. That was too much. I didn't want to cry in front of him. The whole time Jaehyun was silent, I barely noticed him sit beside me. His hand rested on my knee gently and stayed there.

"What happened to your mom?" he asked gently. I frowned and fought back the rage that started to bubble under the hurt. It was still raw for me. I guessed he sensed the tension.

"I'm sorry if that was a sensitive spot. I was just curious. I remember from Mae's...." he apologized. I shook my head.

"No, it's just... heartbreaking to talk about because she died when I was a baby. And my father never talked to me about it. He never mentioned her. He acted like nothing happened and just had a sea of bitches in and out of my life with no clue as to what was going on. I saw a picture of my mother for the first time a few days before I left to come to Seoul. And she was so beautiful... I-I just don't understand..."

My voice broke and it was becoming more difficult to keep tears at bay. The pain and disappointment flooded my chest in waves. I tried my best to not show that I was crying. Jaehyun reached up and held my hand tightly.

"That is traumatizing... I am so sorry that happened to you. It wasn't right or fair. Thank you for sharing that with me. I don't take that for granted," he said. He squeezed my hand in support.

I don't why but that simple action combined with the raw feelings pushed me over the edge. Hot tears rushed down my face without restraint. My vision blurred and sobs shook my body. I don't cry like this. I could usually pull myself together and stop a few tears, but this type of crying, I couldn't stop. I couldn't pull myself together. The thought of even trying to stop crying created more tears and turned the sobbing ugly.

I felt like I had been dropped from a high altitude and shattered into a million pieces. Everything hurt and my chest burned with the exertion of trying to keep myself breathing through the sobs. I was vaguely aware when I felt my body be picked up and readjusted and my face was buried in his chest. I must have been in his lap. I was crying like a child and that made me feel worse because I was being a burden now. I sobbed even harder and buried my face in his shirt more and wrapped my arms around his waist.

I felt so stupid and pathetic sobbing over a woman that I never met and a man that had always been cruel and distant. It angered me. It added to the devastation of how I felt. The new emotion mixed in left a painful mark as it passed. Years of unspoken and buried pain, disappointment, resentment, rage and utter sadness made its way through my body and it made certain body parts go numb. I could vaguely feel Jaehyun soothingly rubbing my back and rocking us back and forth. It was humiliating to be seen like this. He didn't deserve to see this. He had nothing to do with this and I was forcing him to hold me through this heartbreak. That probably hurt the most out of everything I was feeling....

An incessant buzzing noise startled me and my eyes flew open. I sat up quickly and looked around as the room came into focus. My heart was racing and I was panting. When I became aware of my surroundings, I took a deep breath remembering everything that happened. "Hey, are you okay?" Jaehyun mumbled sleepily as he rubbed my back. I must have fallen asleep while I was crying. Jaehyun was behind me cuddling me close and my quick movements woke him up. I looked around for the source of the buzzing. It was my phone. I checked the caller ID to see it was 5am and Han was calling me. My eyes widened and I frowned. "I'm okay. I just need some air. Can I go on your balcony? You stay and rest. I'll be back." I replied as I rubbed his back to lull him back to sleep. He hummed in response, relaxing into the pillow again. I got up and grabbed my phone and headed out the backdoor to the balcony. The buzzing started up immediately after it ended. He was calling back.

I took a deep breath and answered wordlessly. "Fucking finally. You answered." Han growled into the phone. I rolled my eyes.

"I was asleep." I answered plainly.

"An assignment this important and you're asleep!?" If he knew anything about me he'd know that this was the most sleep that I had been getting in my life. It wasn't by much but still. I was already agitated and sensitive, I didn't want to do this.

"What are you asking me?" I questioned trying to keep my tone level.

"Progress report. You haven't been in contact to report."

"Besides, the main family may be bigger than what we originally thought. You didn't tell me that. Other than that, no. I have nothing to report." I told him. He was not happy. He snapped.

"I gave you the police database! What the hell are you talking about?!" Han yelled.

"It hasn't started yet! You sent me on an assignment fucking blind with nothing to go off beside those pieces of paper that weren't useful at all! I'm the one in enemy territory NOT you. I do the hard shit so you can sit on your ass and be comfortable, remember?" I growled in response. My hand tightened on my phone and I felt rage build up again. Whoever said that crying made you feel better lied. The familiar feeling of bloodlust rose up again. The silence was thick and tense.

"Make it happen. I expect an update by the day after tomorrow." he said with finality in his voice and he hung up. I stared down at my phone and resisted the urge to scream into the night sky. Who the hell does he think he is? I never checked in with him during assignments. Why was he calling to check in all of a sudden? Did he forget that I do this constantly? I've been on more assassination assignments than him or anyone else. Did he forget that I'm by myself? I have to think and move carefully in these situations.

We have never had an intense standoff like that ever before. We have disagreed but for it to go as far as it did was astounding. He usually backed off before things dissolved into personal jabs and insults. This was about him. Just as I suspected. It didn't have anything to do with me personally getting revenge for my mother. This was about his revenge, but like the coward he was, he couldn't and wouldn't do it himself. He was weak. He couldn't protect my mother and he couldn't avenge her either. He was worthless. Visions of his decapitated head sitting on a table in his office watching as I burned his body filled my mind. One day I was going to make him pay. He would pay for my mother's death. He was just as guilty as Omega. How he couldn't see that angered me. He would pay for what he did to me. For how he treated me and how he made me feel.

The smartest thing he ever did was train me but it was also the most dangerous thing he ever did. He knew that, so he always made sure to keep my power contained. He gave me leadership but still kept me at a disadvantage to make sure I'd never reach his spot. That's why I wasn't his wakashigira. I remember being so angry with him and holding that sword to his throat that day. I should've killed him when I had the chance. He did it to spite me. In his mind, that was too close to power. To kill him and take over would take time. I wasn't well liked, I'd have to rebuild my image. I couldn't stage a coup because I'd have no support. I'm not irrational in things like this. Me and Code against a force of almost twenty thousand, in the Yamaguchi, that was insanity. I took a few deep breaths to calm my pounding heart and work through the blinding rage.

Did he maybe have a point that I have made shit happen before under harder circumstances? Yeah. But if I slipped up and made a mistake somewhere along the way without realizing it, I could pay for it. And now I had Jaehyun to worry about. He had to remain safe through all of this until I could figure out what to do and where we could go. On the other hand, another hostile 5am phone call with Han after the emotional rollercoaster I was on would end up with Han dead. Logic and careful planning be damned. Especially if he talked to me like that again. Damn the consequences. It was better to get the old bastard off my back for now. I yawned and decided to worry about it later. I was tired and emotionally wrecked. I stepped inside and climbed back under the covers with Jaehyun. He rolled over and pulled me closer, laying his head on my chest mumbling something. I smiled softly and held him as I went back to sleep.

An alarm disrupted the peaceful sleep, and I shifted due to the noise. "Good morning, pretty. Did you sleep well? You had a rough night." Jaehyun asked as he sat up and rubbed his eyes. I groaned and looked up at him. I was truthfully exhausted, but I felt lighter than I ever did before. The crying session and the sleep I got after the call did help. Embarrassed and mortified, but I still felt lighter. "Sorry about that. I wasn't trying to burden you with all of that. I know it came out of nowhere." I apologized as I looked down and covered my face. He chuckled and moved my hands.

"You're so cute." he leaned down and kissed my forehead.

"You obviously needed to let that out. I bet you hadn't cried in a long time. You don't have to be a hard shell in front of me. I'll be here to listen, okay? You're not alone anymore. I promise." He stared down at me and the sincerity in his eyes almost scared me. I nodded wordlessly. He meant it. He wasn't put off by my outburst. He was still in this with me.

"I'll be gone for most of the day, but I'll be checking in on you. There's a driver downstairs if you want to go home. If you want to meet back up, we can." He ran his thumb over my cheek and smiled warmly. I nodded wordlessly again. I was in a state of shock. I still couldn't believe he was here.

"Too much affection?"

"I like it. I'm just still trying to get used to it. I honestly can't believe I am still here. That you're not kicking me out." I said honestly. The reality of the situation was hitting me. I came to a man's house and we didn't have sex. I woke up in his bed and he was talking to me. I've had this situation play out so differently before. I was gone before he woke up or I was leaving right as he woke up. I was still processing everything. A lot happened in a few hours.

"Ohhhhh no. Of course not. That's not what this is. As long as you're comfortable. That's what I care about genuinely." he smiled as kissed my forehead again and got up. He walked towards his bathroom and shut the door.

I got up and stretched and wandered out of the bedroom to the kitchen. I decided to cook something as a way to thank him. It also felt like something I should do. It felt appropriate and right. I hated going to meetings hungry if I could help it, so I didn't want him to experience it. His kitchen was neat and tiny and I almost felt bad as I rummaged through his cabinets and refrigerator. I found ingredients to make a Japanese breakfast dish, tamago gohan. He had a rice cooker too. This would be perfect. I started his rice first and I looked around the rest of the penthouse. He really hyped up my interior decorating skills. He was good too. Everything looked expensive and the accents of the gold went well with the black he chose as his main color. An L shaped black leather couch had a glass coffee table in front of it. Something caught my eye on the table. It looked like there was a case of bullets and a magazine sitting in the drawer of the coffee table. I tilted my head. Now I know why I have guns. Why would he have them? Or at least one.

Curiosity got the better of me and I walked over to the table and opened the drawer. They were in fact bullets and a magazine. They belonged to a Glock to be exact. Holding the items brought me flashbacks. I hadn't even realized how long it had been since I held a gun last. I kind of missed the feeling of one in my hand. I was so distracted by the gun parts that I almost missed the beeping of the rice. I quickly put the parts back and closed the drawer slowly. I snickered to myself slightly at the switch that was happening. A kind of domestic feeling and then the danger of underground life. It would take some work, but maybe I could pull it off. I scooped his rice into a bowl as mine was cooking and added the soy sauce and cracked an eye, putting only the yolk on top. Sprinkling the sesame seeds on top, I noticed Jaehyun poking his head around the corner.

"There you are. I was wondering where you disappeared to." he chuckled as he made his way down the hall and into the kitchen.

"I figured that I'd thank you for last night. So I decided to make breakfast." I smiled warmly. I slid the bowl over to him while I finished my bowl. He looked down at the bowl and stared at it blankly for a minute. "What's wrong? You don't like it?" I asked. My face flushed in embarrassment and a feeling of sadness started to rise in my chest. He looked up quickly and shook his head quickly. A bright smile flashed across his face.

"No, no! It's one of my favorite Japanese dishes! How'd you know?" He leaned over and kissed my temple quickly. I breathed a sigh of relief.

"I've never cooked for anyone before. And it would've really fucked me up if I got it wrong on the first try. I would never do it again." I laughed as I finished my bowl.

"We can eat in the living room." he invited. I tried to keep the burning question in the back of my head about the gun parts. He must be oblivious to its presence. It seemed innocent enough. It was weird to just see the parts but not the actual gun.

Turns out, I didn't have to mention it. He took it upon himself to explain it. "Oh shit. I'm so sorry, Ae Ri. I-I-I left this out. I just didn't have time to register it with the police station, I've been so busy. I hope it didn't scare you." I exclaimed as he scrambled to grab the items. I shook my head and waved it off.

"It's cool. I'm fine. What do you have it for out of curiosity?" I inquired.

"I like practicing shooting sometimes. Having a lot of money and running businesses has its share of dangers as I'm sure you know. I got it for protection." he answered. The answer made sense. I forgot that regular people could still be in danger of break ins and things.

"I get it. Sometimes it is necessary. Ever had to use it?"

"On a person? Yes, but I luckily didn't have to hurt him. A shot near the head in the wall behind can be enough of a deterrent. Some wannabe gangster tried to rob me."

I titled my head impressed that he knew how to use it. "Where's the actual gun? You have the bullets and magazine out here? Why?" I wanted to know for my personal reference just in case I was ever here and I needed to use it quickly. I could move quicker and I was better with a gun, I'm sure.

"The gun is in my room. I keep bullets in convenient places just in case I'm unprepared." he replied. I laughed lightly. He made it sound like this happened often. Was his family hunted down for information or something?

"What kind of business do you guys do?" I joked.

"Remember when I said when we were trying to get into the science realm with the World Expo? There's been backlash. Jealousy is an ugly thing. There's been a lot of stuff going on. Company mainframes trying to be hacked, my house's been broken into. This world can get viscous and I want you to know what you're getting yourself into. So you can back out now, if you want." Jaehyun said as he looked at with an apprehensive look on his face. I guess Korea had its violent streak too. Oh, if only he knew. I was more prepared for this than he would ever know.

"If you can accept me as screwed up as I am. I can accept this. I'm here." I reassured him as I grabbed his hand. He smiled hopefully and held my hand tightly again.

We sat in silence for a while as we ate. "This is really good. The rice is perfect. You're a good cook." Jaehyun complimented. I smiled proudly. It really was nerve racking to cook for him and not be sure how he would feel. It made my chest swell with pride. Maybe I could do this whole relationship thing and be domesticated.

"Where'd you learn to cook? Can you cook for me everyday?" he teased. I rolled my eyes and he grinned.

"I'm serious. I can come to you or you can come here. We can eat together everyday. This is nice." He had a point. Eating together and spending time together was enjoyable. I was getting more and more comfortable with all the affection and the attention. It was a completely different feeling. From isolation to feeling like I belonged somewhere. Sleeping in his arms felt right. Sitting next to him eating felt right. "I'm not opposed to eating together every day." I admitted. "We can go back and forth between our places. Breakfast dates."

The smile that graced his perfect face was my new favorite thing in the world. The smile stretched across his face, making his eyes smile as well. The happiness was clearly visible because his eyes were sparkling. There was something intense lurking in them as well, but I couldn't name it. I didn't realize I was staring until he leaned closer to me.

"You're staring again. Am I that handsome?" he teased as he playfully kissed my nose. I blushed and looked away.

"I'd never tell you that. Your head's big enough already." I smirked as I went back to eating.

"Ouch. Hurtful, babe." He dramatically put a hand over his chest and gasped.

"You'll live."

He chuckled and checked his watch. "Oh shit! I'm gonna be late!" he exclaimed as he hurriedly shoved the rest of the food into his mouth and jumped up. I nodded and grabbed the bowl from him.

"I got the dishes. You hurry up and get ready." I offered as he ran back to the bedroom.

I was washing dishes when he came back down the hall loudly. He paused at the door before opening it and I caught him staring at me. "What?

Aren't you about to be late?" I asked self-consciously. I felt like I was made of glass under his sharp gaze. A small smirk appeared.

"Nothing. It's just…domestic life looks really good for you. You're beautiful in a natural setting like this. That's all." He wandered over to me with a focused look in his eyes. We stared at each other again and a mischievous grin crossed his face.

"In the movies, men get a kiss before they leave the house. Where's mine?" There it was. He was out to make me blush! I rolled my eyes and leaned up to peck his lips softly. It was just like the movies. It was kind of romantic almost.

"That wasn't so bad, was it? You're a natural."

"Are you going to make fun of me all day or are you going to leave?" I swatted at him, and he laughed loudly as he backed away.

"I'm going! I'm going! One more kiss though…"

He pulled me in a deeper kiss and quickly let me go. He waved goodbye and left with a promise to call later. A small smile crossed my face as I finished washing the dishes. A tranquil feeling rested over me and I sat in it for a while. It was quiet externally and internally for a while. I can't remember the last time it had ever been this quiet. But of course, something would ruin it. I groaned in annoyance as the memory of Han's phone resurfaced and ruined the moment. I had to get to work and come up with something to pull off today to get information. The only thing that I could think of was to get into the police database today. And not cause alarm when I do it. I needed to call Code. There were a few hackers in the gang. They had to have something. I rushed back to the bedroom and grabbed my phone and stepped out onto the balcony again. I didn't want to bring that into his home.

My hands trembled as I dialed the familiar number and held it up to my ear. It felt weird calling Code after a while of not speaking to him. "Rose? Is that you?" Code answered surprised. I rolled my eyes, the irritation already filling my chest.

"Who else would be dumbass? I'm not dead, you bastard." I started coldly.

"No I wasn't saying anything by that, ma'am. It's just been a while. How are you?"

"How's everything? How's the expansion coming along?" I said as I looked out over the Seoul skyline. I chose to ignore Code's question. He didn't need to think this was a personal call and I also wasn't about to tell him about Jaehyun. No way.

"We just put a surrogate in Nissan and Yamaha. They'll be putting in bids for leadership at the end of the year. We're almost done purging the 2019 surrogates and the new ones are making their way into position. We just got an expected request from some businesses for help." Code informed me as he shuffled around on the other end.

"Who? What for?" I questioned. It had been a while since a business reached out to us due to the crackdown in Japan.

"Watami and Ginza. The Ukraine war is making seafood hard to get and the prices of flour and wheat are sky high. They're struggling. What should we do?" Code answered. Oh yeah. That was a mess. The Russian gangs stopped working with any international criminal organization when the government chose to invade Ukraine. They were a nightmare to work with anyway. No loss.

"Reach out to some contacts in the Triad and Vietnam. We have a few agents in the US government. See what they can try to do. It may be a long shot but maybe the Americans can try to make something better and not worse for once. Try Turkey and the Italians. The Italians may be the best option. Tell them Rose sent you." I reasoned. I sent him a list of contacts from my phone.

"Understood. Han had asked for some assassinations, I did them and put the money in your account. I took twenty five percent." he informed me.

"I allow it. Make sure you send me the transaction history. Han's a snake."

"Yes ma'am. We're on track."

"Good. I need something from our hackers. And I need it within two hours." He stopped moving papers at the new command.

"Two hours? That's short notice. What do you need?" he inquired.

"Spyware. I need a program that copies systems and steals logins and passwords and lets me put it on a usb drive to access. It needs to randomize the logins I use each time I access it. And I'll need my laptop to be able to start pinging off different computers. It can't be traceable." I explained. He let out a whistle at the request.

"What are you trying to hack into?"

"Police software. Whatever I can get my hands on in this place." I could tell he was pinching the bridge of his nose in worry. But he was going to make it happen.

"Okay. I'll make some calls. It'll get done." he promised.

"I expect nothing less." I hung up and went back inside to take a pair of sweatpants from Jaehyun's dresser.

Breaking into the police station on a whim wasn't one of my best plans. But the timing was probably the best I'd get. I needed to get something today and Jaehyun was gone for the day. So it was perfect. If I could remember what floor the High Profile Crimes Unit was on, I could get in and out. I couldn't go in as Choi Ae Ri. She was still in training and didn't need access to computers yet. I'd need a disguise. Our intern uniforms were different from the regular police uniforms. A police uniform would be easy to get off of someone. Stealing the files was probably going to be the easiest part. The interns were off on the weekends, so I was unsure if the police stations in Korea worked like they did in Japan, the more specialized units were usually off on the weekends. Only one or two people would work, but it was never the whole squad. I could handle one or two people. I just needed to be ready and prepared, and I'd only be able to do that at home.

~Chapter 14~

As Jaehyun promised, a driver was waiting for me outside when I walked out. It was Rowoon from the gala. "Ms. Choi, are you ready to go?" He smiled warmly as he opened the door for me.

"Rowoon. Yeah, I gotta get some stuff done today. So I can't be cooped up all day." I answered as I got into the car. I was really enjoying how the men Jaehyun kept around him opened the door for me and other women. It was refreshing. I knew for me it meant something different than it did for everyone else, but it held the same meaning essentially. That the person was valued. I settled in for the ride back to my place and checked my phone. I saw the files I requested from Code and decided to check them first. The transaction history was long. I missed a lot in the time I was gone. I guess I wasn't aware of just how much I had planned and needed to get done. This assignment threw a curveball into everything, but I was proud of Code for keeping things going. Five assassination payments had gone through and two more were pending. Code did take his said percentage and left the rest in the account. I had to get my percentage and transfer it to my account. I completed that task and opened my email.

I noticed the school email for Ae Ri had new messages and my heart raced in anticipation. I opened the email to see the email for the internship class. The first email was my official welcome letter to the High-Profile Crimes unit. I made it through the final round of testing and next Monday, I would make my way upstairs. I would be reporting to Captain Chae Jum. I opened the second email and I noticed that it was a list of all of the students in the class and their start dates were listed. I raised an eyebrow. Was I supposed to see this? All the students were tagged in the email, so it looks like it was intentional. My eyes scanned down the list and stopped at a girl's name, Park Hayeon. She was one of three people that had a weekend start date and it was for today. I checked my clock and grinned evilly. She was supposed to report at 12:00 and she was in my unit too. It was only 9. I had time.

I pulled up information about the Seoul Metropolitan Police Agency. It was a large building and on the outside it looked like there were officers that stood outside the entrance and they roamed around the building as well. I couldn't tell the amount of officers from the pictures, but that was okay. I could always drive and find out. The wheels in my head started turning quickly trying to piece together something that would work. If I got there before Hayeon, I could just use her uniform and get in and out. No harm done. A quick taser to the back would have her unconscious and it'd be enough time. My phone ringing interrupted my thoughts. I looked down and saw it was Jaehyun. I answered quickly. "Aren't you supposed to be in a meeting?" I questioned. He chuckled.

"I stepped out to go to the restroom for your information. I decided to call you too. And this is the thanks I get? Sheesh." he teased.

"It'll never be easy for you, you know that."

"Obviously. What are you doing? Are you still at my place?" he questioned.

"No. I have some work to do, so I'm on the way home. I cleaned up for you though. I'll need to come back for my dress. I didn't have a bag for it." I replied.

"Just leave it at mine. Never know when I'll have to swoop you away to something big. That was a beautiful dress for you. I'd like to see you in it again."

"A fair point you brought up. Fine. Don't have anyone else wearing it." I warned him darkly. The thought of that created dark thoughts in my mind. The girl would have to die a slow painful death.

"Okay easy there, princess. I'm not sure what that was. But I would never do that. Besides, the dress was tailored to fit you. It was designed for you." The reassurance in his voice eased the tension in my chest and I smiled softly. I chose to ignore the comment about how my voice changed.

It was better to not address it. He didn't need to know about my possessive streak yet.

"That's good. How's your meeting going?" I changed the subject quickly.

"W-W... Okay. It's going well. Boring. We're hearing some pitches to present to the people at the World Expo for the buildings and such." he sighed heavily.

"Sounds like torture. I know what those long meetings are like." I empathize with him.

"Thanks. Hey, whenever I get done for the day, you think I can come over? We can watch movies and hang out? Order take out?" he suddenly asked excitedly.

"You miss me already? Awww...Yeah we can do that." I jabbed.

"Oh here you go. You can say you miss me too, it's okay. Remember? I'm here to catch you. Talked about it this morning?" The thoughts of this morning ran through my mind quickly and I felt like I was melting.

"I kinda do miss you." I admitted softly. It was honest. I did wish we were still laying in his bed and entangled together but we still had things to do. It felt empty to not have him by my side. It was something that I was going to struggle with. I didn't want to be codependent. I couldn't do my job if I was under him all day, every day. If I didn't have a balance, he could get hurt and I could end up dead. Everything was always black and white. These new emotions were introducing me to a lot of gray areas that I didn't know existed and quite frankly it was scary.

"See that wasn't so hard. But I have to go. They're looking for me. I'll call you later, okay?" Jaehyun said quickly. I hung up as we pulled up to my building. I said my goodbyes to Rowoon and hurried inside.

The drive to the station took about 15 minutes and I got stuck in traffic for a moment. It was a weekend, so I expected downtown to be busy. I wasn't prepared for the heavy police that were still around and going in and out of the station. There were still policemen posted on the front steps of the building. My heart pounded in my chest as I stared up at the building. The station was massive. The pictures didn't do it justice. It had to be at least 10 stories tall, maybe more. I turned the corner following the building's west side. Four officers stationed there at an entrance there. Two seemed to be more focused on watching the public streets, looking for trouble. In the back of the building there was a multi level parking deck. I'm sure the parking deck was shared between the station and the massive shopping outlet it was nestled in the middle of. How did I miss that a shopping outlet was here too?! I pulled into the parking deck and saw one police officer at the gate. The back of the police station had an entrance as well and two officers stood watch. This was going to be hard.

I checked my watch. It was 10:30. I had to shift through numerous conversations with Miyeon in my head and in my text messages trying to figure out if she ever talked about Park Hayeon. She knew gossip about everyone and didn't have a problem with sharing it with the world, either. I was able to recall Miyeon telling me that she was an overly prompt person. If she was told to meet at 12, Miyeon said she would get to the destination at least 2 hours in advance. If that was to be believed then she was somewhere here. Miyeon told me there was this coffee shop and she would spend time there. It was on the same street as the station, a few blocks down. I parked the rented car in one of the available spaces in the parking deck. I adjusted my hair under the hat I was wearing. I didn't need anyone to remember the girl with the red hair. This was going to be harder than I thought. I redid the bun and readjusted the baseball cap. I grabbed my black face mask from the passenger seat. A black fanny pack held a taser and a switchblade to use as a weapon if needed. I'm glad I went without my gun today.

As I walked through the streets, I noticed a few plain clothes officers hiding among the people. Damn it. I noticed there were video cameras around the station. The front of the station had three. Cameras and guards why? What was the reason? The eastern side of the building was shaded from the sun and it was a grassy area. There was nothing there but I noticed a security camera there. The camera wasn't moving and the lens wasn't either. There was no little red light to indicate recording in progress nor was there a sign. That could be useful.

I made my way to the cafe Miyeon had mentioned before and walked in. It was a small and quaint little shop. Seemed perfect for those quiet types who just wanted to read books and be alone. It seemed like a place Hayeon would go to. My eyes scanned the room and I spotted her. Her long brown hair was tied in a tight ponytail so she could put on her uniform hat. She wore the typical SMPA uniform. A blue button up shirt and black trousers and her black officer's cap sat on the table beside her. She was about my height and weight, I could fit her clothes. Now to just figure out how to get her out of the building. She was trying to be a police officer, so she could maybe help an innocent bystander who got hurt. I put on the face mask and went up to the counter to order a small latte and once I received it, I went to the table directly behind her wordlessly. I checked my phone and looked at the time. 11:00. I had an hour to get her uniform.

In order to make myself appear normal, I would sit and play on my phone for fifteen minutes and drink the latte. My heart started to pound in my chest and adrenaline started to pump through my veins. This was such an unplanned thing, I was starting to wonder if this was a mistake. I already misjudged how busy the station would be. I didn't realize the station was downtown either. But it was too late, I was in it. I had to see it through. A buzzing on the phone caught my eye and I looked down to see Jaehyun text me asking about what type of wine I liked. It made a chuckle escape me. It eased the rising tension for a moment. I text him back to tell him to surprise me and that I was working on homework. I noticed the girl start to gather her things and I stood quickly and placed my phone in the fanny pack. I breathed deeply because this was going to hurt.

I started to take a few steps forward and purposely tripped myself on her chair as she was starting to stand. The impact of the chair hitting my shin and my ankle caused me to yell out in pain and I frantically tried to catch myself as I crumbled to the floor. The girl and other patrons gasped and jumped to check on me. I whimpered in pain and grabbed at my ankle. She stood and leaned down next to me. "Oh my god! I am so sorry! I didn't see you behind me! Are you okay?" "My ankle! I-I twisted it… Oh god, I just wanted to grab coffee and look around. Just my luck. I should've stayed home." I cried, forcing my eyes to tear up and spill over onto my cheeks to be soaked up by the mask.

"Oh nooo! I'm so sorry! Here let me help you up! Do you need to go to the hospital? Let me help you!" Hayeon exclaimed as she grabbed her cap and put it on.

"Just help me to my car, please. I just want to go home." I sobbed. She nodded and leaned down to help me stand up and to make it believable I hobbled on one leg.

"Can you try to put weight on it? Is it really hard? I can take you there? Did you park on the deck?" she asked. I nodded pathetically. I tried to put pressure on my ankle, it hurt but I could manage. I hissed in pain and nodded.

"I can put enough weight on it, to make it to my car. Just help me there please. Everyone's staring at me and I'm scared. This is embarrassing. I'm sorry."

She waved me off and we started the walk towards the parking deck. "Can we cut between the police and the buildings? I know it's not okay, but it's a shortcut." I whimpered as we began the walk.

"Of course. We can do that. It's totally fine. I work there." she replied sympathetically. I nodded and looked down at the ground, smirking. Too easy. It was a few minutes walk to the station and I sneakily pulled out the taser and held it in my hand, hiding it in my oversized sleeve. We turned the corner on the shaded area of the police station and I waited until we were in the middle and I whimpered out in pain again.

"Can we take a break? My ankle needs a break." I requested as I stood still. She agreed and helped me lean against the wall. I had to be quick, I pulled her into a quick hug and covered her mouth to silence her screams and held the taser to her neck. Her eyes rolled back and she slumped over onto my shoulder, unconscious.

I looked both ways to see if anyone was looking over. Everyone was walking by and minding their business. Heads buried in phones or talking on the phones. People wore headphones and talked with their friends. People are so mindless nowadays. They missed the world around them because of technology, but I used it to my advantage. I breathed a sigh of relief as I quickly sank to the ground with her and quickly worked on removing her shirt and pants. I threw off my shirt and put her pants on over my leggings. I left my black combat boots on and switched my baseball cap for her police cap. I switched over my taser, cell phone and switchblade. She had her badge on her shirt and she had a notebook in her pocket and it looked like she had her passwords and things written down in it. She was one of those people. Rookie mistake kid. I left her there laying in the grass to be found whenever that would happen. I gathered my shirt, mask, fanny pack and baseball cap and stepped out on the sidewalk and walked back past the cafe to throw away the items.

I checked my surroundings and still no one was looking or noticed anything. I walked up to the police station and saluted the officers at the door. They opened the door for me and I walked up to the receptionist. They looked at my name tag. "Park Hayeon. You're one of the interns from Seoul National University. Report to the High Profile Crimes unit. The sixth floor. Captain Chae Jum is expecting you. Room 651." the officer behind the desk pointed. I nodded and made my way to the elevators. The inside was busy and hectic. Uniforms were running to and from across the floor. An attorney was berating three officers about a botched arrest. It was maddening. I was on guard and tense the entire time. No one outwardly suspected a thing. I kept repeating to myself that as long as I played it cool on the outside, I would be fine. My heart pounded in my chest as I entered the elevator and the doors closed on the chaos of the first floor. I breathed deeply and closed my eyes. My hands were starting to sweat and I shivered in anxiousness. Hopefully the floor wasn't too busy there.

I stepped onto the sixth floor and it was quieter than the ground floor. A few people walked the halls but it wasn't horrible. I found the captain's room and knocked. A gruff voice demanded for me to come in and I opened the door. There was a short thin man sitting on the other side of the desk. The captain was a crabby looking older man. He was hardened and stern. He had a stocky build and hair that was black mixed with patches of gray. "Park Hayeon. Lee Minjun. He's your partner and trainer. We're throwing you right in. Your job today is to start investigating a series of robberies that have been happening at jewelry stores. The crew doing it is very quick and efficient. We may be looking at Jopok affiliates." the captain said annoyed. I could work with that. I nodded in understanding and Lee waved for me to follow him. Lee was talkative as we walked to our assigned workstation.

We walked out of the office, and turned right to walk down the hallway. We entered a large office area where there were a lot of tables with computers on them. The office area had an ugly carpet with random colored shapes. We walked to one of the desks in the back left. I noticed there was a back door to the left as well and next to it was a conference room with a large window. "What made you want to be a police officer, Park?" Lee asked in a friendly way. I rolled my eyes.

"I really want to focus on the task at hand. We have a job to do." I snapped at him. He recoiled back and nodded, opening up a few systems on the computers.

"Explain what this is." I requested.

"This is our main database. We keep a database of suspected Jopok and gang members. So here if you get in here, you can see for some people we have photos. This is the main family of the Jopok." Lee explained.

On the screen there were photos of Arsyn, Omega, and Viper. Though their hair colors had changed from when I saw them in Han's files. Arsyn had bright red hair that was cut short into a bob. Omega's hair was brown and a little longer than the short hair he had in previous pictures. He looked younger with that hairstyle. Viper's silver hair was dyed black and it was longer tied into a bun. There was also a fourth box and all there was a tall male figure in a long black trench coat. The figure was facing away from the camera. Arsyn yet again was looking directly into the camera. These spies weren't very good.

"Why is that picture like that?" I asked, pointing at the turned picture.

"No matter what our spy did, they couldn't get a picture of that one's face. It was like they knew the photographs were happening and were trying not to be seen. When we found the film, all his photos were like that."

It was definitely different. The others were almost okay with being on camera and having their photo taken, but this person was trying not to be seen. I wonder why? It was clear Arsyn was going to handle the spy and kill them, so I don't understand it. I saw a small grin spread across Lee's face. "Want to see what we found with the camera?" he asked mischievously. I resisted the urge to roll my eyes. He was annoying. I'm almost positive that I was going to see the dead body of the spy. I nodded anyway. He clicked on a link and sure enough, the mutilated and beaten corpse of the spy's body was laid out on the steps of the station in the front. The film roll was sticking out of his mouth and a handwritten note was stapled to his forehead. The note only said stop and was signed with her name Arsyn.

I whistled impressed. The bitch was ruthless. In order to leave a dead body on a police station's front door, she was cruel and sadistic. Even in examining the injuries on the body, I could tell she tortured the man. I was very familiar with the methods, I've used them personally. He had been beaten, fingers were missing, large fresh scars and wounds were prevalent. She was efficient. She got whatever information she wanted out of him.

"Hey! You didn't throw up or scream. That's no fun. Have you seen this before?" Lee whined as he pouted. I shook my head.

"I've seen a lot of shit. Focus." I answered. I looked back at the photo and an uncomfortable chill ran down my spine. It nauseated me because her work mirrored mine. She had to be eliminated, not just because of what happened to my mother. The two of us simply didn't need to exist on this planet at one time.

He opened a new system and he logged into it. When the page loaded, it was a long list and the heading said 'Possible Jopok Ties'. There were at least 300 companies on the list. "This is the system that we use to keep track of businesses that may be dealing with the Jopok. Money laundering, loan sharking. All of that." he told me. I nodded in understanding.

"These are the big two systems that we use for the Jopok. As you can see there's a lot of work that needs to be done. The robberies have been a part of the latest stream of distractions, we believe the Jopok are using to keep us away from something big that they're planning." He sighed and looked back at the screen, continuing to click through the systems. I checked the clock on the wall. I had been here long enough, I needed to get this information and get out of here. I don't know if the real Hayeon was still unconscious or not.

I glanced around and the office area was empty. I moved behind his chair and placed my hand on his left side squeezing his carotid artery. I slapped a hand over his mouth and nose cutting off his breathing and he was out in a minute or so. I took out the flash drive that had the spyware downloaded onto it and plugged it into the PC. I downloaded the spyware onto the computer and smirked as it finished. Removing the flash drive, I repositioned Lee in front of the computer letting his head rest against the monitor as I stood up and made my way out of the back door. It revealed a stairwell, and I started the long descent to freedom. A quick and clean escape were the best kinds of escapes.

I made it out of the station through the back entrance and I saluted the officers that were on guard there. I removed the uniform once I got into the car, and I sighed in relief and looked down at the flash drive. There better be something on here that I could use or I just wasted two hours of my life for nothing. I checked my phone and saw that I missed a text from Jaehyun. I responded to his message, and I sent a message to Han letting him know I got access to the police databases and I'd let him know what I found. He was seriously lucky I chose to tell him anything. The ungrateful bastard. I pulled out of the parking deck and started the drive back to my house to get ready to see Jaehyun. The thought of seeing him made my mood brighter and I smiled softly to myself along the way.

~Chapter 15~

I walked out of the classroom looking down at my phone. The group chat I was in with Jaehyun's female friends was active for some reason today. I was being tagged in numerous messages, but I never answered until now. I sent a simple waving emoji. Haeun sent numerous angry emojis at my late response. "The girls have been blowing up my phone asking where you have been. Could you answer them please?" A voice sounded behind me. I jumped in surprise and adrenaline rushed through me as I turned to face the voice with my fist raised to strike. I let out a heavy sigh of relief seeing it was Jaehyun.

"What did I tell you about doing that, Nam Jaehyun! Why don't you listen!?" I yelled as I put my hand over my chest, breathing deeply. He was the only person that was able to sneak up on me and I never noticed him. He moved like a shadow sometimes. It was unnerving. He chuckled softly and gave me an apologetic smile.

"I'm sorry, I'm sorry. I just can't help it. It's kind of a rush to see you get so defensive and ready to strike when I scare you." he grinned.

"Your masochism is showing again." He shrugged a little and fell in line beside me as we walked through the halls.

"What are the girls wanting with me?"

"They want to see you. They saw you last at karaoke. You missed brunch with them. A couple of shopping trips, a concert. They're convinced I'm stealing you from them. They really do like you. They're trying to be your friends." he said as he looked over at me with a raised eyebrow.

"Yeah… The chat is muted on my phone. So I don't see it sometimes." I lied. I looked down at the floor feeling uncomfortable.

"What's wrong, Ae Ri? You can tell me. Did you not like the girls?"

"No, there's nothing wrong with them. They're fine." I admitted. It was honest. The girls were all very sweet and they were nothing but kind and welcoming. I wasn't used to it. It scared me. I never had friends growing up. I didn't have a conventional childhood, for one. But I didn't make friends in the training dorms. I wasn't close to anyone except Code and I don't consider him a friend. We work together. We're soldiers that go to war side by side. That wasn't a friend. I was taught that I didn't have friends. I had associates. People I knew. Loneliness and solitude started at a young age for me. It just got worse the more I trained and the more essential I became to Han.

"Then what is it?" he pressed. I sighed in annoyance. He wasn't going to let it go until I opened up. He was persistent.

"I've never had friends. So I don't really know what I'm supposed to do. I wasn't taught what a friend was. I really think sometimes you don't understand how new all of this is to me. You, the girls, your friends. All of this is so... normal. I've never been normal." I replied in a curt tone. He was silent beside me. I sighed heavily, feeling bad.

"That was unintentional. It wasn't for you." I added quickly as I stopped and grabbed his arm. He paused and looked down at me with a soft smile.

"I know. It was your trauma. I get it. We'll work on it. Now keep going." he said gently, throwing an arm over my shoulder.

It was a double-edged sword whenever he was still kind to me after I snapped at him for no reason. I was thankful that he never took it personally but at the same time, I always felt horrible. He didn't deserve it. He always said he knew it wasn't directed towards him and he blamed it on something that I never heard of before. Trauma was a word I heard him use before, but I didn't understand what he meant by that. He never went into detail about it, so I figured it wasn't important. I was just happy he kept talking to me and walking this thing with me. It was still undefined what we were calling this, but we were comfortable with that. Everyone else seemed to want to define it for their own reasons. Sometimes I wanted to change it because Miyeon was still living with her delusional crush on Jaehyun and it was eating me up, watching her shamelessly try to flirt with Jaehyun when she thought I wasn't around. Jaehyun never flirted back, he was still short with her and everything but sometimes he got an obvious kick out of my irritation.

Our dynamic had started to shift. We alternated spending the night at each other's houses almost every night. He bought me a lot of lavish gifts. Clothes were the most common thing he bought me. Reds, oranges, pinks, light blues and other colors were mingled into the black and white that I regularly wore. It took some getting used to it. I wasn't comfortable with all of the colors yet and he told me he just wanted me to have it for whenever I was ready. It caused a few days of arguing because I felt like it was too much and he, of course, insisted that it wasn't too much. It was a me thing. We both knew that. So he kept doing it. Eventually I started to enjoy it. It still felt like I didn't deserve any of it. I didn't deserve any of it because I felt like a fraud. It felt like Ae Ri and Rose were becoming two completely different people. Ae Ri wasn't supposed to be real.

I found myself often thinking of a future with Jaehyun. It was always something crazy like a house and running a business or something of our own. He liked to use the expression building empires together. It echoed in my head constantly. I wasn't Rose playing the character Ae Ri anymore. Ae Ri was her own person. She occasionally went to hang outs and parties with Jaehyun. She talked to people at the police station. Rose had become this completely separate person who worked on the assignment. She was standoffish and distrusting, unfriendly and calculating. She got frustrated when hours of trying to find anything on the Jopok yielded no results. She was the one on phone calls with Han fighting off the murderous thoughts about killing her father slowly.

They felt like split personalities more than anything. Both of them existed within me. I was aware of both of them. It got confusing sometimes because they had similarities too. The emotions I feel for Jaehyun are genuine. That was the same no matter what role I played. I couldn't make them up. I had no experience with them, so I couldn't portray or fake them. The way the sun shined a lot brighter when he entered a room wasn't a figment of my imagination. It did. The safety and comfort I feel with him is unlike anything I have ever felt. I never felt safe. I don't feel safe with

Code. Even after all the time I worked with him. I trust Code to a certain extent. I was starting to trust Jaehyun more than Code. I'd follow Jaehyun into hell with no questions asked if he requested that of me. Jaehyun made me feel like a princess. He treated me like I was fragile. No one had ever done that before. He reminded me that I was human. I forgot that a long time ago.

Everything solidified my desire and need to be here with Jaehyun. I don't know how I was going to make it work. I just had to make it work. If I treated Ae Ri and Rose as two completely different people, then maybe I could. I already operated that way. When I couldn't sleep, I did research and tried to find anything on the Jopok that would help me with my assignment while Jaehyun slept like a baby and occasionally woke up and pleaded with me to come lay down and get some sleep. That was Rose. The only problem with treating them like different people was that Ae Ri had Rose's issues. The worst parts of myself actually became Ae Ri's mannerisms and triggers and personality. My greed and pride, my possessiveness, my coldness. My past bleeds over into Ae Ri and she was supposed to be normal. It was exhausting trying to keep everything straight. But I had to continue this. Not just for my sake, but for his as well because I may be on a collision course with the Jopok.

I started to notice that there were random people who I had never seen before that would be walking and standing outside of my building complex lately. I didn't know everyone in the complex as there were a hundred or more residents, but there was a specific type of person who lived in the buildings and those random people didn't fit the image. They would dress in all black and sunglasses and wear hats and just stand outside on their phones. No one seemed to pay them attention but I did. I noticed they would show up once a week after I used the spyware to access the police systems. They never did anything or said anything. They just stood there. I highly doubt it's a coincidence.

"Earth to Ae Ri. Do you hear me?" Jaehyun's voice broke me from my thoughts as his hand waved in my face and I looked at him.

"I zoned out for a second. What did you say?" I asked. He chuckled and rolled his eyes.

"You never listen to me. I said my design for the new Lotte hotel that the company wants to build, made it to the semi final round. Remember when I told you about the competition?" He reminded me. I hummed in thought.

"Yeah. The competition where if your design was chosen, you'd have your first job after graduation, right?"

"Correct. You do listen a little bit, I see." He smiled widely and the excitement was visible in his eyes. I gave him a small smile.

"I do. Just don't always show it. How are you feeling about it? Think you might win?"

"Of course. I'm good at this, remember?" he chuckled as he pinched my cheek. I swatted him away playfully.

"Well that's good. I look forward to seeing your design win." I grinned as I leaned up to kiss his cheek.

"Let's celebrate tonight. Go out to a nice dinner. What do you think?"

I hummed in thought. It had been a while since we had gone out to a nice dinner. I could use a break from the work and I did miss going out places with Jaehyun. We had both been so busy with work and school that when we were together, we just stayed in and watched tv. It was a complex thing. I didn't necessarily enjoy going out because it was still new to me and I was still very skeptical about the whole thing. However, I liked going out with Jaehyun because he made me feel comfortable and protected. It was something new for me. I agreed to the dinner, excitement filling my stomach. He nodded with a sparkle of excitement in his eyes as well.

"So, back to the topic of conversation. Our friends. They're actually joining us for lunch. So you can see them and talk to them." he said quickly as he helped me into the car. I looked up at him flabbergasted. He grinned slyly and leaned down to kiss me softly. It was disarming and I blushed deeply looking up at him. My heart pounded in my chest as shyness crept in. He winked and closed the door. He played so unfairly sometimes. I shouldn't feel like a little kid around him still. It seemed almost silly at this point given all the time we spent together. I just couldn't help it. It was like once I got comfortable with a new emotion that I had towards him, it started to change and evolve into something else. I couldn't describe it at all. All I knew was that it was becoming all consuming. Being away from him was devastating. I hated the days when I couldn't be around him because he had to work or I had to work at the station. It felt like I couldn't breathe. I only felt better when I was reunited with him. It was honestly terrifying, but I couldn't stop. I didn't want to. And I think that was the most terrifying part.

We arrived at the familiar sushi restaurant and I looked out the window to see everyone already sitting at a table on the patio. A lump formed in my throat and my hands got sweaty. My breath quickened and I was overcome with nervousness. What would they say? Would they even talk to me? I didn't know why I was so nervous or really why I cared, but I did. Jaehyun grabbed my hand and held it tightly. I looked over at him and he gave me a reassuring smile. "Don't look so nervous. You're okay. They just want to check on you. I'm right here with you as well." he reassured. I took a few deep breaths and nodded as he stroked my hand. It made me feel better. I wasn't sure if I believed him, but I was calmer. We got out of the car and walked inside to meet the others.

Jiwoo looked up first and gasped. "Your hair! You dyed it!" she screamed excitedly. Everyone else looked up and Nari and Haeun smiled widely seeing me.

"No way! You didn't tell us!? Is that why you've been a ghost? I love it!" Haeun exclaimed as she got up to hug me tightly. I huffed at the impact and lightly smiled. My hair was no longer maroon, I dyed it after the police station infiltration as a precautionary measure. It took hours to get a brown that I never had and would soften my appearance. The cappuccino brown color worked well with my olive skin and green eyes. It gave me a more soft appearance and the green of my eyes seemed to sparkle.

"Haeun! Let her breath, sheesh. We all missed her. But let her sit down." Nari ordered softly. She offered the two empty seats next to her to us. He gently nudged me to sit next to her and he sat on the other side.

"Where have you been, friend? We missed you! You missed brunch with us." Jiwoo asked softly as she reached across the table holding my hands gently. The girls all looked over at me at once. It was nerve racking. Luckily the boys didn't seem too interested, leaning away from the table and huddling together to see something on Seojun's phone.

"I've been working at my internship and doing some work at the family's business. I didn't mean to worry you guys. I'm not really good at this friendship thing. I've never had friends, so I'm trying to figure it out. I'm just used to doing everything on my own. Life in Korea has been really different for me than it is in Japan." I explained as I looked down at the table. I felt a strange sense of sadness again as I opened up to the girls. I stopped before I could say too much.

"Awww that's not good. I'm sorry, Ae Ri. That sounds really lonely." Haeun said as she frowned deeply. I shook my head quickly.

"Don't need pity or sympathy, it is what it is. I'm just trying to figure it out. I'll try to do better."

"No, this one is on us. Jaehyun didn't tell us that. He said you were really quiet and reserved and we didn't take into account that it may take you longer to open up to us than we expected. It would make sense that you are more comfortable with him than us right now. Hopefully, we can try again. We'd really like that." Nari apologized as she placed a hand on my shoulder. I made eye contact with her and she held so much warmth and maturity in them. It felt like she understood what I was trying to say without me having to say it. I appreciated that. I nodded wordlessly and she leaned over for a hug. Jiwoo and Haeun scurried over to join the hug as well.

"Aw. I'm glad you guys could talk. They've really missed you, Ae Ri. So hopefully we'll see you more?" Minhyun said hopefully. Jaehyun turned to look at me and I smiled softly.

"Yeah. I'll be around more." I said. Everyone cheered and a different type of warmth spread through my chest. It wasn't the same type of feeling that I got with Jaehyun, but it was pleasant. Maybe Jaehyun was right.

"Oh! Before I forget, Jaehyun, did you get that thing I sent you?" Nari asked suddenly as we waited for our check. He nodded in response.

She grinned excitedly and gave him a thumbs up. What was that about? I was about to ask what was happening, but the waiter came back before I could ask. Panic rose in my stomach as I watched them interact looking for some clues. I was scared. I didn't like the feeling of not knowing what was happening there.

"Is everyone free tonight? Want to do karaoke?" Jiwoo invited as she and Seojun stood to grab their jackets.

"We can't tonight. Jaehyun and Ae Ri have dinner plans, remember?" Haeun answered as she looked at the older girl. Everyone looked at her and groaned. I tilted my head, growing more concerned. Was everyone in on it? Did everyone know about the dinner plans before I did? We didn't tell them. What are they plotting? I listened in closer to see if I could pick up on anything suspicious.

"Oops… I wasn't supposed to say anything. Sorry guys!" Haeun giggled as she bowed once. Minhyun rolled his eyes as he put her jacket over her shoulders.

"Come on before you spill any other secrets. Bye guys! We'll call later!" he said quickly before guiding her out of the open fence. I looked up at Jaehyun and he smiled warmly as he held out his arm to me. I took it and we said our goodbyes. I was trying to hold everything in. I felt dizzy from the effort. Maybe I was overthinking and it was nothing serious. But the thought of it being something much worse, was creeping in my stomach. It was making me nauseous as I held his hand and we walked back to the car.

Once we were in the safety of the car, I couldn't hold back. In the logical side of my brain, I knew nothing weird was going on because she was engaged to his best friend. But the feeling that something else was going on wouldn't let up. I didn't know where it came from or why it started. It blindsided me. "What was Nari talking about? When she asked if you got what she sent?" I asked, trying to keep the tremble out of my voice. He looked over at me confused. He turned the car off quickly and turned to me.

"Princess… What's wrong? Why do you sound like that?" he asked with a perplexed expression. I took a few deep breaths trying to calm my racing heart and get breath into my lungs. My hands trembled. I was losing grip on the world around me and I was desperately trying to keep it together. He reached over and grabbed my hands, squeezing them.

"Hey, hey… I'm right here. Breathe. Breathe. You're all right." he called gently. I squeezed his hands back and closed my eyes trying to focus on my breathing. He gently reminded me to breathe over and over again and it took a few minutes before I felt in control of myself again. I opened my eyes and breathed deeply again.

He looked me over a few times before he stopped squeezing but refused to let go. I looked down embarrassed. That wasn't normal and I had no explanation for that. I tried to tug my hands away and he held them anyway. I looked back at him and he wore a worried expression. He raised an eyebrow waiting for me to speak. "S-Sorry. I don't know what that was. I'm okay now. We can go." I said softly. He shook his head and raised an eyebrow.

"You just had a panic attack. And I have no idea where it came from. Has that happened before?" he inquired. I groaned in annoyance. He wasn't going to let it go.

"I don't know what a panic attack is, but yes. Something like that has happened before." I admitted. His eyes went wide and he looked at me seriously.

"Why didn't you say anything?" I shrugged.

"I don't know what any of this stuff means that you're talking about. I don't know what trauma is, I don't know what anxiety is or a panic attack. I barely understand what insomnia is. Those things don't make sense to me. So when you say them, I can't relate to what you're saying. It doesn't click. These things just happen to me and I live with it, Jae. I don't try to understand it. I just go through them. It's like that. I just rather move on please? Please tell me what Nari and you were talking about? That's what I was thinking about." I exclaimed as I threw my head back and closed my eyes, fighting off the tears that threatened to spill over. I didn't need to cry right now. This was embarrassing enough and I hated it.

He sat silently beside me for a while. His thumbs stroked the back of my hands. "I had Nari help work on a surprise for you tonight. That's why I wanted to go out to celebrate today." he offered gently. The realization crashed down on me like a ton of bricks. It was nothing. It was innocent. I made a scene for no reason. *Fuck*. He hates me. He definitely hates me. I looked over at him sadly and the tears I tried to fight back spilled over onto my cheeks.

"I-I-I'm so sorry… I don't know why…I'm like this…. I thought it was something else… And I don't know why… It made sense but my thoughts just ran away…" I cried. I put my head down to hide my tear stained face and he finally let go of my hands. He picked my head up and wiped the tears away gently with his thumbs.

"What were you thinking?" He stared into my eyes with an emotion that I couldn't describe but it was intense and I had never seen it before.

"You were with her… And you were going to leave me for her… That you cheated on me…" I confessed pathetically. The thought of him cheating or leaving me made me feel more broken than I was prepared for. The rage that bubbled under the surface was chilling even for me. It was worse than anything I had ever felt towards Han. Before I could stop it the words left my mouth. "I wanted to kill you both, if it was true." I went rigid in my seat as a small *oh* escaped from him. It was silent again for what felt like hours as we stared at each other again. Tears still stained my cheeks but I could tell from his aghast expression that my eyes told him how serious I was.

His boisterous laugh broke the tension. "You are so fucking cute. Jealousy is adorable on you. How can you be so pretty like this?" he beamed as he leaned over and kissed me deeply. I was stunned. That wasn't the reaction I was expecting. I didn't know what to expect but a kiss and being called cute and pretty was not it. Nonetheless, I returned the kiss as his hands intertwined with mine. He pulled away and grinned smugly.

"You're so cute. I've never had anyone tell me they'd kill me if I cheated. I like it." I raised an eyebrow. It wasn't the first time he said something strange like that, but it looked like the masochism thing wasn't a joke anymore.

"Y-You're weird, Nam. Who says that?" I jabbed playfully.

"The type of person who likes when girls say if you cheat on me, I'll kill you and actually mean it. Like you."

"This masochistic thing isn't a joke, is it? You really like it, huh?" I tilted my head as he shrugged and finished wiping the rest of my tears away and put the car in drive.

"We'll have to find out, won't we?" he grinned as he winked and pulled out of the parking lot.

~Chapter 16~

The only instruction Jaehyun gave me for tonight was to dress pretty. That is all he said. He said it was a fancy new place that his family enjoyed. It was Michelin star rated. I had been to restaurants like that before but not in this type of setting. I felt an overwhelming amount of pressure and I called for help. I watched the group chat ring on Facetime, biting my lip hoping one of the girls answered. All of them did. I breathed a deep sigh of relief.

"Ae Ri! Hi! You're not at dinner yet?" Nari greeted as she appeared on screen. I shook my head and sat at my makeup dresser in my towel.

"I don't know what to do… I was just told to dress pretty. It's a Michelin star rated place. I don't know what to wear…" I trailed off. They all nodded in understanding.

"What do you have?" Haeun asked. I got up showing the dresses I pulled out so far. The first dress was a red strapless corset mini dress with plain black Saint Laurent Opyum sandals. I personally liked the outfit, but it felt plain for the occasion. The girls wanted to see the next one. I pulled out one of my favorite white blazer dresses. It had a wide white belt with a large decorative rhinestone buckle and a small Chanel pin on the right lapel. It was a custom design that was diamond encrusted. I showed the classic and simple white Kate Louboutin pumps.

"You have a lot of designer things. I need to raid your closet." Nari teased as she shook her head playfully.

"That's pretty. But a lot of white. Do you have anything with more color?" Jiwoo asked curiously.

"I mainly wear whites and blacks. Jaehyun bought me more colors." I told them as I opened my closet. I looked at the entire closet feeling overwhelmed. Who would've thought that I would be one of those girls obsessing over what to wear. It was a fucking lot. I sighed heavily, rubbing my temple and letting the girls look inside.

"Wear something Jaehyun bought you. He'd like that!" Haeun squealed. I cringed slightly and looked back at the phone.

"Quiet Haeun. What's that orange one? That one there in the middle?" Nari called. I scanned the closet for the orange clothing, she pointed at. It was a skirt set. It was a wrap style mini skirt and a long sleeved off shoulder shirt. The sleeves weren't tight but they were flowing. The material was soft and silky. It wasn't heavy and the light shimmer of the orange was pretty. I didn't remember this one.

"I don't remember this. He must've slipped it into the closet when I wasn't here." I mumbled as I held it up to my body and the girls said to try it on.

I noticed the tight fit. It was still comfortable. I noticed that the neckline had a medium sized orange rhinestone nestled in the middle and smaller rhinestones lined the rest of the neckline. I looked in the mirror and twirled. It was really beautiful. I turned to my phone and the girls were staring at me speechless. "You look like a princess. I love it! You can wear it with those black shoes! And add some jewelry." Jiwoo smiled warmly. I nodded and looked into my jewelry box to find some silver jewelry. I chose to stack a few rings from Tiffany's on my right hand and on my left wrist I wore a silver tennis bracelet. I showed the completed outfit to the girls after I adjusted the retro Hollywood curls that I tried to do on myself. It was a different look than what I normally wore, but I felt that I should do something new because Jaehyun had something special planned.

"I like it! I've never seen your hair curled before, friend! You look beautiful! Awww!" Haeun cooed as she started taking screenshots. A pleasant feeling spread throughout my body at the compliments. If this was what having friends felt like, I didn't hate it. I felt genuinely supported. There was no animosity or ill intent with them. Nari smiled brightly and gave me a thumbs up. I slightly shivered at the memory from earlier when I thought something was going on between her and Jaehyun.

The doorbell rang and I froze staring at the door to my room. Panic started to fill my chest and I looked over at the girls on the screen. They smiled encouragingly. "You got this, Ae Ri! It's just Jaehyun. You've done this before." Nari pushed gently. *Yeah, but you didn't see the chaos after we left either*, I thought to myself bitterly. What if he didn't like the outfit? What if he was coming over to just tell me he didn't want to see me anymore? My hands trembled in fear and I started to play with the skin on my fingers.

"Ae Ri? Breathe. You're okay. Take a deep breath. Don't panic." Jiwoo said calmly. I turned to look at them and took deep breaths. Once I was centered again, I nodded and waved goodbye to the girls, closing the call. There was a negative feeling in the pit of my stomach as I walked to the door to answer it. I've gone out to dinner with this man before, but this just felt different. I don't know what surprise he had for me. I hated not knowing things.

My hand paused on the front door as the doorbell rang again and I held my breath preparing for the worse. I looked up at Jaehyun and he was looking down at his phone. His attention was caught when he heard the door creak open. Even in five inch heels, I was still shorter than him. His eyes scanned over my outfit and I felt the heat creep up to my face. His phone fell out of his hands and he stared at me with his mouth agape. He didn't say anything, he just stared and that made the feelings worse. The staring was excessive, so I looked him over once to try to calm myself down. Bad idea. It didn't calm me down. It made the heat worse and I felt desire rise in my stomach. He wore a dark red suit jacket and matching slacks with a white button up that stretched tightly across his chest and everything was tailored perfectly to his waist. Why was he so fucking beautiful? It was insane!

It felt like everything was becoming too much. Everything was bubbling up to a fever pitch and I couldn't take it anymore. "Could you say something? You're making me nervous, Nam!" I exclaimed as I looked him in the eye. The tension was suffocating. Jaehyun continued to stare at me but he was blinking now. Did he malfunction in real life? It took several moments of silence before he came to and started to speak. "S-Sorry... I didn't mean to stare like that… You just kind of took me off guard. I wasn't expecting you to wear something I bought you. You look really beautiful. I-I…" he rambled. I didn't care, I was just happy that he was speaking now. I could finally breathe again. He cleared his throat and closed his eyes to compose himself. Once he was together again, a charming smile graced his face and he handed a bouquet of roses to me. I didn't notice that he had anything with him.

"These are for you, gorgeous." he winked. He was back to normal. I giggled and accepted them. They were roses. Lavender roses at that. I had never seen lavender roses in real life. I remembered a conversation that we had before about flowers and I felt my cheeks heat up as I realized he remembered that I liked roses. It wasn't just an alias I used in the Yakuza. I felt a sharp twinge of pain as the memories rushed back. Arisu loved flowers and she used to call me her 'Little Rose'. She would sneak roses into my dorm room without Han knowing because he said they would make me soft and ruin my training. They would fight over it often. Whenever we were in her private garden, she would always tell me that the flower describes me perfectly. *Beautiful to look at but dangerous when not careful. Always guarded and prepared.* Yeah at the time it was cheesy, but it became true the more I grew up. Roses were a soft spot for me and no one knew that. Not even Code. No one had ever gotten me roses before. This was the first time Jaehyun had done it and I was unprepared for the emotions that followed the realization.

My eyes got blurry for a moment as I looked down at the flowers and I hurriedly tried to blink them back. "Hey are you okay? Do you not like them…" Jaehyun asked worriedly. I shook my head quickly. It was the exact opposite.

"No, no. I like them… Thank you. I just wasn't expecting them. Roses are my favorite. And it just… did something to me." I replied as I looked up at him and gave him a small smile. He breathed a sigh of relief.

"I know. That's why I got them. Tonight was the perfect time to get them. I got them shipped in. They fit you well." He gently wiped a tear in the corner of my eye, careful not to mess up the makeup I spent hours on. He shamelessly looked me over again and a sneaky grin crept onto his face.

"You look really good in that outfit. I'm glad I picked it up once I saw it. You look expensive." he complimented as I moved to let him inside. I rolled my eyes and shut the door.

"It's not too many designers at once?" I asked, suddenly feeling self conscious. He shook his head. He turned to me and sat on the couch as he folded his legs.

"I like seeing you show off. Especially when you're with me and wearing things that I bought. It fills me with a lot of pride." he said. I smiled softly. I was relieved that he liked it. It eased the thoughts in my mind. I held the flowers closer to me as I told him to stay there so I could grab my purse and phone. I noticed that Nari sent me a text message outside of the group chat. She was sending me a princess emoji and told me to have fun. I smiled softly and put my phone in the purse. I touched up my lipstick and smiled at my reflection. Turning off my bedroom light, I stepped back out to join him.

"Are you ready to go, pretty?" he asked as he turned to look at me. I nodded my head and looked down off to the side shyly. He could disarm me with a simple compliment, and he knew it. It was unnerving but I didn't hate it. He stood up and walked over to the door, holding it open for me. He held his arm out for me to hold as we started our journey to the parking deck.

When we reached the parking deck, I tilted my head as we walked up to a new car that I hadn't seen before. "A new car or one of your spares?" I smirked as I looked over the red Lamborghini Aventador that was parked in the first parking spot. I noticed the car color and his blazer and slacks were a dark red as well. He was matching the car.

"That's obnoxious, Nam. Matching the car. Really?" I chuckled as I watched the doors slid up to let me in. He rolled his eyes and smirked lightly.

"You're one to talk, love. You have a matching outfit and car too." I raised an eyebrow in confusion. I didn't have anything to match my car. He pointed a few cars down and there was a car just like this one parked next to my G-Wagon. I gasped and covered my mouth. A matching car? There was no way that was real. I stared up at him and he nodded towards it. I walked quickly to go see it up close.

"Do you like it? It looks like you do." he grinned excitedly. He looked overjoyed and extremely proud of himself. I ran a hand along to the smooth red coating and even touching it, I couldn't believe it was real. I never had anything like this before. I talked to him once or twice before about how I'd like to add a Lamborghini to my car collection at some point but I didn't think he'd buy one for me. There was no way I could have seen it coming.

"Jae, I-I don't know what to say... Why? When? How did you do this?" I asked as I turned to look at him. He shrugged.

"You said you wanted one. I figured I'd get it for you." he answered simply.

"What's the catch?" He shook his head gently.

"Not everything has a catch, you know? Sometimes I just want to do things for you. That's not hard to believe, princess. Come on, we have dinner reservations. This wasn't your surprise honestly." he invited as he held out his hand. That wasn't my surprise? Then what was the surprise? I took his hand timidly and followed him back to his car and he helped me in. The first few minutes of the car ride were quiet as I tried to process everything that occurred a little while ago.

"Ae Ri. Can I ask you something?" he said suddenly. I looked at him and the look on his face was full of caution and seriousness. He was trying to find the words.

"Okay. What's up?" I replied. My breath quickened and I fought back any negative thoughts that could rise up.

"Who made you feel so... No. That's not the right way to frame it. What made you so scared of living life?" I could tell he was trying to find the right way to bring up a topic without triggering me.

"What are you wanting to really ask me? It's okay." I told him. He sighed deeply and nodded. "How much hurt is really hiding inside you?

149

What happened to you?" There it was. The in depth conversation, I always dreaded. I sighed and looked out the window.

"I'm guessing you're not looking for a long list of men who did me wrong."

"Whatever you want to tell me. I'm all ears. We got a drive ahead of us. I'm here." he said as he laid his hand on my knee. I shivered and took a deep breath.

"It didn't start there. I was this way long before dating became an interest of mine. My life was unfair and cruel. It always has been. I was homeschooled. I was stuck everyday with my cruel father. You know the thing with my mom. I'm an only child. I don't have a support system to lean back on it. I've always had to pick myself up when I fell. He ruled with an iron fist. It was his way or the highway. It was easier to do what I was told because that's all there was or get smacked around." I answered carefully. I couldn't tell him too much, but it felt good to really get some of this off my chest. But it was like an overflowing dam once I started. I couldn't stop talking. And it made me uncomfortable. He squeezed my hand reassuringly.

"I'm not blind to my faults. I know that I'm not necessarily… a good person. I'm cold and lack empathy for others. I'm greedy and impatient. I need to be in control. I have a mean streak, and I can be vindictive. My love for power keeps me bound to my dad's company." I continued.

"Have you ever thought that you could do something else? Be something else? Why do you stay?" he asked curiously. I sighed heavily.

"I've acquired so much over the years that I've gotten some retribution for what he did to me, right? Power, money. Cars and clothes. Houses. I'm not getting slapped around anymore. We rarely speak. It works, I suppose." It was a true statement. Gaining the position, it did make me feel like I got a small sense of retribution after all Han put me through. I was crucial to his success whether he understood it completely or not.

However, I had started to realize that it wasn't enough. I didn't feel completely vindicated. As long as Han was still breathing, we would still argue. He would still continue to toy with me and use me. I would do the hard work behind the scenes and he would gloat in public about how his vision for the Yakuza was legendary and unique. He would keep true power out of my reach for years to come. He had his succession line already picked out and I wasn't on it. Because of that, I couldn't achieve what I really wanted. True control and power. Freedom.

"From the outside looking in and hearing the way you talk about your dad... There's no way you're content with just having that position. I hope I don't offend you, but you're very intense. Volatile even. Being around him can't be good for you. It never was. How your dad could treat you that way, it's unfathomable to me and I seriously hate that." Jaehyun shook his head sadly and I saw his hands grip the steering wheel tighter. Tension and annoyance visible on his face. Was he upset? For me?

"You know. I envy you. Your family. Your siblings." I mumbled as I looked out the window. I saw his face twist in confusion at my statement from my peripheral. I stayed silent contemplating if I should continue. I could already feel the tears prickling at my eyes and I didn't want to cry. I worked hard on my makeup.

"Please continue, Ae Ri. I'm not judging. I'm listening to you. I want to understand. Honestly." he pleaded.

"You have the freedom that I could only dream of. Choices. Even though you come from an established legacy, you can be yourself. Your family encourages you and cares about you. Your mom sounds wonderful. I imagine that my mom would be like yours from the picture I've seen of her. Hell, even your siblings. For you all to be different, the fact that you guys are so close... I envy it. Your friends. You guys are so close and I feel like an outsider because I can't relate..." I trailed off for a moment trying to gather my thoughts. This was another moment where being vulnerable was difficult for me. The emotions that swelled in my chest threatened to choke me. A lump formed in my throat before I spoke again.

"I never felt safe anywhere. I never felt safe with anyone. So I stayed to myself. And I got used to it. Meeting you was a totally different experience for me. It made me realize just how fucked up I really was. And it scares me because you're practically perfect. A person like me ruins beautiful things. I don't want to do that to you. That's why all of this is hard for me." I admitted as I looked down at the roses in my hand and I played with the petals in nervousness. Saying it out loud lifted a burden off my chest but it stung with the harsh reality of my words. I could never bring myself to say it to me alone.

Han's involvement with my mother ended her life. Han ruined things. He ruined my life. I had been trained to do the same. The countless women he was involved with left with more scars than I will ever know because I was so young. While there were a few marriages in the Yakuza, there were twice as many divorces. It was always in the back of my mind how much danger Jaehyun could be in, if I ever told him who I was really. It kept me up at night more than anything else. I just sucked it up and dealt with it because I could die with my true identity as a secret if it meant protecting him. He would never understand it.

I felt the car come to a stop suddenly and Jaehyun turned to face me. "Have you ever tried to see yourself through my eyes? Because I don't see what you see. Yeah, you're rough around the edges. So what? Everyone has flaws. No one is perfect. I'm definitely not. You've gone through a lot. It's understandable. But look at what you've done. What you have achieved. You're alive. That's a big fucking deal. There are people who aren't alive right now." he smiled softly. I looked over at him confused.

"Remember after the gala when I said I couldn't figure out what it was about you that drew me in? I figured it out." I looked at him curiously. My heart started to pound in my chest as I waited for him to speak.

"You're feisty. I didn't think that was something that I would enjoy so much about you. I like joking around with you. I like watching you grow everyday. You may not see it. But I do. You feel comfortable enough to be open with me. Even if it's just a little bit. I like how you're authentically you. You stay out of the way and stay to yourself. I know it's more of a response to not being used to people, but for me it's such a cool thing because you're not with me to be seen. You don't try to fake it for the masses. You don't keep me around to improve your image or get something out of me. You're independent. You make it very clear that you don't need anything from me or want anything from me. But it just makes me want to give you things. You're confident and fiercely loyal. Even if it's a detriment to yourself. I like our dynamic and how we're different."

He held my hand tightly once he finished talking and I felt tears well in my eyes. No one had ever talked about me like that before. The way his eyes sparkled as he talked about me was unmistakable. There was something intense that lingered behind the sparkle but I couldn't name it. I felt special. Like I was the only person who mattered in that moment.

"While you envy me, I envy you. You don't care about being perfect. I break my back constantly trying to keep up this pretense of me being perfect. I have to be this social butterfly and overly friendly and welcoming because I'm on the student council. I have to make sure that my resume looks perfect, so I'm constantly bouncing from thing to thing to set myself up for a good future. You do what you want. Say what you want. Dress how you want. You have tattoos. You're unapologetic about everything. You don't care about showing off your wealth and money, I try to hide mine to fit in. That's my favorite thing about you. I like how you're fine with being complex and mysterious. Every little thing about you draws me in to you and any time I spend with you, I treasure it…" he added before he took a pause. He sat up straighter and looked me in the eyes with a serious expression and he leaned towards me.

"You have to listen to me and believe me when I say this, okay Ae Ri? I need you to verbally answer. It's important to me."

The seriousness of his tone made me anxious. My mouth went dry, but I forced myself to speak. "Okay. I'm listening." I answered. He sighed nervously and looked at me again. He was starting to disturb me because I rarely saw him nervous. That was more of a me thing. The air in the car was tense.

"I don't give a damn how long it takes, what I have to do, where I have to go… I want you. In every sense of the word. I started to notice it the morning after Mae's. It grew more and more with every interaction. I knew it at the gala and the first time I kissed you. It was sealed when you opened up to me the first time. You trusted me enough to open up and that meant the world to me. Because I had confirmation that you felt something. I just needed a sign." he confessed. Time stood still as I took in the gravity of what he said. He wanted me. In every sense of the word. That meant not just physically.

Jaehyun ran his thumb over my cheek softly. There it was again. That intense emotion that swam in his pretty irises. I got lost in them for a moment. "You're so beautiful, it hurts. You know diamonds are made under pressure. I genuinely believe the most beautiful diamonds are formed under the most intense pressure. And you're the most beautiful one." he smiled warmly and I chuckled softly.

"That's kind of cheesy." I mumbled. He rolled his eyes.

"We're having a moment. Don't ruin it." He poked my nose and I giggled. He grinned and looked at me.

"You're different from anyone I've ever met. You're not easy or simple. You're the only woman I could ever see myself with. And I really mean it. You just have to let me."

I squeezed his hand that I was still holding and I readjusted the bouquet of roses in my arms. The roses were becoming a source of comfort for me during this entire experience. I didn't know what to say. All I could do was resort to teasing him because I felt exposed and transparent. I didn't know what to think or do. Everything he said made my heart race and for the first time I really considered a future with him. It wasn't a fleeting thought, it wasn't just a passing thought. It was an actual consideration about what it would look like. It had always felt like something of a silly pipe dream. It felt like something that I couldn't actually have. I was always aware of my traits and I was okay with them, but I never expected him to be okay with them. I was fine with where we were, honestly. He was close to me and I got to be around him and we spent time together. Nothing would change except putting a title on it. Right? I knew it wouldn't be just a title change. It was going to be major. For me and my emotions everything would intensify and I would have to figure out how to complete the assignment quicker and figure out the logistics of how to integrate everything. This was going to be a ride.

"I'm not perfect. I probably never will be. I don't want to lose you…" I told him honestly. I paused for a moment.

"No one's asking for you to be perfect. I'm not saying that. I just want you." he repeated.

"I'm still going to try. You're the only person I've ever wanted. And it's scary to me. You treat me differently than anyone else. You've never been intimidated by me. You check on me, make sure I'm okay… emotionally. Everything is easy with you and it weakens me. It happened so fast that it still scares me but I feel safe with you. I want us. This. What we could potentially be. I can only see myself with you."

Maybe I was too hard on myself and I had been punishing myself for the shitty life I had as a kid. It wasn't my fault. The world didn't have to be so black and white. Maybe I could have the best of both worlds. I was torturing myself and holding myself back from something I really wanted because I was afraid and unsure. Everything could be figured out. What's a little extra work? Especially when it comes to what I want. A wide smile spread across his face and he raised an eyebrow. "So can I finally tell people, you're my girlfriend? Our gala pictures earned you a few fanboys. I've been fighting the urge to punch lower classmen in the face for weeks." he grinned. I chuckled and nodded.

"Yeah, it's about time Miyeon faced the fact that you'll never want her." I smirked darkly at the thought of her crying when he told her. I wanted to see it in person. He laughed loudly at the jabs.

"Get ready for a fight. She's a persistent one." he teased. I rolled my eyes in annoyance.

"Anyways, enough about her. What about my date? You said I had a surprise waiting for me. I'd like my surprise." I changed the subject quickly.

"I didn't forget. We're here. I wanted to have that conversation first. It was becoming hard to hold in. I was way too nervous." he replied as he got out of the car and came around to open my door for me. I smiled warmly as he helped me out of the car and helped me adjust the roses for me to grab his hand.

~Chapter 17~

The restaurant was located on the 35th floor of the Lotte Hotel and it was really nice. We had never been here before. The hostess led us to a private dining room, and we paused outside of the door. Jaehyun waved the waitress away with a thank you and told me to close my eyes. I closed my eyes, and I heard him open the door and he gently guided me into the room. The room smelled like lavender, and it was warm. Excitement filled my stomach and my hands twitched with the feeling. "Okay. Are you ready?" he asked with excitement in his voice.

"Yes. Hurry up, I want to see." I answered impatiently.

"Okay, okay. Open your eyes." I opened my eyes to see the room lit by candles and I looked around to see rose petals all across the floor and the table in the middle of the room had a bucket with champagne in it and two chairs. Another table by the door had a beautiful gold framed picture of us at the gala and it was the first pose we did. Haeun didn't show us that picture, we only saw the second pose. How did he get this picture? I walked over to it because I almost didn't recognize myself. I picked it up and stared at it for a moment. I didn't take many pictures but compared to the ones I had ever seen of myself, I looked different. The darkness that lurked in me was almost visible in old pictures. It was uncomfortable for even me to look at. I didn't see any of that in this picture. I looked at peace. Maybe even happy. There was a sparkle in my eye that I hadn't seen before. I could see what everyone meant when they said we looked good together. It wasn't an overstatement.

A sudden wave of emotion hit me and I teared up. Who would've thought I would be taking pictures with the man I actually liked? Who just became my boyfriend. It was so unnatural. It didn't feel right saying it yet. I had agreed and I wouldn't take it back but it felt like something that didn't fit just yet. It wasn't uncomfortable, but it was a strange feeling. It was like a pair of uncomfortable shoes. It fit but it was just hard to get used to. I turned to him holding the picture in the opposite arm than the flowers. I could still feel the tears sitting in the corner of my eyes, I just knew I looked like a child. It was confirmed when Jaehyun snickered lightly at me.

"You like the picture? Are you going to treat it like your comfort flowers there?" he jabbed. I sighed in playful annoyance.

"Maybe. I like them both. They're grounding me in reality. Reminds me that this isn't a dream. I'm processing a lot, you know?" I reminded him. He nodded as he offered his hand to lead me to the table. I awkwardly adjusted the picture into my arms with the flowers and took his hand.

He was the perfect gentleman. He pulled out my chair and poured my champagne first. I felt special. I felt important and valued. Even though he hadn't said anything out loud, it still felt honest. It felt completely different than when Han would verbally say it to convince me to keep training as a child. When Han said it was forced and inauthentic. It was like a task that he dreaded. The memory made my stomach twist uncomfortably. Everything with Jaehyun felt like a world of new possibilities and I was starting to look forward to it. "What are you thinking, Ae Ri? You're quiet." he said suddenly as he looked at me with a soft expression.

"I'm still in a state of shock, honestly. I've never been in a real relationship. I've never been treated like this at all. It's kind of overwhelming, but I like it. It's all of the expensive things and luxury that I like, but instead of me doing it for myself. You're doing it. I actually feel like the princess, you keep calling me.This is a lot for me to process, but I wouldn't change it at all. It's like getting new clothes and they do fit, but you have to get used to them. Especially if it's your first time wearing something like it. This feels like that. And honestly for the first time, I feel like I have possibilities and choices. I feel like I have a future. And it's because I chose you. I've gone back and forth with my emotions for a while because I didn't understand them and I still don't understand them, but you make sense to me. You always have. And I want to see what happens." I confessed as I looked down at the picture. I looked up at him and he smiled softly as he watched me.

"We can figure it out together. I'll be with you every step of the way. You didn't deserve any of the things you went through. You don't deserve to deal with the effects of everything you endured by yourself. I want to show you something different." Jaehyun said honestly as he leaned forward and held my hand.

"I'm starting to believe you when you say that." I watched curiously as he stood up and walked over to the table where I got the picture from. There was a small light blue box that was wrapped in white ribbon that I missed.

"You were so distracted by the picture that you missed this. And I'm glad that I decided to hide it there. It was smart. This is for you." he offered. He placed it on the table in front of me. I was more than familiar with the box color and design. It was something from Tiffany's. I readjusted the items already in my hand to unwrap the ribbon and open the box. Inside was a platinum diamond pendant necklace. I gasped shocked and tears welled up in my eyes again as I held it up. It was beautiful.

"This is too much... Why? All of this for me... I don't deserve it..." I couldn't stop the tears falling from my eyes this time. Burying my face in my hands, I sobbed. I'm glad I chose waterproof makeup tonight. I felt his arms wrap around my waist and ran a hand soothingly around my back.

"Because you deserve the world. Simple as that." he whispered as he laid his head on my shoulder. I looked up at him and he gave me a soft smile as he took a napkin and softly dried my tears.

"I'm not trying to buy you or anything like that. I needed to get your attention, so that you would really hear me when I told you I wanted you. You like nice things, so I figured that would do it. The car was me overdoing it but I remembered you saying you wanted one. I didn't tell you I had just bought one. Figured I'd surprise you." he chuckled. I smirked and pinched his cheek.

"You're always planning something huh?" I teased.

"I'm an architect and businessman. I always have plans. It's how I've become successful, remember? You're the only thing that I can't plan for. I'm spontaneous when it comes to you. You've added excitement back into my life. I never know what I'm going to get with you day by day."

"Are you saying I'm unstable?" I narrowed my eyes at him. I was being playful, but he didn't know that.

"Moody is what I was going for but you said it, not me princess." He laughed and kissed my cheek. I melted at the affection.

"You're lucky you're cute, Nam."

He rolled his eyes and stood up taking the necklace from me and moved to put it on for me. He smiled widely at me as he adjusted the pendant.

"It looks pretty on you. I knew it would." he mumbled softly.

"I want to see too. Watch out." I opened the camera on my phone and held it up to take a look at it. It sparkled under the candle light and I looked over at him, smiling stupidly.

"Did I do a good job?" I nodded and I stood up to put down the flowers and photo to hug him tightly. He hesitated for a moment before he wrapped his arms around me tightly.

"You initiated a hug for the first time. You must be really happy right now?" he asked softly. I could hear the grin in his voice.

"Y-Yeah… I'm happy right now. Thank you. This is the best night of my life… Really." I answered truthfully as I hugged him tighter and relaxed into his chest.

Happiness was a rare feeling for me. It was something that was always out of reach for me. It was never reserved for me. For the first time, it felt like things could be different. The world seemed immediately brighter. A rush of excitement coursed through my veins and I could only describe it to the feeling of when I got a new purse. Materialistic things were the closest that I would get to the feeling of happiness. Somehow being with Jaehyun in this way felt better than getting any pair of designer shoes or jewelry. He was warm and he could hold me. He could talk to me and answer me. Material things didn't do that. No matter how tight the clothes fit, it wasn't the same thing as human connection. It was slowly sinking in that he was with me for the long haul. He always had been. Even when he had every opportunity to do the opposite. I would protect him with my life. I owed him my loyalty for that.

"Should we enjoy our date now, princess? No more surprises I promise." Jaehyun said as he pulled back and looked down at me. I looked up at him and smiled as I nodded.

~Chapter 18~

I sat at my desk in my bedroom, staring through the blinds down at the street. The black hooded figure was looking down at the device in their hands and looking around quickly. The figure's head tilted upwards looking at the higher levels of the complex. The strangers were making more frequent appearances. They started appearing a few times a week and they would show up two or three days after I accessed the police software looking for information on the Jopok. Being in an official relationship with Jaehyun caused me to intensify my search for the Jopok to complete the assignment quicker. It was yielding little results.

I would use the internship at the police agency to try to find more information, but that wasn't helping either. The only piece of useful information I discovered was from my classes and it was about Arsyn. She was in fact the equivalent of me in the Jopok. She was the enforcer, the problem solver. She was the one who made sure problems didn't arise. She did assassinations. Other than that information, I had nothing. Any time I got close to finding anything that could be potentially useful, I always ran into firewalls and encryptions. The Yakuza techs couldn't figure them out. On the business links that I would click on, I would only get so far. Someone had been tampering with the files and corrupting them. It was obvious that the Jopok had been meticulous in sabotaging anything the police could use to track them down.

It was maddening. They seemed to have no weak points or slip ups anywhere that I could exploit to get information. The only thing I was certain of was the fact that they were starting to suspect something was going on. The strangers made more appearances when I started to work more in the systems. Over the weeks when I wasn't using the spyware as often, they appeared less often. Now that I was using it almost every night, they came more frequently. They couldn't find me because the spyware pinged off of several different IP addresses and unless they were going to run around the complex and try to find me, they were stuck too. I watched the figure get mad and throw down their device watching it shatter. I was impressed by the Jopok's tech abilities, they were able to find the spyware and then try to track all of the IP addresses, it could ping off. They were persistent. But it always made me smirk when each stranger discovered it was impossible.

I watched the figure quickly retreat down the street from where they came from. I checked the clock and saw it read 3:55 am. They stayed for twenty minutes this time. Every time someone showed up, they stayed for the same amount of time and then got frustrated and stormed off. I wasn't necessarily comfortable with the idea of them being in the proximity of where I lived, but it's likely they traveled all over the city before landing here. And they couldn't trace any of the IPs directly to me. Even with that knowledge it still made me uncomfortable. It made the hairs on the back of my neck stand up. I looked back towards the bed where Jaehyun was fast asleep. Keeping him safe was the most important thing to me. I turned back to the desk and closed out of everything and I removed the flash drive, throwing it into the drawer. I had to be more careful while I searched. Arsyn wasn't going to let her minions give up on figuring out what was going on and who was trying to get access into these systems.

I sighed hard and put my head in my hands. I was growing frustrated by the lack of progress, and I was getting even. "Babe... Ae Ri... What're you doing awake? Come back to bed." Jaehyun whined sleepily. I perked up hearing his voice and turned to him. He was peeking at me from under the blankets. I smiled softly at him.

"Sorry, did I wake you? I was checking on something from work. I got distracted." I replied.

"I'm laying in bed alone and I hate sleeping alone.... So yes you kinda did wake me up. I got cold." He sat up and rubbed his eyes trying to wake up. I giggled and stood up walking over to join him in bed.

"You're a child, you know that right?" I sat beside and climbed under the covers and he cuddled closer to me.

"Is it a hard case?" he asked as he laid his head on my shoulder.

"It's that girl from my class. Park Hayeon. They found her body a couple of days ago. They think it has something to do with high profile crimes." I shook my head sadly.

After the station incident when I took her uniform, she was found by someone and rushed to the hospital. She didn't remember anything, but she wasn't hurt too badly. She came back to class the week after and she was okay. Suddenly she was found dead on the steps of the police station 3 days ago. It was Arsyn's work. I was glad I didn't kill her honestly. But she would've had a less violent death than what Arsyn did to her. Jaehyun shivered at the mention of her name.

"That was sad... I feel so bad." he mumbled. The school held a memorial for her. Miyeon was devastated. Apparently they were really close. I felt a twinge of pain shoot through me but I shook it off.

"Are you okay handling the case?"

"Yeah. I didn't know her well. We didn't interact much. I think that's why they gave it to me and my trainer. I'm just tired." I admitted.

"Well I wonder why? You need more sleep. Are you doing any of the suggestions that I told you about to deal with your insomnia?" he said sarcastically. I rolled my eyes.

"Don't start that. It's too late for all of that."

"But it's serious. You sleep too little, it's not healthy. You need to address the root issue of your insomnia, but you're not ready to talk about your anxiety yet."

I sighed knowing that I walked into this conversation. "I don't have anxiety. I am fine." I told him. He stared at me appalled.

"You really believe that? Some of your breakdowns aren't normal. You're triggered by a lot of things. Remember when we went to that new restaurant and you freaked out because the hostess was really nervous. You overthink all the time. And those moments of overthinking make you really paranoid." He reminded me. I looked off to the side and pouted. Fair enough.

"Exactly. Tomorrow we're resting. Taking a day off. No work, no school. Nothing. We're spending the day in bed." he added as he pulled me to lay down with him. He wrapped me in his arms and pulled me tightly to him. Maybe he had a point. A day off would be nice. I just didn't know how I felt about that with the Jopok actively trying to figure out what was going on. The thought sent chills down my spine and made me tense.

"What're you thinking about? I felt you tense." he said quickly. I shook my head.

"Just tired. And stressed. I need sleep. The reports are long and boring." I lied smoothly. I felt Jaehyun nod softly behind me.

"Do you want to talk about it?" I shook my head again.

"If you ever want to talk about it, I'm here," he offered.

"I know, Jae. You always are." I smiled. He chuckled deeply and kissed my shoulder.

"You're precious. Go to sleep." I nodded and turned over to lay my head on his chest as he hugged me tightly.

My eyes flickered open as I felt the sun's ray hitting me. I groaned and reached out to wake Jaehyun and the space was empty. Jaehyun wasn't there. I sat up quickly in terror and looked around quickly. The clock read 10 am and my heart raced. My breathing picked up quickly and I grabbed my chest. He hardly ever woke up before me and whenever he did, he would still be in bed looking at me. So, him not being there sent panic rushing through me, especially after the events of last night. Through the chaos in my head, I heard the television in the living room playing. I jumped up and rushed out of the bedroom walking down the hall quickly. I approached the living room and poked my head around the corner into the kitchen and Jaehyun was in the kitchen cooking and talking on the phone. I breathed a deep sigh of relief, feeling my heartbeat return to normal and my breathing slowed again. He was safe.

"Areum, no. You're being paranoid again. Okay, okay. I got it. I'll be careful. I'm with my girlfriend. We'll be inside all day. She's not feeling well." Jaehyun hissed into the phone. He rolled his eyes and nodded as the other person spoke.

"Okay. I'll be there. Goodbye Noona." He hung up the phone and I came around the corner completely. He looked up and smiled warmly.

"Good morning, pretty girl. Having fun spying on me?" he smirked knowingly. I frowned and shook my head.

"I wasn't spying. I just woke up and you were gone. I came looking." I answered as I crossed my arms.

"It was my older sister. Her name's Areum." I blushed slightly as he answered the unspoken question in my head.

"You told her about me?" I asked cautiously, stepping into the kitchen beside him. He chuckled and nodded. I tilted my head.

"Obviously. I couldn't keep you a secret. Are you okay with that?" He turned to me and looked me over carefully. I was silent. My mind started to race. Does he want me to meet his family? I've never done that before. I'm not meeting the parents ready or material just yet. I'm still trying to figure out the girlfriend thing. I was *still* getting used to calling him my boyfriend. I have always believed that what was understood didn't have to be said. However, I figured out that regular people really cared about the titles and labels. There was no way I was ready to meet his family. My breathing picked up again.

"You don't have to meet them or anything. I didn't tell them that. I just told them you existed. Breathe. Stay with me. I can tell you're starting to overthink." He held me by my shoulders and he rubbed them gently. He bent down to make eye contact with me. I stared back and the world started to come back into focus. I took a deep breath to center myself again. I nodded.

"Sorry. I'm okay. As long as I'm not being rushed to meet them. I'm not sure I could do that yet." He pinched my cheeks and chuckled.

"Don't worry about it. My sister's just nosy as hell. She can be a lot. Overbearing, over protective. So I have to let things settle with her before anything. My brother Daehyun just exists. He only asked if you were pretty."

"I don't have siblings, but isn't that a default character trait of oldest kids? Overprotective and overbearing. But more importantly, how did you answer your brother? That's what I want to know." I teased as I put my hands on my hips.

"It's still a lot. And of course, I told him you were pretty. The prettiest actually." he answered as he picked me up and spun me around playfully. A joyful laugh came out of me as I clung to him tightly. He paused for a moment and sat me on the kitchen counter and stared at me. He had a goofy grin on his face. I think the sound shocked us both. I didn't think I could sound so happy and giggly. It felt like there was a light shining inside my heart. It was bright and a grin spread across my face.

"Good. I would've been pissed if you hadn't." He stood between my legs and kissed my nose.

"I told the truth. He'll just have to wait and see you. I'm not ready to share you with them yet." he laughed as he fixed my bed hair. I leaned into his touch, relaxing. I was content. The stress of the assignment melted away for a moment. He was my source of comfort. He grounded me in reality when my emotions got jumbled up. This was still new to me, but it felt natural and easy. I worried about how much we would change if we put a title on what we were for no reason. It felt exactly the same except we weren't hiding or holding back affection. We weren't hiding our feelings. We could just live them without being afraid of pushing the other person away. I was starting to believe that I deserved this. I deserved him. I was happy. I have never felt a more pure and innocent feeling.

I was mastering the art of living this double life. Rose and Ae Ri were on two different wavelengths. I flowed seamlessly between them depending on where I was and what I was doing. They were like night and day almost. Rose dealt with Han and his constant questions and all his bullshit, while keeping her cool for the most part. Ae Ri interacted with Jaehyun and our friends like a regular adult. I was content like this. I was doing what I thought was impossible not too long ago. I had Jaehyun and I was doing my job. And I was constantly growing more and more in each area. Jaehyun gave me something bigger and more important to fight for. He fueled my drive and determination to achieve more power and use it to protect him but also seek vengeance. When the Jopok was under my control, I wouldn't need to be stuck to Han. I could overthrow Han. He would be obsolete.

"What are you thinking about, pretty girl?" Jaehyun's voice broke my train of thought and I opened my eyes to look up at him.

"That I think I'm starting to see what happiness looks like." I answered honestly.

"Oh really? And what does that look like?" he grinned. I smiled warmly and brushed my nose along his.

"Looks like you and how natural this is."

"It is easy, right? You were so scared for no reason. Crazy to think it's been almost a month. And here we are." He leaned down and kissed me lightly. I kissed him back and pulled away as I looked up at him. He was precious to me. He was solidifying his place in my life as a necessity. The more time we spent together, the closer we got. I was becoming more comfortable with sharing more personal thoughts with him. The ones that didn't reveal my real identity of course. I found myself settling into a normal relationship and doing normal relationship things. It was completely different than what I imagined. I used to hate seeing couples and people that were so infatuated with each other. And here I am. I enjoyed it more than I thought I would.

I noticed the subtle changes. I had fewer nightmares when he was next to me. I slept more when he was with me. I was becoming more comfortable with his friends, it almost felt like we were friends too. I was becoming softer with Jaehyun. I was opening up to more experiences. We were doing more than just lunches or dinners. He took me on my first weekend trip. I was regaining a sense of my lost childhood through him. We rode bikes in the park, went to amusement parks and water parks. I went to the beach for the first time with him. I felt alive for the first time. I felt like a normal girl. I wasn't a monster completely. Sometimes the changes that I was noticing made my head spin. I felt like I was experiencing imposter syndrome. I didn't feel prepared to take on these changes. I still had moments where I was suspicious and cautious. There were still moments where who I was in Japan showed itself with Jaehyun and I think that would happen forever. I didn't know how to balance both sides.

"I hope you're hungry. I made breakfast. It's not our normal breakfast, but I figured since we're spending the day together, we should celebrate." he grinned. He uncovered the plates to reveal french toast, eggs, hash browns and a variety of fruit. It was the same thing we had the night after Mae's.

"Did you remake the breakfast we had the night after Mae's?" I commented.

"You remember that?"

"Of course. You still never paid the bet. Just thought I'd remind you." I snickered as he rolled his eyes.

"Of course. Money was involved. You'd remember that." he teased and I punched him in the arm.

"You're not funny." I pouted at him. That joke stung a little. Money was all I had for a long time.

"It was a joke, babe. I'm sorry. You hit hard." he huffed in pain.

"I know. That's the point. Gotta keep you in line." I winked and took a few grapes from the fruit bowl.

"Yeah, yeah. Go sit down. I'll bring your plate. You're spoiled rotten, you know that right?" he called after me as I slid off the counter and skipped to the couch.

"Things that I know. And my response is… C'est la vie." I laughed as I kicked my feet up on the coffee table. Flipping through the channels, I landed on a drama with an actor that I had seen somewhere else.

"Feet kicked up on the table? Spoiled rotten. A damn shame. But you're pretty, so I can deal with it." He placed my plate on the table beside me and he gave me a glass of orange juice. I grinned and leaned up to kiss him lightly.

"Thank you, Jaehyun. You're appreciated genuinely." I smiled as I stroked his cheek.

"You're welcome, babe. I know." He went to grab his plate and returned to sit next to me. He scooted close enough to where our thighs would touch. It was something that we always did. We had to touch and have some sort of physical contact with each other. It was our thing. I couldn't explain it. The money comment was circling in my head and bringing down my mood. He had a point. I didn't really buy him things the way he did for me. He said it was a joke, but what if it wasn't? What if he was warning me? I turned to him.

"Would you like for me to buy you things too?" I asked. He raised an eyebrow and swallowed his food.

"Princess, we were joking around. I didn't mean anything by it. I swear." Jaehyun turned to me and his face was full of concern.

"I heard you when you said it. I was asking. I don't want you to feel unappreciated. I saw there was a Rolex store somewhere around here. Want to get matching ones?" I pressed. I didn't want him to think I was selfish. That thought terrified me. Because then he'd leave me. I couldn't risk that.

"Babe really. That's not necessary. I buy you things because I like to. I like seeing you in nice things. Not in hopes of getting something back." he explained. I stared at him as he spoke.

"Matching rolex?" I pressed again. It wasn't really up for debate. I was going to do it anyway. It was just easier for him to agree. He sighed and shrugged.

"Why do I bother? Sure, princess. It'll be nice." I snickered victoriously when he agreed. He shook his head lightly and I saw the blush on his cheeks.

"How about after breakfast, we get dressed and go?" I suggested as I ate some french toast.

"We can do that. You have to wear one of the outfits I bought you though." he agreed as he nudged me. I nodded in agreement. He smiled at that. A lot of things went that way for us. As we got closer, Jaehyun had proven himself to be very calculated and quite stubborn honestly. He was full of pride but still humble. He was very business oriented and had a tendency to treat tiny disagreements as business trade offs. It wasn't bad or anything. It was quite endearing. I got to see him in business meetings and handle important business deals at times and I found his assertiveness attractive. The way he commanded attention and was always perfect made him effective in his area of expertise. He was full of surprises. We continued to eat our breakfast and watch tv for a little bit.

My phone vibrated and I glanced over it. Code's name flashed on the screen and I raised an eyebrow, opening the notification. The text just said 911. He only texted me first if there was an emergency. I glanced over at Jaehyun. He was engulfed in the television. "Hey, I need to take this call. It's from my dad's company." I told him.

"I thought we said no work today?" he reminded me without turning from the television.

"It's not my dad. It should be quick. I'll be back." He nodded wordlessly and went back to being engrossed in the drama. I grabbed my phone and went out on the balcony and called Code.

"You better have a good fucking reason for bothering me." I growled into the phone.

"Boss… There's a situation." he said dryly. He wasn't himself.

"What the fuck is going on? Spill it." He sounded serious. He never took anything seriously. Especially not serious enough to text 911. That set alarm bells off in my head. Worry started to flow through me. It was silent for a few moments.

"I-I think the Jopok know the Yakuza is in Korea…. Specifically you." he rasped. The world stopped. I froze. There was a huge difference between the two things. If the Jopok knew some random Yakuza member was in Korea hacking their systems and fishing for information, that was easy prey. If they knew *Rose* was in Korea hacking their systems and fishing for information, I was a top level threat. I had to be eliminated at any cost in their eyes. That puts everything in jeopardy.

The bliss that I was living in was shattered. The world was crashing down around me. The future didn't seem so bright anymore. I should've expected something like this to happen. But how did they know it was me, that was what I didn't understand. "Boss…. Are you there? Are you okay?" Code asked frantically.

"What makes you say that?" I recovered quickly. I put my hand on my forehead. It was hot. I needed to keep my cool. My heart pounded against my ribcage. My head was starting to pound in pain. I could feel a cold sweat forming. My palms were sweating.

"A few more attacks on some arms deals happened last night. When recon went out, your name was written in blood with a X through it. The attack in Kobe had your picture stapled to the chest of a soldier…" he said carefully. A picture of me!? Where the fuck did they get a picture of me from? My breath caught in my throat and I stumbled forward grabbing onto the railing for support. I was getting dizzy.

"How recent was the picture?" I whispered, not trusting my voice. Tears burned at the corners of my eyes.

"You had black hair in it, so it's older." I let out the breath that I was holding. I haven't had black hair in almost three years. That was the only relief in this situation.

"Whatever you're doing. Be careful. It's not like you to make mistakes. Are you okay? Do you need help?" Code asked genuinely. The question enraged me and I blanked.

"What the fuck are you saying, Code?! Are you suggesting that I'm inadequate?! That I'm sloppy!?" I growled darkly into the phone.

"No-no-no ma'am… I was just asking… I'm trying to help y-" he stumbled through his words. Fear was evident in his voice.

"If you want to help me so damn badly, find out who's doing this. Find the person doing the attacks and catch them. Find out how much they know." I demanded. My heart was still pounding in my chest and my palms were getting clammier by the minute. Then another thought crossed my mind. *Han.*

"Has anyone told Han? Does he know?" I gasped.

"No ma'am. I made everyone vow silence. Any defectors were killed." he confirmed.

"Keep it that way. I don't need to hear his fucking mouth." I let go of the balcony taking deep breaths to calm myself. This wasn't the time to panic. This wasn't the time to freak out. Not with Jaehyun in the living room. Oh my god. *Jaehyun*. I whipped around to see him on the couch watching television still.

It felt like I was having a hot flash. The heat that washed over me and consumed me was unreal. If it was possible, my heart started to pound harder in my chest. He couldn't get hurt. Not at all. I wouldn't allow it. Not after everything we experienced. Not after how much we have grown together. The rage and possessiveness that filled my stomach and chest was too much to bear. Everything started to go in slow motion all of a sudden and then the world started to spin. The excessive calling of my name by Code and the weight of my feelings combined with the gravity of the situation had my head scrambled. It was like my brain was overloading and it couldn't take anymore. Before I could register what happened, I was on my knees toppling over. The last thing I saw was Jaehyun running out of the house to get to me.

I found myself standing in a dark room. My eyes took a minute to adjust to the pitch black. The door to the room was open and there was a long stretch of a hallway. At the end of the hall, there was a faint white light that was floating. I took a step forward and I felt myself stumble and I landed on top of something. I heard a loud crack and felt liquid on my hand. I scrambled back on my knees quickly as I started to smell a familiar metallic tang. Before I could do anything, a bright light blinded me and I closed my eyes to shield them. Once I felt the light on my skin, I blinked a few times. The first thing I saw was the red all over the white room. It was blood. My eyes widened and I scanned the room. There were numerous bodies in the room. I was horrified as I looked down in front of me. I landed on a body. Looking down I saw Jaehyun laying in front of me. I shrieked and scooted backwards in fear. I stared at his lifeless body as I reached out to touch him. He was cold. Nothing like the warmth I knew from him. One of his ribs was pierced through his chest from when I fell on him. His pretty eyes were open wide in shock and terror. Blood leaked from his mouth and it was all over his neck and chest from the cut across his throat.

The anguish that ran through me was unspeakable. I had never felt anything like it before. It felt like I was being torn apart from the inside.

Sobs rocked my body as I grabbed his face tighter and tilted his face towards me. "W-What happened to you… W-Who did this…" I cried as I leaned down and ran my nose along his. My chest burned in pain as I sobbed and tried to keep breathing. It was horrifying. I heard a low gurgling sound behind me and I looked up and turned to the sound. My mother's body laid behind me and blood was flowing from her mouth. She was choking on her own blood as she stared at me. I felt the little breath I had leave me in a rush as I watched her struggle to breathe. I scrambled over to her leaving Jaehyun with a small kiss. I scrambled to sit her up and try to help her clear her lungs. I sobbed and looked down at her. I knew it was too late for her but I didn't want to see her suffer. Despair ran through my body and the sobs kept coursing through me. I watched her choke to death and held her as the blood soaked through my clothes until she went silent and limp.

A broken sob left my body as I held her tightly. I watched my mother die in front of me right after seeing the most important person to me dead. "M-Mom… J-Jae… I-I don't understand this…." I cried. I looked around the room quickly and I saw all of the dead bodies around the room. Faces from old assassination assignments, random women and men, children. I was horrified and I felt like I was going to throw up.

"What the fuck is this!? Where am I!? I want to go home!" I screamed in horror. I was chilled by the voice that responded.

"What do you think, Rose? It's our trophy room! Just a small collection of all the good work we've done. Isn't it nice?" I turned to the opening of the room and stared wide eyed at myself standing in a white blazer dress stained in red holding a bloody serrated knife. That was the knife I used for torture and spite assignments. My breath quickened as I stared at myself. Darkness and evil swam in the green eyes. Bloodlust dilated the pupils. I shook my head slowly cowering into my mother's body.

"No… No… I-I-I've never killed women or children… Not once….I would NEVER kill Jaehyun… You're not real… You're not real… This isn't real…" I stammered as I started to crawl away from the figure bringing my mother's body with me.

An evil smirk stretched across the figure's face and with astounding speed, she was in front of me gripping my cheeks tightly with her bloody hand.

"This is who we are! This is who we have always been! This is who YOU will always be! Designed to be the perfect soldier, the perfect assassin, the perfect tool of destruction. That is ALL! Look at what happened to poor Jaehyun. He'd still be alive, if it wasn't for you. All you had to do was follow orders. Look at him!" the figure screamed as she yanked my face, forcing me to look at Jaehyun's lifeless body. Tears flooded my eyes as I made eye contact with him. "N-No... No... I didn't do it! I protected him! He's safe with me..." I cried as I struggled against the hold.

"Safe!? Who's ever safe with you! Don't be fucking stupid, Rose! That's not what you represent! He was stupid to trust you! Like father, like daughter, remember?" the figure growled in my face. The words hurt deeply. They were true. No one was safe with me. I didn't do protection. I wasn't a security blanket. Sobs racked my body again and I fell to my knees defeated. The figure let go and I buried my head in my hands and curled into a ball. The figure let out a cruel laugh and it rang in my ears repeatedly until I heard my name break through the noise. My head snapped up and I stood up running to the call. It was Jaehyun's voice. I could hear the figure screeching behind me as I ran as fast as I could towards the small light at the end of the hall. The figure was chasing behind me and she was getting closer and closer. I pushed my legs faster as the calls of my name got louder and louder...

I couldn't stop the scream that tore from my throat as I shot straight up and placed a hand over my chest. "Breathe Ae Ri. Breathe. It's okay. I'm right here. Breathe. I'm right here. I got you." Jaehyun's voice grounded me back to reality. He was rubbing my back and sitting next to me on the bed. I panted and cradled my head in my hands. I hadn't had a nightmare in a long time. I held back the tears that I felt threatening to escape. I already passed out in front of him, I wasn't about to cry too. The dream played over and over as the phone conversation played in my head. They knew... The Jopok knew I was in Korea. The spyware had to be what gave it away. I put Jaehyun in danger. He could get hurt. My stomach twisted in knots and I buried my face into his chest. Jaehyun wrapped his arms around my body and held me closer. He rubbed my back gently and I couldn't hold back the tears anymore. He treated me like I was fragile. He treated me better than I could treat myself and I got him into this mess. And I couldn't even tell him he was potentially in danger. I crawled into his lap and held him tighter. He huffed at the tight squeeze around his ribs.

"Stay with me forever please...." I mumbled. He stroked my hair and hummed.

"I can't hear you, pretty. What did you say?" he chuckled. I took a deep breath and looked up at him. I felt so small and soft wrapped in his arms like this. It still felt so different but it felt right with him. He was my safety net. He was worth everything to me. All I wanted was him.

"Stay with me forever, please." I repeated softly. He looked down at me and a warm smile graced his pretty face.

"Where am I going, princess?" He reached up and stroked my cheek gently. There was so much emotion in his eyes that it was almost scary.

"I'll be here as long as you want me," he added.

"Then forever it is." I grinned.

"So be it. Now do you want to tell me what happened out there?" he pressed gently. I sighed and rolled my eyes. He will not let it go.

"Not exactly. But you'll keep asking. My father called from the company phone. Had a huge blow up. Stress and emotions overheated me. I fainted." I lied smoothly. It was necessary. I couldn't tell him what I did. That would put him in more danger. If the Jopok knew that he was involved with me, there was no telling what they'd do. Keeping him in the dark was the safest option.

"What did he say about me? I caught you looking at me. You looked pretty determined. What did he say?" Jaehyun tilted his head curiously.

"He caught wind that I was seeing that 'chaotic, ungrateful bastard' from Nam Industries." He chuckled and shook his head.

"Go on." he encouraged.

"Wanted me back in Japan and away from you. Safe to say to hell with him. He was never around. Can't tell me what to do." I finished. I didn't even want to think about what would happen if Han found out about Jaehyun. He'd probably bitch, and yell and it would eventually escalate into something bigger. That was the least of my concerns, but I was aware of it in the back of my mind. I had to complete my assignment. That was the only way we were going to be at peace.

"Sounds stressful. Your dad seems like a nightmare the more you tell me about him. Why continue to do it?" he sighed. I knew where this was going.

"We talked about this, Jae. I can't let you take care of me. I have to do something. The money makes everything worth it."

He had gotten more adamant about letting everything go and go off grid and start over in Korea. Oh, how I wish it was that simple. "C'mon Ae Ri. You have plenty of money to take care of yourself. If you're so worried about your independence, you could do interior decorating. Start a business. We can do one together, you start your own. I'll help." he suggested. I didn't hate the idea… I never directly owned a business. I had taken them over through surrogacy. But the idea of owning something with him warmed my heart. I grabbed his hand and smiled.

"We could build empires of our own. Think about it. We'd just need a year or two." he said softly.

I could tell he was serious about it. I wonder how much thought he put into this. I tilted my head. "One or two years of me 'taking care' of you isn't so long. I'm sure you could manage." He chuckled and playfully nudged me. I laughed and shook my head.

"I'll keep the offer in mind. No promises. Compromise." I promised. He rolled his eyes and nodded.

"Fine. I'll take it." I smirked and laid my head on my chest. I took a deep breath and sat in comfortable silence with him. I needed to figure this out. I couldn't and wouldn't lose him. I wouldn't lose all of this.

Initiation

~Chapter 19~

I sat at my desk in the police station, clicking through the case file on another jewelry store robbery. There was a tension that sat in the air and it was palpable. The atmosphere was suffocating. Everyone was on edge and uptight. My head perked up as I saw Captain Chae move quickly throughout the office. He was jittery and looked panicked. He was whispering in harsh and hushed tones to certain higher ups that came up the floor. That wasn't like him. He was always callous and cold. He never showed emotions. I looked over at my trainer and he was rigid in his seat. What the hell was going on?

"What's going on?" I whispered. He didn't answer me. He was frozen and staring at the screen unblinking. I huffed in annoyance.

"Officer Kim, what's going on?" I hissed as I punched him in the arm. He hissed in pain and looked over at me.

"Oh shit! Ow! Sorry Choi. Um… Some big wigs from the NIS are coming in. Captain's nervous." The mixed Korean man looked over at me and gave me an awkward smile. He was visibly stressed and fear was evident on his face too. I titled my head in confusion. There was no way. NIS officers came to the office before and the captain did not act like that before. I'm not dumb or stupid. Something is going on. Adrenaline started to sneak into my bloodstream and I prepared myself mentally for anything. I looked around the office and I noticed that almost half of the department was missing. They were here before lunch. I didn't like this. Why did half the team disappear? I heard footsteps clicking down the marble flooring outside of the carpeted office area.

I watched the captain run out to the hallway and stand at attention. I couldn't see who it was from my position at my desk. My desk was located in the front of the office area but it was off towards the side closer to the wall. I adjusted my chair to the right to be able to see a little better. I saw a group of five men dressed in sharp black suits approach. The captain bowed in respect. "Gentleman. Right this way. We can talk in this room." he offered. I examined the group. The sharp dark suits, the sunglasses, the tattoos that poked out from the sleeves raised alarms in my head. I went rigid and felt the color drain from my face. They're not NIS agents. "Isn't it rude to start the meeting without the boss?" a rough and feminine voice suddenly sounded from further down the hall. Suddenly the sound of heels clicking across the floor sounded further down the hall.

The group of men bowed a full 90 degrees and kept their eyes low. I couldn't see her, but a cold chill ran down my spine. My shoulders tensed and the atmosphere shifted drastically. Fear and anxiousness filled the room. Kim beside me went even the more rigid, if possible and the color drained from his face. He was positioned better where he could see into the hallway. Whoever he saw terrified him. That confirmed my suspicion that something was wrong. He was actively trying not to look at the woman. I still couldn't see her but I could hear her. Something told me to put on my police hat and I quickly grabbed it as I listened in.

"Ma'am… It's a pleasure." the captain said, trying to break the tension. The woman hummed. "It would be a pleasure if I were here for fun. But you fucked up." she spit out harshly. The amount of venom she spoke with was chilling even for me. I readjusted my chair and sat directly in front of the computer again to appear normal. The woman was not an upper brass police official. She was something entirely different. The captain led the group into the office space and I peeked over the top of the computer and my eyes went to the female. It was her…

Arsyn was a pretty girl. Her hair was dyed cherry red and she had two bangs that laid free on either side of head. Her hair was pulled into a tight neat bun. She wore designer shades that she removed to look over the area. Clear skin and piercing brown eyes held more rage and danger in them than any picture could capture. She looked to be the same age as when I saw her in the two separate files, but she looked more sophisticated and mature. In the picture I saw in Han's office, she seemed more wild and untamed with power. In the Korean police files, she seemed more rage filled and it showed outwardly. She was a lot more put together and controlled in person. Which makes me think the files were older or she just aged really well and grew up.

My eyes went to the computer screen as her eyes began to look over personnel in the front. I forced myself not to make eye contact with her. I couldn't do anything here, I was outnumbered. That fact didn't stop the rage and despair from rising in me. She had a part to play in my mother's death. She was threatening the security of Jaehyun. My hands balled into fist and my hands trembled in need to hit someone. I was outnumbered and unarmed. When we were in the station, the interns didn't have their guns on them. A sudden realization hit me like a ton of bricks. If she was here, that meant the High Profile Crimes unit was affiliated with the Jopok. Their influence spread through the police. The very unit was designed and created to stop them. At least half of the team was in the Jopok's pocket. *Fuck*. My leg started to bounce as my mind started to race. I screwed up.

The spyware I used didn't filter or search through the logins. It just gave me the information to use. If I used someone's login that wasn't in this room right now that could have been what tipped them off to something being wrong. It drew attention to the spyware. Why didn't I think about that or consider that? A cold sweat broke out along my temple. My heart was drumming along my rib cage. I could hear my blood rush through my body. I noticed the group make their way to the conference room in the back next to the backdoor. Arsyn's black suit jacket flowed in the wind revealing a gun tucked in the waistband of her pants. I breathed deeply once they were all in the room with the door shut.

"Kim… Was that…." I whispered. I knew that it was, I wanted confirmation and had to make it real.

"Welcome to the High Profile Crimes unit. Wouldn't it make sense for the royal family of the underground to be involved in the police? Right out of a fucking movie." Kim hissed out in reply. He had no fucking idea.

"How often does she come? How did this happen?" This was the perfect time to get the information because I doubt that after this anyone will talk about if my suspicion is correct.

"She doesn't handle insignificant matters. She's much too busy and impatient. The idiot handles the small stuff. He comes usually for check ins and collections. They use the station to hold physical money in safes and somehow they launder money through here too. But that's none of your business." Kim informed me. Oh, but it is. I continued to listen.

"The Heiress only comes when things aren't going well. She's the problem solver." I wondered how long he'd been a part of the payroll. Whether he hated it or not. Arsyn being called the 'heiress' was a nickname that I had seen once or twice before. I continued to play dumb though.

"The heiress?" I asked.

"She's next in line for the position of her father. It's kind of a play on the whole thing." Kim explained. I nodded.

"Interesting. So how many are on the payroll? Half the team is gone and I'm still here."

"What you're looking at. Hate to throw you in like this. Chae's going to tell you the details eventually, but I'll break you quickly. When he comes to you, you are clueless and shocked. You are the newest recruit. You've been doing a good job. So Chae submitted your name and he got the okay. Welcome to the club." Kim looked me in the eyes for the first time. There was no hint of sarcasm or joking. He was deadpan. I stared back and nodded.

"How close to the family is the captain?" I dared to ask.

"Whatever they have on him has held him in their clutches for about 15 years, I've heard. Wouldn't call it closeness, but he's their eyes in the station and he has connections in the NIS." he answered looking back at the computer. Political ties too? Damn. The Jopok were just as good as the Yakuza. Kim's body language suddenly changed. He went tense and my head tilted. I focused on what was going on in the background. It was quiet. Before I could speak, Kim warned me to be quiet. Not a few moments later, a glass shattered and I turned to the conference room and looked through the window. Captain Chae was towering under the white board and there was liquid running down the board. She threw something at him.

"Why the fuck haven't you been monitoring the system?! I have at least 50 credentials that have been trying to access private files that only you and this select team has permission to see! Now unless you've added that many people without my approval, then we have a fucking problem. Obviously, you wouldn't have done that, right?" Arsyn screeched as she stood up at the other side of the room staring down at the man. That was not the captain that we were used to seeing. I turned to the computer and bit my lip in thought. I was right. They picked up on the spyware through the logins I was trying to use. I didn't use the correct ones. The silence was deafening as Arsyn stayed quiet waiting for a response from the captain.

"I'm waiting on a response. Or are you so incompetent that you don't know what's happening? I won't fucking ask again." she growled.

"I-I-I'm sorry, ma'am. I slacked off on the monitoring. I was wrong." the captain cried. His voice trembled with terror. That poor man. I almost felt sorry for him. He looked broken.

"Fucking obviously! There's a traitor in the ranks. A spy. We suspect it's the Yakuza's hitman using someone on the team. Find them. That young girl already died. Do you really want to lose anymore people, Chae?" There was a clear warning there.

The woman's voice held a dark tremble of danger and rage in it. So they did know I was here. Code was right. And they know I have something to do with hackings. They just couldn't find me, so they assumed I had a partner. Find and flush out my partner, it'll lead them to me. A classic plan. I've used it before. The jokes on them though. It's just me. It was good that I was still hidden behind my undercover alias but this was a bad spot to be in. They were going to be on guard and observing everything. I had an advantage though. Now that I know what their defense is, I can plan around it. The captain was close enough to Arsyn that he had to have knowledge about the headquarters, their business and everything. I could just force him to tell what he knew. Easy. I couldn't help the excitement that coursed through my veins and I fought to keep the grin at bay.

This was the first lead I had in a long time. The hopefulness that followed behind the excitement was a relief. I could get ahead of them and plan how to infiltrate and kill them one by one. That means Jaehyun would be safe. There would be no lingering threats and then I could figure out what to do about Han. The thought of Han sent a wave of annoyance through me. He was going to ask a shit ton of questions. A lot of whys and I wasn't too interested in answering any of them. It was going to result in a fight. I really didn't need that, but Jaehyun was worth everything to me. I had never considered what would happen if I got booted out of the Yamaguchi. What would that mean for me? Not having access to the money or the power. Just being a normal person like him. The thought of being normal kind of sickened me. I didn't want to be dependent on Jaehyun and wait to get a legitimate business up and running. I could stay in the drug business, it gave me the amount of money I was used to. The time and planning that would take to rebuild those contacts outside of the Yakuza would be hard. I would lose more leaving the Yakuza. It would be better to overthrow Han with the Jopok under my control and my gang in support of me.

I rubbed my face and looked at my computer screen. I heard the conference room door slam shut and Arsyn and her men walked to the front of the office space. She paused and turned back to address everyone. "For whoever the traitor is in this room, just know, I will find out. And you will die a slow and painful death." she warned. She looked over at each person in the room and I felt when she looked over at me. I didn't look up. I felt her watch me for a moment and I held my breath. It was like time stood still. I peeked up from under the hat and I saw her turn and leave without another word. I held back a laugh at the deja vu. I've said that exact same thing to people so many times before. It was a strange sight. I never saw another woman with as much power, money and apparent skill as me. It was admirable but it didn't feel right at all.

Seeing Arsyn in the flesh and being in the same room with her proved how dangerous she was. It was tangible. She was volatile too. It was like looking in the mirror and I didn't know how to feel about that. I'm pretty sure her journey to the top was just as hard as mine. She wasn't going to be an easy kill. She was going to put up a fight. She was going to be tough to find. The only way to bring her out of hiding was the death of her father or brother. If her brother was an idiot like Kim said then he should be the easiest to find. I noticed Kim got up from his desk and I looked over at him. "Want to get lunch together, kid?" he offered. I gave him a fake smile.

"Thanks, but I have to finish an assignment." He shrugged and nodded as he walked away. I grabbed my phone and headed towards the back exit of the room and called Jaehyun. I was late for my daily lunch call with him. He answered on the first ring. "There you are, princess. Late lunch today? I was getting worried." Jaehyun chuckled. He sounded genuinely concerned. That was weird.

"We had a couple of NIS visitors at the office today. It was a long meeting." I replied with a warm smile spreading across my face. It meant the world to me knowing that he knew my schedule and got concerned when I deviated from the plans. Because I was the same way. He reciprocated what I gave him.

"Ah, I see. Well hopefully it went well. So…. I wanted to ask you something." I tilted my head and hummed.

"What is it?"

"Well two things really. Miyeon invited us to a party tonight. Want to go? And the second question. Next weekend I have to go and do some business with my family. We have really important World Expo and real estate deals that I have to be there for. I was wondering if you'd like to come with me?" Jaehyun offered with a slight tease in his voice.

"Why is Miyeon having a party?" I asked. I wasn't purposely ignoring the second question. I just needed a second to think so I could figure out some things. If he was gone, then I could start planning to find out the captain's address and things. I sat on one of the steps as I spoke to him. Miyeon was always having some sort of party or event. She was an only child with a shit ton of money and parents that gave her whatever she wanted, thinking it was love. It was inevitable.

"Well, she's celebrating a business. She's opening a boutique." Jaehyun chuckled.

"Well, she'll finally shut up about it. Okay. I'm fine with going."

"What about the other question?"

"I don't know if I'm ready for that yet, Jae. It's still a hard thing for me to wrap my head around. I don't feel ready yet... I'm sorry, I know it's-" I started and he interrupted me gently.

"Ae Ri, Ae Ri. It's okay. It's okay. I just wanted to ask. I'm not pressuring you. It's okay, pretty. I'll miss you though. I hate sleeping alone." he laughed. The sound made me laugh as well. It was so pure and it grounded me when I got caught up in the job and in my head.

He was always so understanding and kind. It reminded me constantly of the urgency of the assignment and how quickly I needed to complete it to protect us.

"When will you be home? I miss you. It's lonely." he whined playfully.

"Where are you?" I giggled.

"My place. It's my house tonight, remember? We spent the past week at your house. The white of your house makes me nervous. I don't want to mess it up." I really enjoyed how comfortable we had become with each other and how close we continued to get. Each other's houses had become home for us personally. We each had a key to each other's houses. It made me get better with hiding my weapons and assassin tools now that he had free reign of the house, but I wouldn't change it at all. It felt right. I never felt like I belonged anywhere before, not honestly. But I belonged next to Jaehyun. Everything was better with him.

"I get off at my regular time. I only leave early if something changes. Why are you home so early anyways?" I questioned. We usually got home around the same time.

"They canceled my last two classes. Teachers had emergencies or something. So, I'm all alone at home. Skip work and let's spend the day together. We can have fun before Miyeon's party tonight." The smirk was evident in his voice.

"Tempting offer. Are you sure we'll make it to the party if we have fun? We've missed events because of it before." I grinned as I looked down at my nails.

"You just started to like Miyeon truthfully. It will not bother you if we miss the party. Stop being so difficult. Come home now." The growl in his voice let me know that I took the teasing far enough. I chuckled and stood up, walking back inside to grab my items.

"Okay, okay. I'm on the way." I smirked.

~Chapter 20~

"How long are you going to be gone?" I asked as I sat on the edge of Jae's bed. A small chuckle left his lips as he looked up at me through the mirror.

"Don't pout. I'm only going to be gone for the weekend. It's two days. You look like a lost puppy." he teased. I caught my reflection in the mirror and I did look like a lost puppy that had been kicked. It was pathetic. That was embarrassing.

"Well it's just that we usually go everywhere together. We're a package deal. That's your fault." I jabbed in response. He turned to me and folded his arms. He raised an eyebrow and he smirked.

"You're one to talk. You act this way anytime I mention leaving. You're such a baby. It borders the brat territory. And I asked if you wanted to go, you said no. Remember princess?"

I pouted and rolled my eyes. He was right honestly but I'd never say it.

"You like it though." He walked to me and cradled my face in his hands gently.

"I do. Because I'm the only one who can deal with you and all the chaos you come with." He winked and leaned down to give me a chaste kiss. He had a point. At this point, it was almost sad how he saw right through me.

"I just miss you sometimes. You can be good company." I smirked as I looked up at him.

"Good company? That's a funny one. You've officially entered brat territory." He turned to finish packing.

"I'm sure you'll find a way to entertain yourself. You're a smart girl." Jaehyun smiled softly as he zipped his bag.

"I will. I just don't like it. You're exposed out in the world, without me. It's not a fun thought." I replied. He looked back at me and he raised an eyebrow.

"Exposed? I'll be with my family and some business men. I've known them my whole life practically. I'll be fine. You stay out of trouble while I'm gone."

"I never cause trouble. I am innocent." I smiled. He laughed loudly at that.

He was going to join his family and finalize those business deals. I still told him I wouldn't go with him because I genuinely didn't want to intrude on his family time. I wasn't ready to meet them still, but there was an alternative reason why I wasn't going. I was going to get the information I needed to find the Jopok and finish my assignment. I had been stalking Captain Chae and I got his address, so I was going to pay him a little visit.

"Innocent? Sure if you want to call it that. Come give me a hug. I have to go now. If I'm late my mom will kill me." He opened his arms and smiled warmly as he waved me over. It was a natural response as I ran into his arms and held him tightly. I genuinely would miss him with every fiber of my being. I had no reason to be paranoid. There were no signs or warnings that came in about the Jopok knowing about his existence. That comforted me, but I just didn't like him being away from me. I can't protect him. He was the safest with me.

"Are you sure you don't want to come with me? You don't have to meet the family. I have a hotel room in Busan, you can stay there while I'm gone." he offered as he held my waist.

"I don't want to be that girl. I'll be fine. I swear. And I don't want to be cooped up in a hotel room all day while you work. I'm too pretty for that." I chuckled.

"If you say so, princess. I'll be home Sunday. Are you staying here or at your place this weekend? Just need to know where to drive after four hours." He looked down at me and smirked lightly.

"I'll probably be here waiting for you. But I'll sleep at my place." I answered.

"Gotcha. Be good. I'll see you when I get back. Get some sleep, it's still early." He leaned down and caught my lips in a deep kiss. I wrapped my hands in his hair and tugged him closer. He was going to miss me too. Probably more. He just played cool.

He squeezed my ass to break the kiss. "Ever the tease, Ae Ri." he panted as he ran his hand over my hip. I smirked as I watched his eyes darken. I ran my hand through his hair and tugged on it again. A growl left his throat as he stared at me.

"Y-You started it." I whined breathlessly. He leaned down and nipped at my shoulder and neck teasingly. I whimpered and ran my nails down his chest and I felt his muscles ripple as he shivered.

"Fucking hell... I'll tell mom I had a problem with the car. Come here." he growled as he pulled me into a messy kiss as we shuffled backwards to the bed again. I didn't know what to call it or how to describe it, but I knew I was falling into something deep with Jaehyun and it was permanent.

I sat in the blacked out sedan a few blocks away from the house. Captain Chae lived fairly modestly for the money he was bringing in with his ties to the Jopok. His wife, two children and himself lived in a two story single family home in Gyeonggi Province. It wasn't luxurious or expensive. It looked normal. Nothing about it was different from the other houses on the block. The same boring brown and white. The neighborhood was quiet and peaceful. Not much happened from the week of observation I conducted. I liked that. It meant that people minded their business and didn't interact. The clock read a little past midnight and I was still waiting for Chae to return home. I heard that at least twice a month, he sent his wife and kids to Jeju Island for the weekend so they could spend time with her family. If the rumors were to be believed, the captain used the free time to sleep around with men and women. I didn't care to investigate the rumors, but it was interesting information because that could be what the Jopok have on him. I got lucky and I overheard him tell someone today that he was seeing the family off after work. I was already planning to pay him a visit today and I was prepared for the wife and kids to be there, but an empty house with him alone is so much better.

Boredom and restlessness started to set in. I had been here since ten. Luckily I saw the familiar black Hyundai drive up the road and pull into his driveway. He got out and grabbed his belongings as I slid out of the car and shut the door quietly. He didn't hear anything because he had his headphones in. He approached his front door and started to fumble with his keys for a little while. I took a deep breath and centered myself as I put on a face mask. I readjusted my baseball cap as well. I looked around and saw the street was still empty. My heart started to pound so hard in my chest, I could have sworn that he heard it. My hands were tingling in excitement. Waiting for the perfect moment when he would unlock the door was crucial. I heard the door click open and I rushed forward and wrapped my arm around his neck and my hand flew up to cover his mouth and I put the gun to his temple.

"Say a word and you die." I growled in his ear. He nodded and opened the door and I led him inside. I closed the door back with my foot and I let him go, continuing to point the gun at him.

"I want everything you know about the Jopok. Headquarters, everything." I demanded as I glared at him. He faced away from me still with his hands up. He turned to face me quickly and spit at me.

"I'm not telling you a fucking thing!" he yelled.

I rolled my eyes and shot at his feet. He jumped back losing his balance and fell to the ground. I aimed the gun again and shot a few centimeters away from his hand that was trying to hold himself up. "We can do this the easy way or the hard way. I'm not in the mood." I growled. He looked up at me and I could see that he was conflicted. He looked over at the bullet holes beside him. Defiance danced in his eyes.

"Your wife and kids can come home and find your dead body or you can tell me everything you know. Choice is yours." He cowered against the wall in the hallway as he stared in the hallway. I smirked as I fired another shot near his head and he ducked the opposite way and screamed. The fear and panic growing in his eyes made me smirk. Pride filled my chest as the familiar thrill started to course through my veins. It had been so long since I had seen someone look at me like that. The fact that I held their future in my hands gave me a high that was indescribable. Everything made sense at that moment. Adrenaline started to tickle my spine. Arsyn may scare him but I was an enigma. He didn't know that I was a fate worse than Arsyn. A wicked grin spread across my face as the pleasure and twisted feeling of joy boosted my ego.

"I'm not telling you anything." he repeated as he looked up at me. My smirk grew more. I fired on the other side of his head. He jumped again.

"You won't? Are you sure about that?" The defiance in his eyes died a little. He was starting to contemplate it. His jaw set hard as he looked up at me.

"The Jopok is the last of your worries right now. I'm offering you the option to at least see your family one more time once I leave here. I'd take the opportunity I'm giving you." I warned him.

Chae was stuck between a rock and a hard place. He was dead either way. Arsyn was sure to kill him once she got wind of the death of her brother. I would kill him if I didn't get what I wanted. At least telling me what I wanted to know would extend his life by a few more days. He knew I was the better choice. The defiance died more. "I can't... I have too much to lose..." he whimpered pathetically. He looked down at the ground. I rolled my eyes, irritation reaching an all time high. I turned the gun around and pistol whipped him. My patience was wearing thin. Torture it is. He cried in pain and doubled over.

"You brought this on yourself." I kicked him in the stomach and started to stomp on his stomach and legs. Once he was clutching his stomach, I dragged him along the floor to the kitchen by his hair. One hand reached up weakly to dig his nails into my hands in an effort to get me to let go. He was pulling against me and screaming and it aggravated me even the more. I turned around and kneed him repeatedly in the top of his head. I could hear the blows that landed on his jaw and cheeks. That loosened his grip until he let go. Once he was compliant, I turned to the stove and turned on one of the burners letting it heat up.

"Tell me what I want to know!" I screamed as I put my knee in his chest and pressed down. I pistol whipped him again. He screamed in agony and shook his head weakly. I yelled in frustration. It shouldn't be taking this long to get this information out of him. The crunch that his nose made as it broke under my fist added to the adrenaline. It had been a long time since I felt alive like this.

It felt like a drug. Looking down at the bigger man broken before me sent a tingle down my spine. The power I held felt so right. I missed it. It was easy to get lost in and to let the power take over as my body went on autopilot. The familiar darkness consumed as I kept swinging my fists and the gun inflicting more damage. Causing more pain. The sound of pain and bones cracking and feeling blood splash onto my clothes and my cheeks sunk me further into the dark space. There was a fleeting thought of how much I missed and needed violence. It was the only thing that I understood fully. It was only when I heard whimpers of what sounded like an address did I come back to reality. I blinked rapidly and looked down at Chae's bruised and bloodied face. His left eye was swollen shut. His nose was off centered leaning too far to the right. Swollen and busted lips. Bruises and open wounds leaked blood.

"Repeat it." I growled as I shook him.

"T-T-Two bases… S-Seoul… A warehouse… red light district. V-Viper there... Northern Seoul… Drugs, arms there… Other… base…" a cough cut off his sentence.

"Don't you fucking die on me! Address!" I demanded shaking him roughly. He mumbled the northern Seoul address. I programmed it into my head.

"Where's the other base? Hurry up!" I screamed. I didn't need extra information. I can find that out myself. He mumbled the last address before he lost consciousness. I dropped his unconscious body and looked around the kitchen. There was blood on the floor and some had splattered on the oven door. I looked down at my hands and I saw that his nails tore through my gloves and they had busted open from the punches I threw. He broke skin. I groaned loudly in annoyance. I had to clean that now.

I stood up and made my way through the house until I found a bathroom. I was looking for hydrogen peroxide, a nail kit and bleach. I had to clean his nails because from the scratches on my wrist, he probably had skin cells under his nails. I didn't need any issues. I also had to clean up the excess blood. It was an extra 20 minute cleaning process. I finished and looked down at Chae's broken body and suddenly Jaehyun's face appeared in my mind. I audibly gasped and shook my head quickly. The vision made my stomach twist and I almost threw up. I finished cleaning and checked to make sure everything outside was still calm and quiet. When I got back to the car, I threw all of the bloody clothes into a black plastic bag before I got in. Another inconvenience avoided. I looked up at the mirror and I saw droplets of blood splatter drying onto my skin. I definitely needed a shower.

Before I drove off, I wrote the addresses down in my black notebook and then I started the ride home. I was still running off adrenaline and I could feel the anger and darkness swimming in me still. It was only then that I realized how heavy the feeling was. The darkness lingered and it felt like it was just waiting for the next moment to emerge again. It was sort of unsettling. I never noticed it before. I needed to figure out how to come out of this state after assignments, because Jaehyun would know something was up. The flashes of Chae's body lying limp on the floor played over and over in my mind. The more I saw the images, the darkness seemed to grow stronger. I craved more violence and my hands twitched on the steering wheel in restlessness. It was hard to explain why I felt so invincible. I just did. I felt untouchable. The feeling was addictive.

I would have to work harder than I thought to keep this part of my life a secret from Jaehyun going forward. When I completed the assignment and took over the Jopok, I could take a break from the assassinations and the violent side of the lifestyle. At least a few months before I went after Han. Give myself time to figure out how to decompress. My thoughts were interrupted by the ringing of my phone and I looked down to see Jaehyun's name. It was a reflex at this point to answer.

"Hello?" my voice was rough from the screaming and yelling. I cleared my throat.

"Hey pretty girl. I knew you were awake. Are you okay?" he chuckled lightly.

"How'd you know I was awake? Yeah I'm okay."

193

"It's 3 am and I'm not there. And you haven't heard me tell you good night. So of course you're not asleep yet. I called to see if you had even tried yet."

"No, I went for a drive. Trying to clear my head. Might get a snack." I giggled at his answer. Talking to him was starting to tame the storm that raged inside of me. He stayed quiet for a moment.

"Are you sure you're okay, Ae Ri?" he asked again with a serious tone. How was I supposed to answer that? I couldn't just tell him what happened, but he wasn't stupid. He knew something was wrong.

"I miss you… I don't like being without you. You're not here to make me feel better." I answered truthfully.

"We can talk about it if you want. I'll stay up with you to sort through it."

"Don't you have to work? I don't want to keep you up. I'm an adult. I'll be fine. It's no big deal."

"That's not important. It's a late meeting tomorrow. I don't have to do the activities in the morning. It's just a bonding thing. Now talk to me. What's wrong?"

"I-I… I don't know. My thoughts aren't kind to me… I keep replaying bad shit over and over again. And even though there's no immediate threat, I keep thinking bad shit will happen. I keep trying to prevent it from happening. I never feel at peace by myself." I found myself admitting. I figured talking about something else that lurked underneath the surface was my best option.

"Did you have another nightmare?" I looked at the phone.

"How did you know about my nightmares?"

"It's kind of obvious. When you fainted and woke up screaming when we were off. You had a nightmare. But you said nightmares? Plural? That wasn't a one off thing? You never told me that. Why didn't you say anything?" He reprimanded me. I grimaced as I unwillingly told him more information than I intended to.

"I told you. You make me feel better. I don't have nightmares when I sleep with you. When I'm alone, yes. Back in Japan they were often. Almost daily or every other day." I confessed.

"What do you have nightmares about?"

I paused, unsure of how to answer him. Telling him that they were violent would make me seem crazy. I chose the safest option.

"My childhood. My father appears in them a lot. My mother's death. Anything really. A lot of stuff." I pulled into my building complex and parked the rental car next to the other two cars. He sighed sadly.

"I think we need to start having serious conversations about your mental health. Not me just mentioning them to you. Have you ever heard about mental health?"

"Nam Jaehyun, I don't know the meaning of those words. I didn't grow up like you. No one gave a fuck about me. No one cared about my feelings. So I learned not to as well. It's harsh, but it's true. I lived a completely different life than you. I didn't make any of this up. I swear." I promised.

"I never said you did, Ae Ri. That's not what I was saying. It just sucks. I hate that you felt that way and that you had to do that. I'm here to walk this journey with you. It's going to be okay. We will figure it out together." I could hear the conviction in his voice and it felt different this time. He has said he would be here for me many times before but when he said it this time it felt personal. Almost as if it was his new life mission.

"Do you think you can sleep with me tonight?" I asked shyly. I could hear the smile in his voice. "Not such a dumb idea now is it, princess?" he teased. I rolled my eyes and blushed lightly. We had slept on FaceTime together a few times before we officially became a couple and I always thought it was a stupid idea. Because we could just sleep together in real life, but he didn't want to make things complicated at the time. So me asking to do it now was quite ironic.

"I will hang up right now."

"And I'll call right back. But sure, pretty. We can." he replied.

"Okay. I just got home and I want to take another shower and see if it helps me get sleepy and then we can call."

"Sure, sure. I'll be here."

I climbed into bed after setting my phone on the pillows where he would usually sleep. Jaehyun had already laid down and had me set up on the bed. He smiled softly. "Comfortable now?" I nodded and adjusted my pillow.

"I am. How was your day? Any contracts signed?"

"Most of the day was my mom's. She wanted a family day without the business talk. By the way, she chewed me out because I was extremely late. In case you were wondering. So thanks for that." Jaehyun sarcastically noted. I raised an eyebrow and shook my head.

"I don't remember that being my fault. You made a decision and I was along for the ride." I teased.

"Of course you enjoyed the ride, because my siblings are convinced you're a cat because of the claw marks now. So I will never hear the end of this. You owe me."

"Fine. Let me know how."

"Oh, I intend to. Very soon." Jaehyun chuckled. He yawned right after.

"Go to sleep. I'll be right here." I offered. I'm sure he was tired.

"Not until you fall asleep. You won't go to sleep if I do." I rolled my eyes and giggled as he watched me carefully. He was probably right. I was physically tired but mentally I still couldn't turn my brain off.

The negative emotions had lessened a lot but I still was running through tomorrow's plan and trying to process the whys and hows of everything. "My brain won't be quiet. It's hard." I frowned. My thoughts ran on a continuous loop about numerous things all at once. It was chaotic and loud. My mind had always worked like that. He nodded in understanding.

"Close your eyes. I'll try something." he offered. I closed my eyes, and he started singing softly to me. It took a few moments to realize it was the same song from karaoke a few months back. A small smile crossed my face as I relaxed further into the bed and I started to drift off to sleep. Before I slipped into unconsciousness, I heard him whisper that I was beautiful.

~Chapter 21~

I awoke to an alarm going off that wasn't mine. I heard Jae shuffling to turn the alarm off. My eyes opened slowly to see him sitting up and rubbing the sleep away. He glanced over at the phone to see me and broke out into a wide grin. "Good morning sunshine. You actually stayed on the call the whole night." he smiled.

"It wasn't horrible. It was actually comforting and kind of cute. It felt like you were here with me. And I appreciate that. Thanks. The song from karaoke was a nice touch." I admitted. I couldn't lie that turning over and seeing his face through the night was comforting. I didn't like that it didn't give me his warmth, but it made the loneliness easier.

"I knew you would like it eventually. What are you doing today?" he asked as he got up and grabbed his phone to bring to the bathroom.

"Probably to go to the mall. Spend some money. Work on a report. Whatever I can get my hands on." I answered as I sat up and leaned against the headboard enjoying the sight of him shirtless. Part of that was true. I was going to spend money today. I purchased the matching rolex I promised him a while ago. I had to go and pick them up. I had some time before it got dark because tonight I was going to the Jopok headquarters.

If I was lucky, someone would be there and I could eliminate one of them. I wasn't going to get my hopes up, but I was going to be prepared just in case. Jaehyun's laugh brought me from my thoughts. "Impulse buying again? You have a problem." he commented.

"Doesn't happen often enough to be considered a problem." I replied matter-of-factly.

"Once a week is a problem."

"It's not that often."

"That diamond necklace you bought last week. And the week before that you bought another car. The same model except in the brighter red color." he reminded.

"I bought you stuff too. What are you saying?" I defended myself.

"That's not the point, princess. I'm just saying you have impulsive tendencies and we should figure out why."

He chuckled at my silence. He was right. Since I had met him, my impulsive tendencies got worse. I had more clothes and shoes here than I did back in Japan. It wasn't until he said that I realized how bad it had become. I looked around the room and at the purses and shoes and clothes that I had all over the place. I had a tendency to spend money when my emotions were scattered and discombobulated. When I thought about it, that was the only time I bought anything. Even when I was younger, I spent money when I wasn't feeling like myself. Why did it seem to be all the time though? I shook off the thought. "Duly noted, Nam." I rolled my eyes and he chuckled.

"It's something to think about, princess. Just watch your spending. You go a little haywire sometimes. Grab something pretty to wear at least." he smiled playfully.

"Sure, sure. What's on the agenda today?"

"I have a meeting with some investors with my dad and siblings. Then a meeting with some organizers for the World Expo. Then a dinner where hopefully we are closing on a few land and building deals. If all goes well, you'll be sleeping with a very wealthy man." He looked over at the camera and winked.

I laughed out loud at that. "I think I already do that. But congratulations in advance. I'm proud of you." I told him honestly. He worked really hard for his family's business. It was difficult to watch him stress over everything he was juggling. Between school, his competition, student council and his family's business, I was astounded that he spent as much time with me as he did. I was grateful for it too. He stopped shaving for a moment and stared at me through the phone. His eyes sparkled and I could see the tears collect in the corner of his eyes. "Why are you crying, Jaehyun? What's wrong?" I asked quickly as I held the phone tightly in my hands. Worry and panic rushed through me at the sight of him crying. He shook his head and blinked the tears away quickly.

"You said you're proud of me... You've never said that before. That means a lot to me, princess. Thank you."

The relief and pride in his voice was evident. I calmed down and a small smile spread across my face. It was the first time I had ever said that to him. I really meant it. He was the only thing I could be proud of. The staredown was intense. It made me almost shy. I couldn't break away from it though. There was something in his eyes that captivated me. I had seen it before. Whatever emotion that was there had intensified in that exact moment and I wished I could understand it. I wanted to. It was unfamiliar and beautiful at the same time. He looked at me with this sparkle in his eyes. Like I was worth something. It became too much and I broke eye contact first. "Shouldn't you be getting ready instead of staring at me?" I reminded him bashfully. He snickered slightly and I blushed as I covered my face. God, I felt like a little kid. This was humiliating.

"You got me there. I'll let you get your day started. I'll call you later, okay?" I nodded in response and waved as we hung up.

I breathed a sigh of relief and placed a hand over my chest. My heart was fluttering and I took a minute to calm down before I got up from the bed. Once I was calm, I called Code.

"Yes ma'am?" Code answered on the second ring.

"I have two addresses. See if you can get some sort of information on it. Internal layouts hopefully. These are the addresses of the Jopok headquarters." I told him, smirking. He was silent for a moment.

"Who did you kill to get that information and how did you kill them? I need details." he gasped.

"Police captain on their payroll. I beat him. Pistol whips, fist, stomps... Didn't get to the torture part before he told me what I wanted to know. He may be dead. I left him unconscious in his house. His wife and kids will find him. I'll let you know."

"Damnnnn… In his house? No torture though, that sucks. That's the best part. He was weak. I hate that. It's no fun." he huffed in annoyance.

"Yeah, I know. He broke fast. It was an easier clean up though." I admitted. It was an easier clean up than what I normally had to do. Chae's nails took the most work to clean.

"Fair. Torture is hard to clean up. Okay, let's do this. What's the address? I'll do some research and get back to you."

"I need it done. I ride tonight." I informed him. I could almost see him pause and stare off into space.

"That's short notice, ma'am… I'm not doubting you. It's just that there hasn't been any proper surveillance. No recon. You'd be going in blind. Respectfully, I think we should wait." Code said warily. I growled low in the back of my throat.

"I don't have that type of time. It's gotta happen tonight. Do whatever it takes. I expect information before the afternoon. Am I understood?" I demanded harshly.

"Yes ma'am." he agreed. I hung up and ran a hand through my hair. I was definitely pushing it. I knew that. I was moving recklessly. I knew that. It had to be tonight though. Jaehyun was gone, so I didn't have to worry about him. The element of surprise is on my side. No one knows about Chae and they wouldn't know until at least Sunday night. So that meant Arsyn was still running off of unconfirmed information. I had to be strategic about this.

Maybe Code was right, though. Maybe it would be better to hold off and let more recon happen. It wasn't just about me anymore. I had to protect Jaehyun. I can't protect him if I'm dead or captured. He would be worried. He didn't need that stress added on top of everything he had going on. Fucking hell. This was the first time I ever feared or was nervous about a plan. I never second guessed myself. No. No. Overthinking gets me nowhere. It gets people killed. I need to see what information Code gets me. This was the best option I had in a messy situation. It had to happen tonight. I sighed loudly and got up and proceeded to get on with my day. I had to go pick up the watches before I left tonight. I had put off getting them for long enough. Might grab something nice for myself too. Spending money reminded me that I was untouchable and cleared my mind.

I was walking out of the rolex store when my phone rang and it almost took me off guard. I looked at the ID and answered. "What?" I questioned.

"Got some information for you. I did some digging and found someone who could maybe help. I got in contact with an ex Yamaguchi member. Turns out he's in Korea right now. He does the deliveries for a small gang that the Jopok uses to smuggle drugs into the country. Remember Kenji?" Code answered with an excitement clearly in his voice. I paused for a moment. I hadn't heard that name in a long time. Kenji was one of the men that I surpassed when I was given the saiko komon title. He wasn't too happy about it and he forgot his place. It was the first time I saw yubitsume in person. I still remember all of the blood that sprayed everywhere and his wails of pain. He wasn't in the syndicate much longer after that. His wife got sick and he didn't want to be away from her. I was probably twenty two or twenty three the last time I heard anything about him. "He's a delivery boy? What a fall from grace. Isn't he in his mid fifties or something? What the hell?" I asked.

"Yep. It looks like his wife was Korean and when she got sick, they headed to Korea. He went off the grid and tried to do his own gang thing, he got hurt and his own gang turned on him and overthrew him. Made him a delivery boy." Damn, that was cold. To be bitched by your own gang that you created? Sad.

"All he had to do was mind his manners." I sucked my teeth and shook my head sadly.

"Boss, you made him cut his finger off. A humble reminder." Code snickered.

"Exactly my point. But anyways. What does this have to do with anything?"

"Right, sorry. He knows those addresses pretty well. He's been there a lot. He can help. I got an address for you."

"Hold on." I pulled out my phone and put the address in. "Tell him I'm forty five minutes out. It's in a poorer part of the city." I put the bags in the back of the truck and climbed into the driver's seat.

"He's expecting you. I'll keep looking for information." he explained. I hung up and pulled out of the parking lot and sped off down the road.

Pulling up to the address where Kenji lived was like stepping into a different world. It was a run down apartment building. It was three stories and the white paint was yellowing and the building looked like it was falling apart in some areas. Trash was spilling over out of the dumpsters and onto the street. The smell was horrid. A pack of starving stray dogs ate some of the food in the trash. I pulled out my gun and shook my head. How could a gang live like this? Pride is such a foolish thing to have when one is poor. Just earn some standing with established an organization or earn a way in. It has to be better than this. I touched nothing as I began the cautious walk up the steps to the second floor. At the end of the hall on the second floor, a haggard gray haired man sat on an old milk crate. He smoked a cigarette as he stared out into the distance.

The sound of my heels alerted him to my presence. His head turned faster than the rest of his body. Wrinkles and crow's feet made him look much older than I remembered. He looked bad for his age. He stared at me for a moment before he struggled to his feet and bowed to me awkwardly. He looked to be in serious pain. I nodded once in acknowledgement. "Kenji. It's been a while." I said as I walked to stand in front of him.

"It has been a while, ma'am. You look beautiful, if I may compliment you." Kenji said in a low, tired voice.

"Of course. Things are certainly different now. This is what the great enforcer Kenji became after he left?" He looked down at his feet in shame.

"I am so sorry, saiko komon. I am so, so sorry. I regret that day so much. I-I was jealous. You were the best person for the position. You were the only one who could expand the mission. I was young and dumb. I was cocky and I stepped out of line. I apologize." I hummed in mild annoyance.

"You were in your early 50s, old man. Not really young and dumb anymore. But that's not important right now. You have information that I need." I said as I looked down at his broken form. He looked up at me and nodded quickly.

"Yes, of course. Whatever you need. If you'll follow me." Kenji agreed as he opened the door to his apartment. Stepping inside, I cringed at how small it was. It was the size of my closet at most. The only upside was that it was cleaner than the outside. A small table was next to his bed and there were blank sheets of white paper. One piece of paper had a drawing on it. He followed behind me and sat in the only chair and started shuffling through the papers.

"Code told me that you needed the layouts of those addresses. I see the red light district building often. It's really a warehouse but its front business is a strip club. There's two floors. The first floor is the club itself. The place where the dancers dress and get ready in the back, that's where they hide the drugs. Under the floorboards. In the walls. The offices are on the second floor. Viper's office is there. Arsyn has one there but it's pretty much empty, so they use it as an extra storage room. Whenever she's there, she's giving orders. She's doing inventory or collections. There's a lot of other buildings around it that they use as warehouses too. They hold the drugs they smuggle in. Fentatyl, cocaine mostly. This building is painted red and black and you have to use the back entrance. You have to go around to get to it. They closed up the front entrance," Kenji informed me as he pulled out a blank sheet of paper and started drawing.

"There's always two guards outside and inside, there's always workers combing through the club," he added.

That's bold. Keeping the product in plain sight like that. The red light districts still had a lot of traffic. And it was a club as well, people were in and out of the place. It was smart though. I had to give them that. I knew plenty of strippers who did cocaine to make it through shifts. It was grueling. "What about the other one?" I asked. He sighed and pulled out the already completed drawing. It looked like he drew a map of a campground or something. "This northern Seoul address is something entirely different. It's complicated. It's an address for a community of hanoks. This I believe is the actual headquarters. Where things actually happen and everyone goes to. Problem is, I don't know which hanok. I've only been in one of the hanoks. There's probably twenty or more in this lot, I suppose. I went inside of the first one by the road. It's built like a maze. There are so many twists and turns and rooms. I've gone to one conference room, but I walked through six or seven sections to get to the conference room. There's so many entrances to get inside but finding your way around is tough." Code answered. He flipped the paper on the back and started to draw the inside of the hanok he went into. There were a lot of hallways and twists and turns. It was confusing to look at. How the fuck was I supposed to figure this out? And he wasn't even sure if that was the main building. I didn't have time to visit every building.

"How did you get inside anyway? Did they escort you in or something?" I questioned as I looked over his shoulder at the paper.

"Yeah actually. So the compound is separated from the rest of the area. When you drive down the road that the compound is on, you immediately come into contact with guards. They protect a few miles of road before you get to the compound. It's easier to escape Alcatraz than to infiltrate the compound. You're amazing, Rose. You truly are, but this is next level." Kenji warned. I glared down at him, offended.

"You've been gone for years, old man. You don't know what I'm capable of. I've just gotten better over the years." I said it confidently, but I honestly didn't feel so confident. This was going to be a test. The Jopok were something entirely different. I have never been on an assignment where the targets were so hard to find. Even if they were rival leadership. Omega was clearly talented before he rose to power. I crossed my arms across my chest and looked down at the drawings again.

"The only way to get anywhere near the compound is to be snuck in by someone or to be invited. And they check the cars before they let you in."

"Of course they do." I added sarcastically.

"Okay. So you sneak me in and we don't get caught."

All the new information was seriously diminishing my confidence. This went from messy to an absolute shitshow. Where could I hide in a car that couldn't be checked? That was insanity. "I won't be back there for another month or two, ma'am." he confessed. I stared down at him flabbergasted.

"What the hell! Why?" I exclaimed as I threw my hands in the air in frustration.

"They switch out the crews every delivery. My gang doesn't go back all the time."

"These bastards are good… Do you have anything good or useful for me to use right now? Anything helpful." I groaned.

"I'm sorry ma'am. Nothing really. Hm… Well maybe this can be helpful. I overheard some Jopok members saying that they were interested in trying to get in on the action with the World Expo in 2025. But that's all I have."

My eyes widened at the mention of the World Expo. Oh god… Jaehyun's family was involved in the World Expo and they were signing deals this weekend. It felt like the world stopped and I started to zone out as my thoughts started to race. Was he sitting in a room with Arsyn right now? Signing a deal with them, that would cost him everything. My heart pounded in my chest and I started to hyperventilate. I had to make sure he was okay. I grabbed the papers from the table and ran to the door. "Ma'am…!?"

"I'll be in touch." I exclaimed as I threw the door open and made my way down the steps as quickly as I could without breaking my neck. I reached the car and jumped in calling Jaehyun. My palms were sweating and trembling so much that I kept dropping my phone. The amount of dread that coursed through me was paralyzing and it got worse the longer the phone rang without an answer. He never took this long to answer normally. My thoughts started to spiral. Did they capture him? Did they find out? How did they find out? As my thoughts spiraled, it became harder to breathe. Tears spilled over onto my cheeks and covered my mouth to try to calm down.

At the last moment, the ringing stopped and a deeper voice answered. It wasn't Jaehyun's voice and it worried me more.

"Hello Jaehyun's assistant, Daehyun speaking." the voice answered. He didn't have an assistant, it must have been his brother.

"H-hi… I-Is Jaehyun available? I'd like to talk to him." I said as calmly as possible.

"OH! You must be the cat! Haha! You're a real person! You're the girlfriend! How are you-" Jaehyun's voice cut in from the background.

"Hyung! Put it down! Give me my phone! You're scaring her!" Jaehyun yelled. I heard a scuffle and the distinct sounds of punches being thrown and groans of pain. When Jaehyun answered he was a little out of breath.

"Hey pretty girl. Sorry about that. He jokes around a lot. Ignore him. How are you?" Jaehyun panted softly. It felt like the world had been lifted off my shoulders and I sighed in relief. He was all right. He was safe. I heard him close a door and it got quiet. I could finally breathe.

"Ae Ri? Are you okay? What's wrong?" he questioned with concern, lacing his voice.

"I just had a nightmare. I'm fine. Just needed to hear your voice. Are you okay?" I answered, wiping at the tears that escaped.

They were grateful tears. An amused smirk crossed my face as I realized just how much I was stuck with him. It felt like I was constantly discovering just how much Jaehyun meant to me. It felt like there were so many layers to the way I felt. And I still hadn't reached the end.

"Oh my god, Ae Ri… Do I need to come home? Did you take a nap? What happened at the mall? Please don't cry…" his voice was full of sadness. I didn't realize that I was sniffling. That was what gave away that I was crying.

"N-No, I'm okay. I promise. I-It was a dream. I just needed to know you were okay. I'm sorry. I know it's dumb."

"It's not dumb. You're important to me. I'd drop everything for you, you know that. I love you-"

It was deathly silent. You could hear a pin drop. I stared down at the phone. There it was. That emotion that lurked in his eyes, that I could never understand. That emotion that I couldn't figure out. There was no going back. Everything had changed. I felt it in the pit of my stomach. The words sat on the tip of my tongue. Everything was screaming at me. The voices were loud in my head, despite the silence in the car. I didn't understand the feeling. I couldn't comprehend it, but it felt right. It felt like the answer to everything that's been happening. A lump formed in my throat and I could've sworn I was choking. The reason why I was so protective over him, the possessiveness I felt. The way he made everything better. The safety I feel with him. The reason why everything felt right with him. It's what I saw in his eyes. That mystery emotion that I couldn't figure out when I stared into his eyes. That was it. He loved me.

Tears welled up in my eyes and a knot formed in my stomach. "A-Ae Ri... I-I'm so sorry... I didn't want to- Oh my god.... I-I don't know why... I'm sorry... I wasn't trying to spring that on you. Oh my god... What the fuck, dude!" Jaehyun was fumbling over his words and he was clearly distraught. He was terrified and panicking. Even when he confessed his feelings, he was still worried about me. Why couldn't I say anything? Why was I sitting here frozen? This was supposed to be beautiful, but why did I feel so stunned? Shocked? Fearful? This moment was single handedly the best moment of my life but I felt crippled. Thoughts of my childhood, thoughts of past assignments, thoughts of every drug deal, thoughts of what I did to Chae all came rushing back to me and I felt a cold sweat break out along my forehead. I felt like I was falling apart. I was in uncharted territory and I was lost. I didn't know what to do. I was vaguely aware of Jaehyun's rambling on the other end of the line. Some of it was directed to me, most of it was to himself. I had never heard him so discombobulated and unfocused.

"C-Come home... Please..." I wheezed out. He kept rambling, he couldn't hear me. I tried again. Still nothing. I forced myself to speak louder and he stopped abruptly and went silent.

"I'm on my way. Are you at my house?" he asked. I heard a room door open and close and things move around.

"Yeah." I answered.

"I'll see you soon."

208

"Yeah." I hung up and started the car, speeding off back to civilization.

~Chapter 22~

I stood out on the balcony, overlooking the skyline in Jaehyun's penthouse. The sun was setting, and it was supposed to be peaceful. I was hoping it would calm me down. I was hoping it would give me a chance to gather my thoughts. It did none of that. The storm of conflicting emotions and horrible memories mixed in with Jaehyun's profession of love for me. I was a wreck emotionally. I hadn't felt this broken since that night I cried in Jaehyun's arms. Since I saw my mother's picture for the first time. There was a deep satisfaction that burned in my stomach at hearing Jaehyun say he loved me. But at the same time, I felt so undeserving. I've seen and done things to people that were too horrendous to say out loud. I've used force and coercion to get what I wanted for years. I disregarded people's feelings and their lives because I can't empathize with them. If I wrote my life out on a sheet of paper, I'd have more sins than I could be forgiven for. I was the true definition of like father, like daughter.

When Jaehyun was compared to me, he was an angel. He had no faults, he did everything right. He was perfect. He was kind to people, he gave to people. He was friendly and joyful. He had a family who loved him. He had friends who loved and adored him. I never fit into his world. But I was starting to. I was starting to become comfortable with integrating into his life. I was living a life that I had always thought was impossible for me. Jaehyun gave me peace and stability. Jaehyun loving me was something that I didn't see coming. I couldn't predict this. I couldn't prepare for it. I knew I would do anything to keep him with me. I would do my best to be perfect for him. I would live a double life to keep him safe and keep him with me. I still stand by it.

I heard the door open and I turned to see Jaehyun standing in the bedroom looking at me through the glass door. He stood there and the trepidation was radiating off of him. It was awkward between us for the first time. No one moved or said anything. I nodded for him to join me outside. He only moved then. We stared at each other for a long time. His pretty brown eyes were stormy. They didn't have the same sparkle in them. He looked unsure. Not the usual confident man that I saw. He took a deep breath and looked down. "I didn't mean to make you uncomfortable. I'm sorry. I was caught up in my head and in my emotions and... it just came out. I know it's-" Jaehyun started, but I cut him off.

"Did you mean it?" He looked at me and he almost seemed offended. When he saw the seriousness of my expression, he softened.

"Of course, I mean it. I've tried to show it in ways that I thought you would understand. It's been a lot of work and I've been sitting on it for so long. It's been eating at me for a while now. You called me crying, it just did something to me. And for you to just tell me that you needed to hear my voice... It meant the world to me. I've been so proud of you because I've watched you make small steps to try to express how you feel about me and it just makes me smile like an idiot. I know that this is new for you and you're trying to figure this out still. That's why I never said it before." Jaehyun explained as he walked closer and reached for my hand.

"If I was to sit and talk about just how much shit I've seen and endured as a kid, you wouldn't believe me. You'd wonder how I wasn't inside a psych ward. I don't have a guide through this, I'm battling things in my head constantly. I wasn't perfect before you. I probably never will be, but I am trying to be perfect for you. I constantly feel like I don't deserve any of this. None of your attention, your care... Your love. I'm trapped in my head. It has nothing to do with you. It's me. It really is. I don't want to unpack that with you. It's dark and you don't deserve that or need that. It's hard to voice." I confessed. Jaehyun nodded as he listened to me.

It was deeper than me trying to keep a secret. It was the darkness and the pain that I couldn't verbally explain because I was slowly starting to become aware of how bad it was. I knew something was wrong because getting to this point with Jaehyun was difficult. My inadequacies with relationships and never having them made it a struggle to admit and understand that I was starting to like him. Once I admitted it, I was perfectly content with having him in my life even if he wasn't mine technically. Then the possessiveness started to rear its ugly head. And just having in my life wasn't good enough anymore. People thought they still had a chance. I knew my feelings were morphing into something, but I couldn't figure out what it was. Then we became official and I was pleased. My feelings were and still are continuing to grow and I'm almost positive they replicated his. I just didn't know how to say it. I didn't know how to reciprocate it or embrace it.

Jaehyun's hand cradled my face and he stared at me. "I'm willing to listen. To anything you have to say." he said encouragingly.

"I feel like I'm out in the middle of the ocean and there's a storm happening. Rough winds, heavy rain and the only thing keeping me afloat is a piece of wood. Out in the distance there's an island and it's safe, there's a little house there and I can see it. If I can get to the house, I'll be safe. I know it. I can rest and get through the storm. The piece of wood is steady and stable. It's strong. I'm still miles away from the island but I'm going to get there. I know it. I'm determined to. It's just going to take some time." I explained to him. I knew the analogy wasn't the best, but it was what I could come up with at the moment.

"Am I the house on the island? The piece of wood is your emotions, and the storm is all the other stuff going on in your head?"

"Sometimes I forget you can read me like a book," I said.

He smirked lightly and shrugged. "It's my job. So, tell me what the analogy means since I decoded it. It's only fair, you know?" he teased lightly.

I sighed knowing it was coming. "You're not alone in the way you feel. I just don't know how to say it yet. And I don't want you to get mad. I don't want you to feel like I don't. I don't want you to…leave me. You're the only thing in my life that has brought me any happiness. Made me feel like I was worth something. Made me feel human. It's just the shit I've been through… makes it hard." I sighed and took a moment to breathe.

"I hate it because I should just get over it. It's in the past, it's not happening currently. So, I should be glad about that right? But it's not that easy and I'm not understanding why. It's annoying to deal with. And when

I try to ignore it, it gets worse." I looked up at him and he smiled sadly at me.

"I would never be mad at you. I'd never leave you. You will always have me. No matter what. I'm still willing to wait and stand by you. I understand this is all new to you. Now in response to the second part. You have to be ready to have that conversation to understand why. I've mentioned it before, but you weren't ready to talk about it. Are you ready to do that?" Jaehyun replied and he led us over to the rail of the balcony.

"If it helps me figure this out. It's getting annoying." I grumbled. The constant battle was getting tiring. It was getting old. It was pissing me off because I didn't want to deal with it. Truthfully. I had enough to worry about, with getting the assignment completed and making the next steps. Dealing with my complicated emotions was becoming a nuisance.

"You don't heal by ignoring things. You don't get over things by ignoring them. That's not how things work. You've been traumatized. Trauma is a deeply disturbing or distressing experience. It sticks with you. Typically for years. It can lead to a lot of things like anxiety, PTSD. You have trauma. Plain and simple. From your dad. It's possible that not growing up with your mom had an affect on that too. But for sure, your dad is where it comes from."

Fucking Han. He was truly a disease. He ruined everything he touched. I wasn't surprised to hear that though. I knew that it had everything to do with Han. That was apparent. But hearing what I went through being described as trauma was strange. Trauma was always physical to me. Gunshots, baseball bats to the skull, cutting off fingers. "I wasn't aware trauma could be emotional. I thought it was only physical. Get knocked around enough times, you hear it enough." I commented as I leaned on the railing. I could feel his stares on the side of my head.

"What's anxiety and PTSD?"

"Anxiety is just what it says. Excessive and persistent worry and fear about everyday situations. An anxiety disorder is repeated episodes of that feeling that happen without control. Sometimes it's sudden and can hit a peak within minutes. Typically called a panic attack. PTSD is a disorder where a person has a hard time recovering after experiencing or witnessing something terrifying." he explained. There may be something in what he was saying.

"Any… symptoms? How do you know if that's what it is?" I questioned quietly. He placed a hand on my shoulder and rubbed it softly.

"Symptoms of anxiety…trouble sleeping; feeling nervous, restless and tense; an increased heart rate; hyperventilation. PTSD commonly has nightmares, emotional detachment, unwanted memories of the trauma, heightened reactions. Anxiety can be a symptom of PTSD too." Welp. There it is. A bitter chuckle left my lips.

"That explains a lot, huh? Why I'm so fucked up." I replied. I stood up and turned to go back inside.

"Ae Ri, wait! This isn't your fault. None of this is. You can't blame yourself. That's insane." He quickly followed me inside and stood off to my side as I looked down at the dresser where he had our picture framed. Angry tears spilled down my cheeks. He was right. It wasn't my fault. It was his fault. It was all Han's fault. He was always screwing me over. He did everything his way without any consideration for anyone else but himself. He had no boundaries. He crossed every line repeatedly. The rage and bloodlust started to bubble underneath the surface.

"I wish he was dead…" I said out loud. The shock flashed across Jaehyun's face for a brief moment before it settled back into a neutral expression. The venom that coursed through my veins felt like fire burning my skin everywhere it went.

"You don't have to let him win, Ae Ri. You can heal from this and move on. You don't have to stay like this. It'll take work. But this is something you can get through. I will be here every step of the way. If you're not ready to tell me everything right now, that's okay. We take it one day at a time." Jaehyun said softly as he took a step closer. I looked over at him and anguish filled me. He didn't deserve this. He didn't need all of this.

"Why do you put up with me? I don't understand. You have so much already going on, you don't need a wreck of a girlfriend like me. You can be with anyone else. Be with someone who's normal. Someone who doesn't have all of these… problems. Someone who won't give you so much hell. You left your business meetings early. That couldn't have gone over well, by the way… I just don't understand why. Am I a charity case to you?" I cried as I looked back down. Looking at him physically hurt. Not in a bad way, but I felt like I wronged him. I didn't do anything to cross him, but I felt like I did. I hated it.

"Because you're special. Because I feel safe with you. You never needed me for anything. You never wanted me for anything. When I met you, you weren't the slightest bit concerned about who I was. You didn't want me right off the bat. That intrigued me. I was smitten from the start. Then we started to hang out everyday. I started to learn more about you. Your confidence is unlike anything I've ever seen. When you found out what my family did, you didn't get weird on me. You shrugged it off. Even when I've shown you that I'm willing to take care of you for you to get away from your father's business, you still tell me no because you want your independence. You're stubborn. You don't listen. You're short tempered at times. You speak without thinking sometimes, but I find it adorable. Your mood swings are still unpredictable, but I find you cute even then. You live and die by your own sword," he started as he walked beside me and lifted my head. I leaned my head against his hand. He smiled softly and wiped my tears with his thumb.

"You know as I think about it. I don't think you'll ever have to say you love me because I know. You've managed to be upset about this entire thing because of how this affects me. You think I don't notice you watching me sleep when you get up in the middle of the night. Or when you can't sleep, you'll sit on the edge of the bed or at your desk or in the chair in my room and make sure I'm okay. It was weird at first but now I like it. It's cute. You sleep more around me than you do when you're alone and I know that for a fact. You just have to make sure I'm safe first. Your possessiveness is another big indicator. But it's not unhealthy really. Only if you think the girl has a crush on me. But that's not so bad anymore now that we're together. You're trying to figure it out and that's commendable. There's a lot of people who wouldn't try after what you've been through. You're the strongest person I know. You have never been a charity case." he continued.

Even though he was teasing in some of the comments, I could feel that he was sincere. The love in his eyes was apparent and it was unrestrained. After months of trying to hide it, he was done with that now that it had been said. I appreciated that about him. He was sincere in everything he did and said. It was hard to be guarded around someone who was only honest and had no bad intentions. Especially when everyday was spent with them. I couldn't even come back with something to tease him with like I normally would when things got too deep emotionally for me. I was stuck on him saying he felt safe with me. I took a lot of pride in that.

"You feel safe with me?" I repeated as I looked up at him.

"I do. You're not the only one who has their scars. Growing up with money makes it hard to tell who's really your friend or who's there for the money. I've been burned a few times. By past ex girlfriends and past friends."

"You have tons of friends though. Everyone likes you. What do you mean?"

"I'm cordial with people. I'm friendly. Doesn't mean everyone is my friend. I'll talk to anyone. That doesn't make them my friends. Seojun, Seunghyun and Minhyun are my friends. The girls they've become friends. Well, except for Nari, she was my friend before.. That's why I introduced you to them. That's why they're the only ones you see me hang out with on a consistent basis. Other than that, I'm with you." he grinned. When he said it, I started to realize that he was right. I hadn't seen him hang out with anyone except them. He interacted and spoke to people at school, but that was it. We happened organically.

"You're the only thing I've ever gotten right, Nam Jaehyun. I'm trying to keep that going." I told him.

"You'll get the hang of it, princess. I believe in you." he teased as he leaned down and kissed my forehead. I gasped lightly as I remembered his gift.

"Oh before I forget. I got you something." I walked over to the closet and grabbed the bag from his closet and waved him over to the bed with me. He followed me and sat next to me as I smiled proudly and handed the bag to him.

"You didn't... There's no way. Ae Ri, I told you it wasn't necessary..." he exclaimed as he took out the signature green box. He chuckled as he opened the box to look at the Rolex.

"A Datejust 31? I don't have this one. Did you get one too?" I smiled at his reaction and pulled out mine. I got myself the Lady Datejust. Both watches were yellow gold and diamonds. His was bigger at 31 millimeters than my 28 millimeters and his dial was an olive green color and mine was diamond paved.

"That's a nice piece, princess. You did a good job. I like how they're the same but still different. Look at you being symbolic." he playfully pinched my cheek.

"You really like it?" I confirmed.

"I do, I promise. I honestly forgot all about this. I wasn't worried about it. So thank you, sweetheart. It was really sweet of you."

It made me feel really good that he liked the watch. And the fact that I surprised him made it all the more worth it. Maybe I wasn't ready to say the word out loud yet, but hopefully my actions would continue to show it. I couldn't lose him. I suddenly remembered that I needed to ask him about the meetings. The Jopok were trying to get in on the World Expo business. I had to make sure he was safe. "How were the business meetings? Anything exciting happened?" I asked him quickly.

"Oh, they were great. I meant to tell you, but you know all that happened. We signed all the deals so you're sleeping with a very wealthy man now." he answered with a wide grin. He was beaming.

"Oh really? I thought I already did that." I teased.

"You could humor me, you know. Come on." He playfully whined in annoyance.

"Okay, okay. How wealthy?"

"2 trillion won was made for the business. 10 billion won goes back into the company, 2 billion won is in everyone's pocket. Not so bad for a day and a half of work, I suppose."

"Not bad at all. Congratulations, I'm proud of you. Was it just you guys at the meeting?" I inquired curiously. I kept my voice neutral like I was being mindless with the questioning.

"Yeah, just us and the same old guys. Boring as usual." he answered. Okay, they weren't there at that meeting. They will likely try to find another way in. Right now, I was content with having him back home with me where he was safe. I could figure everything else out later. I wouldn't worry about it right now.

"Can I ask you something, Ae Ri?" Jaehyun asked after a few minutes of comfortable silence. I hummed in response.

"Would you be willing to meet my mom? You don't have to meet anyone else yet. Just my mom. I've been thinking for a while that maybe it'll be beneficial... I know it won't replace your mom, but maybe it'll give you someone who you can talk to. And she's been dying to meet you. She asks a lot about you." His voice was extremely careful and I could tell he didn't want to upset me. However, under the surface, he was hopeful that I would say yes. Maybe he was right... It could help me.

"Okay... I'll do it. I think it's time." I agreed. It had been months and he did tell me he loved me, it felt like the next logical step. He smiled brightly and leaned over to kiss my cheek quickly.

"Thank you, princess. I can't wait for you to meet her. She's going to be so excited. I'll call her tomorrow."

His excitement was evident and contagious. I found myself hoping for the best.

"Do you want to order delivery and watch tv for the rest of the day? I'm tired from the long drive and I can only imagine how exhausted you must be." he offered as he placed the boxes back in the bag and put them on the dresser. I smiled softly at his consideration and nodded.

"I'd like that a lot." I replied.

Initiation

~Chapter 23~

Officer Kim came running into the room full speed with a terrified look in his eyes. He looked around the room and started talking to himself quickly. I looked up at him and raised an eyebrow. His nervous energy was making the hairs on the back of my neck stand up. Arsyn must be on the way. And the full team was still in the office. That wasn't good. He caught my eye and pointed at me. "You have to help me get the office clear of the ones who don't belong here. She's. Pissed. Off." he said gravely. Terror was evident in his eyes.

"How do we do that? Where do we send them?" I asked quickly. As easy and nice as it would be for her to get locked away for years, I wouldn't be able to kill her from behind bars. So I couldn't have that. He ran to Chae's office and grabbed two clipboards and threw one at me.

"These are the assignments he usually sends them on when she's coming. You take half and I do the other half. We got an hour." he hissed.

"What's going on? Where's Captain Chae?" I asked cluelessly.

"Hospital. He was attacked over the weekend. He's in a coma." I gasped in pretended shock. I was somewhat surprised that he wasn't dead after what I did to him. That would explain the uproar. We worked for the next hour sending people on made up assignments and patrols.

It had been an hour exactly and we heard heavy stomps coming down the marble flooring quickly. The temperature dropped in the room. We all sat rigid in our seats as Arsyn stormed into the office. She stood at the entrance for a few moments, fuming and her eyes scanned the room. Her eyes paused on me for a moment, and I looked at her from underneath my police hat. After a few moments, she continued her scanning. The tension in the air was so thick that it could be cut with a knife and it was suffocating. She let out a primal scream and picked up a chair by the entrance and threw it across the room. It slammed into the wall and everyone on that side moved out of the way. She flipped over the first workstation she came to and she screamed again. She looked more like a wild animal than she did a human. A strange sense of deja vu hit me as I watched her. I've had that same reaction to something not going my way hundreds of times. I've rage killed during some of those episodes and I knew she was capable of that. I watched her from the corner of my eye as she continued her rampage through the office.

"I asked you idiots to find the traitor and SOMEHOW CHAE ENDED UP IN A FUCKING COMA OVER THE WEEKEND!" she screeched as she threw a mouse at an unsuspecting woman that had looked away from her. The mouse made a thud noise as it hit her in the side of the head. Wow, she used anything as a weapon for punishment too. That's oddly familiar too.

"Somebody better tell me something. Who was with Chae before he left Friday? And someone better say something or bodies are dropping." she growled as she pulled out her gun. Terrified gasps and whimpers spread throughout the group. I wasn't near Chae Friday, I overheard the conversation. I tapped Kim and whispered to him.

"Wasn't Chae talking to two higher ups before he left?" I asked him.

"Hm… yeah. And then two other captains not with us." he added.

"Then someone should say something before there's dead bodies all over the floor." I suggested.

"Say it then."

"Chae never spoke to me. I'm still clueless, remember?" I hissed at him under my breath.

"Damn it. Fine." Kim answered.

Kim called out and answered her with the names of the people he was last seen with. She calmed down slightly. "They're giving you all a replacement captain for right now. I'll be communicating with you all through encrypted emails. Since he was incapable of finding the rat among you all, I'll have to do it myself. Get to work. And clean up this mess." she warned us as she stormed out. We all watched her leave and I let out the breath that I didn't know that I was holding. I needed to get out of this internship as quickly as possible. Anytime she shows up, she looks at me like she's trying to figure me out. She's never made any type of statement or hinted that she knew my secret, but it unsettled me. With Jaehyun being home, it was hard to do long stakeouts and do recon on the warehouse location. That was the only place I could realistically get to. Even if I was to do recon, it wouldn't be helpful because who would be there. Kenji hadn't gotten a call for a delivery yet, so I was forced to wait.

"She's going to be more down our throats than ever before. It's going to be a nightmare. Did you choose to extend your internship into the summer, Choi?" Kim asked as he collected the clipboards.

"I haven't decided yet. I have a few more weeks to decide. I might." I answered. I was hoping that I would have had more system access but Chae never officially brought me into the fold with Arsyn's crew, so my credentials wouldn't work in the systems. Whenever I worked, I had to use Kim's credentials. So if I didn't have anything within the next few weeks, I'd have to extend the internship, in hopes that I would get another lead to the Jopok. Using the downloaded spyware was too risky because it would lead trackers to the building complex and I know she's on high alert right now. I would have to lay low and wait for another opportunity to present itself. I didn't necessarily like it, but it was the safest and smartest move to make.

"Having you around has been fun. I like working with you. You're a good kid. Inquisitive and analytic. You have potential." Kim complimented me. I smirked and grabbed my stuff.

"Don't tell me you've gone soft, old man. What happened to you hating all the interns?" I joked.

"You're the only exception. Consider yourself lucky."

"Sure, Kim. I'll see you later."

"Headed out early? What's the rush?" he asked curiously.

"Meeting my boyfriend's mom for the first time. We're going to dinner. I need to get ready." I replied. The excitement brought a warm smile to my face.

"Finally? That's good. Well you made her wait long enough. Run along." He waved me off with a nonchalant goodbye and I laughed as I walked out of the back exit to the garage.

"Jae! Come here!" I yelled frantically as I stood in my bedroom and stared at the four outfits that were on the mannequins. I heard his footsteps pound on the floor as he raced to my room.

"What's going on?!" he exclaimed in concern. He stood at the entrance of my room and stared at me.

"Which one?" I gestured to the outfits. His shoulders dropped.

"Really, Ae Ri? I thought something was wrong! Why'd you scream like that?" He leaned against the wall and put a hand over his chest in relief.

"Something is wrong. I need help choosing. So, help me." I complained while gesturing again. The first mannequin showed off the spaghetti strap burgundy silk mini dress. It was plain but from what Jiwoo said plain can be good for a first impression. The second mannequin showed a bright red pants set, with flare pants and a red wrap shirt tied in a bow on the side. It revealed a lot of skin on top. So I wasn't too sure about it, but Haeun said that it looked good. Nari chose a more sensible outfit, a white long sleeved V-cut silk dress with a wrap design and a bow tied in the front. The last outfit was a black off shoulder midi dress with a lace overlay.

"Probably no pants. It's still warm out and I have another place, you can wear that. Hm, wear that burgundy dress. It's one of my favorites and you always wear the nicest accessories with it." he suggested. I turned to the dress and pulled it off of the mannequin and put it on. He helped me zip the back up and placed a gentle kiss on my shoulder.

"You might want to hurry. It's almost seven right now." I gasped and looked at him.

"Why didn't you say anything, Jaehyun!"

223

"I didn't want to disturb you. You were taking a lot of time to get ready and you looked so peaceful. It was cute." He grinned and quickly ran out of the room before I could throw something at him.

"Come back here! Help me! Grab me some shoes! Make yourself useful!" I grabbed a pair of dangling gold earrings and a matching gold necklace. Jaehyun's loud laughter filled the room as he entered and went over to my closet. I removed the rollers out of my hair and let the curls fall. I admired the length of my hair. I usually kept it short to my shoulders, but it had been growing a lot and it reached past my shoulders now. I kept the cappuccino brown color still. It had really grown on me.

"These are so cool, Ae Ri! Here, wear these! The little wraps are snakes. Women's shoes are creative." He excitedly showed me the pair of burgundy Rene Caovilla stiletto sandals. I forgot I had those.

"I haven't seen those in a while. Those actually will look nice with this." I agreed. He helped me slide the shoes on and he looked up at me and smiled.

"You look beautiful, princess."

"Thank you. You look handsome. This is a good look. You did well, sweetheart." I looked in the mirror and turned around once. Jaehyun had gotten really good at helping me get dressed and choosing pieces for me. I found it endearing because it was a testament to how close we had gotten. As I touched up my lipstick, I noticed he was fully dressed. He wore a dark blue long sleeved button up and tan slacks. He recently got a haircut so he was back to his shorter length. He had a crew cut with a side part and I was a fan of it. I did miss his longer hair but he insisted on the cut, so I had to support it. I still felt like the entertainment industry missed out on him. He was gorgeous and in some weird way he got prettier day by day.

"I like the dark blue and tan combo. You look handsome. You really should have been an actor or model." I complimented him. I kissed the corner of his mouth lightly and grinned.

"Is this going to be distracting for you? We're going to dinner with my mom. You need to behave." he smirked as he kissed my nose in response.

"This is why you don't get compliments. They inflate your ego." I grabbed my matching purse and walked past him out of the room. He laughed obnoxiously and followed.

"You're fun to tease, what can I say? You always make it easy."

The entire car ride I could feel my stomach twist into knots. Anxiety filled my chest and I spent the entire car ride playing with the edge of my dress. I have been in shoot outs and surrounded by men three times my size trying to kill me. I was more nervous now than I ever had been back then. Jaehyun spent the ride reassuring me and keeping me calm. We pulled into the parking lot and I froze for a moment. I'm meeting my boyfriend's mother. That was a sentence that I never thought I would say. Getting to this point with him was one thing but this felt like something else entirely. This felt like I was taking another step into something I didn't understand. From what people have said about mothers they tend to know everything. They can see what other people can't see. What would she see if she looked at me? I feared the possibilities.

"Hey… Stop that. You will do great, Ae Ri. My mom's excited to meet you. She will love you." Jaehyun encouraged me. I looked up at him and smiled softly. He believed in me and he believed in this. The excitement in his eyes was evident. I had no choice but to believe him.

We followed the hostess down the hall to our private room that his mother reserved. The host opened the door and bowed to us and left us. Sitting at the round table was a woman with waist long bone straight black hair. She was slender and wore a white pantsuit with a brand name stiletto heel. Her diamond earrings dangled and caught the light every so often. Her aura radiated power. She sat straight up and she was looking down at her phone texting. "Mom, we're here." Jaehyun hummed playfully. The woman looked up and a wide beautiful smile graced her face. She didn't look a day over thirty at the latest. Her skin was flawless and her features were sharp. She had a beauty mark under her right eye and full lips. That was why Jaehyun was so damn pretty. He looked like his mother. Just like her. Her light brown eyes held maturity and warmth.

She stood up to hug him. She was much shorter than her son and it was sort of adorable. Jaehyun was a giant. "There's my baby boy." she teased as he rolled his eyes. She giggled brightly as she pulled away and looked at him. I stood behind him and watched them interact. The familiar feeling of envy washed over me and I looked down at my nails. I didn't want to interrupt their moment.

"Not in front of my girlfriend. Mom, this is Choi Ae Ri. This is my mother Park Iseul." he introduced as he gestured to me with a proud smile. It took me a moment to remember that Korean women didn't take their husband's last names like they did in Japan. I bowed respectfully and Iseul scoffed.

"Stop the formalities. Come here! Give me a hug!" she exclaimed as she pulled me in for a hug. I stood there stunned for a moment before I embraced her back. She smelt like vanilla and she was warm. When she felt me hug her back, I felt her squeeze me tighter. It was intentional. She squeezed me, almost like she was trying to pull me together. All of my nerves and uneasiness just washed away when she hugged me. Is this what mother's hugs felt like? I only felt safe in Jaehyun's arms but this was a close second. I was fighting back tears and I felt like the craziest person because I just met her and I was almost in tears.

She pulled away too soon and gave me the brightest smile. "You're absolutely beautiful. Jaehyun, you got lucky. I used to tell him, he'd never find someone prettier than him. I was wrong apparently." she giggled.

"Thank you so much. You're beautiful as well. He gets his looks from you. You guys are twins." I complimented her genuinely. When they stood side by side, they looked like twins.

"Oh, stop it. Come sit. Please. I ordered Dom Perignon. Are you a fan, Ae Ri?" I nodded and we followed her. He pulled out our chairs like the gentleman he was and his mother smiled proudly. "He turned into a perfect gentleman. I'm so proud." The pride and joy radiated off of her. It tugged at my heart strings. Would my mother look at me like that if she was alive? The endless possibilities ran through my mind as I responded to her.

"He is a good man. The best one I've ever met. You did an amazing job."

"Thank you. Jaehyun tells me you guys go to school together? What do you study?" Her attention turned fully to me. She held eye contact with

226

me and she had that same sparkle in her eyes that Jaehyun did. It was disarming. I smiled softly in response.

"Law. I do an internship at the Seoul Metropolitan Police Agency." I told her.

"Oh my god. You want to be a police officer?" She looked shocked.

"No ma'am. I want to practice law. I just took it for an in depth look at the system."

"Oh good. I was going to tell you that you were too pretty for that." his mother laughed and shook her head.

"That's not nice, mom. There are pretty police officers I'm sure." Jaehyun commented as he sat down in the empty seat.

"I doubt that but whatever you say, son. Well, I'm curious now. Because I heard you were a good interior decorator and you helped run your family's business. Why law?" She was a curious one.

"Interior decorating is just something I like. I guess it's a hobby even though I never studied it. I decorate my homes and offices. I'll help do Jae's soon. I don't want to spend my entire life under my father. I want my independence, so I chose school and law by myself." The lie was easy to tell now.

"Ah, I understand." Iseul nodded. A knowing look flashed in her eyes and I appreciated the fact that she would let it go.

"What kind of business does your family do?" She changed the subject quickly.

"International business. It's based in Japan. International trade, some shipping." I answered. She nodded impressed.

"All of that and school, I'm impressed. You sound extremely busy. Any siblings?" I shook my head in response.

"Just me and my father."

"That must be lonely. I come from a big family. My grandmother made me promise that I would never have just one child. So when I had my first born Areum, it was a certainty that she'd had a little sibling. And then came Daehyun and then Jaehyun." Iseul smiled brightly as she talked about her children. I could only shrug in response and chuckle lightly.

"It has its advantages. Never had to share my things. So that was fun." I joked. I ignored the shot of pain that shot through my heart. Maybe if I had siblings, I wouldn't have been so lonely but maybe it was a blessing in disguise. No one else was scarred by the shit Han pulled. I took a sip of my drink as the waiter came in and he took our orders for appetizers.

Once the waiter left, Iseul started the conversation back up. "So how did you all meet? And how long have you been dating? I saw Mae two weeks ago and she said she saw you all together months ago." she said as raised an eyebrow and crossed her arms. Jaehyun nearly choked on his drink. I looked over at him and chuckled.

"We met at the airport in Japan. We started talking before the plane boarded and once we landed, I took her to Mae's. She just happened to be there that night, mom. We have spent a lot of time together. The rest is history." he recovered quickly and smiled warmly.

"We had a nice time and then suddenly I couldn't get rid of him. He's my little nuisance now." I teased him. He rolled his eyes and his mother laughed loudly.

"Oh, he was always clingy. It's his charm. I remember when he was a baby-" Iseul started.

"Mom! Let's not start with the baby stories." he interrupted with a pleading voice.

"That explains a lot. Noted." I commented and I turned to wink at him. He blushed slightly and took a sip of his drink.

Iseul looked between us and a wide grin spread across her face.

"Oh you two look so cute together. Jaehyunnie tells me all the time about how he couldn't see his life without you. Once you graduate, will you be staying in Korea?" she asked hopefully. It was my turn to almost choke on my drink. The entire thing threw me off.

"He says that about me? Really?" I looked over at him and his face blushed brighter. I couldn't contain the warmth that filled my chest.

"Oh yes! All the time! He's gone so far as to look at private houses-"

"Mom! Please! Not right now!" Jaehyun whined as he covered his face. He was blushing so hard that his ears were bright red. I tilted my head in confusion and shock. Private houses for...us? The warmth spread to the bottom of my feet and to the top of my head. He really saw a future with me. I believed Jaehyun when he said it, but there was a part of me that still doubted. Hearing his mother reinforce the things he's said to me and tell me that he's been looking at houses for us in the future, it silenced any doubt.

"If Korea is where he is, then so will I. If it's in America or Japan, I'll be there." I declared as I reached over and held his hand under the table. I squeezed it and he returned the action as he held it up to kiss as he looked me in the eyes. The emotions in his eyes burned bright and I could only blush in response.

"Wherever you want to go. I'm there. Why settle for one place when you have money?" he added.

"Real estate overseas is a good investment. We have property all over the world. Money is the key to having the world at your fingertips." Iseul smirked as she raised her glass for a toast. She was right. We toasted her in agreement. I figured it was a good time to ask questions to get to know her, since she seemed to like me.

"If I may ask... Are you also active in the business?" I was curious to know based on her statement. She came off as a woman who liked to live a privileged life and she didn't mind working for it.

"I am, yes. I actually handle expansion opportunities for the business. However, I studied economics and real estate. Commercial real estate is what I love, but I do private real estate too. When I met my husband, I took an interest in business so I went to school for it. It's a funny story because he wasn't my husband yet, he was just a kid I knew from school. He was running some little businesses then. We got close. Before I knew it, we were attached at the hip. We built empires together." she explained.

The blinding smile that graced her face showed that she was genuinely happy. She loved her husband and her family. The envy burned brighter in my heart. I felt bad for feeling so envious because it wasn't his intention with this. Jaehyun was just trying to do something to help me. He thought it would make me feel better. It just wasn't happening right now. She wasn't my mother. Iseul was kind and inviting. There was nothing wrong with her. She was wonderful. Maybe she and my mother would've been friends. From what I saw of my mom, she gave off the same aura. I just would never know for myself. A small smile appeared on my face hearing the expression that Jaehyun had used before. It was sweet.

"So that's where the empire thing comes from. He says that all the time." I commented. She looked at him shocked.

"Mom has a way with words. Besides the family business, she's into poetry and shit like that." Jaehyun chuckled as she shrugged and looked down at the menu. She slapped his shoulder.

"Language, Jaehyun. But yes. I'm the artsy one in the family. Everyone is all business. Such a shame really. Trying to get them to attend an opera performance is like pulling teeth." Iseul rolled her eyes and took a sip of her drink.

"It's not fun, mom. I'm sorry. It's not for us." Jaehyun groaned as he shook his head. I laughed and watched them interact. I tried to keep my expression neutral as visions of me and my mother sitting and talking and joking around with each other like that. Visions of my mother sitting at the table and how she would possibly interact with them played in my mind. A deep sadness sat heavy in my heart as it fully hit me that Jaehyun would never meet my family. I would be forever known as that poor, sad girl with no family. I internally sighed at the pity that would come with it. I felt cheated. I had no one. I was always going to wonder if my mother would have liked Jaehyun. All of these things that I was going to experience with Jaehyun, she wasn't going to see it. That realization rocked me to my core and it stung. I kept my face neutral as I tried to fight back the tears that threatened to fill my eyes. Not right now.

"Ae Ri. Did you hear me sweetie?" Iseul asked as she rested a hand on my shoulder. I came back to reality and smiled at her.

"I'm sorry. I zoned out for a moment. Daydreaming again." I noticed the waiter standing next to her looking at me.

"Are the courses I ordered okay?" she repeated softly. I looked down at the menu and nodded.

"Oh of course, I trust your judgment. I've never been here. It's fine." I agreed as I gave a warm smile to get them off my back. The waiter nodded and collected the menus and thanked us before he left.

"So, Ae Ri. Tell me about yourself. I've talked enough. What is something that I should know about you?" she asked as she folded her hands under her chin and looked at me. I hummed in thought. What is there to tell? My life was fucked up. I was pretty fucked up. I guess a semi honest and transparent answer would suffice.

"I'm new to all of this. But I'm trying and learning. I raised myself pretty much after my mother passed. My father was out running the business. He threw himself into work and I was left behind. But despite that, I am going to be the best I can be for Jaehyun. He's safe with me." I promised her. She chuckled a little.

"I don't doubt that at all. But it didn't have to be about Jaehyun. What makes you, you?" she tried again. I hummed in thought for a moment.

"Hm… My drive. My loyalty. I'm the only woman that reached a status inside the business. And I didn't get it by being his daughter, trust me. I worked my ass off for it. I'm rebellious and confident. I'm opinionated. It makes me who I am. A diamond in the rough almost." I told her more confidently. She smirked lightly and her eyes took on a more mischievous glint.

"That felt more genuine. I like it. Women in our family take up space. We are seen and heard. We aren't perfect but we are authentic. I just wanted to see if you were that. I accept." Iseul folded her arms across her chest and she looked over at Jaehyun and nodded in approval.

"Oh don't let the quiet nature fool you, mom. She'll fit in just fine." Jaehyun smiled proudly and looked over at me. He held my hand under the table and leaned over to kiss the side of my temple. The soft and innocent look returned to her eyes and a warm smile returned. The quick change almost gave me whiplash trying to keep up. I kept my expression calm and looked over at Jaehyun and shook his head. *She does that sometimes. Keeps you on your toes,* he mouthed. Before I could press the issue further, the waiter came in with a cart with our food on it.

~Chapter 24~

"Ae Ri! Jaehyun! You guys finally decided to finally show up! Where have you been?" Miyeon exclaimed as she ran up to us as soon as we entered the mansion. Miyeon was having another party to celebrate the end of the semester and the start of summer, even though the semester was over in June and we were already one month into summer. This was a common thing I had discovered. She spent the summers partying and blowing through money. It wasn't too different than during the semester honestly, but that's none of my business. Her hair was dyed black, and she looked different. I had only seen her as blonde. She hugged us tightly and stepped back examining us.

"You got a tan. Where have you guys been?" she questioned as she put her hands on her hips.

"Hawaii. The Maldives. Dubai. We've been traveling since the semester ended. We got back a few days ago." Jaehyun shrugged. He looked over at me and I grinned.

Classes ended and Jaehyun had the idea to travel and take an extended vacation to unwind from the stress of the semester. He didn't want to take summer classes and I decided to not extend the internship because I wasn't getting anything from it. Chae retired because his injuries were too severe, and the doctors couldn't clear him. So, I would never get access to the police systems for myself. Using the spyware was way too risky and I got rid of the flash drive to be safe. I still had contact with Kenji but his crew hadn't been used by the Jopok in months so I was at a standstill with the assignment, so I figured maybe I should take a break too. I never took a vacation and Jaehyun being Jaehyun, put together a month and a half long vacation. We traveled to places that I had never been to and we bonded. It was worth it.

To be away from everything and everybody was the best thing. I could never get away and do whatever I wanted. The voices in my head were silent for the longest time and I didn't feel so anxious. I didn't have a single nightmare the entire time we were gone. I felt like a new person. From what I was discovering and learning about these conditions, I knew they didn't go away that easily but for the moment it was nice to just be at peace in my own head. I didn't have that luxury normally. It was an adventure everyday with him. Miyeon's jaw dropped.

"No way! You guys decided to just live it up, huh? Did you have fun?" she asked excitedly, pulling us into the house. The house was packed but there was still plenty of room to move around comfortably. The place was massive. She led us into the kitchen and offered us both a beer. Looking out of the glass door in the kitchen, I saw a DJ set up outside as far away from the pool and hot tub as possible. People were relaxing on pool floats or sitting on the edge of the pool and talking. The pool had to be the length of a soccer field. I never saw Miyeon's house in the daytime and it was even more impressive in the daytime than at night.

"It was relaxing." I answered for us both.

"Good. You both look really good. You guys don't look so uptight. It's an improvement!" she joked. I rolled my eyes and Jaehyun chuckled.

"We did look stressed. Pictures tell a lot of stories, princess." Jaehyun agreed.

"Enjoy yourselves, okay. We got all night to enjoy the weather and plenty of drinks. Here's to a great summer, friends." We toasted her and downed the beers she gave us. It was a party so we may as well have fun.

My phone ringing repeatedly roused me from my sleep. I reached over and grabbed it, cutting the sound off and checking the caller ID. Kenji's name appeared and I groaned sitting up. Jaehyun was fast asleep. He got kind of drunk at the party, so we called it a night at midnight and came home to crash. It was 3:45 am and Kenji was calling this late. He had a reason to be calling. I checked on Jaehyun again and got up and went outside onto the balcony. I answered groggily, fighting off the dizziness and nausea. "Saiko Komon, I have something to tell you! I just finished the

234

delivery for the Jopok and Arsyn was there!" he exclaimed. I winced at him yelling in my ear.

"Stop yelling. I can hear you. What did you get?" I hissed.

"Sorry, ma'am. I heard her on the phone talking to someone else. They'll be attending the Nam Industries end of the quarter party. All of the children and her father and his wife." All of the dizziness and nausea went away in a second. I was sober in a matter of two seconds. I was silent. I couldn't speak, I couldn't think. I felt numb.

Part of the reason we came home in the beginning of July was so that he could get ready to start making the preparations for the event. They usually had the party the third or fourth week in July. The parties were a big deal for the company, it was to celebrate the achievements of the company and thank their partners, investors, staff and employees. They also used it as a way to gain new partners and investors. It wasn't unheard of in this world for mafia members to attend big business parties like that. It was just as much for them as it was the company. I attended my fair share of the parties to foster a business relationship or to renegotiate business terms. I've also attended them to complete assassination assignments. My mind was racing and I vaguely heard Kenji speak.

"Saiko Komon, did you hear me?" he asked quietly. I hung up on him. I sighed heavily and sank down onto the ground.

My only chance to kill the Jopok comes right after I went on a relaxing vacation, cleared my mind and when I will be meeting my boyfriend's family on the same night. Just my luck right? I finally got the courage to say yes to meeting the rest of his family after spending time with his mother and now I was going to have to jump through hoops to complete the assignment. It sent chills down my spine as I realized that Jaehyun would be in harm's way. There was no way I wouldn't be recognized. The only saving grace I got at the police station was my police hat. I could hide behind it. In public, I didn't have that luxury. Anxiety rushed through me as I realized the other daunting reality. Jaehyun would know I wasn't normal. This entire double life that I was leading would be exposed.

My chest tightened and my stomach twisted. I felt nauseous. Arsyn would see me and she would immediately go after Jaehyun once she saw us together. She'd immediately know that he was my weakness. Determination and possessiveness rushed through me as I tightened my grip on my phone. Jaehyun had to be protected no matter what the cost was. If it meant blowing my cover then so be it. Arsyn had to die first. The conviction hit me hard but the fear hit harder. I started to think the day would never come when I would find the Jopok because of all the roadblocks along the way. I almost forgot about the entire thing while I was on vacation. I was becoming content with living this life with Jaehyun. I should've known it was going to go up in flames. I didn't get happy endings. What would change now? I felt my heartbreak at the thought of Jaehyun finding out that I wasn't who I said I was. What if he hated me because he loved someone who wasn't real? Would he believe me if I told him that my emotions and stories were real? Why would he? I would rather lose everything and have nothing than be without Jaehyun. My pride be damned. Jaehyun was more important to me. An even worse thought crossed my mind, what if Jaehyun was seriously hurt or killed? The thought made me hyperventilate. I felt my palms get sweaty and my hands trembled.

"Okay, okay. Focus Rose. We're built for this. This is what we're trained for." I whispered to myself. I did train for this but I didn't feel so confident. I was a realist. This wasn't going to be painless. I was going to get hurt. Either physically or emotionally. Any idea that I tried to come up with to try to keep my identity a secret and complete the assignment, it didn't make logical sense. I would have to get comfortable with the idea of revealing who I was in order to keep him safe. Maybe if I explained to him why I had to lie, he could understand that. Explain to him how this wasn't a choice I made on my own. He could understand that. I didn't lie to him about any of that. The problem would come if he asked me to leave the lifestyle behind. I couldn't say that with confidence. How was I supposed to do anything else? What could I do? Even if I opened a legitimate business with him, it'd take years to actually get set up and take off. What was I supposed to do with myself all that time?

I don't think I could just sit around all day. I had to do something. Having him take care of me wasn't an option. I couldn't let him do that. He said that he appreciated me because I didn't want him for his money.

Leaving the lifestyle would mean I would have no income. I couldn't live that way. He would get tired of taking care of me. I would lose so much more by leaving the lifestyle. It would be a slower loss and that would hurt significantly more. I groaned loudly and looked at Jaehyun's sleeping form on the bed. Sometimes I wondered if all of this was worth it. I was avenging my mother's death and that had to be done. It was more than them taking her away from me, it was all of the possibilities that they took away from me. How different could my life have been if she was alive and there to raise me. How different would Han be? Would I hate him just the same?

As I sat in my thoughts, I didn't notice that the door opened. I looked up and Jaehyun's sleepy form blinked at me. "Why are you outside?" he yawned. I smiled softly at him as he rubbed his eyes. His hair was messy and his cheeks were still red from the alcohol.

"I'm thinking. What are you doing awake? You look like a child standing in the doorway of their parents' room." I replied as I looked up at him. He squinted at me and rolled his eyes.

"Haha. Very funny. You were nowhere to be found. So I came looking for you." He walked outside and came to sit beside me. I leaned my head on his shoulder and he kissed the top of my head. He was home for me.

"What are you thinking about? What's got you worried? We just got back from vacation." he asked, concerned.

"Don't worry about it. I'm fine."

"That's not how this works, you know that."

"I am fine, really…." I paused for a moment and took a breath. He sat in silence with me and waited for me to finish.

"You know you're the most important thing to me, right?" I continued. He chuckled softly and nodded.

"I don't want to lose you. I couldn't bear the thought of losing you. You've changed my life and I never really thanked you for that. You put up with a lot dealing with me and my issues. I know it's been an adjustment for you and you've been patient and you still are. So, I thank you for that.

It means the world to me." I told him as I looked up at him. He looked down at me and gave me a bright smile.

"Everything's worth it whenever I get to hear you express your feelings. I'll always be right here, princess." he promised as he kissed my nose. I always felt soft when he did that. It felt like all of my problems melted away with a simple kiss. If I was honest, I still didn't understand how we got here but I wouldn't change it for the world. I had to figure out a way to keep my identity a secret. I didn't want to run the risk of losing him. There had to be a way. I've gotten out of life threatening situations before, this was no different. Code. I could call Code. It was a perfect idea, but I wasn't too keen on it. I know he wouldn't need an explanation or anything. He would do it because I asked. I just didn't want any help on this for selfish reasons. But it was an idea. I let the excitement and relief show on my face and he laughed loudly. "What are you thinking about? You look like you just found the answer to world hunger. What're you so relieved about?" Jaehyun asked.

"You. I just came to a realization that I'd risk everything for you. If it came down to it." I answered. He raised an eyebrow.

"Where did that come from?" I wasn't supposed to say that out loud. I recovered quickly though.

"Honestly, I was thinking about my dad. Our last conversation wasn't a good one. Words were exchanged. That's all I'm gonna say. I'm fine." It wasn't technically a lie. The last conversation Han and I had was ugly. We hadn't spoken in almost a month or so and he was furious that I didn't have a death to report. I was five months into my assignment and it wasn't completed. The longest time I had been away on any assignment ever. It was the same manipulation tactics, the same slip ups, where he proved that this mission was about him and not me. I called him a selfish bastard and told him it was his fault that my mother was dead. He was weak. I still remember the deafening silence on his end. I remembered the labored breathing on my end. I remember the coldness of his tone as he told me to contact him when the assignment was completed and hung up. I listened to the beeping of the phone for a long time after that. There was no turning back at that point. The damage was done. The line in the sand had been drawn.

"Okay, okay. I'll drop it. But come to bed. It's late. I would like to get some sleep before I go back to the office. I can't sleep without my pillow." Jaehyun relented and he winked at me. I giggled and nodded and allowed him to help me up.

"You're the biggest baby I have ever met, you know that right?" I teased as I followed him back inside.

"You love me regardless." He grinned and wrapped his arms around me tightly and laid his head on my shoulder. He always reminded me of a koala when he did that. I found it adorable. It was one of my favorite things in the world about him. It reinforced the entire thing for me. I had to do this mission. If I didn't go through with it, I could run the risk of Arsyn trying to find me. And she could find Jaehyun. It was bigger than my mother. It was bigger than vengeance. It was about the future that I could have with him. I lost enough. I had no choice but to call Code. It was going to give me the best chance of success. I felt more confident about the situation, so I decided to get some sleep. I had to start training again. It had been a while since I had seen combat. I didn't lose it, I just needed to sharpen up. Arsyn had been working for months. I've been resting. I let my eyes close and I drifted off.

I found myself in a familiar living room where everything was white. The walls, the couch, the rug on the ground, the white blazer and pants I wore. The couch was facing towards the front door and I was in the back of the room. I looked around the room and my mother was standing at the window beside the couch. My mother's long brown hair was put in a tight bun and she was wearing a similar outfit to mine. I approached her and stood next to her. She remained silent. She was looking out the window. Her expression looked concerned. I looked out the window and I saw Jaehyun standing outside and he was facing away from the window. He was dressed in a black sweater and cargo pants and black combat boots. I followed his line of sight to a high gate made of red brick and there were black metallic rods that opened up to let cars in. The window looked at the brick, it was strategically placed where no one could see inside the house. But we could see a part of the gate and the street was visible from my point of view. I could see part of a black SUV in front of the gate.

My eyes widened as I started to panic. That was one of the SUVs the Yamaguchi used. I rushed outside and ran around the side of the house. As I approached Jaehyun, I noticed that he had a gun tucked in the waistband of his pants in the back. I ran forward to stand next to Jaehyun. He had the same concerned look. I was in a better position to see more details on the SUV. I noticed that some paint was messed up on the passenger door. There were spots of red paint all over the door. My heart started racing and adrenaline started to rush through me. That was a car I used back in Japan. It was damaged from an assignment Code and I went on a year ago. Our escape wasn't so clean and painless, we scratched the passenger door on a building trying to evade a side sweep from the pursuing cars. Why was it parked outside?

There was a heavy suffocating feeling in the air. It felt like time stood still as we waited for something to happen. The sound of the car door opening sent my body into an automatic response. I grabbed the gun from his back pocket and pushed him to the ground and positioned myself in front of him. I aimed the gun and took a breath to steady my hand. I was shaking in fear and anxiety trying to figure out what was happening. The door opened fully to reveal my face looking at me through the gate. With fiery red hair and darkness swimming in the eyes, she let an evil grin spread across her face. She stepped out of the car dressed in a red blazer and pants. She had the same bloody red knife and I fired once. Twice. Three times. The satisfying thud of the body hitting the ground relieved me. Until I heard another car door open. Then another. And another.

In seconds, there were fifteen doppelgangers of me standing outside of the gate and smirking at me. I looked down at Jaehyun and back at my mother and she held the two babies in each arm and a diaper bag was on her shoulder. Jaehyun's eyes followed mine. "Go. Run. I'll take care of this." I demanded. He shook his head quickly.

"I'm staying with you. We'll do this together." he disagreed. I jumped slightly when they started shaking the gate trying to get in. I looked back at him frantically.

"Please! Go! Take mom and get out of here! I'll cover you! I'll meet up with you!" I yelled. The shaking of the gate got louder and louder and the metal groaned under the force. Tears lined my eyes as I looked back towards the gate and saw that it wouldn't hold. I turned back to Jaehyun and he looked conflicted.

"Please, go… Protect them… I-I love you…" I begged. He looked at me wide eyed and tears filled his eyes and he nodded.

"I love you too. Come home… We need you." he said through his tears and he stood up quickly and kissed me hard.

He pulled away and stroked my cheek before he took off around the corner and entered the house. I watched him grab my mother and one of the babies and talk to her. They gave one last look at me and I nodded once telling them to go. They ran from the window and I let the tears fall as I watched them leave. My heart felt like it was tearing into a million pieces. I turned to the gate and watched as it gave way and the small army breach. It looked like they had doubled in numbers from when I first saw them. I aimed the gun and started to fire as they started to filter in. It felt like the more I shot down, the more that appeared. I didn't have enough bullets, I was going to be surrounded soon and I'd have to fight my way out. Tears streamed down my face faster as the realization hit like a ton of bricks. I didn't stand a chance. Not with a hundred of me that I was going up against. I kept firing until I heard the dreaded click signifying it was empty. I dropped the gun and sank to my knees as they all ran towards me with their knives raised. The first two reached me and swung at me…

"Ae Ri! Wake up!" Jaehyun yelled. I woke up screaming as I looked around the room. I panted and put my head in my hands and Jaehyun wrapped his arms around me and rubbed my back. I took deep breaths to ease my racing heart and fight off the terror that ran through me.

"What the hell were you dreaming about? I tried to listen to what you were saying, but I couldn't tell." I looked up at him and he was staring at me with a worried look. I shook my head and laid my head on his shoulder.

"It was nothing. Just a nightmare. I'm fine." I told him. He looked at me with a raised eyebrow. We stared at each other for a moment, communicating silently. He sighed after a few moments.

"Fine, Ae Ri. Whenever you're ready to talk I'm here. Are you okay though? Want some water?" he offered. I nodded in response and he leaned down and kissed my temple and he stood up to go to the kitchen. I sighed deeply and looked around the room. Why was I always the bad guy in my dreams? I'm sure if I told them to Jaehyun he'd say there was some deeper meaning to it that I needed to figure out. Probably would bring up therapy again. If only he knew how crazy that would be.

He reappeared in the room with a glass of water and handed it to me as he sat beside me again. "Hey, I know we've had this conversation before. But I'm gonna bring it up again. Have you considered therapy? You have pretty frequent nightmares and I really think you should consider therapy. This isn't healthy." he suggested. I fought the urge to roll my eyes. I knew it was coming. I really did appreciate that he cared that much about me and how I was. It just wasn't something that was for me.

"I told you therapy's not for me. I'm not crazy." At least. Not really.

"Okay one, you're not crazy if you get therapy. It's perfectly healthy. However, my second point, you absolutely are. But for completely different reasons." he teased. I punched his shoulder in response and he laughed loudly.

"That doesn't help your case, you know? Judging me." I told him.

"The therapist wouldn't judge you. They listen and give advice. Some can actually diagnose and treat. Maybe a therapist can help you figure out why you're so attached to a life that you hate and want to leave, but you won't." I looked over at him confused and he grinned. What the hell was that? The statement left me speechless because he wasn't wrong. I had never considered it or put it into words like that. I couldn't let him know he was right.

"That sounded like a low blow." I said as I rolled my eyes playfully.

"It wasn't. Not necessarily. Just an observation from over time. It's clear as glass that you hate your dad for the shit he's done to you, but you won't leave the company. You still have an open line of communication with him. That attachment is there and you won't fully heal until that's severed. It's something I learned a while ago. Sometimes severed ties are necessary for your growth. A therapist is a good investment. Think about it." he grinned as he stood up and walked into the bathroom.

The truth of his words stunned me for a moment. I hated how he could see through me sometimes. I had to remember that he didn't understand why it wasn't that easy. I couldn't just leave like that. Han wasn't going to accept that. I knew too much, he'd rather have me killed. He's said it before. Dying before I handled the unfinished business between us was not an option. I was going to get my revenge. As much as I hated it, I was stuck with Han. A sinking feeling appeared in my stomach and I frowned deeply. I stood up and walked into the kitchen and looked at the clock on the wall. Fifteen minutes to nine. I decided to put on some coffee for Jaehyun so that he could have it as he walked out the door. As I waited for the coffee, I took out my phone and started scrolling through websites looking for an evening gown for the party. Jaehyun said I could pick the color. I had to choose red because that was the color I always wore during assassination assignments. It was fitting for the occasion.

My thoughts were interrupted by Jaehyun entering the kitchen and I looked up at him. He was dressed in a nice collared shirt and a pair of slacks. I looked him over once and he grinned. "It's rude to stare, you know?" I rolled my eyes and gestured to the coffee.

"Just for that, get your own coffee. When's your meeting?"

"In thirty minutes. I should be back early today. Want to do something with our friends later on? Seunghyun and Nari say they have to tell us something." Jaehyun remembered as he put a lid on his coffee cup and turned to me.

"Yeah, that's fine. I'll reach out and see what the plans are." I agreed.

"Stay out of trouble. I'll see you in a little bit." He leaned down and kissed me quickly and saluted me playfully. I smiled softly and walked out to the balcony to call Code.

The sleep was evident in his voice. "B-Boss… Y-You're calling… It's early." he answered. I heard him get up and start moving around the room.

"I need something. The Saturday after next, could you get to Korea?" I inquired.

"Product's moving in. I have a few deals and purchases that I have to do. Why? What's going on?" I checked my watch and cursed under my breath. The middle of the month was when shipments came in and went out. Arms, drugs, occasionally humans if Han got his way. I shivered at the memory.

"I found a place where the Jopok will all be in one place. I could use an extra hand." I said calmly. I was freaking out inside. My hand tapped against the railing gently. Money was more important. That couldn't be postponed.

"I can send one of the elites. They're on standby. Just came back from an assignment. I got Ace, Danny and Yong ready to go. You can get some help." he yawned as I heard him flipping through papers.

I completely forgot the elite soldiers. When I first took my position, Han gifted me eight specialty trained foot soldiers. They were almost as good as me. Excellent marksmanship, fearless and trained in hand to hand combat. Ace was the one I was most familiar with because he worked with Code and I on an assignment a while ago. He was a little better than the other two. "I want Ace. Give him a heads up he got a mission. I'll call him." I decided.

"Texting him now. Let me know when you're ready for the number." Code replied obediently. I hummed in acknowledgement and typed in the number as he read it out. I sighed out loud as I saved his number in my phone.

"Are you okay, boss?" he asked suddenly. I looked at the phone in confusion.

"What do you mean?"

"I thought you'd be more excited about this. You don't sound excited." I paused for a moment, debating on what to say. The words sat on the tip of my tongue about the worse case scenario.

"It's not that. I've got an idea and it's risky. It could maybe get me killed one day." I told him.

244

"When do you not tell me your risky ideas? We do this all the time." Code reassured me.

I internally sighed. He didn't understand the gravity of what I was about to say. "I want to take over the Jopok. Combine them with us and overthrow Han." I told him. The silence was loud.

"A coupe?" Code simplified breathlessly. I hummed in acknowledgement. He didn't immediately shoot down the idea or disagree, so he found it intriguing.

"I figured things were getting worse with Han. He kept asking if I heard from you. I told him no. I always knew Han would fuck up with you…" He mumbled the last part under his breath.

"I wouldn't have the support of any other Yamaguchi clans and the Jopok would give me the numbers needed for a coupe. And they're good. So the soldiers must be good too. Once I find the leadership and eliminate them, I may need help getting them in line."

"Sounds like a good idea. It may actually work. It'll take time but it may work. The end of an era to let the rose grow. Poetic. I'm by your side every step of the way." Code promised. I slightly smirked. He was a loyal soldier and I appreciated that.

"A loyal soldier as always. I'll be based in Korea and come to Japan when needed. You make sure things run smoothly over there." An evil grin crossed my face as the visions flashed in front of my eyes. It was perfect.

"Ah, you took my advice and started to live a little now you like it over there. Don't wanna come back. Okay, we can work it like that." he chuckled. I rolled my eyes.

"I'll keep you updated." I said plainly and hung up the phone. I called Ace and he answered on the first ring.

"This is Ace." the smooth tenor voice on the other end answered.

"It's me." I replied.

"Yes ma'am. Code told me I had a mission." He was proper and all business. I liked that.

"You're assisting me with an assignment to eliminate the Jopok head family. I'm sending you the profiles now. Be aware Arsyn now has cherry red hair from the pictures I am sending you." I told him as I sent over the profiles I downloaded from the police database. He paused for a moment and checked his phone to check the files I sent to his phone.

"The Koreans? Okay. There's a person on here, who we can't see their face. Why?" Ace asked.

"That's the unknown third child of Omega. The Saturday after next the entire family, all of his children and his wife will be at the Nam Industries party. That's when we strike. We have to be discreet and silent. No unnecessary attention needs to be drawn. I'll get you a ticket and we will meet when you arrive. Try to arrive a day early, so the meeting can happen. I'll be busy Saturday all day. We will be communicating through our regular headpieces we use." I explained.

"Understood ma'am. I can do that." Ace agreed.

"Our main priority is Arsyn. If we take her out first, everyone else is an easy target. If you see her first, do not hesitate. If I find her first then I'll take care of it. Whoever you see afterwards is fair game."

"Okay. Should I seek her out first? What if I come across someone else first?"

"You can handle them. I just want them all dead before the night is over." I clarified.

"Understood."

"Let me know when you get your ticket. I'll be in contact." I told him as I hung up the phone.

I sighed out loud. There was no turning back now. It was hard to process how I was feeling. I had this overwhelming sense of uneasiness about the whole thing now. I had made my decision though and I couldn't turn back or change it now. I just hoped I was making the right decision, and it didn't bite me in the ass.

~Chapter 25~

"Jae… Jae… Jaehyun… Hello? Jaehyun!" I yelled at the phone screen sitting in front of me. He jumped slightly and looked up from his laptop into the camera again. He blinked at me a few times. He was zoning out again. He was at the office for the last-minute preparations for the party. I was just getting out of the shower, and I took a moment to help him organize his calendar for the rest of this month and next month before I ran more errands.

"You zoned out again. Why don't you just take a break?" I said as I took his appearance in. He looked tired and the bags under his eyes were heavy. Stress was evident on his face. We were counting down the hours to the Nam Industries party, and he was having a hard time. He was trying to make sure his PowerPoint presentation and the speech that he had to give at the party were perfect. I was stressed because I was soon going to look my mother's killers in the eyes and get my revenge. I was also going to meet the rest of Jaehyun's family at the same time. In the same location. Anxiety, excitement, fear and all of these emotions were swimming in my stomach, and I was fighting to contain it all. I didn't want to stress him more than he already was.

He groaned loudly and ran hand through his hair, messing it up. I sighed softly. I hated seeing him like this. It was sad. He wasn't his usual cheerful, joking self. He was short and easily annoyed when he was stressed. I knew he didn't mean it, but that was my thing. We both couldn't be short and easily annoyed when we were stressed. He wouldn't let me help with the big things, but small things he was okay with like helping him get organized for the next couple of months. "Sorry Ae Ri. Where were we?" he yawned.

"You should at least take a nap. How much better do you think your presentation will get? It's already in depth and explanatory. You'll have plenty of new business partners." I suggested. He chuckled tiredly.

"Later. We have to finish this. You have to run errands soon. Did you get your workout in?" I laughed softly because he had already asked that earlier. It wasn't a workout necessarily, it was a sparring session with Ace. He arrived in Korea earlier than expected and he was being useful by helping me train. I was proud to see I didn't lose anything after the months of inactivity.

"You really need sleep. I left to workout while you were getting ready to go to the office." I reminded him. He gasped lightly in shock and shook his head.

"You may be right. I may need a nap." he admitted.

"Exactly, so let's hurry. You were telling me that you needed to register for classes and Seunghyun and Nari were graduating. When's that?"

"Registration is August 8th. They graduate on August 14th. We have to be there. They'll be pissed if we miss it. Then their graduation party is the next day."

"Okay. I wrote it down. What else?" I asked as I jotted everything down in his calendar.

"We are good for right now. That's all I have for now. Thank you for your help, princess. I appreciate it," he answered. I nodded and looked over at him and closed the calendar.

"Okay. Now take a nap. I need to go and get these errands done. What time are you going to be home?" He yawned again and checked his watch.

"Probably 3 or 4, we need to eat before we go. There's only appetizers and hors d'oeuvres and a whole lot of alcohol at these parties." I chuckled at the comment. That would be useful tonight.

"I'll be back before then. We can get dinner."

"Sounds like a date, princess. I'll see you then." he smiled tiredly. I nodded and waved him off the phone as I hung up.

I stood up and quickly threw on a pair of shorts and a shirt and grabbed my car keys. I did actually have errands to do before the party tonight. The biggest errand I had to run was to meet with Ace again to run through the plan for tonight. We didn't get the chance this morning during training. I also needed some makeup and to get our outfits from Rachel. I grabbed my sunglasses and the box I had set by the door for Ace. I left the house and drove to meet Ace at the cafe we decided upon.

After a fifteen-minute drive, I pulled into the parking lot and I walked inside. Ace was seated in the back in a booth and his black hair was neatly tied in a bun and his intense black eyes made contact with mine. Everything about him was intense. He never laughed or smiled. He was a man of few words. He served in the military back in Japan and when he got out, he never transitioned back into civilian life. He met Han and the rest was history. As I approached, he stood and bowed in respect and I nodded in acknowledgement.

"Ma'am." he greeted with a blank expression. I sat down at the table and placed the box on the table.

"Ace. I want to go over the plan for tonight. I brought you something to help you blend in and I got your ticket." I replied as I slid the box over to him. He opened the box and looked inside.

Nam Industries was extremely strict about the guest list to their end of the quarter parties because it would reveal new business projects and deals that were being worked on. They didn't want to risk their ideas being stolen. I took a phone call for Jaehyun and there was a guest that wasn't going to be able to make it due to a family emergency, so instead of telling him, I stole the ticket and saved it for Ace. Getting him in would be painless. I got him a tuxedo just in case he needed one and there was an earpiece in the box as well. He remained quiet.

"I don't have to tell you how important this mission is. You know that it is. I need you to remember your targets, but I need you to protect one particular man." I explained as I pulled up a picture of Jaehyun and sent it to his phone. He looked down at the picture that flashed on his screen.

"If any Jopok members get near him, kill them. I don't care what you're doing, who's around, that is your main priority at that moment. He is to be protected at all costs." I told him seriously. I saw the subtle flash of confusion on his face but it was gone just as quick and he was back to his blank expression. I chose to ignore it.

"Understood." he agreed.

"That earpiece is just like the ones we normally use. The party starts at nine. Get to the hotel early and start recon. We need to know exits, the surrounding areas, everything. Boiler rooms, anything that can help us. This isn't going to be easy because we will surely be outnumbered. Arsyn isn't going to allow her whole family to be in one area without extra security. Bring your silencer, we don't need any accidents. Bring your combat knives too just in case."

"Understood. I won't let you down."

"I expect nothing less. Text me whatever information you get." I told him as I stood up and he followed behind me.

He followed me outside and opened my car door and I got in.

"Ma'am?" I looked down at him and I could tell he had a question. It was all over his face. He was just hesitant to ask because he feared my reaction. I was known for being quick tempered and hated being asked too many questions. Orders were to be followed; no explanation needed.

"You may ask one question." I allowed him. He breathed a soft sigh of relief.

"The man we need to protect. Is he an asset to the mission?" I paused for a moment. That was a strange way to ask who he was. I shrugged it off though.

"He is an asset. He helped me locate them. I told him that I would protect him." I answered him. He didn't need to know any more information than that.

"Then I will protect him with my life as I will you." He closed my door and stepped back and bowed in respect again. I pulled out of the parking lot as he stood back up and headed to Rachel's store.

I rode in silence as my thoughts raced. With Ace's help, my chances of success were significantly higher, but what if something went wrong? There were so many unknown variables, something could go wrong. It was apparent that Arsyn was crafty. She could have something up her sleeve that I couldn't prepare for. I didn't have the police connections anymore to keep tabs on her, so I was going into this blind. What if something happened to Jaehyun? What if they went after him instead of me? The thought had my stomach in knots. What if they went after his family? I hadn't met them yet and I really didn't want our first meeting to be after I saved them. That couldn't be explained. I sighed deeply and I felt my palms start to get sweaty. This was the first time I felt like this about an assignment.

Every so often the thought of just calling everything off crept in. I pushed it away though. This was for Jaehyun. This was for my mother. I couldn't give up like that. A loud car honk brought me out of my thoughts as I pulled into the building complex sharply. I cut someone off when I made the turn because I almost missed it from being in my thoughts so much. I sat in the parking space for a moment and all of the thoughts in my mind got louder and louder. The louder it got, the more my heart started to race and all of the emotions I tried to hide started to bubble to the surface.

I screamed into the silence of the car as I started to slam my hands on the wheel and dashboard, not caring that I hit the horn more than once. It was the only way I could purge everything that I was feeling. I couldn't have all those emotions lingering into tonight. I had to be focused and alert. I leaned my head on the wheel and breathed deeply. It wasn't loud anymore. I felt slightly better. I took a moment to compose myself. I sat up and looked at myself in the side mirror. Tear stains littered my cheeks, and my face was red and lips chapped. Grabbing a tissue and wet wipe, I cleaned my face and grabbed my ChapStick to rub on my lips. I steeled my resolve and put on my sunglasses as I stepped out of the car.

Walking into the store, I looked around. Rachel stepped out from one of the backrooms a few moments later. "Oh, hi Miss Choi. Are you here for your outfits?" she greeted me warmly. A small and stiff smile crossed my face.

"Yes I am. Big night tonight." I tried to sound normal but my voice was slightly hoarse.

"Mr. Nam was telling me. The quarter end party and meeting the family at the same time. That's a big deal. Are you excited?" She was beaming at the question. I wish I could relate. It got lonely having to carry the burdens of my job by myself.

"Nervous. But that's to be expected, right?" She giggled as she walked to the backroom for a moment. She came back out with a bottle of champagne and a glass.

"It is to be expected. I was nervous meeting my husband's family for the first time. You look tense. Glass or no glass? No judgment." Rachel said as she offered the items with a sympathetic look.

"Is it obvious?" Damn. Am I that much of a mess? I sighed as I took the bottle after she opened it and I brought it to my lips chugging the bitter liquid.

"Yeah, just a little. Want to talk about it?" she offered. I released the bottle, gasping a little.

"Not really. This makes things better. As long as I can take it." I joked lightly.

"All yours, missy. One moment. I made some adjustments to your dress. I really hope you like it." I tilted my head in curiosity. She grinned mischievously and disappeared into the backroom again. I sighed lightly, well if it was a disaster, I could always kill her. I guzzled more of the champagne from the bottle as I waited for her. A pleasant warmth spread through me as the alcohol started to do its job. She returned with two garment bags and she unzipped one of them. The long ruby red gown was now a sparkly ruby red color. I gasped in shock and stared at the dress. It was a strapless sweetheart neckline and the silhouette was a mermaid. She held up the dress and I chuckled at the long split up the left side.

"I couldn't have you in a dress without your signature split. It didn't feel right. And the ruby red color was beautiful, but I saw this sparkly red material and I knew you had to have it. What an impression, right? And I added… Matching gloves!" Rachel squealed excitedly as she handed the gloves to me. They were made out of the same material, and they sparkled too. I tried the gloves on and they fit perfectly. They were fairly long and they stopped past my elbows. I was thoroughly impressed. When Jaehyun said she would actually be making our custom outfits for tonight, I got a little nervous. I knew her as the stylist who chose clothes, not necessarily made them. He asked for me to trust her and I'm glad I did. Her design was so much better than the original one I chose. It was a simple spaghetti strap ruby red evening gown originally. The new design was attention grabbing and it honestly would work better practically.

I could hide weapons better and access them quicker if I needed to do so with the split up the side. It gave me more movement and freedom to maneuver. "This is epic. I'm really surprised. I really like it. You're talented." I told her genuinely. She blushed brightly and looked down at the dress in admiration. She seemed really proud of it.

"Thank you. It's my favorite design that I've ever done. It photographs well so prepare for the best pictures ever. Do you want to try it on?" she smiled softly. I nodded. I wanted to visualize the weapons placement and I was genuinely curious to see how the dress fit. She waved me over to the viewing room and I finished the rest of the champagne, placing the empty bottle on the counter. She helped me into the dress once we were in the privacy of the dressing rooms and I audibly gasped in surprise. It looked better on me than I could've hoped for. The lights of the store made it sparkle a little more and I smiled like a child. It was beautiful. The material was light and airy. It wasn't heavy. I could wear a garter and hide a knife on the inside of my left thigh if I wore a holster. My hair would have to be down to cover my earpiece so I couldn't bring the knives that I disguised as thin hairpins. I was going to bring a purse so I could bring a small gun and a small silencer. I would bring a more powerful one and strap it to the right calf with the other silencer. That would be the best way to position the weapons.

"Miss Choi? Are you okay?" Rachel asked as she tapped my shoulder. I focused back on her and she smiled softly.

"Sorry, I got lost in the dress. I like it so much." I lied smoothly.

"It is very distracting. You look gorgeous. How do you feel about silver shoes?" She showed me a pair of silver ankle strap open toe stiletto shoes. I hummed and nodded, agreeing to try them on. Her eyes lit up as she saw the shoes, dress and gloves together.

"This is the look?" I teased her. I was hopeful because I really liked the way the outfit looked together as well.

"You know it. Let me take a few pictures for my portfolio please? One second!" she squealed as she scurried off to grab her camera. I chuckled and checked my watch to keep track of the time. I still had enough time to get to the makeup store. She came back and took a few photos before she helped me out of the dress and took it to put it back in the bag.

I rejoined her at the desk and she had the garment bags laid on the counter and the receipt tapped to it. "I was supposed to pay?" I questioned.

"Mr. Nam took care of it a few days ago. He said don't tell you. He even paid for the adjustments even though I told him not to. I wanted to do it. But he insisted." Rachel shrugged and laughed as she cleaned off the desk. I rolled my eyes and grabbed the bags.

"He doesn't listen."

"I don't think it's that. I think he just really loves you. It's endearing. He comes in here all the time to buy you things or to ask me to pick out whatever I think you'd like and he'll just swipe the card. He talks about you to anyone who will listen. I've never seen him so happy." My cheeks heated up at the thought of him telling random strangers about me. I looked down at the two bags in my arms. Everything had to go right tonight. There was so much riding on this.

"Jaehyun is the only good decision I've made in my life. It's not easy for me to say it but the feeling is mutual. I just wish I could tell him that." I admitted quietly.

"That you love him? He knows that. But it doesn't hurt to say it out loud. You're safe with him. Safer than you've ever been in life. You don't even realize it."

I felt her place a hand on top of mine and she soothingly ran her thumb along the back. I looked up at her and she smiled warmly. I couldn't help the smile that crossed my face. She was rooting for us. She supported us. It was encouraging. "You're a good person, Rachel." I told her. That was the best thing I could come up with. She laughed and nodded once.

"You are too, Ae Ri. You'll do great tonight. Have fun." She sounded like she really believed that. I almost believed her too.

~Chapter 26~

"**A**e Ri! Are you almost ready? We're already running late, princess. Can I see you yet?" Jaehyun called from the living room. We were at my place, and I was in the bedroom fixing my hair to cover the earpiece completely. My hair was in curls and I pinned it up to lay over my right shoulder for the night. The gun and knives were hidden and secured into place. It was never a comfortable feeling and it was always risky, I just got used to it after all of the years of doing it. The silver purse sitting to my left held a smaller nine-millimeter gun and extra rounds. My phone went off and I looked down to see Ace send me another text.

He went to the Lotte Hotel right after we left the cafe to do recon on the building and he was texting me updates. There was a basement floor where the laundry room and the electrical units were. It was almost built like a maze, he told me. Different areas and sections. I found that strange. That wasn't a normal design for a basement floor. I opened the new text message he sent, and my breath hitched for a moment. He saw Arsyn walking through the basement floor. She was on the phone and she mentioned me by name. She told everyone to be on guard. I groaned deeply in my chest and leaned over the counter as my stomach churned. She knew. She knew I was in Korea. My heart started to race in my chest and the room started to spin. I took a moment and closed my eyes tightly, willing myself to calm down and collect myself.

I breathed deeply and opened my eyes making eye contact with my reflection. Dilated pupils stared back as anticipation started to fill my stomach. It felt like the walls that I built around the darker parts of myself were starting to crumble and I was forced to watch all of the violent memories and feel all of the bloodlust as it rushed through me. The familiar darkness started to swim behind the green of my eyes. It had been so long since I felt like this. But at the same time it felt comfortable and familiar. I couldn't deny that it felt unsettling at the same time as well. To go so long without having to fight for my life or take someone else's had more of an effect than I realized. I took a deep breath and closed my eyes again so I could gather my thoughts and center myself. When I looked at myself again, I looked more normal. I nodded in approval and grabbed my clutch and left the room.

Jaehyun leaned against the wall by the door and he looked up from his phone as he heard my heels click on the floor. His jaw dropped and he stared at me wide eyed. I grinned at his reaction. I figured he'd like it, I wasn't expecting him to be so speechless. He continued to stare at me for a while without speaking. I felt my cheeks heat up the longer he stared at me. "Did you malfunction again? Say something." I reminded him as I looked down at the floor.

"You look stunning… Red looks amazing on you. I'm glad she didn't go with your original dress idea. This is beautiful, princess…" he rambled as he held out a hand to bring me closer. I smiled shyly and took his hand, allowing him to spin me once. His eyes couldn't focus on my face, they roamed and lingered a second too long on exposed pieces of revealed skin.

"Is this going to be distracting for you? We have to get through the night. I'm meeting your family. You have to behave." I teased. He looked at my face and swallowed thickly. A mischievous grin graced his face as he shrugged.

"It's a long party. I'm sure we can make some time to misbehave." he smirked as he leaned down and pressed a kiss to the connection between my shoulder and neck. I playfully pushed his shoulder.

"That's a bold prediction. Shouldn't we get going? You said we're late." He groaned lowly in annoyance and nodded.

"I mean if you want to be responsible, yes. Rowoon is downstairs already. But, he wouldn't mind waiting longer." he raised an eyebrow and winked at me as he tugged me closer. I allowed him to place a few small affection pecks on my shoulder and neck before I pushed him away gently.

"Later. We need to go now." I reminded him as I stepped away from him and gestured to the door. He rolled his eyes and huffed in disappointment.

"You're mean. Fine, let's go." he agreed as he opened the door and let me go first.

"Don't be a child. This is a big night for us." I smiled as I pinched his cheeks on the way out of the door. He chuckled and followed me to the elevator. I took a moment to look him over as we rode the elevator down. He wore a black tuxedo but instead of a white shirt, he wore a ruby red shirt to match me. It was his way of showing that we were together. I tried to convince him that it wasn't necessary, but he insisted. It was the little things like that. He was worth every risk I was about to take.

The Lotte Hotel in Seoul was a normally calm place, but today it was hectic and the employees were scrambling around. It was understandable. Seven hundred of the world's most powerful businesspeople were all in the Crystal Ballroom. Every upper management member from Nam Industries; foreign businessmen and their plus one; investors; potential business partners; employees and staff were in the building. We pulled up to the hotel entrance and Rowoon came around and opened the door for us. With a thank you, Jaehyun helped me out next and we made our way inside. I squeezed his hand tightly as we entered the building. I took in the tall ceilings and luxuriously decorated lobby. The amount of money that was walking around was apparent.

I scanned the area quickly to see if I saw any Jopok members. I didn't see any on the floor. "Are you ready for your first Nam Industries party?" Jaehyun asked as he intertwined our fingers. I nodded in response.

"I can handle the party, it's your family I'm worried about," I answered. He laughed softly and kissed my temple.

"You'll do great." We started our walk through the lobby and I felt a sudden shot of adrenaline rush through me. The hairs on the back of my neck stood up. Goosebumps raised on my arms. The room got colder. Arsyn was here. Somewhere. The energy in the room shifted and my eyes scanned the room again. Finding nothing, I looked up again and realized that you could see the upper floors. People were leaning against the railings looking down at the lobby. I scanned all of them and then I saw a woman turn around from the railing quickly and walk away on the fifth floor. The fiery red hair was pinned up into a bun, but some strands were laying free. I caught the back of her black halter top dress. It was her. I knew it. I didn't see her face but I knew it.

We entered the Crystal Room and Jaehyun was immediately hounded by an older foreign man with a shaved head. Jaehyun was taken off guard but he was the perfect gentleman, still polite and respectful. I chuckled to myself as he introduced me and I shook the elder's hand. I didn't remember the name. I was on a mission. I took out my phone and texted Ace where I had seen Arsyn. His voice came through the earpiece. "I'm on it, ma'am. I'll be back." he confirmed. My anxiety was at an all time high. I didn't actually have a way to confirm that it was actually her. I could've been seeing things. I took a deep breath and looked around the ballroom decorated in sleek black and gold decorations.

There was a stage in the front of the room with a black curtains and a gold banner with black lettering that welcomed everyone to the event. Black and gold balloon arrangements were placed systemically at the corners of the room and by the doors. It looked elegant. His family had a thing for decorating spaces too. It made sense. Music played over the speakers and a few people swayed to the music playing. The waiters and waitresses were dressed in normal white and black attire but their vests had Nam Industries written on the pocket as they served hors d'oeuvres and champagne. I grabbed two glasses from one of the trays and held one of them for Jaehyun. The two men were still talking, so I nudged him and he looked down as he took the glass with a thank you.

My earpiece squeaked to life. "Ma'am. Are you sure it was the fifth floor? I can't find her. Did you see where she went?" Ace said. I could hear the slight pant in his breath as he walked around. Fuck. My heart started to race as I frantically scanned again. Where did she go? I didn't see any red hair anywhere in the room, but I saw a man with silver hair standing by the stage and he was looking around the room as he leaned against it. He was visibly more muscular than anyone else in the room. It was Viper. He looked even more muscular than the photos I had seen of him. How was that possible? I tapped Jaehyun on the shoulder lightly.

"I'll be right back. I'm going to get an hors d'oeuvres." I told him. He nodded and smiled warmly as he kissed my cheek and went back to his conversation. Once I was far enough away, I spoke to Ace.

"I got Viper in the ballroom. Arsyn is here somewhere. Get back here." I hissed. I moved through the crowd of people, ignoring the people complimenting me keeping my eye on Viper. He hadn't seen me yet.

I felt my chest constrict slightly as the realization hit me. I was really in enemy territory. If Viper was here, then that was definitely Arsyn. All of them were here. I felt a nervous sweat start to form along my temple. It got too hot, too fast. This was happening. I could complete my mission. Adrenaline started to pump through my veins faster and my fingers twitched at the thought. I just had to survey the area. I noticed that in each corner of the room, there was a group of three or four men in suits and they were on their phones and drinking and talking. That was a clever way to disguise their security. I downed the champagne in the flute to ease my anxiety. I passed by another waitress and grabbed another glass.

"Where's Viper? I'm back in the ballroom." Ace's voice broke my thoughts.

"By the stage. We got security in the corners. We have to be careful. We need a distraction or something. Or they have to go first," I replied.

He went quiet for a moment, then mumbled a curse under his breath. "Fuck. You weren't kidding, this won't be easy. Viper's built like an ox."

"No, it will not be. Keep an eye on Viper, let me know if he talks to anyone. Watch his moves."

"Got it, ma'am." I started the walk back to where Jaehyun was and I scanned the area again, searching for Arsyn. She was nowhere to be found from what I was able to see. When I reached Jaehyun again, he was talking to his mother. She smiled warmly as I approached and gave me a hug.

"You look gorgeous! I love this dress! Eye catching and sexy. I love the matching colors. Are you enjoying yourself so far?" Iseul excitedly spun me around and held my hands.

"Thank you so much. It's beautiful here. I'm taking it all in. It's a new environment. I'm almost nervous." I answered her honestly. She giggled and waved her hand.

"It gets easier over time. I get nervous still and I have to kick this whole thing off in a few minutes. I greet everyone and then I have to introduce everyone."

"We'll be supporting you mom. Want me to walk you to the stage?" Jaehyun offered as he held his hand up to her. She smiled proudly at him and nodded.

"I will take that. Don't forget, Ae Ri." she reminded him. He laughed and offered his arm to me, and I took it.

"I will never forget her. She'd kill me." I playfully punched his arm.

We walked towards the stage, and I stopped in the front as they continued to the back of the stage and he helped her up the stairs. The music faded out slowly and Ace's voice sounded in my ear.

"Arsyn at nine o'clock." he rasped. My eyes widened and I stopped breathing for a second. My heart thumped hard as I turned slowly to see her standing along the western wall with her hair in the same bun as before. Her dress was a plain black silk halter top ball gown, and we made eye contact. She was already staring at me. Cold piercing brown eyes stared me down and I stared back. How long had she been here? What did she see? A wicked smirk crossed her face, and she looked up on the stage as Jaehyun led Iseul to the front of the stage. Oh god. No. No. She saw that. It felt like the wind was knocked out of me and my stomach sunk.

"Be on alert, Arsyn saw my informant and his mom. She's planning something. I know she is." I hissed as I stared at her. She waved to one set of the guards, and they approached her quickly. I knew what that meant. I groaned under my breath.

"Look alive Ace. She called security. I'm in front of the stage." I told him.

"Coming," he replied. I watched the security walk to the back of the stage and my heart pounded as I watched them surround Jaehyun when he descended and led him away.

"Ace, is there a back door to this room? The guards took him." I gasped. I tried to keep my composure calm and when I looked to find Arsyn, she was gone. I felt someone tap my shoulder twice. I knew it was Ace because that was my clan's sign to identify each other in the field.

"An emergency exit. It leads to a small hallway. The door to the basement floor is out there. They must have the alarm system off."

I growled lowly. "Did you see where Arsyn went? I lost sight of her."

"I did too."

"Fuck it. We need to get him. I made him a promise. Lead the way." I demanded. We made our way back through the crowd in order to not draw attention to ourselves and we would go the long way around to get to the exit. Rage started to bubble up in my chest each step I took. Arsyn had taken Jaehyun. I wasn't observant enough. All of my preparation and planning didn't take this into account. I let him out of my sight. It was my fault. My eyes scanned as I walked and I noticed the other groups of security were walking through the crowd too. Fuck. She was willing to make a scene in front of all these people. She was willing to risk exposure.

"We got company. The guards are roaming. We gotta hurry."

"I see them. Travel along the wall where Arsyn was. More people on that side. We should be able to get behind the stage. Iseul's voice carried on in the background as she did the welcome and told the story of the company.

We made it to the wall and calmly walked alongside it, watching everyone closely. We got past the front of the stage unnoticed and we were able to get behind the stage as well. There we ran into six of her security. I pulled my knife and charged at one of the men. I blocked the punch he threw with my clutch and stabbed him in the stomach twisting the knife and dragging it upwards. He coughed and blood flew out of his mouth and some hit me in the face. I ignored it and pulled my knife away as he dropped to the floor and I immediately turned to the next man I saw that was on the ground moving and I stabbed him in the chest, effectively ending his movement. I turned to see the other men were already on the ground and Ace had his gun out and he fired, killing the last man. He brought his silencer, so I didn't hear any of the gunshots. He nodded and we escaped through the backdoor.

I took a moment and replaced my knife back in its holster and grabbed my gun out of the clutch and grabbed my spare magazine and tossed it to Ace. "Stay close if possible. I may need more ammo. How many guards were down here when you came?" I panted. I caught my breath as I untied my shoes and took them off.

"It looked like she had all of the ones I saw in the ballroom. But I'm sure she called in more reinforcement, since she saw you. I'd be ready for anything and everything." he answered.

"Always am. Everyone down here dies. Secure the informant at all costs." I stood up and took a deep breath centering myself. The bloodlust I felt was stronger than anything I had felt before. Jaehyun being in danger unlocked a side of me that I had never seen before. It felt like the weight of the world was resting on my shoulders and I felt fragile. I felt something more than being scared or being terrified. Those didn't describe how I felt. I rushed towards the door to the left that said employees only and I heard Ace's footsteps follow behind me.

~Chapter 27~

The steps that led to the basement floor were steep and it was muggy and humid. It was hard to breathe. Whoever had to work down here I felt sorry for them. This was miserable. The steps were made of uneven concrete and pieces dug into my bare feet as I descended. Despite the discomfort I pushed through. This was about Jaehyun. It was eerily quiet except for the hum of machines and our footsteps. I aimed my gun as I scanned the open area to our left. There was nothing and no one from where we were. "Which way?" I whispered. We were at the bottom of the steps and the basement extended in either direction. It was dimly lit in either direction and it looked the same. He pointed to the left wordlessly. We started walking in that direction.

The atmosphere was tense, and it was a long time before we found any signs of activity. We rounded seven corners and traveled through several intersections. This basement floor was designed like it was used for more than just storage. It almost looked like an office area. There were rooms with doors and in some of those rooms there were computers and desks. And we weren't close to an exit or anything. We were passing by an area with three rooms when we heard voices. I raised my hand to stop us and listened. "What do you mean you can't find her!?" a male voice yelled. Another man answered and it sounded like it was coming from a phone.

"She had help, we think. One of the security teams is dead behind the stage. All of them."

"WHAT! Arsyn's going to have a fit when she finds out! She's going to have my fucking head!"

"Check down there with you. We have people checking the hotel proximity. They have to be somewhere, Chan." the voice on the phone said.

"Where's the kid? Is he secure? Arsyn said she'd be looking for him. It was imperative to secure him." the one now known as Chan questioned.

"We got him. Everything is still going on as planned. Omega is in the ballroom now with the wife. We got eyes on them."

My eyes widened at the news. Omega was here with his wife. Everyone really was here. My fist clenched tighter in anger. The opportunity to destroy the head of the snake was back upstairs. I looked back at Ace and he stared back at me and mouthed the words I dreaded. The assignment. It was hard to breathe and my chest rose and fell with the exertion. I was conflicted. I couldn't do the assignment knowing Jaehyun was in danger. He was all I could think about. I had to find him and make sure he was okay. Killing Omega and his wife meant nothing if Jaehyun was dead or hurt. This was to secure our future. That's what made me keep looking for them. That's what all the work was for. It was for him. I felt hot tears start to fill my eyes making them blurry.

Thoughts of my mother and what could've been played in my head. I remembered sitting at all of the dinners with Iseul and Jaehyun and wishing she was there too. My childhood with all of the random women coming and going out of my life. The abuse I suffered at Han's hands and in training. The opportunity for revenge was walking around upstairs, living life. He was collecting money and terrorizing Jaehyun's family. He didn't deserve that. I wanted my revenge. I wanted him to suffer. I wanted him to suffer just as much as I suffered. I wanted him to die in my hands and with my sword. As I sat in silence and thought, I didn't care about the how as much as I did about making sure I got the satisfaction of seeing his dead body. I turned to Ace and told him to go. "Kill them." I whispered. He looked confused for a moment, but he nodded and took off in the opposite direction, leaving me alone. I was going to find Jaehyun and get him back, no matter what it took.

I peeked around the corner to see how many men I was dealing with. I saw eight men and they were dressed in black suits and ties as well. They were all focused on looking at something on the table. It looked like a map and Chan was assigning them sectors to investigate. I raised my gun and fired off four shots, hitting the four with their backs to me. I hid again as everyone jumped and panic started to ensue among the men. "What the hell guys! Get up, that's not funny!" a higher pitched male voice said.

"Idiot, they were shot! Rose is down here! Find her!" Chan yelled. The silencer did its job.

I heard the feet start to pound on the ground towards me and I stepped back and aimed. I could hear Chan calling for backup and then I heard Arsyn's voice cut in and she said in a chilling voice, "I'm coming."

I fired as the remaining men passed by me, and I emerged from the corner. Chan stared at me wide eyed as I crept towards him. "Where is he?" I demanded. The man stood up from the chair and backed away from me stumbling.

"I-I don't know… I don't have him." Chan stammered.

"Liar." I growled as I ran full speed at him and pinned him to the ground and grabbed my knife holding it to his throat. I pressed it to his throat and growled.

"Tell me where they're holding him, or Arsyn will be the last of your worries."

"You'll be doing me a favor by killing him actually. I was gonna replace him. But looks like you took out his replacement. So I'll have to choose another." A chill ran down my spine as I realized who had joined us. I seethed at the new voice and ran the blade across his throat and stood up facing her.

She was ninety centimeters away from me. Much closer than we had ever been before. A dangerous glint flickered in her eyes and the callousness took me off guard for a moment. "So you're the great Rose that everyone speaks so highly of. It's nice to officially meet you." she said smugly.

"Arsyn." I spit back at her. I felt my heart pound in my chest. Looking at her face to face was surreal. The danger and controlled madness radiated off of her. It was tense, the only noise was the soft and faint gurgling of the man behind me choking on his blood. He went silent after a moment.

"I wondered when I'd meet you face to face, outside of the police station that is. You're a tough one to find. You're just as good as they say."

"Where is he?" I growled. She raised an eyebrow at me.

"Where is who?" She grinned darkly. I took in a shaky breath. My anger was reaching a boiling point, and I was starting to twitch. I wanted to kill her. I remained silent. She was toying with me and I refused to fall for it.

"Oh! You mean Jaehyun? Well, why does that matter to you? How do you know him? Used him to find me, huh?" Arsyn folded her arms across her chest. She took a few steps closer.

"You seem really concerned about him. What's the deal? Do you actually like him? Pretending to care about him?" she continued to tease as she walked closer. I waited for her to come closer before I struck.

"Do you know anything about him?" She stopped a few centimeters in front of me and smirked. I glared at her wordlessly, not listening. She laughed at me, and her eyes closed for a second. I took my shot. I lunged at her and swiped at her with the knife. I caught her across the cheek before she caught me with a sharp punch in the gut. We both staggered backwards and her hand touched her cheek and she stared in horror at the blood.

"You bitch! My face! How dare you!" she screamed. She reached down and tore the bottom half of her dress off to reveal a garter with a knife as well. She lunged at me, taking a pointed shot at my midsection. I sidestepped it barely and caught her arm with my right hand and I brought my left arm around to try and stab her in the side but she was quick. She headbutted me and I staggered backwards discombobulated for a moment. I felt the blood pour out of my nose. I hoped it wasn't broken, I couldn't explain that to Jaehyun. I was able to move before she could plunge the knife into my shoulder and she only grazed me.

I knew I had dropped my knife in the hit and I swung my fist, catching her in the jaw and the side. She staggered backwards clutching her side and she dropped to one knee for a second. I rushed her again and kneed her in the face. Payback for the headbutt. She yelled in pain and fell onto her back and I jumped on top of her, starting to swing wildly. She blocked a lot of hits and suddenly I felt pain in my back where my kidney was. She kneed me hard enough to send me into shock for a moment. I rolled off of her and she jumped up and started kicking me in the stomach and stomping on me. I covered up the best I could, but one shot in particular caught me in the gut and left me breathless.

"Is that the best you got Rose! Huh! I thought you were supposed to be unstoppable!" she screamed. At the teasing, I found a reserve tank of energy and I kicked my leg out to trip her and she collapsed, smacking the ground hard. She huffed in pain and I stood up quickly, shaking off the dizziness and I dragged her up by the arm and threw her into the wall behind me. She groaned in pain as her head smacked against the wall and she slumped over. I stormed over to her and put my hands around her throat and started to squeeze. She gasped in shock and her nails started to dig into my arms to fight me off. It stung, but I was on a mission.

"Where is Jaehyun? Tell me and I'll kill you quickly!" I demanded as I pressed her into the wall and squeezed harder. Her strangled gasps came out quicker and she started to beat on my arms. Her face started to turn red and I stared at her. I demanded to know where Jaehyun was again. Her lips started to mouth words and I loosened my grip some.

"What?"

"Surprise!" a deep voice said from behind me and before I could turn to see what was going on, I felt something strike me in the back of my head and the rush of pain was agonizing. Darkness lined my vision and I couldn't keep a hold on Arsyn's neck. I watched as my hands fell from her neck and she got farther from me before the darkness consumed me completely.

My eyes fluttered open slowly and I tried to make sense out of what was happening. My eyesight was fuzzy and I blinked a few times trying to refocus. Once I could see clearly, I looked around. I was in a room with a hardwood floor and I looked in front of me and there was a large mahogany desk in the center of the room, along the back wall. There was a door behind the desk. The wall behind the desk had numerous plaques and awards on it. It hurt my eyes too much to try and read them. I continued to look around and the room looked like it belonged in a traditional hanok. I gasped lightly as my eyes widened and I stood up quickly, fighting off the dizziness. I looked around the room for my weapons. Of course, I didn't have any. I looked around the room for something to use as a weapon. I found a sword on the wall behind me and I grabbed it just in time to see the door behind the desk open.

I got in a defensive position and stared as the person stepped in the room. The man walked in with his head held high and he wore dark sunglasses. Thick black hair was combed back and slicked down perfectly. He wore a sharp black tuxedo and a bowtie. He looked over at me and a small smirk played on his face. He was muscular with broad shoulders and he was tall. He sat at the desk and sharp hazel eyes stared me down. My breath hitched slightly as I made eye contact with him. Omega. He was more handsome than what his profile pictures gave him credit for. It was tense as we had a stare off. He sighed loudly and shook his head. "You left me quite a mess to clean up, Miss Rose. If you wanted to meet me so badly, you could have just waited. Why go through all that trouble? You were in bad shape when you got here. I had my personal doctor patch you back up. You and my daughter got into a nasty fight. I hope there's no hard feelings, she can be a little... hot headed. Especially when she's trying to prove a point." he spoke to me in a calm voice as if he was trying to calm down a growling animal or a child throwing a tantrum. It pissed me off. It felt like he was making fun of me.

"Where am I? Why did you bring me here? Where is Arsyn and what coward attacked me from behind!" I yelled as I readied the sword. The door behind him opened again revealing Viper. He laughed boisterously as he took in the sight of me with the sword.

"You just woke up and you're already holding another weapon? Damn. You're something else. Sorry about the vase over your head. It was kinda necessary. You know? Given the situation. You got the upperhand and the choking and stuff." he waved a hand dismissively as if the whole thing was a misunderstanding. I raised an eyebrow in confusion. He was the exact opposite of Arsyn.

269

"Where is Jaehyun! If you've hurt him, I'll kill you! Where is that bitch Arsyn! Where is she!" I yelled as my voice started to raise in pitch.

"Patience, Miss Rose. All will be answered soon. Just relax. He's fine. She's fine." Omega singsonged lightheartedly. What was wrong with these people? Is this a joke to them? Was I a joke to them?

The door opened again and Arsyn walked in covered in bruises. A bruise on her jaw from when I punched her and bruises around her neck from when I choked her. A bandaid on her cheek from the first cut. She glared at me as she folded her arms and stood at her father's right side. Two out of the three kids. Where was the third one? I shook my head focusing back on the issue at hand. "Where's Jaehyun? I won't ask again." I demanded as I raised the sword into an offensive position and Arsyn moved to grab a weapon too but Omega stopped her.

"Stand down," he ordered and she relaxed again. He hit a button on a keypad and said come in. The door behind me began to open and I trembled lightly, unsure of what I'd see. Jaehyun walked in unscathed and completely fine. No scratches or dirt on him. I was relieved and I fought off the tears that threatened to spill over. I wouldn't cry in front of them. Jaehyun scanned the room and his eyes landed on me and his jaw dropped. Then a small smirk and chuckle tugged at his mouth. "Oh what trouble did you get into, princess?" he asked playfully. He stepped forward and adjusted my hair that had been placed in a ponytail. I kind of chuckled and shook my head. I stepped in front of him to shield him from their gazes.

Omega stifled a laugh. "Aren't you curious to know where my third child is?" he asked playfully. I raised an eyebrow. Why did that matter? A sinking feeling crept into my stomach.

"W-where is he?" I stammered.

"Behind you, bitch." Arsyn answered harshly as a wide smirk crossed her lips. I froze and the sword fell from my hands and I stared at all of them. I felt all the air leave me as I took in the information. No, there's no way. It can't be. There was no way that was true. The door behind Omega opened again and Iscul walked in.

"Ah, there you are beautiful. Come sit. We're meeting Jaehyun's girlfriend finally." Omega smiled widely as he grabbed her hand. It felt like

I had been sucker punched. I looked behind me at Jaehyun and then at Iseul and Omega and then Viper and Arsyn. They did favor each other. He looked like his mother, Arsyn looked like her father. Viper was a mixture of his parents. The common feature was the sharp features. Sharp eyes, sharp noses.

I trembled as reality hit me like a ton of bricks. How did I not see any of that? How did I miss the signs? He had a gun. I was speechless. He had an older sister and an older brother. He was in school. The profile pictures of the third son were never of his face. It was purposeful, he was being mindful of the cameras. He was protecting his identity. I felt so stupid.

"Y-You're the missing son…" I mumbled as I looked up at him with confusion. My heart was shattering into a million pieces.

"I didn't want you to find out like this… I didn't think Arsyn was right. I swear I thought she was crazy." Jaehyun said as he threw his hands up.

"Your father killed my mother…" I gasped as the realization dawned on me. I fought back the tears that threatened to overflow.

"Out. Arsyn and Viper. Now." Iseul commanded. I was grateful that she did that, I didn't want Arsyn to see me cry. I heard their feet shuffle and the door closed.

"Who told you that?" she asked. I looked up at her and my heart broke even the more and I crumbled to my knees. Jaehyun followed me to the floor and tried to hug me and I jerked away.

"Don't touch me! D-Don't…" I cried and I could see the hurt flash in his eyes. He looked at his parents and my head fell into my hands.

"I had nothing to do with your mother's death. I promise you." Omega said. I looked up at him through the tears and his figure was blurry. I blinked away the tears and sniffled as I looked at him. What was he talking about?

"You were born in 1997, correct?" Iseul asked as she came around the desk and squatted down in front of me. I nodded.

"Our family didn't come into power until 1998. Our daughter was four or five, Viper was born in 1995 and Shadow-Jaehyun, was born in 1996. The old leader died in August of 1997 from a heart attack. That wasn't us." Omega explained patiently from his desk as he looked down at me. I searched his eyes for any sign of a lie and I couldn't find one. But there was something else there. I couldn't place my finger on what it was. I looked at Iseul and searched her eyes. I couldn't find any lie in hers either. I was even more confused. I was captured by the enemy and they told me they didn't kill my mother? Would they lie to me? There were more of them than me. It didn't make sense.

"Then why did Han say that… Why did he lie…" I muttered out loud. I thought back to all the years of hell with him. All he did was lie. All he did was manipulate. It was about the money the whole time. I knew it. He manipulated me and my emotions. I felt myself seething with anger and hatred again. Han was not to be trusted. Never was.

"Do you know what happened to my mother?" I asked as I looked between them. Iseul shook her head, and she was being honest.

"I will help you find out. Whatever it was, Han was involved." Omega said. There was a fire in his eyes that I didn't expect to see. He was almost angry. But I saw no lie in his eyes when he said Han was involved. I started to think so too. I was born in May, so the timeline didn't make sense. They couldn't have done it.

"Why do you want to help me?" I inquired. I saw them both look at Jaehyun who was still beside me with his hands folded in his lap and he looked like a sad puppy that had been kicked.

"Our son clearly feels something deep for you. And you feel something deep for him. He wouldn't rest until he got the answers for you. So, I'll carry that burden for him." Omega said simply.

"Is that all?" Omega slightly chuckled and shook his head.

"You're a quick one, Miss Rose. It's no secret, you're talented. It's no secret that you are the greatest asset to Han. Without you his empire would crumble. But I know Han. I know him very well. He fears you. He fears the power you hold and the greatness you hold. He's holding you back. You know it too. So why stay? When over here with us… You'd be valued and treated with the respect you deserve. Jaehyun is here. And we'd never try to hold you back. Allow me to make you an offer that I think you'd like." he explained. I looked up at him and he leaned across the desk seriously.

"Join us," he offered. My eyes widened and once again I felt like I had been sucker punched in the stomach. I was stunned.

"Jaehyun, I'll extend the offer to you as well. Get back to me in two weeks. Take some time to think about it." Omega said as he stood up and turned to wait for Iseul. She smiled softly and leaned forward to kiss me on the cheek and she kissed Jaehyun on the forehead and she stood up and walked out with Omega. We sat in a tense silence. I turned to Jaehyun and he was looking at me still and toying with his fingers.

"I guess we have a lot to talk about, huh?" I said softly. He simply nodded at me.

~Chapter 28~

J aehyun led the way outside and I took in my surroundings. There were numerous hanoks surrounding us, but they looked much larger than the typical ones. From what I could see there were seven or eight arranged in an upside-down U shape and the one we came out of was at the center of the slope. In the middle of the open space was a beautiful pond. It was large and on either side there were walkways that followed the upside down U shape and it allowed people to walk into the hanok of their choice. There was beautiful greenery and colorful flowers around the water. There was a bench close to the water to sit on and we sat there. It gave a small area of peace and tranquility in the chaos that was happening. Koi fish swam in the pond peacefully.

"So, you're an assassin? From the Yakuza. You're not really a businessman's daughter." he inquired.

"The Yakuza is like a business. He is the kumicho of the Yamaguchi gumi. I hold the saiko komon title," I answered.

"Ah, that's what you mean by being the only woman that holds a position of high rank. Makes sense. That was clever."

"What did you mean when you said you didn't believe Arsyn?"

"Remember when the NIS came to visit you at work? I knew it wasn't the NIS, that's why I was so concerned about you not calling on time. Areum left and called me asking questions. It was a theory then. She was certain after the Chae incident. I got a warning about the potential presence of a Yakuza member in Korea earlier than that."

"That conversation in the kitchen that I walked in on." I remembered.

"The one you eavesdropped on, yes." he teased. I glared at him and shook my head. Not the time for jokes.

"Why didn't you say anything?"

"Because I didn't believe her. Didn't believe her for a long time because I mean, my Ae Ri? Sweet, precious little Ae Ri. An assassin from the Yakuza. It just didn't make sense. The anxiety, the PTSD. Assassins just don't feel anything from everything I know. Areum doesn't feel anything. We have other assassins who are just cold. Callous. But now that I'm thinking about it. It does make sense. You see a lot of shit. When did you start?"

"I started training in this lifestyle when I was a child. I could shoot a gun before I learned how to ride a bike. I entered our training program at the age of four or five and I was in combat classes. I trained in just about every martial art you could think of. The program was brutal and when I wanted to quit, Han smacked me around. He was ruthless. The shit with my father is so dark that if I told you everything, you'd be surprised." I admitted.

"So that's a real thing? I've heard mentions of the Yakuza training program. She listed it as a reason why she trained so hard. So you've done this all your life. That's why you're stuck. You've never lived a life outside of the underground world." Jaehyun said, disappointment evident in his voice.

"Honestly a lot of the things that I've done with you, it was my first time. Going to the beach, the vacation, shopping at the mall, amusement parks, dates, even having close associates or friends. All of this is so new to me. I've never experienced it. I never had a family. Dinner dates or trips with my family. I envy you." I shook my head sadly and looked down at the koi fish as they swam around.

"So I have to ask you, what is it that makes you stay in this lifestyle? Anytime I ask you to just leave everything behind and start over with me, it's always a no. Why?"

"What else am I supposed to do? Honestly. I've done this my whole life. I acquired great power and wealth at twenty. I like the money and power it gives me. The freedom, the control. The violence makes sense to me. It's the only way I've been able to channel my emotions. Not having it for the past few months has been hard." I answered honestly.

"Your fainting spells. Makes sense. I commend you for your acting skills. You played your role really well. I was definitely fooled. You were holding a lot of secrets." he smirked slightly. I grimaced at the comment. That stung a little.

"When you put it that way, it sounds bad. I don't like that. I didn't plan to meet you. I didn't lie to you just because. I had no idea who you were. You weren't included in my files. Even when I started working at the station, there was nothing about you. All of the pictures were of your back dressed in a trench coat. I've never seen you in a trench coat. And it's not like you told me. I had reason to hide. You were a normal college kid who just had money and a secure future. And I did try to keep you at arm's distance. You bulldozed your way in." I defended myself. He shrugged at that.

"That's a good point. I was going to tell you at some point."

"I debated. I went back and forth on telling you. I didn't want to scare you off. I figured I could complete my assignment, take over the Jopok and then use the combined strength of the Jopok and my clan to overthrow Han. There would be no one to threaten us then. We'd be safe. I could maintain my power and status. The wealth. And I'd have access to the violence whenever I needed it."

"Those were some seriously big plans. What was your assignment anyways?" Jaehyun asked curiously.

"To kill the head family of the Jopok. Omega, Viper, and Arsyn. I found out about a mysterious third child and a wife later on. But they automatically became targets too. And there were times where I forgot who I really was and I became Choi Ae Ri and she wasn't real. But I got lost in it. She lived the life that I wanted, but could never have. I enjoyed it but I still felt out of place because it wasn't real technically but it became real. I grew a strong liking towards Haeun, Nari, Jiwoo. Miyeon too." I answered. I paused for a moment to gather my thoughts. There was so much I had to say and I had to explain because I didn't want to lose him. I didn't want him to think that I lied to him about how I felt because that was real.

"I'm here, Ae-Rose. I'm listening." he encouraged placing a hand on thigh.

"The only thing I was sure about and that I knew was real was you… And what I felt about you. I knew when my feelings started to grow and change, I just couldn't describe it or put it into words as it happened. All I knew was that it was happening. I liked it and I knew I couldn't lose you or let you go. Even now I think I'd die if you were to leave me. I fell in love with you and I couldn't stop it from happening…"

Everything went silent after the words left my mouth. I stared down at the pond and wished the ground would swallow me whole. A lump formed in my throat and the prolonged silence sent insecurity and panic coursing through my body. Why was he so quiet? Did he not feel the same now? Did he get tired of waiting to hear that? I felt his hand brush against my cheek and wipe away a tear. I didn't realize that I started crying. I looked up at him and he smiled softly.

"Thank you for saying that. It means the world to me, princess. I never said I was going anywhere. This changes nothing between us. I still want you just as much as I did when I first met you. You just have to tell me what you want to do. And I'll be there every step of the way. Do you want to continue in the lifestyle or leave it behind and we start over?" He spoke to me in a gentle voice and I paused for a moment. I didn't understand the gravity of the situation until he framed it that way. Either option got me away from Han but only one would get me the revenge on Han that I wanted. Possibly. The other option took me away from the lifestyle completely and I became a civilian. What would I do as a civilian?

"I-I don't really know… It kind of took me off guard. Did he really mean that when he offered it? Why did he offer you the choice? Aren't you already in?" I inquired. He shook his head.

"I chose not to go active when the choice was offered. Areum was part of the reason why I decided not to. She dedicated her life to it and it turned her into something I didn't recognize. She never dated or had a boyfriend from what I know. It didn't look like she was living life. And she has all the potential in the world. Daehyun never had an original idea of his own. He's more of the brute strength guy, no real brains. He didn't have much drive or desire to do anything outside of this. I wanted to form my own path. I wanted to live a normal life as a college kid. Date, travel, make mistakes, have friends. It felt like I couldn't do that and be active in the lifestyle." he answered. He took a moment and chewed on his bottom lip. I tilted my head in curiosity. He was debating something.

"I'm not saying I am perfect. I'm not saying I haven't done things for the Jopok. I've done illegal business things for the organization. I've been the front man taking Nam Industries into different sectors of the economy and helping it establish its footprint in things like finance and international trade. I've done some money laundering, loan sharking. I've connected Areum to drug dealers in large corporations, helped her find places to smuggle it into and ways to ship it out. I've used family ties to get what I wanted. My father and mother never treated me any differently for not choosing to go active and I'm thankful for that."

I was stunned. I didn't know that was an option. I didn't think you could choose whether or not you followed in a parent's footsteps in this lifestyle. It was always expected. It always happened that way. Any deviation or attempts at deviation was met with punishment in my case. His father still talked to him and accepted him. He still cared for Jaehyun. Omega seemed like a good father. "He gave all of you the choice?" I clarified. He simply nodded as if it was the most normal thing in the world.

"I've never heard of that... Your father sounds like a good man. Allowing you the freedom to choose." Definitely better than Han.

"He's a good man. We grew up in a happy home. My dad rarely yelled. He was stern, yes but he was gentle. He trained us all in combat and things like that. He made sure that we knew how to shoot and made us resourceful but we also got to play with kids our ages and we went places as a family and he loved my mom so much."

I kept my expression neutral. What Jaehyun was telling me completely shattered any knowledge and teachings I had about the Koreans. They weren't hateful or vile. They weren't abusive to women and children. As I thought about all the things I learned, it sounded like that was what the Yakuza was. It sounded like Han was talking about himself and the Yamaguchi. He was abusive to women and children. He was involved in human trafficking and the clan that he directly oversaw would kidnap women and children and sell them. I remember finding that out and being genuinely speechless. But it was one of the first incidents that started to show me who Han was.

"You know the more I learn about your father, the more I want to hurt him. I want to hang him from a flagpole and watch him suffocate to death." A dark look crossed his face for a moment as he looked down at the pond. I looked back at him slightly stunned at the comment. I had never seen him upset. I couldn't help the bitter laugh that escaped me.

"You're too kind. I want his head hanging on a wall." I sighed. He looked back at me and grabbed my hand.

"This revenge means a lot to you, doesn't it?" I took a deep breath to settle my nerves.

"It does. I can't leave this life behind until Han pays for everything he's done. I have to figure out what happened to my mother. This is the only way I can figure out what happened."

"Then that's what we're doing." My eyebrow raised and I looked over at him quickly.

"What the hell are you talking about?" I demanded.

"We're joining the Jopok." he answered.

"No the hell you're not. This isn't a game. This is serious. Didn't you just say you chose not to pursue this lifestyle?"

"Just because I chose not to go active, doesn't mean I can't change my mind. I'm ready to go at a moment's notice." he chuckled.

Uneasiness rushed through me. Thoughts of him in danger and being shot at made me sick to my stomach. I felt my mouth go dry. Did he continually train? How was he ready to step in at any moment? When did he find time to train? I suddenly remembered the gun from his house. That was his weapon of choice. I couldn't help the stunned laugh that escaped me.

"What's so funny?"

"I missed the signs. All of them. To be as great as I am, I was blinded by emotions." He snickered and shrugged.

"Looks like I'm a good actor too. Or we were both blind. Either way I'm ready."

"Absolutely not. I disagree. It's not safe. You have school and your friends. Your projects. You can't leave that behind." I reasoned with him.

"Who said I was leaving any of that behind? I'm the king of multitasking, remember?" he countered. He had a point.

"I don't want you to get hurt. I'll worry about you all the time."

"And I'd worry about you. We might as well be together and watch each other's backs. We'd be unstoppable together." It was becoming difficult to reason against him. We'd be right beside each other as usual and he wouldn't have any better protection than me. Still, I was going to put a stop to it.

"You're new to this. Training isn't like being on the field. It's different." I explained to him.

"Good thing I have some practice then, huh?"

I groaned in annoyance at his unwavering. "You're being ridiculous, Nam." I whined.

"No, you are. My mind's not changing. If you go active then I do too. If you choose to leave it behind, then I'll disassociate from the illegal businesses and only do the legal businesses. The choice is yours. By the way, my real last name is Cho. Nam is the last name we use in the public to hide." Jaehyun declared as he stood up and looked down at me. The tone of his voice told me that it wasn't up for debate. He had made his decision and he put the ball in my hands to decide our fate. The realization put more weight on my shoulders than I had ever felt before in my life. It wasn't just about me anymore. My decision would have a ripple effect. I internally groaned, he wanted it that way. He extended a hand to me, and I looked up at him confused.

"It's late. Let's go home. I have a car that I leave here. Are you coming?" He asked as I stared out at the pond blankly. I nodded and grabbed his hand and stood up with him. He helped me stand up and he led the way out of the pond area. We walked through a grassy area, and I saw other hanoks positioned in similar arrangements off in the distance. The compound had to be sitting on acres of land.

"Is this all the headquarters? How big is this place?" I asked out of curiosity. He hummed for a moment before answering.

"About 2 acres and yes. We have offices, some training quarters, places to sleep and live for those who need it, we hold some drugs, money and gold here. It's set up to be huge, so no one person will know where everything is. Everyone knows which hanoks have the weapons just in case." he replied.

"Well prepared, I see." I looked around at the buildings as we walked a little longer. I saw that we were getting close to the road and ahead of me I saw a building that wasn't a hanok. It was made of brick and had a large gray door like it belonged to a garage. We approached it and he typed in a number on the keypad and the door slid up. We stepped inside and it really was a large garage. It was surprisingly two stories and there were cars packed inside and a small office was off in the corner and a person jolted awake as the door slid closed again. The man stood and bowed.

"At ease, Junwon. Just came to get my car and I'm leaving. Go back to sleep." Jaehyun waved him off. The man sat back down. Each car was black but it was a different model and make. We walked further into the garage and in the back there were five cars separated from the rest of the cars. I noticed each one was a Lamborghini Aventador just in different colors. Black, blue, white, silver and bright green. He leaned down and reached under the blue one to pull out keys and unlock the door. "A blue Lamborghini too? The red wasn't enough?" I laughed.

"It's the family's favorite brand. Can never have too many." he replied. He helped me into the car and got in after me and we started the long drive home.

Charnaye Conner

~Chapter 29~

The past week and a half was torture. How Jaehyun was able to sleep so peacefully after everything the night of the party was a mystery to me. It was another sleepless night for me. My insomnia was the worst it had been in months. Nothing would help me sleep. Not even being in Jaehyun's arms. It seemed like sleeping in them made everything worse. The lack of sleep was causing the feelings of anxiety to grow more frequent and whenever I was able to sleep the nightmares got worse. I honestly didn't know what was worse. The time where I didn't know what was wrong with me or now because I know what's wrong, but I don't know how to fix it. It was cruel.

I heard movement behind me, and I looked back at Jaehyun's shirtless figure lying in bed fast asleep. He was on his stomach under the blanket and without looking I knew his arms were folded under the pillow. It was his default sleeping position. It hadn't fully sunk in that he was the son of the enemy I had been taught to hate and sent on assignment to kill. All of the fantasies that I had of us living in peace was shattered. It was impossible to even imagine leaving the Yakuza. It was almost unheard of. The people who left the Yakuza were no longer useful to the organization, so they were allowed to leave but not without consequences. They were beaten or tortured, sometimes even killed. Han wasn't going to just let me leave, high ranking officials didn't leave. They retired but they were still at the mercy of the Yakuza. At a moment's notice a retired official could be called and answering was mandatory or it was death. I couldn't retire. I wasn't old enough; Han wouldn't allow it anyways. Everything went through him.

The decision should have been easy, it should have been clear cut. It wasn't. I was battling the part of my brain that was hardwired from years of training that kept telling me it was wrong to leave. It was against the rules. The voice sounded robotic as it repeated itself in my head. The pledge I made at a young age in each martial arts class. To protect and preserve the way of life. While the voice played over and over again, there was another part of me that screamed for my freedom. It was more logical than the other one. It screamed for a new start. It reminded me that Jaehyun was permanent in my life. He was the only constant in my life. It told me that my revenge on Han could only happen if I joined the Jopok. Then there was a third voice that always crept in whenever I thought logically about how Jaehyun would join too, and he would be in danger. I groaned softly as I put my head in my hands and rubbed my eyes. I was exhausted. I took a look at the clock, and it read four am.

"We need to get you to a doctor. You've gone seventy-two hours with six hours of sleep. This isn't healthy." I jumped slightly hearing Jaehyun's voice. I turned to him and he was leaning against the headboard with his arms folded.

"When did you wake up?"

"I've been listening to you for about an hour and a half. You talk to yourself. I never noticed that before." I raised an eyebrow. Talking to myself?

"You can't tell me you don't know that you talk to yourself."

"In my head. Not out loud."

"You need sleep then. Because you must not be aware of it. But anyways, let's talk about it." he said as he got up from his spot and sat on the edge of the bed in front of me. I sighed and looked away from him. I felt the tears fill my eyes despite my attempts to swallow them down.

"It's not fair. There's no reason to even still be considering what the Yakuza teachings say or what Han taught me because it never benefited me or included me in the 'family' he loved to preach so much. But yet that's all I keep hearing repeatedly. Then there's the side of me that's logical. I know it's a necessity. This could be my only chance at the revenge I want. You're here and that's the most important thing to me. But the idea of you joining because of me doesn't sit right. To uproot your life like that, it feels wrong. I don't want you to resent me for it." I admitted as the tears fell down my face. He sat quietly waiting for me to continue.

"You want to know what frustrates me and what's been frustrating me the past week and a half. The lack of control I have over all of this. I'm used to having everything under control and going the way I orchestrated them. I've spent all this time trying to figure out how I could achieve all of my goals without dragging you into my mess and I can't figure it out. I can't force myself to be comfortable with a normal civilian life. I keep trying to silence the hardline voice in my head that's been dictating my life for years but it won't shut up. It won't let me be at peace. I know what I need to do and I know what I'm going to do, but this is the first time I've ever had so much anxiety over a decision…" I looked down at my nails as I took a deep breath to settle myself.

"If you know what you're going to do then why continue to think about it? You're torturing yourself with what ifs that you can't prove. Nothing has happened yet. We still have to answer the invite. We haven't jumped over that hurdle. How are you worrying about steps four and five when we haven't done step one? Take it one day at a time. I know it's easier said than done because of the anxiety but breathe. Embrace the freedom that's in front of you, princess." Jaehyun said as he grabbed my hand and stroked it. I looked up at him. Freedom. I had never considered that word before. When he said it, I could tell he had a different meaning of freedom than I did. It meant more than money and power. I was too exhausted to try to decipher at that moment. I remained quiet, waiting for him to speak again.

"Why are you so worried about me joining? I have the training. You're not holding a gun to my head saying I have to join you. It's a choice I'm making for myself. You'd be willing to be something you're not and not do something you need to do because of me?" He sighed disappointed at my silence.

"That's not fair or healthy. You shouldn't sacrifice your wants and needs for anyone. Not even me."

"Let's not call it that. It reminds me of how shitty my life was." I said quietly. It was a sacrifice that I didn't want to make. It was easier to tell myself that I had no choice in the matter. It wasn't a lie, it helped lessen the pain for me when I was younger. Feelings of bitterness and rage coursed through my veins for a moment. Once those feelings passed, shame and embarrassment caused my cheeks to heat up.

There was a part of me that hated that he was finding out so much about my past through context clues and conversations because it was embarrassing. Everything I put up with, the disrespect and the unfair treatment I had to endure because of Han's position. There was a part of me that felt like a fraud. I struggled in my relationship with Han because of the power dynamics but when I had subordinates, I ruled with an iron fist. There was a part of me that was grateful though. He could use context clues to fill in some of the blanks that I left out. I didn't have to sit back and recount every horrible memory in order to tell him how messed up I really was. It was indirect but Jaehyun understood. He never forced me to go into explicit detail. He never pressed for more information than what I gave him. I appreciated that.

I wasn't prepared for how well he would take everything. Nothing could have prepared me for that. When the darker parts of my upbringing started to come out, he didn't run from me like I thought he would. He still felt the same and if anything, he was less reserved with his negative emotions towards what I went through. He had made more than a few comments about wanting to skin Han alive or watch him be tortured slowly. I was amazed by how sweet it was. He still looked at me with stars in his eyes. He was proving that it didn't matter what happened, he would always stand by me, and it meant everything to me.

"You know I've never known you to be the one who cares about the rules. Or follow them. Come to think of it, I've never known you to care about what other people say either. You've been doing what you want since you've been in Korea. I'd like to think I've seen the real you and I know you pretty well. You're overthinking something that you're going to do anyway. Don't torture yourself for something that makes you happy. Especially for something that will make you better and help you heal. Besides, you're too pretty for that." Jaehyun tilted my head up and gave me a small smile as he stroked my cheek softly.

He had a point. I was torturing myself over something that I was going to do. I wouldn't choose anything over him. I always knew what decision I was going to make in my gut but everything that would come afterwards made me nervous. We weren't going to ride off into the sunset like everything was fine. I didn't want to drag him into the mess. I sighed and grabbed his hand. "Aren't you the slightest bit worried about what happens after this decision is made? Did you think about that? Because that's what my concern is. I don't want you to suffer because of me. I don't know what will happen." I confessed. He shrugged nonchalantly.

"Obviously I have. I'm not naive. We'll get through it together. No matter what happens. I'll be right by your side until the end." Jaehyun chuckled.

"I don't know if I admire or fear your arrogance, Cho. You have no experience in this, remember?" He rolled his eyes and stood up and moved to the open space on the left side of the bed. He made a come here motion with his fingers and got into a fighting stance. I raised an eyebrow.

"What do you think you're doing? Is that a challenge?" I laughed loudly at him. It wasn't to be mean; I was genuinely amused.

"You keep doubting me, so I say we settle this. First one to be pinned for three seconds loses?" A cocky grin crossed his face and I shook my head.

"You're going to get hurt. I'm not doing this with you. You'd be embarrassed."

"Are you sure about that? Because you sound scared. Areum told me that you weren't that strong of a fighter. Is that why you won't fight me?" he smirked mischievously as I glared at him. Arsyn saying that I was weak enraged me and I stood up and stood in front of him.

"Your sister's a liar! She would've been dead if your brother didn't hit me in the back of the head while my back was turned! You're an idiot to believe her. I'm better than she will ever be!" I snapped. His grin widened.

"I don't know... You're the greatest assassin to ever live, but you won't fight little old me? Sounds like she's right to me..."

I saw red and before I could stop it, my fist raised, and I took a swing at him. He leaned back avoiding the hit that would have connected with his jaw. I stared blankly. He moved quickly. That should have connected. He winked. "Want to try again?" he teased. I grumbled in annoyance and took my left fist and aimed for his stomach. He grabbed my left hand and shook his head.

"You have to be more creative than that, princess." He was making fun of me. I scoffed and kicked him in the stomach. He hit the wall and I heard him groan in pain and he clutched his stomach and sank to his knees. I yelped in concern and rushed over to him.

"Are you okay? See that's why I said you're not meant for this. You hit harder things than walls in this lifestyle. Why are you-HEY!" I yelled as he swept my legs from under me and straddled my waist and pinned my shoulders down and started to count quickly to three.

"Rule number one. Never let your guard down in a fight. Thought you knew that, Rose?" he snickered.

"You tricked me! Get off!" He laughed slightly and let me go and stood up and stepped back to give me space.

He gave me an annoying smirk and waved me forward again. I hummed under my breath, slightly embarrassed. He took a defensive stance and I charged at him throwing calculated punches and kicks at him and he blocked each one. I growled in frustration as he continued to block each hit even as they got wilder and more aggressive, he continued to block each one. I started to look for weak and vulnerable spots and in my search, I somehow missed him stopping a punch by grabbing my right wrist because I found myself pressed face first against the wall with an arm pinned behind my back. It happened so fast I couldn't defend myself.

"For being so great at this, you make careless mistakes. Letting your emotions get the best is the second most basic rule of combat. And never take your eyes off of your opponent." he whispered as he kissed my temple and chuckled. I jerked around in irritation, ignoring the burn in my shoulder from how tight he was holding. He laughed slightly at my struggling.

The whole thing was upsetting me because he actually had some potential and training. He moved too fast to not have been trained at one point. He wasn't a rookie. He was able to keep up with me, and if that wasn't bad enough, he was making fun of me for it. I used my right leg to push off the wall and it caused him to lose his footing and his hold on my arm. I used the momentum of the push to flip over him and when I landed, I swept his legs from under him, and he landed hard on his back and I quickly moved to put him in an arm bar before he could recover. He yelled in pain as he rolled over trying to break the hold. "Shit! That hurts! An arm bar, seriously babe?" he groaned as he squirmed trying to get out of the hold. I grinned in satisfaction hearing him whimper in pain. It made me feel vindicated.

"Looks like your emotions got the best of you, huh Jae?" I called as I watched him struggle with a small smirk.

"If I didn't know any better, I would say you were enjoying this. Is this a kink of yours?" he laughed slightly through the pain. He finally got enough momentum to roll completely over and essentially curl me into a ball as he stabilized himself on his knees and he winked at me. The awkward position caused me to loosen the hold on his arm and he counted to three again as my shoulders were pinned. He laughed loudly at my expression and let me go again.

"I would say since I pinned you twice, I'm qualified." he reached out his hand to help me.

"I got it." I ignored his outstretched hand and stood up on my own. He just chuckled and shook his head.

"Pouting about it won't make you right, princess." he teased. I wasn't as irritated about losing as I was everything else. No matter what I said he would point to this moment as saying that he was qualified and capable. I hated it. This wasn't for him and it didn't matter how qualified he was.

"I still disagree. This isn't something you want to do." I stated. He rolled his eyes.

"You have to come up with something more concrete. If I didn't want to do it, I wouldn't be having this conversation with you. Are you ready for bed now?" I sighed deeply.

"This job changes you. I don't want to see that happen to you." He turned to me and sighed softly as he put his hands on my shoulders.

"There it is. You finally told me the real reason. I was wondering how far you were going to take this. Talk to me. What do you mean?"

"This job has a lot of dark parts in it. It stains and taints you. Being involved in it makes you callous and cold. Untrusting. The world doesn't shine and sparkle when you've seen the things that I've seen. Do the things that I've done. It's dark and cold. It's lonely. I don't want you to experience that. You're the only example of good that I have in the world. I told you a long time ago that I ruin beautiful things. If you join, it would just be another example of that. And I'm trying to save you."

I felt the tears fill my eyes and I looked away as I tried to keep them at bay. The pain that coursed through me shook me to my core. The thought that Jaehyun would become anything like me haunted me. Especially since it wasn't necessary. He didn't have to see what I saw. He was pure. He had all the potential in the world, and I didn't want to see him lose everything. I didn't want to change him. It didn't feel right. It didn't feel good, and I couldn't accept it.

"Your environment doesn't dictate who you are. You can choose to be something different. You can do a job and live a completely different life outside of it. I won't change. I promise. Do you trust me?" Jaehyun ran a thumb over my cheek, and he looked me in the eyes waiting for an answer. The emotion in them was intense and I could only nod in response.

"Then you have to trust the process on this. There's a reason why I have to do this. I just have to figure out what it is. But it will be alright."

"I hope you're right on this Cho Jaehyun. I hope you're right." I leaned my forehead against his chest, and he wrapped me in a tight hug.

~Chapter 30~

"You've been quiet back here. Are you okay?" Jaehyun called from down the hall. I remained quiet for a moment until I saw his reflection appear in the mirror in front of me. We made eye contact in the mirror, and he slightly smiled.

"You had a choice. You can't be mad at me because I'm doing what I said I would do." he reminded me. I rolled my eyes. He had a point, but I still didn't like how he decided to join too. Today was decision day. We were meeting Omega and the rest of his family to give our decisions on joining the ranks of the Jopok. I had been dreading this day since I found everything out. I predicted that it would end up with both of us joining, but I had some foolish hope that I could convince Jaehyun to decline. A stupid idea really.

"I'm about to make the most life changing decision that I could ever make. Why wouldn't I be okay?" I replied as I adjusted the white and pink blouse I wore and left some buttons undone. The sarcasm and bitterness in my voice wasn't intentional, it had been like that for the past few days.

He walked into the room and kissed my cheek quickly. "You'll be grateful for this one day. You'll see," he said as he rubbed my shoulders and adjusted the necklace I was wearing. He was always so sure when he said it. I was sure that I would always hate the decision he made. It wasn't worth the argument; we were minutes away from the meeting and there was no going back. Their headquarters had similar rules as the Yakuza headquarters. It was a business or business casual dress. I wore a white and pink short set that Jaehyun bought for me and he was dressed in a white polo and khaki slacks.

"You look really pretty in this. Aren't you glad I bought you colors, princess?" he grinned slightly and I allowed a small chuckle to escape. He was trying to ease the tension that I felt and I did appreciate it, but it wasn't that easy for me. I was an outsider to them. I didn't know what position I was going to have. There was nothing certain about this. I was leaving behind established power and status for something unknown. I didn't have the patience to work my way up from the bottom. I had gone through that once before. I couldn't share any of this with Jaehyun, he wouldn't understand. It was his family. He was guaranteed to be treated well. I wasn't. I sighed internally as I felt him squeeze my shoulder softly.

"Let's do this," I agreed and he nodded and he led the way to the front door.

We had been at his place the whole day trying to get everything in order for the new changes. He had to work on a few projects and change his proposed class schedule for his last semester. I spent the day getting Choi Ae Ri back overseas on an academic leave of absence. There was no need to keep Ae Ri in the world when my cover was blown. We told his friends that I was transferring schools so they wouldn't be seeing me around campus anymore and they were sad, but they were hopeful that they would continue to see me when they hung out with Jaehyun. There was a part of me that was hopeful. I had become fond of the group over the past few months. I never had a life outside of the Yakuza so I didn't think anything would be different here. I didn't really believe Jaehyun when he said that he would maintain school and a social life outside of the Jopok, but he was so confident and sure I just let him believe it. The reality would set in soon enough. As we rode the elevator down to the parking garage, I held onto his hand tightly and stood close by him. He kissed the top of my head and rested his chin on it. "I love you. I always will, you know that, right? No matter what happens," he whispered.

I leaned against him and nodded. Everything felt heavy. The gravity and seriousness of everything was starting to hit the closer we got to the parking garage. He was still nonchalant about this entire thing. I just didn't understand how.

The car ride to the headquarters was silent and I swear I could hear my heart pounding in my chest as the landmarks started to look unfamiliar to me. My palms started to sweat and I fought to keep my breathing under control. I couldn't shake the anxiety that was rushing over me but I sat in the passenger seat expressionless. I didn't need to look weak at this moment. I knew I was making the right decision. I just couldn't shake the feeling that making this decision would have consequences. "Breathe Rose. You're literally turning red in the face." Jaehyun reminded me. I let out the breath that I had been unknowingly holding. I looked over at him.

"We don't have to do this. We have other options." I rolled my eyes as he repeated himself for the hundredth time. He still didn't get it.

"Correction. YOU. You don't have to do this. I have to. I don't have skill sets outside of this lifestyle, remember? I can't just go the straight and narrow road. I've done too much and seen too much."

"It's not too late to change. There's still the interior decorating business. Two years tops. You're a CEO. Power and money."

"Two years of doing what? Sitting around bored? Doing nothing? Letting you take care of me?" I fought to keep my voice level. I know he really believed in this fantasy where I lived a civilian life, and I just couldn't do it. I know he wasn't trying to be pushy or annoying, but it felt that way. It was what he wanted for us, and I couldn't give him that.

"Whatever you want. You want to run one of the businesses? Hell, two or three. I can use the help. There's money and power there too. Finish school. Be normal. Go to therapy. Heal. The sky is limitless. You have more than enough money. I'd hardly be taking care of you. I have more than enough money, so if you happen to run out, I'll cover you then." he offered. He looked over at me and he just looked so nonchalant. I couldn't read his emotions. The frustration and irritation spilled over.

"Why don't you just say what you want, Cho Jaehyun? Why are you being like this? You want me to mold into what you want. Just say that." I snapped at him. He didn't respond to the outburst. He sat quietly and continued to drive and that made me madder. So, I continued.

"I can't be this domestic and homely girlfriend that you want! I can't live a quiet and normal life. Everyday I'd be looking over my shoulder, thinking that my time in the organization is going to sneak up and bite me in the ass! I can't protect you if I'm outside of the lifestyle. You're the reason I'm doing this! We will never live a life of peace if I don't do this!" I yelled at him.

It was tense and quiet for what felt like forever. The car pulled over to the side of the road and I stared down at the floor. He was silent beside me. The atmosphere was suffocating, and I wished he would say something. Did I go too far? Did he finally realize that I was too much trouble? Suddenly he just chuckled and let out a sigh of what sounded like relief. I looked at him stunned by the reaction. "I'm not going to tell you what to do. It's your choice. What I want is for you to be safe and happy. I want you to feel safe and secure. I didn't mean to keep pushing my ideas on you. I can understand why you feel like this is your only option." He reached over and grabbed my hand and held it tightly. He turned to face me and the look on his face was serious. I shrunk back slightly from the intensity.

"I don't want you to change. I love you as you are. Even when you are short tempered and moody. I'm not trying to morph you into something you aren't. I genuinely thought I was giving you ideas that would help you. I just want you to be healthy in every aspect. I just know being tied to the Yakuza and being tied to your father is not good for you. I never cared what decision you made. I just wanted you to feel like you had options. And I want you to be confident and secure in whatever decision you make. If this is what the decision is, then we stand on it. We don't look back on it. We move forward."

I rolled my eyes slightly at the joke at my expense. I sighed in annoyance. He was right. If this was the decision, I was going to make I had to be at peace with it. The consequences would be the same whether I joined or not. So, I may as well have an advantage and access to resources. Maybe I could do damage to Han before he could figure out what happened. Obsessing over it wasn't going to make the situation better. Everything I wanted and everything I was trying to do was unprecedented. Leaving the Yakuza without any warning in order to get the revenge that I have wanted for years. While doing that, I was trying to keep my most prized possession safe from the potential consequences of my actions and he was throwing himself into the fire with me. It was insane. It was on brand for me though. Create chaos wherever I go and ruin lives in the process. It was the story of my life.

My life was the product of decisions that people had made for me. I never got a say in any of it. I just had to deal with whatever I was given. This was my chance to make it all stop. This was my chance at freedom. All I had to do was follow someone else's orders for a little longer and then I would be free. I could start living my life. Jaehyun and I could live in peace. The thought of Jaehyun and I on a beach somewhere calmed my racing heart. "Do you promise not to hate me?" I questioned him softly. He shook his head.

"Never could and never would. I'm by your side," he promised as he held out his pinky.

I allowed a small giggle to escape at the childish action. I locked my pinky with him, nonetheless. This would be our new life then. "Headquarters, then?"

"To the headquarters."

I watched as he pulled onto the road again and we continued our journey. I watched the scenery change from the luxurious city into more open fields and more construction areas. It was definitely the poorer side of the city. The Jopok were smart for picking this area for their headquarters location. No one would think to look out this far. We were at least forty-five minutes from where we lived. There were some abandoned buildings and a few hanoks and rundown apartment buildings out here. The hanok compound didn't look out of place. I started to notice police cars scattered around and I froze in panic. "They're our people. We're entering our territory. We have police on the payroll who guard the first few miles before we actually reach the compound. Keeps out unwanted visitors. They're guards essentially." Jaehyun explained and I relaxed. He knew a lot more than what I thought. We turned down a street and drove a little further and passed by some officers on foot. They all stood at attention and saluted the car as he drove by. I tilted my head in question.

"Every guard knows my family's cars and license plates by heart. We all drive Lamborghinis and have designated colors for identification." he answered my unspoken question. That was a genius system. I thought back to the Lamborghinis that I saw in the garage when we left the first time I was here.

"So those cars were all your family's? Not yours?"

"Correct. The green one is Daehyun's. The silver is my dad's. The white is my mom's. The black is Arsyn's. Because of course it is. The blue one is mine that I leave here. It's the business car, if you want to call it that. The guards know that I have a red one as well because that's the one I usually drive." he explained.

My jaw dropped stunned at the coordination and careful planning that they had. No wonder it was so difficult to find them. They were proficient at secrecy and hiding. I watched the compound come into view and he took another turn down a road into a dead end and I saw the garage from before. A different man stood outside, and the door was already open for him. He nodded in acknowledgement and drove inside, and we went towards the back of the building again and pulled in the available space next to the green car. As we parked, a thought crossed my mind. "Hey! So, when you bought me a matching car, that wasn't you being romantic and stuff? It was intentional. And here I thought it was special. A shame." I was slightly kidding but it did sting a little. He knew beforehand.

"Hey, don't do that. Don't pout. It is special. We have matching colors. We are the only ones who do. And that means everyone knows you're mine. If you ever drive here without me, they'll know it's you and they have your license plate already. We can get you another color if you want for business too." he offered as he pinched my cheek. I swatted him away playfully and we started the journey to the headquarters.

~Chapter 31~

As we approached one of the organized hanok sections, I looked around slightly confused, not seeing the pond. "Pond is on the other side. This is the official entrance inside. The pond's in the back. Four burly guards stood at attention and when they saw Jaehyun they bowed deeply. He nodded in acknowledgement and led the way inside. The inside seemed much larger than the outside. I observed the numerous twists and turns we made. It really was like a maze. Seeing it in person, I had to admit that the craftsmanship and design was brilliant. We stopped at a closed door labeled CH10. We made eye contact and I nodded. He opened the door, and it was a conference room. Viper sat at the U-shaped table in the middle of the room and grinned when he saw us. There was a door on the back wall. It was directly behind the chair in the center. Must be Omega's seat.

"Oh hyung. Where's everyone else?" Jaehyun asked as he walked ahead of me. I held onto his belt loop out of protectiveness. I wanted to make sure he wouldn't go too far.

Viper noticed this and raised an eyebrow. "Easy Rose. He's fine. No one's out to hurt you guys. Well except Arsyn that is," he laughed boisterously.

I looked at him fully and scowled. His silver hair was dyed a lavender color and he favored Jaehyun a little more with the lighter hair color. "I'm not too worried about her. She would've been dead if it wasn't for the sneak attack," I told him.

"Sorry about that again. I was just doing my job. Didn't know we'd be here now. No hard feelings?" He grinned playfully and winked at me.

"I'm not surprised you were lurking around to save her ass. She should be grateful."

"You'd think she would be, right?" Viper complained as he shook his head.

"Bitches get lucky one time and they suddenly think they're worth something." I heard Arsyn's voice and I turned towards the door in the back to see her walk in. Our eyes met and the malice was palpable in her eyes. I scoffed.

"Bitch please. Lucky? You were on the verge of blacking out, that's why your brother came to your rescue. If you were as good as you claimed, he wouldn't have been lurking around." I growled at her as she stood at the right chair next to Omega's.

"Insignificant tramp. If I wanted you dead, you'd be dead. Always remember that." she snapped back at me.

"Whenever you're ready to try, let me know. Would love a round two." She jumped over the table, and we approached each other at the same time. Neither of us moved as we stared at each other. It was deadly silent, and the tension could be cut with a knife. We were waiting for the other to slip up to take advantage of the mistake. She was a little taller than me, but it didn't matter, neither of us were backing down. I heard Viper's whistle rang out in the silence and he laughed again. I heard a punch connect somewhere and he huffed in pain. Jaehyun must have hit him.

"That's enough. That's not what we're here for." Omega's booming voice rang up in the room. Neither of us moved still. We continued to maintain eye contact and let the animosity simmer between us.

"I said stand down both of you." he repeated with more bass in his voice that time. It was an order. Jaehyun quickly stepped between us, and he raised his arms in defense. "Let's take a moment and chill, okay ladies? Everything's fine. We're all cool. Noona please sit down. The sooner we finish up, the sooner we can all leave." he suggested calmly. Arsyn looked up at her brother and grimaced. She took a step back and went back to her seat. He let out a sigh of relief and turned to me.

"Let's just get through this, okay?" he said softly. I nodded and took my place beside him. Omega sat at the head of the table with Iseul seated next to him on his left. Arsyn sat to his right and Viper sat next to Iseul. His arms were folded over his chest and he watched us intently. Jaehyun nudged me to bow and I quickly followed his lead.

"I'm going to cut to the chase. No need for the formalities. I extended an invitation to you both to join our ranks. And I was generous with the time of consideration. But the day has come to finally give your decisions." Omega announced. The varying reactions of Arsyn and Viper let me know that he didn't run this by either of them and they felt completely different about the situation. Viper had a stunned expression that morphed into an amused laugh. He watched as Arsyn essentially lost her shit. She was clearly agitated and not pleased with the situation. The petty side of me was pleased to see that my presence vexed her so much. It was an unexpected plus to doing this and I felt a little better. Jaehyun placed a hand on my back in support.

"I accept." I said boldly as I made eye contact with Omega. He failed to hide the small smirk on his face that showed he was pleased. He nodded once in response and looked at his younger son.

"Jaehyun?"

"I'm finally home." he announced proudly. He seemed almost excited. Omega's smirk couldn't be contained then. He was ecstatic.

"Excellent. I'm glad you've decided to join us. Keeping with our tradition of accepting new members, I will open the floor to the family for comments and voting." Omega offered as he looked at the other members of his family.

"On the topic of Cho Jaehyun, alias Shadow, entrance into the organization. Raise your hand if you're in agreement," Omega said.

It was no surprise that everyone's hand went up. That made sense. Omega nodded.

"On the topic of Yokoyama Aria, alias Rose, entrance into the organization, raise your hands." My eyes widened slightly. How did he know my real name? That wasn't public information. I'd have to figure that out later. Everyone's hands went up except Arsyn's. That didn't surprise me though.

"Arsyn. Are you voting no or abstaining from voting?" Iseul clarified.

"This is insane. A Yakuza member in our ranks? This is a horrible idea and I'm not going to say yes. I don't even want to entertain this. We don't know her. We don't know where her loyalty lies." Arsyn answered as she folded her arms across her chest and glared at me. Viper snickered and everyone looked towards him.

"You have something to add?" Iseul inquired.

"I personally think my dear sister is looking at this from a selfish viewpoint. The addition of a former Yakuza member would strengthen us. Think of the business connections we could have access to. The family's power grows. Her experience could help us out. It seems like your jealousy is interfering with your logical thinking, noona," Viper answered. An irreverent grin spread across his face.

Jaehyun dropped his head in his hand and sighed softly. The rage and annoyance radiated off of her. I could see her face turn red and her fist clench tightly. A dark glint crossed her eyes as she stared her brother down. He was completely unfazed by her reaction. It was obvious that he had done this before. Omega hummed in thought. "Understandable concerns Arsyn. What to do?" he wondered. He looked at his wife and slightly frowned.

"An initiation mission. Have them prove themselves. Test Jaehyun's skills and see what he's capable of. Test Rose's loyalty. Kill two birds with one stone." Iseul suggested. His eyes sparkled at the idea.

"I like it. Great idea. We'll do that. We'll address Arsyn's concerns and see what they look like in the field. Okay Rose and Shadow. Before you become full members, you will complete an initiation mission. You will get your orders soon. Be on the lookout for them. Once that's completed, we will go forward. Until then, everyone's dismissed." Omega declared. Iseul nodded in agreement and stood up as her husband helped her up and they left the room.

It was silent again and the rest of us looked around awkwardly at each other. Arsyn's jaw was set hard, and she continued to stare at Viper. He was still unfazed. "You guys want to get dinner?" Viper offered cheerfully and he smiled at me. Jaehyun chuckled as the awkwardness died off.

"I could use dinner. I'm starving after the entertainment. You coming, Areum?" Viper extended the offer to her as well. She scoffed and stood up quickly, knocking her chair over.

"You're a fucking idiot," she growled and she stormed out of the room slamming the door behind her. It rattled the entire room. Viper laughed even harder than before.

"Why do you have to aggravate her like that, Daehyun?" Jaehyun scolded him. His brother shrugged and stood up.

"Because it's fun. Until she seriously injuries me or kills me, it'll be that way. Besides that's what brothers are for." the elder smirked.

"So, two broken ribs weren't serious enough? A fractured wrist?"

"I'm not dead yet, little brother. So, the mission continues. But enough about her, let's get some barbecue? How's that sound? Rose can come too. Let's celebrate! My treat."

Jaehyun looked back at me and I shrugged. The night couldn't get any weirder, so what was the harm in that. Viper clapped loudly and ran over to carelessly throw his arms around our shoulders.

"I know a place. I'll race you guys there!" he yelled excitedly. With him so close, you could see the wild and mischievous look in his eyes. Something told me that he was like that naturally.

"No racing. The police are out tonight. Take it easy," Jaehyun warned.

"They gotta catch me. Keep up." Viper winked and made his way out of the conference room.

"Is he always like that?" I questioned.

"Yeah... I wasn't lying when I said he was just there. All his serious thoughts go to the gym with him, and he leaves them there." Jaehyun sighed. He was one of those meathead gym guys. No brains, all muscle.

"A meathead with money and power. A dangerous combination."

"And he's reckless as hell."

"You have an interesting group of characters in your family." I commented. Jaehyun laughed as he shook his head. He led the way out of the conference room, and we made our back to the cars.

The restaurant that Viper invited us to was obviously a popular place for criminals to hang out at. The restaurant was packed with loud men and they were talking loudly over the alcohol and the grills. The workers were all women and they were bringing out bottles of soju and other alcohol for the crowd. Back in Japan, the Yakuza had places like this but I stayed away from them. We sat in a private room in the back of the restaurant.

"So I'm looking at this kid as he pulls out this small as hell pistol and points it at me. And he's shaking. Scared. He tells me to give him the money and then his boys run up wth guns too. So now I'm excited, right?" Viper laughed as he took a shot of soju.

"This was in the red light district? Near one of the clubs?" Jaehyun asked for clarification. Viper nodded.

"Don't worry they're dead. I'm just telling you the story. Now shush, let me finish."

I zoned out for a second and looked out the window of the private room. A group of men were standing up and singing at the top of their lungs. The restaurant was busier than I expected it to be. It was a little after one in the morning. "Hey, you okay?" Jaehyun asked as he rubbed my back. I looked back at them and nodded.

"Just observing. I haven't been in a hang out spot. It wasn't my style back in Japan." I replied.

"The Yakuza didn't have places like these? What a shame." Viper frowned as he took another shot.

"There were. I just didn't go. There was a clear distinction between me and the underlings."

"Oh that reminds me. What were you for them? It was always unclear. You were the assassin, but you held a position and we could never figure out what it was." I paused for a moment debating on if I should tell him. I accepted the offer to join, it would be wise to start being transparent. It felt wrong to give that information up still. It still felt like something I should keep to myself. I wasn't even a full member yet. We were enemies two weeks ago and now I was fighting to secure my spot among their ranks. Viper looked at me expectantly with a small grin on his face. I sighed internally and answered.

"Saiko komon. I ran the clan in Tokyo."

"Why do you call it a clan by the way? I've never asked. I always thought they were called families." Jaehyun jumped in with a question.

"I've never called it that. It's not a family to me. It's business. It's what I do... or did. I was paid well."

"Well, we are family here. And I am excited to have you and Shadow here. I've been hoping to see him finally stop bullshitting around and come back to where he belonged. Little bro was gone for way too long." Viper laughed as he put Jaehyun in a headlock and ruffled his hair. Jaehyun protested and swatted him away.

"I belong wherever I choose. Stop acting like I wasn't here when you guys needed me. I just didn't want the violence." Jaehyun defended himself.

"Well, that's funny. You got with an assassin? That's literally her life. Why did you choose her? Is she the one you told us about? Did you believe Arsyn?" I tilted my head in slight confusion. Did everyone know?

"Wait, all of you suspected me?" I questioned. Viper and Jaehyun looked at each other for a moment.

"We all thought Arsyn was crazy. Honestly. She has this tendency to run with conspiracy theories and be paranoid. I think dad was the only one that humored her and heard her out. She spent a month and a half trying to prove Choi Ae Ri wasn't real and couldn't. She went insane trying to prove her point. She started to notice some stuff with the police and somehow her brain connected Choi Ae Ri and that. She started looking at the police roster and there's the name again." Viper chuckled as he remembered something.

"She visited the station two times before she actually saw you. The third time she went, she came home and doubled down on her theory. We just let her have it. When the Chae thing happened, she was positive. I got fed up eventually and said fine I'll bring you to the company party. So, it was floating around for a while. But no one really thought she was right." Jaehyun added as he shrugged and took a shot. I nodded in understanding. Arsyn was relentless. I had to give her that.

A sense of pride and a soft feeling grew in my chest as I realized that Jaehyun thought the world of me. Even as he heard earth shattering news about me, he didn't believe it and he chose to see the best in me. The me that I showed him. Even after finding out the truth, he chose to stick by me and completely change his life to fit into mine. When I thought about it, that was the sweetest thing anyone had ever done for me. "Speaking of Chae, did you do that to him?" Viper asked quickly.

"I needed information," I shrugged.

"You and Arsyn are just alike. Sadistic and violent. You guys should talk, you'd be great friends." he chuckled. An uncomfortable silence was the only response he got from me. Never in a million years. I heard Jaehyun snicker beside me.

"You underestimate their stubbornness. We'll have to wait on that one," he added, and I punched his arm softly. Viper looked between us for a moment and a small grin spread across his face.

"What're you smirking about?" Jaehyun asked.

"It's crazy to think that this is *the* Rose that people fear. It's different. A bloodthirsty assassin turned expensive domesticated girlfriend. How did you manage that?" Viper answered with a laugh. I picked up the scissors on the table and threw them. He moved just in time for them to lodge into the wall.

"Don't cross the line." I warned him. He stared at me wide eyed and looked over at his brother.

"Dude! She almost killed me! Do something!"

"But you didn't die. So, you're fine. Maybe you'll stop joking around so much." Jaehyun grinned as he took a bite of his food.

Viper scoffed and shook his head. "You're *that* type of boyfriend? Girl can do no wrong, huh?"

"None at all. She's perfect," Jaehyun smiled warmly at me and adjusted a strand of hair for me. I would never get over the fact that even after everything he saw me as perfect. He still felt the same and he stood on everything he said. Everything felt like a dream. There was no way this could be real. He didn't know everything that came with my position or everything that I had done but he overlooked all of it. He still stood by his decision to be with me. I felt shame creeping into my stomach. I didn't deserve it. There was no way I could repay him; I could only give my life to protect his. Viper made a gagging noise.

"Okay, okay. Enough of that." he complained. I glared at him and looked around for something else to throw. Jaehyun laughed and grabbed my hand softly.

"He was teasing, princess. No more throwing things. You may actually hit him. We're still waiting on our induction." he chuckled. I rolled my eyes and leaned back against the wall.

Sharing a meal with Viper wasn't horrible. He joked around a lot and didn't have any major opinions on anything. He was playful and nonchalant. He acted as if I had been around forever. He only talked about fighting, girls, money and working out. He was almost welcoming and friendly. It was drastically different from Arsyn's abrasive and serious nature. Jaehyun's face planted onto the bed in his room. I shook my head. He had a drinking contest with his brother, and I couldn't tell who won because they were both stumbling out of the restaurant. Arsyn wasn't too pleased to hear my voice on Viper's phone telling her he needed a driver. I'm not sure what made her madder, the fact that we all went out together or the fact he got so drunk that he needed her help. Nevertheless, she showed up like a responsible older sibling and took him while I drove Jaehyun home.

I was washing my face in the bathroom when I heard him calling for something. "I don't understand what you're saying, Cho. Go back to sleep." I called back. I was genuinely exhausted from the lack of sleep and that was all I honestly wanted to do, but my brain was too busy trying to process everything that happened the past few hours. It took a few hours for my life and everything that I had ever known to be flipped upside down. It was a decision that I had made but I couldn't help but feel lost. Everything that gave me value was essentially gone. My position, my power… It was unsettling. I felt emptier than I ever had before. I felt like a child again. I was transported back to the Yakuza training camps on my first or second day. Confused, unsure and completely unprepared for what was about to happen. Viper wasn't exactly a help in telling me what to expect. He was that guy that had a leadership role but didn't deserve it. He got it through the right connections. Arsyn was definitely going to be no help. Jaehyun wasn't either. I wasn't sure if I trusted Omega. The only option I had was Iseul and I'm not exactly sure how much she knows.

I sighed under my breath at the situation I got myself into. "Rose… How are you so good at drinking alcohol? You drank just as much as us but you're fine. How? Why?" I turned to see Jaehyun's drunk figure leaning against the door. His eyes were red and squinting from the bright bathroom light. His cheeks matched the red in his eyes and his face was swollen a little from the alcohol. He would complain about that when he sobered up.

"You gotta remember I'm the only woman in Yakuza leadership. Not being good at drinking could've been disastrous. And meetings are full of alcohol," I replied.

"You mean were?"

"Huh?"

"You said you are the only woman in Yakuza leadership. You meant you were," I paused. I didn't realize that.

"Oh yeah. Force of habit. Sorry. That'll take time to get used to not saying." I looked down at the sink and finished washing the rest of the cleanser off my hands. When he said it like that, the feeling of emptiness got worse. I fought to keep the tears at bay. I really was nothing without that title. That was my identity for years. The Yakuza was my identity. Who was I now without it? All I was left with was a bunch of issues that I became aware of and no outlet or knowledge how to figure any of it out. All I had was Jaehyun and he had a lot on his plate too. It wouldn't be fair to him to have my weight too.

"Hey I'm drunk, not stupid. What's wrong? When you realized your slip up, you got this look in your eyes. Talk to me." Jaehyun asked as he laid his head on top of mine. I didn't have the words to explain it right now.

"It was just a realization. That's all. Nothing crazy. All of this is new. Just give me some time, I'll be okay." I replied as I rubbed his back and smiled at him through the mirror. He blinked at me a few times. I could tell he wanted to protest, but he couldn't figure out how to because he was drunk. He pouted.

"I'm too drunk to fight right now. We'll come back to it."

"Whatever you say. Now come on, brush your teeth and let's get you back to bed. You can barely stand up and you're heavy." He sighed and used his remaining strength to brush his teeth and we climbed into bed.

After a while of silence, I heard Jaehyun mumble something. "You're mumbling. I can't hear." "Did you have fun tonight?" he repeated. I raised an eyebrow.

"With your brother?"

"Yep."

"He's interesting. He's what I expected from what I've heard about him. Young, dumb and rich. He doesn't have much to contribute. I prefer him over your sister, that's for sure."

"Areum isn't so bad. You gotta give her a chance. You two would be a force to be reckoned with together. The world would crumble at your feet." He giggled at that.

I rolled my eyes. "Keep dreaming, Cho. Keep dreaming."

Silence filled the room again as I felt him drift off to sleep on my chest. I looked down at him and I felt my chest warm at the sight. He looked at peace and his features softened while he slept. Now that I had seen his siblings, I could see the youngest sibling's features on his face.

There was a softness to his sharp features. There was an innocence in his eyes that didn't exist within his siblings. Probably due to him choosing to stay away from the violence and chaos of the lifestyle for so long. The family was beautiful, that was undeniable. I was intrigued by how different they all were as well. Raised by the same mother and father, they all turned out differently. I guess that's a benefit of having parents; a kid can grow up and have freedom to choose their path. They all had different roles. Arsyn was the no nonsense leader. Viper was the brawns. Jaehyun seemed to fill the brain position with his education.

Their personalities were contrasting. Jaehyun was responsible and kind. He was diligent and considerate. A little mischievous at times, but he knew when and where to draw the line. Viper was reckless and lighthearted, but he was brash. He joked around too much. He crossed the line constantly. Arsyn was... too much like me. It was uncanny. She was cold and unapproachable. She was short tempered and hostile. The worst thing about all of that was she knew it. She knew she was all of those things, but she didn't give a damn. She confused me. She had both of her parents, so why was constantly like that? It made no sense.

When I thought about where I would fit into the group, it was difficult to imagine because Arsyn and I were going to continue to clash. It was no secret that we hated each other's guts. The reasons were petty right now, but I'm sure we'd find other reasons later on. What would happen if we fought one day, unrestricted and I killed her? I could kiss my plan for revenge goodbye, that's for sure. Jaehyun would never forgive me, and I could lose him forever. We would have to interact as little as possible to ensure everyone's safety. Viper and Jaehyun had a lot more optimism and hope for us than we did. Omega knew what I did, I doubted he was going to use me somewhere other than what I was designed for. Which was bittersweet because I don't want Jaehyun to be exposed to that side of me. I was terrified of what he would say. I wanted him to remain as untainted as possible. He shouldn't have to suffer because of me.

~Chapter 32~

Aweek or two had passed since our meeting with his family. Life had returned to normal in some ways. Jaehyun was back working and had registered for classes. He found out he won the architecture competition from the school semester, so he was riding on a high from that. Without having my assignment to work on anymore, I felt more lost than ever before. I sat at home all day with nothing to do and it was the worst. The silence was not kind to me. My mind constantly replayed my worries and every traumatizing memory it could pull from the depths of my mind.

Memories that I kept locked away for years. Years of abuse, violence, and anger played over and over in my mind. If it was even possible, my insomnia had gotten worse because I was having nightmares again. It all felt like a cruel cycle that I couldn't escape from. It had gotten so bad that I resorted to bothering his friends to turn my mind off to find some peace. The girls were more than happy to have me around again after not seeing me for a while. However, it was difficult to get back into the swing of hanging out with them again because they didn't know who I really was. After everything had come out, Jaehyun and I just accepted things as they were and adjusted. I had to figure out how to be Choi Ae Ri again and keep up the illusion. I found that the more I thought about how our lives had changed, it was overwhelming to process.

It didn't help that there hadn't been any mention of our initiation yet, so we were waiting. As the days passed, it felt more like a looming threat. There were no clues or hints to tell us what it would be. It made me anxious. I prayed it wouldn't be something extremely violent because I still didn't want Jaehyun to be thrown into the lifestyle like that. That would be too jarring for him, and I doubted if he'd be able to handle that. I know that we talked about accepting the decision that he made, but I still hated it. I always would. My feelings wouldn't change. I wanted to protect him.

"Hey Rose, are you awake?" Jaehyun called from the door of his bedroom. I turned over and looked over at him. He sighed softly and walked over to the bed sitting beside me.

"I sent you in here hours ago to get some rest. Did you sleep at all?" I shook my head wordlessly.

"This is getting really unhealthy. We need to get you to a doctor seriously. A therapist or something. You can't live like this. You're not sleeping."

"I'm not crazy. I don't want someone looking at me in pity. I'm fine. I'll be fine."

"That's not what therapists do. They're there to help. They help you process things and work through them. It can be helpful to help you move forward. May even help you deal with your anxiety and PTSD," he explained as he ran his hand through my hair.

"That just sounds like too much work. I don't have time for that," I complained.

"So, you're willing to leave me behind?"

I looked up at him quickly and frowned. "I'd never leave you. Especially not to something that's in my head. What are you talking about?" I questioned.

"Not sleeping can kill you."

"I've been tortured before. There are worse things that can kill someone."

"Not the point, Princess. It can eventually kill you and I don't want that. So please if you won't see a therapist at least let me get you medicine for the insomnia. Please? If you love me in the slightest bit, you'd take the medicine," he reasoned.

"That's low. Fine. I'll take the damn medicine." The grin that broke out on his face was infuriating, but it wouldn't be him if he wasn't a nuisance at times. He had been bringing up the topic of therapy a little more frequently in the past few weeks. I guess I wasn't doing a good job at hiding the chaos in my head.

"You'll thank me later. But anyways. Are you still up for going to Nari and Seunghyun's graduation party?"

"Yeah. I said I'd go. Don't want them to think I bailed. They'll text and ask questions," he chuckled lightly and nodded.

"Let me know when you're ready. I'll be waiting on you."

I pulled myself together to look presentable in front of Nari and Seunghyun. "Ae Ri! Jaehyun! You guys made it!" Seunghyun yelled excitedly as he ran up to us with Nari in tow. Nari smiled brightly as she saw me.

"Ae Ri! You're not sick anymore! You look amazing! I'm glad to see you're not sick anymore. How are you feeling?" she asked as she hugged me.

I gave her my best smile and nodded. "Feeling better, thanks. I haven't seen you as much the past few weeks," I replied.

"Sorry about that. Graduation and getting ready for this party has been hectic. And we've been getting our passports and visas ready. Trying to get set up in the US has been hectic. Jiwoo and Haeun always let me know when they saw you. I was worried about you."

"I figured they did. Sorry I didn't stick around too long after your ceremony."

"You came and that means the world to me. I know big events aren't always your thing."

"Still trying to figure out this friend thing." I admitted.

"You're getting the hang of it. Don't worry. Come on. The others are here, they'll be excited to see you!" She pulled me deeper into the party as Seunghyun and Jaehyun followed us laughing. As expected, Jiwoo and Haeun were just as excited to see me.

It was a few hours into the party and Jaehyun and I were standing outside taking a break from the loud noise. My eyes scanned the party, looking for nothing in particular. It was a force of habit. Now that my secret was out, I could tell that old habits were resurfacing. It was customary to be aware of my surroundings at all times. "You know just because your secret is exposed, doesn't mean you have to resort back to your old ways. Nothing's changed about the people around us." Jaehyun said.

"It's a part of me. It comes with the territory." I told him.

"Not every aspect of our lives has danger in it."

"But the possibility for it to slip in is always there. I never had anything to protect back in Japan. Nothing worth protecting. I was always alone. I have something to protect here. And there are innocent lives involved here." I looked out at Nari and Seunghyun talking to Minhyun and Haeun. Jiwoo and Seojun were at the dessert table talking to Miyeon and a man I had never seen before. I sighed softly at the realization that they had no idea of the potential danger that was out there.

"What are you trying to get off your chest? I can tell you want to talk, but you won't say it." Jaehyun looked over at me and leaned against the rail in front of us.

"I'm worried. About all of this. I know you said we accept the decision and move forward, but this is hard for me. I feel bad..." I confessed.

"About?"

"Dragging you in this. Dragging the others into this. Uprooting your life."

"Guilty? Is that the word you're looking for?" I paused for a moment. I knew what the word meant, I had just never used it before. But it fit the situation and how I felt.

"I've never felt guilty before... This is new to me... and I don't like this emotion."

"I'm sure you don't. Emotions tend to scare you sometimes. But feeling guilty means you did something wrong. What did you do wrong?" Jaehyun looked down at me and I raised an eyebrow.

"Didn't I just answer this question?" I groaned in slight irritation.

"Not really. Because you didn't force a gun to my head and tell me to make the decision. How can you feel like you did something wrong, when I made a decision for myself and ignored your pleas or advice to not do it? If you think about it logically, it doesn't make sense. The others don't even know anything about us. I never told them anything about me. So they certainly don't know about your background. So why do you feel like you did something wrong to them?" he inquired.

"You must not have listened when I told you I ruin beautiful things," I reminded him.

He shook his head and frowned. "You should have more faith in yourself and your abilities. I'm still here. Our friends are still here. You spend so much time downplaying yourself and being cruel to yourself when you're doing your best with what you've been given. So you can't be that bad."

"I hope it stays that way." I mumbled. To whatever or whoever is out there, I could only hope things don't change. Jaehyun was the only thing that meant something anymore. He was the only lifeline I had now. Everything else was broken and would never go back to the way it was. He turned my body to face him, and he stared at me for a few moments, looking for something.

"I didn't change my plans to not be with you through whatever awaits us. I have every intention of going through this with you. Until you get tired of the lifestyle or until you find the answers you need. Until you find whatever fulfillment you're looking for, I'll be right here." he promised. The intensity in his eyes startled me for a moment. It almost sounded like an oath. The ringing of his phone interrupted the intense stare off. He looked down at his phone and he took a deep breath.

"It's my dad," he announced. My jaw set and I nodded once in understanding. It was time. An unfamiliar darkness entered his eyes as he answered the phone. I could hear Omega's muffled voice on the other end, but I couldn't make out what he was saying. The conversation was fairly short.

"We'll be there," he agreed and then he hung up. I waited as a tense silence rested over us. He looked at me and the darkness left his eyes, and he was back to himself. The transition almost gave me whiplash.

"The assignment is ready for us. We will meet tomorrow night at eight," he informed me. I let out the breath that I didn't know I was holding. This was happening.

"Did he say what it was?" He shook his head in response.

"All he gave me was the place to meet at. He wants us to meet him at the restaurant where we had dinner with mom for the first time."

"Is that normal?"

"Not from anything I have seen." I looked out at the party happening out in front of us and my heart started to race. Why would he want to meet in a public place like that? And it was out of the ordinary? What was he planning?

"You look like you're about to pass out. What're you thinking about?" Jaehyun pressed.

"Everything's really changing. The deja vu is hitting me hard right now. Feels like when I was thirteen, when I got my first assignment…" I replied. The memory of standing in front of Han and him sliding the first black envelope across the table to me in front of his second in command and his saiko komon at the time flooded my mind. He called me to meet him at the Yakuza affiliated restaurant and that was the day my life changed forever. Having another experience like that just felt like a cruel sense of irony. It made me second guess the entire thing, but I couldn't turn back now. Too much had already happened.

"Want to talk about it?"

"Not really. I'd rather not tell you about how at thirteen years old, I got sent on my first assassination."

I could almost taste the venom that leaked out when I spoke. It was not directed towards him. I couldn't help it. The memories scarred me for life. Han's lack of concern when I came back to headquarters beaten, bruised and covered in a mixture of blood irrevocably changed me in an instant. I knew where I stood in his eyes. "You were thirteen…" Jaehyun repeated. I shook my head, and he went quiet. We stood in silence as I tried to collect my thoughts. Haeun decided that was the perfect time to run up to us.

"Y'all have had enough private time. It's time to rejoin the party and have fun." she declared as she handed us a plastic red cup with a dark liquid in it. The smell of alcohol was strong in it.

"What is in here, Haeun? Is it straight alcohol?" Jaehyun complained. She grinned mischievously and shook her head.

"There's juice in there too… I think. I told Minhyun to put juice in the punch." She put a hand to her chin in thought. I rolled my eyes and shrugged. It was better to risk liver failure than continue to feel any of the complicated emotions. I chugged down the liquid, ignoring the burn. Obviously, she ignored the rule that white and dark liquors do not belong together. The taste of tequila and Hennessy did not go together.

Haeun cheered loudly as I held the cup back out to her. "Choi Ae Ri is the queen of drinking!" she yelled as she tilted the cup over in disbelief. Jaehyun looked at me stunned and I laughed lightly. She would expect the same thing from him now.

"Jaehyun… Jaehyun… Jaehyun! Jaehyun!" she chanted loudly.

"Why do you encourage her chaos?" He groaned. He shook his head and chugged the drink as well. Her joyous squeal when he completed the task was almost cute.

"See? That wasn't so bad."

"It was disgusting. You're trying to kill everyone. How did you get away with this?"

"We snuck it in. Seunghyun's on his third cup and he has no idea." she smiled. I raised an eyebrow.

"Oh no we just made this batch really quick. We had another batch that was better, and everyone's been drinking it. We're just waiting to see what happens."

"So, you decided to poison us first?" Jaehyun questioned.

"You were always my favorite to mess with. Come on. Let's see how this goes." Haeun invited. We looked at each other and shrugged. It would be entertaining to see. So, we followed her to join the others.

~Chapter 33~

Jaehyun and I sat in silence outside of the restaurant in the car. The atmosphere was tense, and my leg bounced because of the anxiousness. He placed a hand on my thigh to stop it. "You're making me nervous when you do that," he said calmly. I looked over at him and he smiled slightly. He was so calm about all of this. He got dressed like it was a regular family dinner. No hint of hesitation or anything. If he was nervous, he didn't let it show.

"This is your family. How am I making you nervous?"

"You're acting like something bad is happening. It's just work. It's like the first day." He laughed a little at his own joke as I rolled my eyes. He had moments like his brother. Not taking things as seriously as he should.

"Oh, come on, princess. Relax. I'll be by your side the whole time. This is just going to be an adjustment for us. But we're a team. We'll get through it. I got you. Can you trust me on that?" he reassured me as he squeezed my hand.

I nodded slightly. Trusting him was the easiest thing he had asked me to do during the entire ordeal. A sense of calm settled over me as I squeezed his hand back.

"If I never said it before… I'm glad I met you," I told him.

"I know. It's nice to hear it out loud though. Because it's the same for me too. I'd choose you every time," he grinned. He tapped my nose, and I scrunched it in response. He chuckled again at the action and motioned for us to get out of the car.

"We'd better get inside. We're pushing it close." he commented. I took a deep breath and nodded as he came to open my door.

We followed the host down the hall to the private room that his family reserved. They stopped at the last room on the left and knocked on the door. A muffled reply was returned. The host opened the door and gestured for us to enter the room. I felt my heart hammer against my chest as I followed Jaehyun into the room. Omega and Iseul sat at the head of the table dressed in matching black suits. Their white button ups were unbuttoned at the top the same way too. It was admirable the way they showed their unity and affection for each other. Viper sat next to his mother in a white short sleeved button up and black jeans. He saluted us as we walked in. A vexed scoff sounded, and my eyes automatically rolled knowing it was Arsyn. She sat next to Viper with a scowl on her face as usual. As always, she was being a bitch.

We made eye contact as I walked up to the table and Jaehyun pulled out my chair for me. My own expression hardened as I stared at her. Neither of us looked away. It was a power game to see who would break first. Animosity and tension bubbled under the surface. A small sigh escaped Jaehyun as he sat next to me. "Please don't start, ladies." he whispered. Neither of us moved.

"Areum, how could you be so rude to our sister-in-law?" Viper snickered as he tapped her shoulder.

"Don't touch me, idiot. And stop using my real name." she growled. She never broke eye contact. Omega cleared his throat loudly and that was when we looked away from each other. He didn't say anything as he looked around the table at everyone. It was deathly silent, and his expression was unreadable. After a few moments, he called a waiter into the room and ordered two bottles of wine.

Once the waiter left, it felt like hours had passed before he said anything to us. Anticipation hung in the air and suddenly the corners of his mouth lifted into a grin. "Thank you for joining us, Rose and Jaehyun. I know this is a little different than what you expected, but Iseul thought it'd be good to have a little family bonding dinner to celebrate tonight." Omega said as he gestured to his wife. She smiled warmly.

"If I can interject. What exactly is happening here?" Arsyn inquired as she raised an eyebrow and looked at her parents. Oh, she was not going to like the answer to that. Viper grinned mischievously and before anyone could say anything, he spoke.

"You really don't know? Shadow and Rose are getting their initiation assignment tonight." he answered. Her expression dropped and she stared at her parents blankly. I could see her face turn red and her left eye twitched. Her mouth opened and closed rapidly, and she pinched the bridge of her nose. She was furious. I held back the smirk that wanted to cross my face as I watched her malfunction.

"Really, Daehyun? Was that necessary?" Jaehyun hissed as Iseul slapped him in the back of the head. Viper only cackled in response. Omega shook his head slightly and sighed.

"That was not supposed to happen. Oh well. This is a little bit of a different setting than how we normally do this and it was because I knew something like that would happen." he said calmly as he poured himself a glass of wine. I looked at Arsyn and she was composed again. Her face wasn't red anymore but the fury in her eyes was undeniable. She was completely caught off guard by the news. It almost made me laugh to know that my presence pissed her off that much.

"Is everyone done with their outbursts? I'd like to continue." Iseul said as she looked over at Arsyn and Viper. A stiff nod and a wave of the hand was what she got in response.

"Well, a quick overview of the family roles and positions. Jaehyun this may be a refresher to you, Rose this may be new to you. It might not be from your old affiliation. Arsyn, the oldest, is the listed right hand to Omega. She controls our Busan and Jeju Island operations. She is our assassin. She's our equivalent to you back in the Yakuza. Viper, the middle child, is the left hand to Omega. He trains our foot soldiers. Trains new guards as well. He oversees our arms bases in Daegu and Seoul. Anything really dealing with weapons and fighting and training is his area. He also has some dealings in the night life operations we do. Clubs, bars, etcetera." Iseul explained. I could sense Arsyn's uneasiness with the amount of information she was telling me, but Iseul seemed to not care.

"Our Shadow-Jaehyun-he handles the legal business ties. He has been a huge help in getting us into markets that we couldn't reach before, like architecture. He's heavily involved in our real estate and manufacturing areas. He helps in finance too. He has some government ties too through school and business. I am listed as the COO of Nam Industries. I oversee all the operations all over the world and I choose the next expansion opportunities. Omega is of course the CEO and the leader of the Jopok." she finished as she gestured back to Omega. He smiled as he applauded her.

"That was a nice summary, my dear. You covered it all. Well like she said. Everything runs through me. I approve and deny. Authorize assignments and expansion. Ensure that the Jopok stays strong and powerful. Easy enough, right?" he smirked slightly. I nodded wordlessly. I looked over at Jaehyun. To be classified as an inactive member, he was more active in the lifestyle than what I thought. Everything the legal businesses do can't be completely legal. That was impossible.

"I'm guessing the inactive status only applied to the violence and the illegal activities?" I questioned out loud. I was genuinely curious, because I didn't know the answer to that anymore.

"Well… Yes and no. I've been in some shootouts, fights if I was needed. But for the most part, yeah. Maybe I helped facilitate one or two illegal trades." Jaehyun shrugged as he took a sip of his wine.

"I've seen your parts of weapon of choice, then?"

"Yes, you have." I nodded in understanding. I felt like kicking myself because I missed so many clues and signs. I got lost in a character that wasn't real and I missed so many obvious things. I could only chuckle as I looked back on it.

"I can't believe that I fell for that lame excuse you gave me." I chuckled.

"Yeah. That wasn't my best lie, but now that I look back on it. You weren't scared. That maybe should have been a red flag. I missed it too. I guess we were both blind." he teased as he reached under the table and held my hand again.

Iseul laughed brightly. The sound was welcoming and eased the tension. "Love will make you blind. But things happen as they should. It's the beauty of life." she commented. Something about the way she said it made me feel like there was more she wanted to say but she chose not to. She looked over at her husband and he grinned like he was in on what she was hinting at. It was unnerving and slightly irritating because what did they know that they weren't sharing? As I scanned the table, their children seemed just as confused as me. Especially Arsyn. Seems like they didn't tell their right hand everything. An unsettling feeling started to form in my stomach and I chose to down my glass of wine to calm my nerves.

Omega was in no rush to give us our assignment. We sat through appetizers and the first and second course without a mention of the assignment or any more lifestyle talk. It was awkward as hell. Viper, Jaehyun, Omega and Iseul talked among themselves like a regular family. Arsyn sat silently in her seat frowning the whole time. She only spoke to try and discourage her family from revealing too much personal information. She was still in a sour mood from earlier and every now and again, I caught her glaring a hole into the side of my head. If I didn't feel like an outsider already, Arsyn was intent on making sure I did. She was overworking herself, I didn't need her help to feel like I didn't belong. I already felt that way.

Iseul tried her best to make me feel comfortable and include me as much as she could. The issue was I couldn't relate. I didn't have fun memories with my father. No memories of my mother. No siblings. Watching them interact like a normal family despite what they did, it made me jealous. Then a rush of guilt followed behind it. I shouldn't be jealous, but watching all of them interact hurt more than just watching Jaehyun and Iseul interact when I first met her. I felt even more out of place. He had a complete family. He was loved his whole life. If Iseul's statement was true that things happen as they should, then my life had to be a sick joke. Because what did I do to deserve feeling like this? And why did this feel like the hardest thing in my life? Experiencing these feelings was ten times worse than any beating, torture or gunshot. At least I could identify and understand those. I knew how to treat physical wounds. Emotional wounds were harder to identify and understand. And they felt impossible to treat.

Omega clearing his throat brought me out of my thoughts and back to reality. "All right. I kept everyone in suspense long enough. Let's get down to business. Rose and Shadow. Your initiation assignment is a debt collection. Shadow, check your phone and it'll be there." he announced. I wasn't accustomed to hearing his family call him by his alias when all I ever knew him by was Jaehyun. They were able to swap between both names seamlessly. Jaehyun picked up his phone and I looked over his shoulder to see what he was doing. He opened a text message containing a file. A debt of 1.3 billion won was owed to the Jopok. My eyes widened. How does someone get away with that much debt? And they're still alive? What needed that much funding?

"That's a lot of money to owe. Who the hell owes that much and is still alive? You guys don't kill over money?" I asked snarkily. Jaehyun nudged me and cleared his throat as he scrolled down the document. Two pictures appeared further down with the names Sato Haruto and Sato Kiyo. I examined the pictures. The man was an elderly Japanese man with light brown eyes and white hair. Prominent smile lines and crow's feet joined with regular signs of aging on his face. Something about him felt familiar. I couldn't tell how though. The woman in the picture underneath looked younger than the man. She was maybe late forties, early fifties, while the man had to be in his sixties. Her black hair was cut into a pixie style but the front was longer. Her face was round and high cheekbones caused her eyes to disappear when she smiled. Her eyes were a chocolate brown color. Something about her felt even more familiar and again I couldn't figure out why.

I read the information under the pictures. They owned a few doctor's offices and a medical transport company. The money they borrowed had accumulated interest over time. "I remember them. They had those older twins and she had a little kid with her, right?" Jaehyun asked after some silence. Omega nodded.

"It's been a while since we've seen them. It was last in 2012. That was when they first came to ask for the loan. They wanted the money to start the first and second office. Business took off for them. They opened a few more and the transport company. They stopped making payments about a year ago and we've been kind for long enough-" he started to answer.

"Why the hesitation?" I interrupted.

"Who told you to speak? How dare you interrupt my father, you stupid-" Arsyn suddenly stood up as she glared at me. A sharp glance from Omega silenced her outburst. I rolled my eyes and looked over at him again.

"One of their children went missing last year. I'm a father too. We were supposed to hear from them at the end of last year. But nothing. So we're here now. I've been meaning to check in on this but I've been busy. So I figured why not have you all do it." Omega stated plainly. I nodded wordlessly.

That type of kindness was unheard of to me. I couldn't count the number of times, I've executed people in dire situations and they needed mercy. Sometimes their pleas were the last words they ever said. The concept of mercy and grace were not concepts that I was familiar with. I was not taught those things. The fact that Omega valued them because he was a father was admirable. He held onto his humanity. The differences between Han and Omega were becoming more obvious the more I interacted with him. Omega had compassion because he could relate to others. Han had me and all it seemed to do was make him more cold, especially as I got older. The feeling of bitterness and jealousy rose in my chest and I quickly tried to focus back on what Omega was talking about.

"We know they live in Tokyo but they have property in Osaka as well. We haven't found them in either place. Your mission is simple. Locate and retrieve the money." Omega said simply. I raised an eyebrow at him just ending the sentence that way. No alternatives? No threats?

"What if they don't have the money?" I asked.

"Call me. We have other ways to collect debts." The simplicity of the sentence gave more away than what I cared to ask. I knew what it meant. Jaehyun turned to me and I took a deep breath, the acceptance part was next. My palms started to sweat with nerves, and it felt too hot. Accepting an assignment from someone other than the Yakuza felt wrong. It felt like a burden, but nonetheless I nodded.

"We won't fail you." Jaehyun agreed. There was no way out now. The deal was sealed.

"I hope not. I'll be in contact soon with your flight details. You're dismissed."

We stood and bowed in respect before we left the room. The walk back to the car was silent and it felt heavy. Every step felt like I was walking through quicksand. I was going back to Japan. I doubted that it was a coincidence. I couldn't be seen. "You look like you're about to throw up. Are you okay?" he questioned as he leaned against the door of the car. He crossed his arms and looked down at me. He wasn't wrong with the observation. I felt sick.

"My first assignment with the Jopok sends me back to Japan into territory I was known in. I can't tell if this is a set up or your father's attempt to flex his power." I replied as I toyed with my fingers. I couldn't find the words to describe how I was feeling exactly. I couldn't describe it myself really. My stomach was in knots and I felt almost dizzy. It felt like a boulder had been placed on my chest and it was crushing me.

"I thought Tokyo was your territory. You controlled Osaka too?"

"No, Osaka was someone else's territory. I did a few assignments out there. Mainly assassinations under Han's orders. There was a period of time where there was tension between the two syndicates. I'm known out there." I rubbed my eyes as exhaustion started to creep up on me.

"And I know the Satos from somewhere. They look familiar. I can't remember how. I don't think I've done business with them, though. It's irritating me." I added. My mind was racing. I was trying to process all of the new information and sort through the memories that never left me alone. I felt drowsy all of a sudden. My body chose a bad time to let me know it was finally ready to rest. I couldn't sleep now, there was too much going on now.

"You really don't look good, we should hold off on trying to figure it out. You need to rest." Jaehyun said as he placed a hand on my back.

"I'm fine. I'm just thinking. We need to start planning. I do not want to be in Japan for too long. The more we plan, the more chances of success we have." I stretched trying to get my body to wake up. I stumbled slightly and a look of concern crossed his face.

"Absolutely not. You're going to sleep. You've been awake for too long. We will worry about this when you wake up."

I rolled my eyes. When I want to sleep and have nothing to do, my insomnia won't let me. When I needed to do something, my body and brain insisted that I sleep. How convenient. "I'll be alright." I tried to convince him as I yawned. He shook his head and opened the car door for me.

"You're going to sleep. It's not up for debate." he stated. His voice told me that he wasn't going to hear anything more on the topic. All I could do was scoff in disbelief as I got in the car.

~Chapter 34~

"You got your passport and paperwork?" I called out to Jaehyun as I finished packing my bags. His laugh sounded from the living room.

"Rose, I've traveled before. Before this assignment and this life. I got it," he called back.

Fair enough. I was still nervous though. Omega called us bright and early this morning to let us know we had an afternoon flight to Tokyo. It didn't feel real that I had to go back to Japan because I didn't think I would be doing it so soon. Especially not with Jaehyun. I wanted to keep him as far away from who I was before. I couldn't predict what would come up as we began our assignment. He knew what I did for the Yakuza, but I never actually went into explicit detail about how often I did my job or everything it included. What if he couldn't handle it? What if I was too much of a monster for him to overlook? What if he left me? The thought made me nauseous, and I shook my head to clear it.

"What were you thinking about? You did the head shake thing." Jaehyun's voice interrupted my thoughts.

I looked up and he had entered the room and leaned against the door. I was starting to realize why he was called Shadow. He moved quickly and quietly.

"I was thinking about my old house in Tokyo. We can use it as a hideout while we're there. It has all the furniture and stuff still there. I'm sure I still have some weapons left there too." I told him.

"Is that safe? Wouldn't that be a bad idea? The Yakuza would know, right?"

"No. No one knew where I lived. Only my right hand and my assistant. And they know I'm in Korea on assignment."

"Which one is Code?"

"My right hand. How do you know about Code?" I inquired.

"The name appeared on your phone once or twice and I saw it. Didn't want to pry." Jaehyun answered with a grin.

"Starting to realize why you're called Shadow. Because I could've sworn I kept that a secret."

"That day you fainted the first time. I noticed your phone vibrating and you picked it up."

He shrugged and chuckled as I looked at him with a raised eyebrow. "They hung up quickly when I grabbed your phone to tell them what happened. So I didn't talk to them." he added. I sighed slightly. I hoped that wouldn't bite me in the ass eventually.

"It could've been worse, I suppose. Code never asked who you were. So, I may be okay," I reasoned.

"Another question. You said all of your furniture was in Japan? So, all of this in your place is new?"

"Of course, it is. Why wouldn't it be?"

"The money you could've saved... Why?" Jaehyun complained as he folded his arms across his chest.

"The shipping and logistics were annoying. I didn't want to deal with it. The easy solution was to buy new stuff in Korea. Sell it when I left. You've got to remember this wasn't part of the plan. You, joining the Jopok. This assignment. All unplanned." I reminded him.

"You would've left and gone back to Japan? Even with me here?" He playfully pouted and put a hand over his chest. I rolled my eyes.

"No. I would've figured out something. Traveling back and forth all the time was on my list of ideas. I thought about staying and running my clan from here. Kidnapping wasn't off the table either." I grinned.

"Sometimes your possessiveness is adorable. Other times, I worry about it. But I love you as you are. I'm kind of honored you'd jump through hoops like that to kidnap me," he laughed.

"Your ability to just be calm whenever you hear something that is meant to be outrageous is uncanny. I'll never understand it."

"I'm adaptable. It's a strength. And if I may say, I don't think you understand the concept of duality. People are complex. Everything's not black and white. And you're going to drive yourself insane if you keep trying to put the world in black and white terms. Don't torture yourself that way." Jaehyun said as he pinched my cheek. I chuckled and swatted his hand away. He was unfazed and wrapped me in a tight hug as he looked down at me.

I took a moment and looked up at him, admiring his features. His beauty mark stood out under his eye. Full pink lips curled into a small smile. His hair had grown out over time and it was to his shoulders. He kept it tied up in the back with a few pieces free to frame handsome face. His sharp features looked amazing with the long hair. Sometimes just looking at him calmed me down. I would never understand how I ended up with something so beautiful, but I wasn't going to question it. I was just thankful.

"Enjoying the view?" he teased as he kissed my forehead.

"Looking at you makes me feel better. Your hair looks good at this length. I like it." I answered as I smirked lightly.

"Well, thank you, princess. But you can't pull on it right now. We have to finish packing. Maybe at the airport, we can arrange that." He winked at my flushed face and walked off to leave the room. I shook my head and went back to packing.

The check in process was painless and we had an hour and a half to kill before our flight left. We walked into one of the bars and sat at a table by the wall looking out at the packed airport. "So, I was doing some research and I found out something interesting. The Satos suddenly disappeared from the public eye around the time their kid went missing. They stepped down from their CEO and COO positions and new people took over." I whispered to Jaehyun as I showed him the articles.

"Yeah, I saw that. I got addresses. Maybe the new leaders can tell us some information on why they left so abruptly and where they could've gone," he replied as he sent me two addresses. I raised an eyebrow. How did he know to do that?

"I'm not new to this. I'm sure you already checked this and know but I'm going to say it anyway. I looked to try to find any missing information on that missing kid. And there's not a single photo of her online. Not even a name." Nothing on the missing kid?

"The only time I've seen rich parents not upload pictures of their missing kids is if the Yakuza has them and they're held as ransom. It's a tactic used to force someone to pay off their debts."

"You think they owed money to the Yakuza too? But why? That doesn't make sense. The Satos were making money. The yearly reports that were put out for the hospital showed that they were making more money than other hospitals." Jaehyun looked just as confused as I was.

"Could've been a quick scheme to bring in more money by one of the leaders of a syndicate or something. They could've just been the unlucky ones who were chosen." I replied.

"The Yakuza just use people randomly for money?"

"Yeah. It's not uncommon. I've done it to businesses. Never to families. I'm not a fan of kidnapping. It usually leads to trafficking and I hate that even more. Han's big into it." I answered truthfully. He hummed in response and I appreciated that he didn't push the issue further.

"Well that complicates things. How do we go forward now?" Jaehyun asked after a few moments of silence.

"Let's just work the theory that the Satos borrowed from the Yakuza. We need to figure out who they could've gone to. Because it didn't come from the Yamaguchi. It had to be another syndicate."

"I didn't think other syndicates of the Yakuza had the financial resources to loan money. You don't hear about the other syndicates a lot."

"I didn't either." I looked down at my laptop and chewed on my lip in thought. Who could've loaned the Satos that much money. They would have needed millions of yen to fund whatever project they were working on.

"Do you know anyone from the Sumiyoshi or Inagawa?" Jaehyun suggested.

"Not really. I may have a contact in my office. But I don't think they could afford that. Now Kobe Yamaguchi maybe could. That's a better guess." I corrected him.

My mind raced through anything that I could find to help us. I knew many people but the problem was I wasn't social enough to build a rapport with people. "Kobe Yamaguchi? What is that?" Jaehyun whispered as he blinked at me in confusion.

"You never heard of that? Oh yeah… You were out there being normal, I forgot." He rolled his eyes at the tease.

"Yeah, yeah. Whatever. Spill it."

"In 2015, there was increasing tension surrounding Han's continued leadership because he was bringing me more into the politics and leadership side of the syndicate. Apparently to some of the men, there was a huge difference between me being an assassin and doing deals and trades every so often. A young woman in the inner circle pissed some people off. Pissed them off enough to go form a syndicate in Hyogo. There's been some violence over the years. But since I eliminated the top leadership back in 2016, 2017, it's weakened them a lot. Persistence pays off though. They merged with some smaller syndicates to help rebuild." I explained nonchalantly. I hadn't told anyone that story besides Code.

He snickered slightly and took the laptop back. "You just stir up trouble no matter what you do, huh princess? Causing a major rift in the Yakuza's most powerful family? Impressive."

"It wasn't just me. They had other reasons to."

"Like what?"

"Han's leadership." I giggled. He shook his head slowly.

"It was you, princess. It's okay. Weak men are intimidated by strong women. That's not your fault." I laughed at the comment because there was a lot of truth to his statement. I did cause chaos wherever I went and whatever I did. I chose to ignore the guilt that stirred in my stomach when I thought about what I did to him and his life.

"Well, do you think the splinter group would do it? How could we find out?"

"Maybe. It's worth a shot. I can see what I can get, I just rather not go to the headquarters." I sighed. That was such a risky thing to do. I just wanted this to be a low profile thing, it was a debt collection. One of the easiest assignments. However this was turning into something complicated.

"You didn't keep any files on a computer at your house? Paper files?" Jaehyun asked, puzzled.

"Not in relation to other syndicates. Only our files, if any at all. If you're good with computers feel free to search my deleted files. Maybe you'll find something." I told him. He nodded in response. The overhead speaker announced our plane had arrived and it would board soon.

"Let's take a break and relax. We'll get back to work once we land and get something to eat." he suggested as we packed everything up and made our way to the gate. My mind raced as we walked the short distance. There were so many variables and complexities to this already. I couldn't help but feel uneasy about the whole thing.

"Do you think we'll get this done without any issues?" I asked quietly.

"If I have any say in it, yes. If not, I'm in this with you and I have your back." Jaehyun promised as he squeezed my hand. It reassured me and calmed me down.

"I'll protect you with my life then." I declared as I squeezed his hand back tightly. He held my hand up and kissed the back of it.

"Same here, beautiful."

~Chapter 35~

O nce we landed in Tokyo, we rented a car under Jaehyun's name and began our journey to my old house. I was trying to hide how uncomfortable I was. My stomach was unsettled, and I felt nauseous. A cold sweat started to break out along the back of my neck and my chest moved with the inhale and exhale of my breath. Tokyo never felt like home exactly. It was a place that I was comfortable in. I spent so much time in the city, it was natural. Being here now, I didn't feel that comfort like before. A feeling of dread settled over me. I was apprehensive about being here again. I felt antsy. The air felt thinner than I remembered.

"How does it feel being back in Japan?" Jaehyun asked as he looked over at me. I chose to keep how I felt to myself.

"It's complicated. I honestly was never planning on bringing you here. Hell, I wasn't planning on coming back." I admitted quietly.

"Why? Was there nothing good about living here?"

"Nothing's wrong with the city. It's a beautiful place. It's busy and life moves fast. I just never got to enjoy it. It wasn't in the cards for me. And besides, you aren't here. You're in Korea, why would I come back here?"

"Well, since you brought it up. What do you think about living together?" He glanced at me quickly to see my reaction. I was taken aback. I tilted my head and bit my lip for a moment. Live together? I had never lived with anyone as an adult. The last time I lived with another person was when I was in the dorms with the other Yakuza kids that were training or studying. I hated it. The moment I could leave at 16 I ran.

"I haven't lived with someone since I was a kid. I don't know how to do that…" I whispered as I looked at him. I couldn't explain why I felt so nervous and unsure. I was around him all the time and I wouldn't want to be anywhere else but beside him. The thought of living together terrified me. What if he got tired of me? What if he hated me? He raised an eyebrow and chuckled.

"Love, you do realize that we practically live together now, right? We just swap places. I was just thinking it'd be easier and nicer to have a place together. To call home." he said gently.

"Fair statement."

"If you don't want to, it's okay. Don't feel pressured. I was just suggesting it. I understand. I was just looking at places and found some that I think you'd like. It changes nothing if you say no." He smiled warmly and reached over to grab my hand.

The hopefulness in his eyes couldn't be hidden. I half thought Iseul was joking when she said he was looking at houses. I couldn't believe that he was seriously thinking that far ahead. Even with all of my issues and everything going on, he was still committed to this. The warmth that flowed through my chest made me blush. It didn't feel real. "What's on your mind? I can see your mind spinning. Talk to me." Jaehyun gently nudged me.

"Just checking to make sure I'm not dreaming. I don't know much about relationships, but I've heard that moving in together can change a lot of things. I don't want us to change. Are we ready for that?"

"Well, no you're not dreaming. This is real life. And I think we are, yes. We've been through a lot, I think the only change for us could be us getting better together. That's how I see it. But if you need to think about it, then that's fine. I'm in no rush. I'll be here whenever you're ready." he answered as he kissed my knuckles.

"I'll compromise with you. We can look at places together." He nodded in agreement. There were parts of me screaming to say yes and I wanted to, but I could hear the voices that were saying the opposite.

I felt unqualified. What if he wanted me to change? I wasn't a housewife. I couldn't be that. If we lived together, he would see everything about me. There would be no hiding. He'd see my training sessions, the way I worked on assignments, all of the weapons. I couldn't hide any of that if we lived together. The idea of being that open and exposed frightened me. I genuinely didn't know if he could handle seeing me while I worked. I wasn't the same person when I was preparing and training. I didn't want him to fear me. I didn't want him to look at me differently. I internally sighed as the realization hit me that there was a lot of work I had to do.

We pulled up to my old house and I had to fight to keep my emotions in check. As I stared up at the black and gray villa, it didn't feel the same. The silence was too loud. It was eerie. It didn't feel like the sanctuary that I once had. It felt dangerous almost. It made me anxious. My heart pounded in my chest as I looked up at the building. A lump formed in my throat and a chill ran down my spine. I knew it was empty because no one knew this house existed. It was hidden in a forest a few miles away from the road and that was intentional as well. I just couldn't shake the uncomfortableness.

I jumped slightly as I felt a hand on my shoulder. I turned to see Jaehyun recoil as he tilted his head. "Are you okay?" he questioned.

"Sorry. Yeah, I'm okay. It's just… different being back here." I lied. I hated the way my voice quivered slightly. There was no way I was going to open that can of worms. I couldn't explain what was happening. All I knew was that it made me nauseous being back here. I was fighting the urge to cry all of a sudden. I was on edge. I wanted to go anywhere else but here. I felt Jaehyun's eyes on me and I rolled my shoulders.

"We should get inside. We have work to do." I told him in a steadier voice. He nodded and followed me out of the car.

"Go ahead inside, I'll get the bags."

I nodded and walked up the stairs to the porch and stood in front of the door. I paused. I could hear my heart hammering in my chest. I could hear the blood rushing in my ears. The house felt menacing. I felt frustration start to fill my chest. It was a building. It was my house. Why was I feeling like this? It was not logical. Despite knowing that, my hand trembled as I punched the code into the keypad. My breath hitched as the door unlocked and I pushed it open. The door swung up slowly and the door creaked noisily. The stale air was the first thing I noticed. No one had been here since I left. That was good. It was still safe.

I took a shaky step inside and looked around. Almost six or seven months of stillness had allowed for some dust to collect on the plastic sheets that covered the furniture. The furniture was in the same spot, untouched. The hole in the wall from the knife I threw at Remi was still there and I shivered at the thought. Memories came flooding back to me. Late nights on the couch watching live stream torture sessions of captured enemies and traitors to get information. Sleepless nights where I cleaned every weapon I owned. The rehearsed fight sequences I went over again and again in the living room. The target practices I conducted from different positions in the house on dummies outside in the forest. All the times I treated wounds and bandaged them by myself, the nights I stared at the wall, wishing I could sleep but couldn't.

"Do you want to talk about it?" Jaehyun's voice broke through the memories, and I sighed as I looked over my shoulder. He was standing next to the closed door and the bags were sitting beside him. I shook my head.

"I'm fine. It's taking a minute to get used to being here." I answered. I watched him take a few careful steps towards me.

"Is it okay if I hug you? You look like you need one." He paused a few feet away from me and opened his arms as an invitation. I stared at him for a moment, contemplating. Before I knew it, I crashed into his chest and buried my face as I held him tightly. Hot, frustrated tears ran down my face as I sobbed.

It felt as if I was physically falling apart. It felt like my heart was tearing into pieces. I felt raw and exposed in a different way. It felt like the walls were closing in and my chest was constricting. Terror flowed through me and it made me cling to him tighter. Every time I tried to pull myself together, I ended up crying even more. I didn't understand what was happening. My emotions were all over the place and I tried to keep it together, but I failed. I felt Jaehyun squeeze me tighter into his chest and it just made me cry harder. He gently rubbed my back and I felt worse. My knees gave out and he easily adjusted and caught me and guided us gently to the floor and he adjusted me onto his lap. I was vaguely reminded of the first time I cried in his arms and it broke me even the more.

I awoke with a start and found myself in a dark room. The floor was freezing, cold and I shivered slightly as I moved into an upright position. It took my eyes a moment to adjust to the darkness. I could just barely make out a sliver of light outside of the room. It was barely enough light but I could tell there was a hallway outside of the room and the room had no door. There wasn't enough light to reveal if anything was in the room with me. I was on the floor, so I slowly ran my hands on the floor in front of me to see if it was safe to walk and as I felt a few feet in front of me, my hand came into contact with a warm liquid. I could smell the faint metallic scent and I knew immediately it was blood. I jumped back as a bright light flashed suddenly in the room and my eyes squeezed close.

After a few moments, I opened my eyes and blinked a few times. The room was pure white but there was blood splattered across the room. The walls were covered in it. As I looked around the room, there were dead bodies all over the room. I choked on the air that I was trying to inhale. My heart dropped as I took in the men, women and children that littered the floor. Some of the men's faces I recognized from past assignments, but I didn't know any of the women or children. I didn't take those assignments. I looked in front of me and saw the puddle my hand landed in and when I looked further, I saw it was coming from... Jaehyun. I felt the air leave my body as I stared at him. He was covered in blood from a slit throat.

The scream I let out was something I had never heard before. I crawled to him and cradled his face in my hands. His eyes were wide open, frozen in shock or fear. The light in his eyes was gone and he was ice cold to the touch. "J-J-Jae... W-what happened... W-Who did this to you?" I sobbed as I picked him up and held him close to my chest. He was dead... Someone killed him and I wasn't there to protect him. I looked around the room frantically to try to find any clues. I didn't find any clues, but when I glanced behind me, I saw my mother's lifeless body a few feet away from where I had previously been sitting. She was covered in blood as well. I felt like I had been sucker punched. I sobbed harder as I tried to drag Jaehyun's body with me a short distance to hers.

More tears blurred my vision as I looked down at her beautiful features. Her throat was slit, and I felt sick to my stomach. My body racked with sobs as I leaned over her body. I was a mess. I was distraught. I felt more fragile than glass. I was hanging on by a thread. My emotions were all over the place. Rage and despair swapped off as the primary emotion, confusion and dizziness followed closely. "What the fuck is this?! Where am I!? Who did this?! Show yourself coward!" I shrieked as I looked around for anything to use to make sense of this. The voice that responded chilled me.

"What do you think, Rose? It's our trophy room. Aren't you excited? A collection of all the good work we've done." I looked over to the doorway and my breath stopped as I saw myself in a white blazer dress stained in blood and a knife with serrated edges dripping blood onto the white floor. I froze as I realized the voice wasn't mine, it was Han's. Darkness and evil swam in the green. Bloodlust dilated the pupils. My blood ran cold and I felt my body tremble under the relentless gaze.

I shrunk back as I held Jaehyun and my mother tighter to me. "No... No... I've never killed women or children... I would NEVER hurt Jaehyun... Let alone my mother... Y-You're not real... T-This isn't real..." I stammered. My voice cracked from all of the crying and the fear coursing through me. A wicked smirk stretched across the figure's face and before I could do anything, it was in front of me gripping my face with its bloody hands. The jagged nails dug into the skin of my cheeks and I whimpered in pain.

"It's so pathetic watching you try to run from who you are. Trying to play pretend and fit into a world where you don't belong. All you do is ruin lives, you don't deserve a happy ending. Did you really think you'd get away from me after *everything* you've done? Do you really think you'll get any happiness after what you've done? THIS is who you are. Who you have ALWAYS been.Who you will ALWAYS be. Like father, like daughter, remember? The perfect soldier, the perfect fighter, the perfect assassin, the perfect tool of destruction. Innocent people get hurt when you forget who you are. Look at poor Jaehyun over there. He was happy before you came along. Now look at him dead. All you had to do was follow orders." Han's voice growled at me as my figure forced me to look down at Jaehyun's lifeless body again.

I whimpered pathetically as fresh tears spilled onto my cheeks as I was forced to make eye contact with him. I felt powerless and broken. It was like I had been beaten and bruised and the figure kept poking at all of the bruises at once. I sniffled as I tried to defend myself.

"I protected him... He's safe with me-"

"Safe!? Who is ever safe with you? Don't be fucking stupid, Rose. He was in danger the moment you met him and forgot who you were. You knew that, but you're so selfish and greedy that you didn't care. You didn't care about the consequences. You didn't care that you were putting him in danger. You just wanted what you wanted. Typical of you. He was a fool to trust you. Just another body on a long list." The words stung. They cut deep because it was true. No one was safe when I was called. I was selfish. I couldn't let him go even when I knew I was getting too close. I was possessive. I was obsessive. Sobs racked my body again and I collapsed into a ball as my shoulders slumped and the figure let me go.

The cruel and belittling laugh rang in my ears. The figure continued to taunt me and repeat all of my flaws as I continued to fall apart. Suddenly I started to hear my name be softly spoken through all of the noise. The call got louder and louder and I started to realize it was Jaehyun's voice. Before I knew, my head snapped up and I was scrambling to my feet to run towards his voice. I jumped over the bodies littering the floor and ran out of the room as fast as my legs would carry me. I could hear the figure let out a blood curdling screech behind me as my legs carried me to the faint white light that got brighter the closer I got....

I screamed as I sat upright clutching my chest and panting. The room was dimly lit by the lamp on the nightstand. I was in my old bed and as I looked around, I saw Jaehyun sitting on the side of the bed with a troubled look on his face. "As soon as we get back, you're going to therapy. You were having another nightmare. What is going on?" Jaehyun said seriously. He tried his best to hide the frustration but it was clearly there. I chewed on my lip as he stared at me. What was I supposed to say? Where did I begin?

"I'm not a fan of the house anymore. It holds bad memories. And I'd rather not relive them. My dreams don't agree." I answered. He stayed quiet and waited for me to speak again. Of course he would.

"Who I used to be… Who I still am, I guess. It's coming into conflict with who I'm trying to be with you. That's the best way I can describe it. I don't have the vocabulary for all this shit. And it's pissing me off. I'd like to just focus on the assignment so we can get the hell out of here."

The venom in my voice wasn't intentional. It wasn't directed towards him. I was frustrated because I couldn't articulate what was going on. I didn't understand what was happening. I didn't know what to call it. It was hard to explain to him because he would never understand. He couldn't. It was a fact. I would never wish he did. I'm glad he had the life he had. Communicating became difficult at times because whenever he asked me what was wrong, I was never able to explain it. I was just as confused as he was. He could try to use medical terminology to explain it, but I didn't get it. It was too complicated and trying to pinpoint how my actions and feelings fit into all of the different categories made me angry. I wasn't patient enough to figure it out. There was too much to do. It was easier to deal with things on my own and ignore it. I had to protect Jaehyun until I could bring down Han.

A sad smile crossed Jaehyun's face as he moved to sit next to me. "I don't want to frustrate you. I'm sorry. I just want to understand what is going on in your mind. I know I probably won't understand it all but I want to try. I'll never understand what you went though, I know that. I hate watching you constantly suffer and I can't do anything about it. I know that the concept of someone genuinely wanting the best for you is outrageous, but I really do." he said as he held my hand. He took a moment before he spoke again.

"I see a future with you. I'm certain about you. That's why I care so much. I've had dreams about our future together. Visions about it. You're happy in those dreams. You're healed in those dreams. We have a really beautiful life together. A dog in the mix." He chuckled softly and I couldn't help but laugh too. A dog in this lifestyle? That would be a first.

"I'm really hoping that one day you'll get to see yourself that way too. You aren't what someone did to you. You aren't your past. You can be something different if that's what you want. And I really hope that you realize that. I can't do it for you. But I'll be here every step of the way until you do."

I was speechless. I didn't know what to say to that. Something about him saying that he essentially couldn't fix me or get me to see myself differently made me feel like crying. It was almost as if he realized it at the same time and he was heartbroken by it. He couldn't fix me, no matter how much he wanted to. No matter how much I wanted him too. It wasn't a possibility. I couldn't understand why that felt so heavy to me but it did. It was disappointing and frightening because it felt like a burden that had been placed on my shoulders. Except this burden felt heavier than anything I had ever felt. I looked over at him and I could see tears lining his vision slightly.

"Don't look like that. I'm still by your side. You just have some work to do. And it's not going to be easy. It's going to be hard. But I will be here when it gets hard." he smiled as he wiped tears from my eyes. I didn't realize that I was crying. I couldn't explain why this felt much bigger than just a conversation. It felt like a warning. Or a piece of advice. I couldn't wrap my head around it at all and it was becoming frustrating to make sense of it all.

"It's okay, princess. Let's regroup and we can talk about it later. I have those addresses. Want to start there?" he offered. I nodded and wiped my face with my sleeves. I was thankful that he was understanding enough to not try to push me when I was already fragile.

~Chapter 36~

After getting ourselves together and gathering all of the intel we needed, we were outside of Shimizu Jiro's house. He and his wife had taken the CEO and COO positions after the Satos disappearance. The promotion had made him extremely wealthy. He and his wife had moved into a luxurious three-story house with a pool on the top floor and a glass ceiling to match. They enjoyed midnight swims according to their profiles on the hospital's page. And we were right on time. From our position in the tree next to their house, we could see the couple enjoying wine as they relaxed. The curtains were open so the moonlight could enter the room. They were in their own little world.

"I think we should have a pool indoors if we ever build a house. That setup is nice." Jaehyun commented as he looked over at me with a slight smirk. I rolled my eyes and chuckled.

"Yeah, as long as there's not a tree anywhere nearby where enemies could watch us from it." I added. He nodded and shrugged.

"Anyways. Got a game plan on how you want to do this, newbie?" I teased. Jaehyun smirked and winked at me as he repositioned himself to hang from the tree branch with his hands.

"Through the front door. Keep up, princess." he whispered as he dropped down into the front yard. I chuckled and followed his lead, dropping to the ground silently as well. We put on our face masks and made our way to the front door. Jaehyun picked the lock on the door and quietly opened the door and let me inside first. He entered after me and quietly shut the door back.

Soft music played throughout the house. "Yeah, we definitely need the pool vibes. They're having fun," Jaehyun whispered. I drew my gun and nodded.

"Should we ruin the party?" I grinned back.

"Hold on. Let's look around first. See if they got anything on Sato." An interesting approach. I usually forced people to tell me everything. I didn't like to research while on the job. He apparently did. I wandered over to the living room to go through the stack of papers on the table. A letter caught my eye because it listed Sato Kiyo's name as the sender, so I grabbed the letter and picked it up to read it. The letter was dated two months ago in June. She wrote it to Shizimu's wife. Sato said that things were getting bad for them. They were running out of money and time was running out. The letter mentioned that Hana and Hiro were in the US and Yua was still missing. They couldn't keep searching for Yua and try to make the payments.

My eyes widened. They did borrow money from the Yakuza. But the letter didn't seem to hint at Yua being taken by the Yakuza. So if the kid wasn't taken, then what happened? The letter concluded with asking if the Shizimus could help by sending them money. Jaehyun came from down the hall, holding a laptop. I motioned for him to come here. He walked over and I showed him the letter. "Those are the kids' names. The twins Hana and Hiro, I remember them. Yua must be the youngest. So it looks like you were right. A syndicate gave them money. To find the kid?" he whispered. I shrugged. I gestured to the laptop.

"Patience. I got it. So, I got into the guy's laptop. He left all his stuff open and he's the type to write all his passwords down. And leave them out." I rolled my eyes. Old people. It's crazy how often that happens. But it makes the job easy.

"There's been numerous payments going to this company called Lee's. Website says it handles personal documentation, like passports, notaries and shit like that. But it seems to be a front business. Because we're talking about 13.7 million yen payments. And they've done it ten or more times." he whispered. The business name sounded familiar.

"It's definitely a front business. But let's go ask." I whispered back as I motioned towards the stairs.

He nodded as he put the laptop back. The music was still playing, they were none the wiser. I made my way up the winding staircase, moving up to the second level. I pulled the gun from my holster. Jaehyun met me on the second level and he put a hand on my shoulder and tapped it twice to announce his presence. I paused for a moment because he knew that gesture as well. I thought it was something only the Yamaguchi did. He was definitely trained. I nodded as we kept climbing the second set of steps. I peeked over the edge of the third floor and the elderly couple were embraced in a hug swaying in the water. We silently entered the pool area, guns pointed. I clicked the safety off on my gun and it was loud and it cut through the music. I smirked at the terrorized screams.

"Relax! Relax! We're not here to hurt you. We need some information. Once we get that, we're gone. So let's work together, okay?" Jaehyun cooed as he lowered his gun and kneeled next to the pool. They nodded.

"Good. Sato Haruto and Sato Kiyo. You were in contact with them not too long ago. Where are they?" he asked gently. They looked at each and were silent. The silence irritated me.

"He asked you a question. I suggest you answer it. He's being nice. I'm not." I growled, aiming at the woman.

"W-We don't know! I swear! All we know is that when we took over their positions at the hospital, they said they were going to travel and move. Kiyo was diagnosed with breast cancer last year." Haruto stuttered.

"Is that why they stepped down? What about the missing kid?" Jaehyun asked.

"It was a combination of both. Yua went missing the following week after she got her diagnosis. It was a month later that we started getting letters. They told us that her cancer was aggressive and likely to spread. They were spending millions on her treatment and then on top of that Yua went missing. They made a deal with the Yakuza to pay them to find Yua. We hear from them every two months. In the last couple of letters, money was so low that they actually asked us to pay the Yakuza so they'd keep searching. We did that. Kiyo was getting sicker and not doing well. The bills were piling up at the hospital." Kiyo explained.

"That's what the letter was talking about. They couldn't pay the medical bills and pay the syndicate. Did they tell you who they went to? What area were they in when they reached out for help?" Jaehyun said as he looked back at me.

"At the time she was being treated at the Cancer Institute Hospital of JFCR in Tokyo, so it could have been there." Kiyo answered.

"That's not true. Couldn't have been in Tokyo. Lie again." I hissed as I clicked the gun again. They yelped in fear and shrank back. Jaehyun held a hand up to me.

"Hold on. Let them try again. Come on guys. Think harder. We're in a time crunch. I really don't want you all to get hurt. Focus. What area?" he said soothingly to them. The differences in our styles were glaringly different.

"They were in Kyoto. That's where they were when they asked for help." Haruto chimed in.

"That's the Aizu Kotetsu-kai… How did they get that type of…" I paused and lowered the gun. They formed an alliance with the Yamaguchi-gumi back in the 2000s. Of course, I wouldn't have had anything to do with the deal. It went through Han. Realization hit me.

"That's why I've heard of Lee's. That's a front business Han formed years ago. That's what we use to forge documents and it's the security headquarters. People pay the protection fees there." I groaned as I rolled my eyes.

"How long ago was this? When did they reach out for help?" Jaehyun asked calmly.

"They reached out in February of 2021 when they got nowhere with the police." Haruto answered.

"And we're here more than a year later and the kid hasn't been found yet? Either they're dead or they've been taken." I said plainly. The woman gasped in shock and she began to cry. Jaehyun looked back at me and made a face. I shrugged.

"You did well. Enjoy the rest of your night." Jaehyun winked as he stood up and he gestured for us to leave. We turned to leave the way we came out. Once in the car, I sighed disappointed.

"You have to go to the Yakuza headquarters?" he asked.

"Unfortunately. Those files are going to tell us where the Satos are. Or at least they'll tell us where the kid is and we can track them that way." I answered. As I answered, my stomach twisted in an uncomfortable way. A chill ran down my side. Something felt wrong. I couldn't figure out what it was but I could feel it.

"This is the weirdest collection I've ever heard of. Areum and Daehyun never talk about debt collections being this hard. I don't know if I like it." Jaehyun said suddenly.

"Agreed." The entire situation made me uncomfortable. Why did Omega give us this assignment? Did he know something we didn't?

Jaehyun sensed my discomfort and rubbed my shoulder. "We'll deal with it tomorrow. We need rest. Let's head back. I'm starving. Where's a good place?" he offered.

"Convenience stores. That's where I usually got food. I'm a wanted criminal here, remember? I don't go to too many places." I reminded him.

"Still? It's been months. You'd think the cops would give up."

"I've been on the most wanted list for years. They're persistent."

"Oh. A lot of things make sense. That's why you don't like crowded places. Got it." Jaehyun said as he nodded in understanding.

"Yeah. Being inside was the safest option for me. The government will never say it out loud because they don't want to seem like the monsters they truly are, but there's a kill on sight order on me. If an officer were to see me and be able to confirm it's me, they can very well shoot first and ask questions later." I told him. His head turned so quickly to me that I heard his neck crack.

"What? That's illegal. That can't be true."

"Compared to the things that I've done, they see it as fair." I shrugged. It was silent for a little bit before he spoke again.

"Can I ask you something, princess?" Jaehyun asked quietly. I could hear the hesitation in his voice. I looked up at him and hummed.

"I don't like the way you sound. I'm concerned, but okay."

"Do you like what you do? Do you like being an assassin?" I sat back and sighed. I remained quiet as I tried to think of what to say. I never thought about it like that. Is this something to like? I didn't even know how to answer the question.

"I honestly can't answer that. It's been my job for so long that I can't do anything else. I started as an assassin when I was thirteen. After about a year, I became numb to it. I became numb to life in general. I spent my life in the training dorms. Han didn't care about anything other than me becoming the perfect Yakuza member. I wasn't human to him. I was a project. He was only proud, if you want to call it that, when I got excellent marks in combat training and target practice. I was expected to be perfect. That's all I know. I prefer the money and the power over the actual assassin work. If that answers your question." I admitted as I looked out the window.

"Do you ever imagine anything different for yourself? Do you think this is all life will ever be?" Jaehyun asked. I wondered where this was coming from. I chose to not ask.

"I'm twenty five. Logically, I know I'm still young. But sometimes it feels like my life is over. Even if I were to leave this, it's going to follow me forever. Han isn't going to let this go. Eventually he's going to figure out I abandoned my position. And he's going to want revenge. If he finds out about you, he will come after you. I can't even imagine leaving this life until Han is dead." I answered.

"Why would I be his target? I just want to understand. You're always so guarded when it comes to talking about your past. I think it's time you tell me."

"Because that's the only way he could ever break me. It's impossible to hurt someone who is used to torture and physical pain. I've never had anyone that I gave a damn about except you. Death was always around me, so I don't fear it. But now that I have you... I could lose everything, but not you. He would know that. As much as I hate to admit it, it's really like father like daughter."

"Understandable. So let's say that Han is dead. Do you imagine a life different from this?" Jaehyun repeated his question.

I took a deep breath and looked out the front window. "I never thought about it. I wouldn't want you to be in this lifestyle. If that meant, I had to leave it in order to get you to leave it, then so be it. I would maybe just sell drugs and arms. Keep revenue coming in. We could travel the world. Honestly, I never thought about the future until I got with you. All I'm sure is that you're in it. I'm beside you. And I'm happy with you. I don't know what happens that leads to that, but I'm determined to get there with you. No matter what it takes." I admitted.

"Okay, I'm in the future. That much is obvious. But that's not what I meant. I'm talking about you personally. Every answer had something to do with me. Where do you see yourself? Do you see yourself free from your past? Healed? You can't put your everything into me. That's not healthy." Jaehyun said as he looked over at me concerned. I raised an eyebrow. What did he mean by that? I had never been asked what I wanted, so I didn't know what to say. Everything that I had ever done was for someone else. It was for the Yakuza. When I met Jaehyun, everything I did was for him.

"I've never been asked that before. All I ever wanted was money and power. I got the money. The power." I replied.

"There's got to be more than that. You're too smart for that. I'm not going to judge you, I swear."

"I'm serious. The only other thing I ever wanted was... my mother. But she's dead. So I can't have that. But I could have revenge. He took her away from me. For the times that he embarrassed me. For the hell he put me through. I want the life that I should've gotten. At least the fucking option. I didn't get a choice. Everything was chosen for me. But, of course I can't have that. That time is gone. It's always like that. When I want something for myself, I can't have it. Because it's too late or because someone said I can't have it or do it. So I think I got to a point where I just stopped wanting things. That's why it's hard to answer that. How am I supposed to *heal* from something like that? How am I supposed to begin to do that?"

I hated the way my voice quivered with the emotions that I couldn't describe. There were too many to list. Rage, angst, grief, sorrow, regret… Every imaginable emotion flowed through me and for the second time, tears fell down my face and they wouldn't stop. Even with the anguish following through me, I gave him a sad sarcastic smile. I felt pathetic. I had to be the worst assassin in the world. Assassins weren't crying over their dead mothers, they weren't crying because they were doing their job. They followed orders and did what they were paid to do. I laughed bitterly as I threw my hands up. "I'm a fucking mess. Look at me crying. This is pathetic…" I scoffed.

"I can't sit here and say I understand everything you've gone through. I won't say that at all. But I can tell you that you're being so unkind to yourself by holding onto all of that. Especially when it wasn't your fault. I really can't take your pain away from you, princess. I so wish I could. It was something that I had been trying to do and I think I did more harm than good. You try to hide behind me because you want to run from your emotions and your past. You're better than that. You won't get better that way." Jaehyun said as he used his sleeve to dry my tears. I looked down at my nails as he spoke.

"There's so much to you that you haven't discovered because it's buried under all of your pain and anger. And it's completely valid. I am not taking that from you. You recognize that you are valuable and you were treated less than valuable. You are right to be angry and be hurt. I'm not trying to deter you from anything you want to do. I'm not asking that from you. But I am asking for you to give yourself a chance to find out who you are without the pain and anger. To find out who you are. You are so special. You truly are. You are so much more than what people have made you feel like. You're so much more than the job you do. I can tell you that all day but you won't believe it. Unless you could see it for yourself. I know it doesn't make sense, but sometimes things happen to show you how strong you are. Sometimes things happen because you need it to grow. And it fucking sucks. It does. But the healing can be such a beautiful thing, if you let it be." Jaehyun smiled softly as he titled my head up to look him in the eyes.

"That's a lovely story honestly. A beautiful message too, but let's be honest, that's for the girls you're used to. The girls who have never had to lift a finger to get their next meal. Never had to go through anything." I sighed.

"You're worthy of happiness and a beautiful life too. Your past doesn't have to define you. It doesn't have to keep you from loving yourself. You just have to take a step towards healing. There's a quote I heard one day that the soul has the capacity to prevail through it all. I have to find the rest of it but that's what I remember of it right now."

I rolled my eyes. "How can you make up a quote like that right now? I thought this was serious." I teased.

"Hey! I didn't make it up. It's a real quote. I'm hungry so I can't think of it all right now. I'll find it and show you after we eat." He pinched my cheek softly and pointed towards the convenience store we pulled up too.

"This one has onigiri and fried chicken." I said I pulled my mask on.

"You're not going to eat that together, are you? That's chaotic as hell."

"Isn't that what our life is? Chaotic. It sounds fine to me."

"Well, when you put it that way. Sure, what the hell... come on." Jaehyun put the mask on as well and we went into the store.

~Chapter 37~

The clock read 8am as I stared out of the window and watched the sun rise. I didn't sleep well. I had been awake since 6 because the nightmares became too much to deal with, so there was no point in trying to sleep again. I just chose to stay in bed and stay in Jaehyun's arms. I tried to figure out what other ways we could find the Satos instead of me having to go to the headquarters, but I was coming up empty. It was a nice distraction because I had no energy to try and decipher what the nightmares meant. I felt Jaehyun stir behind me and cuddle closer as he mumbled my name sleepily.

"Morning Mr. Nice Guy," I quipped as I referenced last night with the Shizimu's. He chuckled slightly.

"You get more accomplished by being nice. Look at the information we got. And no one died. No fighting. Quick and easy." he replied. I turned over to face him and he was already looking at me. I rolled my eyes at the statement.

"Now if they call the police then what? No witnesses works best."

He leaned up on his elbow. "That's cruel though. Why kill when you have the information already?"

"The police. They're no longer useful. Why keep them alive?" I tilted my head in confusion. It was just what you did. I had no intention of going to prison for the rest of my life so I was taught to get rid of anyone that gave me information, so I could continue to work in secrecy and protect myself. It made sense. Most of the time, I was doing them a favor. The people I tracked down usually were just as bad as me. I was saving them honestly.

"They're people. They have families. Lives. People are more than pawns in our lifestyle, princess. I know that's a foreign concept, but I think it may be something you need to learn. I think it may start to change the way you see life." I hummed as I turned the light on in the bathroom to brush my teeth.

"Never really thought about that." I admitted quietly. I never took a moment to think about the other person. I was trained to focus on the assignment, that's it. I was taught that considering another person could be the reason why I got caught or killed. I paused for a moment as I looked back at Jaehyun sitting on the bed. The weight of that sat on my chest.

I guess I was going to have to see that for myself. I felt my stomach twist in knots. I could protect him. If anyone could prove that wrong, it was me. I had to protect him no matter what it took. It was because of me he chose to go active in the lifestyle. I turned his life upside down, the least I could do was protect him with mine. "You okay in there? You've been quiet." Jaehyun called gently.

"Trying to sort out my thoughts. I would rather focus on the assignment." I replied.

"Okay. Do you think you'll have any issues getting into the headquarters? Seeing as you've been gone for so long?"

"I shouldn't. As far as they know nothing has changed. I'd still rather go at night. The guards won't be there. Han isn't there at night either. I just need to be in and out. Find the documents on the Satos and I can get back to the car without incident. I'll need you to park far enough away. I don't want to risk anyone seeing you." I sighed internally.

The thought of returning to the headquarters sent chills down my spines. My hands felt clammy and my heart pounded in my chest. Han was a creature of habit, I doubted his routine changed in the months I had been gone. At least I was hoping so. I was too volatile and on edge to see Han. It would create more problems. I wasn't in a position to go to war with the Yamaguchi right now. It was just us and he had no experience. It would put him in danger. I was brought out of my thoughts as Jaehyun entered the bathroom and put his chin on my shoulder. "I'll be there if anything goes wrong. You know that. Don't worry. Want me to look at tickets for the train?" he offered.

"Yes please. I'll find the rental. We need the darkest tint possible. The sooner we get this done, the sooner we'll find the information we need and we can get the hell out of here."

"Agreed. But first, we need food. Any suggestions for around here?"

"Didn't we talk about this already? Convenience stores." I reminded him.

"Not to be dramatic, but this is hell. When we get home, we're going out to dinner. I'm tired of noodles and origini and fried chicken." he whined as he left the bathroom to throw himself back onto the bed. If he thought a few days of living like this was hell, he wouldn't understand how the last six years of my life had been.

We were able to catch one of the last trains from Tokyo and it put us in Kobe at 11pm. We had another forty-five-minute drive after we got to Kobe. The ride into the city was fairly quiet. As we started to make the turns to get to the headquarters, it was even quieter. This should be painless. Internally, it was anything but quiet. My heart was pounding so hard, I swore Jaehyun could hear it. Because my heart was beating so fast, I could almost hear the blood rushing through my veins. I was starting to sweat. I kept my face neutral and unbothered on the outside. I didn't want Jaehyun to be worried.

"We're five minutes out. How should we play this?" Jaehyun announced.

"Put on this hat and when we pull up, park in front of the door and come open my door. Bow ninety degrees. That way the cameras don't suspect anything. You'll be another one of my clan members who brought me to the office. Once I go inside, go park around the corner. I'll be back." I said as I handed him a baseball cap. I had to dye my hair again so that I would resemble my old looks and the cameras would register me as a familiar person. I couldn't find the same maroon color, so I ended up with a more cardinal red color. A little brighter than what I originally was. Dying my hair again this color was emotional. I had to lock myself in the bathroom and silently cry as I waited for the color to take.

"I'm an underling. Cool. Can do, Boss." he saluted me playfully. I rolled my eyes.

"Shut up. Look alive. It's up here on the right." I directed him. He pulled along the curve and put the cap on and kept his head down as he walked to my side of the car and pulled open the door for me. He bowed as instructed and I stepped out of the car and nodded once in acknowledgement just like I would any other subordinate.

"I'll be here if you need me." he whispered as I walked past him and went up to the door and I typed the code in. It made me anxious as I watched from the corner of my eye and saw the car drive off. I was relieved because everything went off without a hitch. He was safe. The building was empty. My combat boots made soft thuds as I walked towards the elevator and eventually got on. I toyed with the keys in my pocket as I watched the numbers increase, all the way to the thirty-fifth floor.

Once the doors opened on the floor, the halls were just as I remembered. Han's office door still felt large and imposing. Even with no one here, the atmosphere felt just as hostile as I remembered. I grabbed the correct key and took a deep breath as I inserted the key and twisted it. The office door opened and I stepped into the office and closed it back. The moonlight gave me enough light to get to his desk and turn on the lamp. He had moved his desk slightly but it was relatively the same. I sat at the large mahogany desk and the feeling of power was intoxicating. It radiated from the chair. It felt like a fog started to cloud my vision. It was something I truly missed. It felt like a blissful high that was easy to get addicted to.

I shook my head to clear the fog and logged into the computer. There were hundreds of files and in each file, he categorized every document under a letter in the English alphabet. I had advised him before it wasn't smart but did he listen? No. I opened the file that was labeled finances and opened the document labeled S. I started scrolling through looking for anything with the Sato name. He was predictable like that. After some scrolling, I found what I was looking for. A graph tracking the amount of money the Satos paid. I almost felt bad for them. All that wasted money to never get their kid back. I started to wonder if the parents had accepted that the kid was dead or were they holding out hope for a miracle that would never come.

I kept scrolling not seeing anything about their location, it just tracked their businesses and I came across the contract that the Satos signed. It wasn't until I saw something with Sato Yua's name that made me pause and focus.

Sato Yua initiated May 31, 2021

"What the fuck? They found the kid and made her a member? Where was she assigned?" I mumbled. I suddenly felt on edge and I was sweating again as I scrolled down.

Assignment: Tokyo

My eyes widened as the breath left my body. My sector. I jumped up from the chair and looked over at the podium near the back of the room. The large blue book sat closed on the podium. It was a Yakuza tradition that when someone joined the organization, their name was written and registered in the record book. Each syndicate had their own. There were several of them over the years. I slowly crept to the book and my stomach flipped with each step. I opened the book with shaking hands and flipped to the S section. The book was organized by last names and on each page, everyone was listed categorized by the date of joining. The date of joining; the syndicate; then the birth name, last and then first; and then the alias name.

2021/05/31-Yamaguchi-Sato Yua-Remi

I stared down at the page in shock and it felt like the wind had been knocked out of me. Remi. The Remi that worked as *my* assistant. The Remi that Han pushed off on me to train and almost got me killed on several occasions. Her parents owed money to the Jopok, but she was here? She was the missing Sato kid? She was kidnapped? My mind was racing trying to piece together a story that didn't make sense. In some ways, it made sense, in other ways it didn't. I had always said she didn't fit the lifestyle. She was way too bubbly and ditzy and clueless. That was why. She didn't belong. I fucking knew it. She was forced into this.

I was fuming. I didn't know who to direct my anger at. There was so much happening at once. The familiar anger from the day Han surprised me with Remi when I came to the headquarters came rushing back. I took one look at her and I knew she didn't fit. I tried and tried to persuade Han to let her back on the street, take her to an orphanage, something. Hell I even asked if he would put her into the training dorms. He refused. Of course he refused, he kidnapped a kid. That asshole. All the moments when she ruined assignments with her carelessness and stupid decisions. The amount of times she almost got me killed while I was working. Was it on purpose? Did Han try to use her to kill me? I gasped out loud and covered my mouth as I slammed the book close.

I stormed over to the computer and tried to stop my hands from shaking as I sent the document to myself. I kept myself calm enough to try and find any mention of the parents. There wasn't any. That pissed me off more. I closed the document and turned off the computer and the light and left the room. I needed to find Remi. She was going to pay off her parent's debts. Whether she had the money or it was with her life. I didn't care how. Mission complete. I tried to ignore the tugging in my stomach. *She's innocent in all of this. It's not her fault.* I banged my head on the elevator wall trying to will the incessant nagging away. I just wanted out of Japan, but I couldn't leave without completing the assignment. My emotions started to bubble up and it felt like the pressure was constantly rising in me. I could feel the incoming migraine as I walked towards the exit of the headquarters.

"Boss? You're back?" I froze in my tracks as Code's voice filled the silent lobby. I cursed under my breath and tried to calm myself down. This wasn't supposed to be happening. I took a deep breath as I shuddered and turned to face him slowly. He was standing in front of the second set of elevators. Panic coursed through me as he jogged to meet me.

"I needed to get some stuff, so I flew in for a little bit. I'll be leaving soon." I told him as I tried to keep my posture.

"The assignment isn't done yet?" he asked, puzzled. I fought to keep the annoyance at bay.

"Obviously not. They're just as good as we are. This wasn't as easy as I thought."

"What happened to Ace? Did things not go well?" I hadn't even thought about Ace since everything happened. What happened to him? He was likely dead, but I should confirm that.

"It didn't. He was captured and I haven't found him yet." I sighed as I rubbed my temple. He tilted his head clearly intrigued.

"Oh shit... That's not good. Do you need my help? I'm free now. I could get my stuff ready."

"No! No. I need you here. Things have to keep going. The assignment has become personal and I need to do it alone." I ordered as I looked down at the ground.

"Personal? That's new... May I ask what it is? I'm only asking because I need to know how long I'm running the show around here. I'll need some help here soon and Remi's been helpful, but it's time to bring out the big guns for the next plans."

His chuckle was full of mischief and excitement. I took a deep breath. As I stood across from Code, I felt guilt rush through me and some panic because burning ties here left me with nothing. I wouldn't have access to as much money as I do now. Code had been the only constant in my life for so long and whether I considered him a friend or not didn't change that. I had never lied to him before. He was the only person I could ever be honest with. I guess all those years meant something and I never realized it. I still couldn't tell him what was going on, he would tell Han and I wasn't prepared for that fight yet.

"Han told me they killed my mother. I've found evidence that says otherwise. I need to figure it out." I admitted. The look of shock and confusion was evident on his face, but there was something else that he was hiding in his eyes. I knew Code well enough to tell when he was holding something back. I raised an eyebrow.

"I've heard that rumor before. I'm sorry I never told you." he confessed as he bowed in apology. I nodded in response.

"Heard which part?"

"Both. That's why I never said anything." Code clarified as he folded his arms. He was visibly uncomfortable. I couldn't shake the feeling that there was more to it. It didn't feel right. It wasn't that it didn't make sense, Code was older than me by a few years so it made sense that he could have heard the rumors before.

"Why didn't you say anything?" I inquired. He sighed heavily.

"Han told me not to. It was an order. He said he would tell you when the time was right. I guess he decided to wait until you were in your twenties to do it. I never agreed with it, it was wrong. But an order is an order. That's why I spent all of your training and development with you and following you through it. I was supposed to be done with you after you left the dorms, but I wasn't going to leave you without a small sense of stability in your life." Code looked genuinely disappointed, but as I looked in his eyes there was more to the story. He was hiding it from me and it angered me.

"Would you lie to me after all these years?"

"I'd follow you into war blindly and without questions asked. I'm on your side. Why would I lie to you?" We stared into each other's eyes, and I saw the familiar spark of determination and devotion in his eyes. Whatever he was hiding, he didn't want to tell me or he *couldn't* tell. I couldn't tell which one it was. Either way, it pissed me off because why wouldn't he tell me? Why wouldn't he want to tell me? I felt all of my emotions rise to the surface and I fought to push them all back. I was going to explode at any moment, and I just wanted to leave the situation.

"Choose whoever you want as your wakashirga. I'm giving you my position. Lead well," I told him. His eyes widened.

"A-Are you sure? I understand you're angry with me, but this is an overreaction. You don't have to be drastic and rash." That did it.

"Drastic and rash? I'm not a fucking idiot! You're hiding something from me! I've known you my whole life and you've been there, and you won't be honest with me. I'm so tired of everyone knowing something that I don't know and refusing to tell me! Is my life some sort of joke to everyone?! You know what… I don't have time for this. Continue as you have been." I yelled. I caught myself before I said too much and turned to walk away.

"I-It's not that… Boss! Wait!" I heard him calling after me and I pushed my legs to sprint out of the building and run around the corner to find Jaehyun parked on the left side.

"Hey, how'd it- You're crying. What happened?" Jaehyun questioned. I quickly wiped my eyes and groaned in annoyance at the smeared mascara and eyeliner. I felt so confused and conflicted and angry. Code knew something I didn't; Omega always seemed like he knew something that I didn't; and Iseul did as well. I heard Jaehyun's voice trying to get my attention and it added to the noise already going on in my head. It was too much.

"Jaehyun please! Give me a minute. I'm trying to decompress. I found out too much information in the last 30 minutes." I snapped at him. I rubbed my temples and sniffled as I tried to calm myself down with deep breaths. It took a little bit of time before I felt centered again. "Remi is the missing Sato kid." I stated.

"Remi is?" Jaehyun tilted his head.

"My assistant. I was supposed to train her, but she didn't work out as an assassin. She was essentially my left hand. The Sato's paid all that money for nothing. They were never going to get her back. Han may have used her to try to kill me."

"Wait… what? How did you conclude he used her to kill you? Didn't you say that she didn't work as an assassin?"

"It would've looked like the most normal thing. An accident."

"Hold on, Rose. I'm not trying to say anything by this but don't you think you might be being a little paranoid? Why would he wait so long to kill you? It's been six years. You were in that position for six years. And if that was true, he can't reach you now. You're not there." Jaehyun reassured me calmly. He had a point.

"I saw Code. He's hiding something from me. I told him that I was still on my assignment and gave him my position. Told him it had become personal because the Jopok killed my mother. I told him that there was evidence that Han lied too. He told me he'd heard that before and that he was sorry he never told me. But I saw something in his eyes. He was hiding something. Like he knew something I didn't. The same way Omega and Iseul look. Everyone seems to know something except me. And no one will tell me anything. Like my life's meant to be a big secret. Like I'm not good enough to know what the hell happened in my past. Why does everyone know something I don't?" I confessed as I looked over at him.

"Do you know something that I don't, Jaehyun? About my life?" He physically recoiled away from me.

"I joined the same day you did. I don't know anything more than what you do. But I do know for a fact that the timeline of your mother's death doesn't line up. You would at least know your mother, if my father had done it. You would've had a year with her. So simply based on that timeline, it couldn't have been done under his leadership. That's the truth. I've been researching. Just be patient, please. I don't have an answer for the who and why yet. Do you trust me?" he replied gently. It was hard to miss the hurt in his eyes at the accusation and I felt guilty.

"I didn't mean to come at you that way... I'm just under a lot of pressure. I do trust you. I know you wouldn't lie to me. Just being back here is a lot to handle. I'm ready to be back in Korea."

"Did you find out anything about the Sato's? We can get this done if you did."

"No, but I know where Remi lives. We were told to collect the money. Kids are fair game."

"Fair statement. We show up and get this over with. We should let you calm down and then do it tomorrow."

"She lives in a small place in the Chiba prefecture... I just can't believe I didn't catch it sooner. She's a mixture of both her fucking parents. That's why they looked familiar." I shook my head slowly.

Silence filled the car for a little while as we drove back to the train station. I was trying to process so much. I was still confused, irritated and angry. But the feeling of guilt was settling in my stomach as I thought about Remi. I was cruel to that kid. For her to be so young and go through everything she had gone through. Her mom gets sick, she gets kidnapped, then she's suddenly thrown into my world, and I use her for target practice. I was impatient and abusive. I treated her the way Han treated me. I felt sick to my stomach. I was always aware of the similarities between Han and I, but when I had to confront them, it hurt more than I wished to admit.

"You okay, princess? You're quiet. I thought you'd be in better spirits with the possibility of going home so close." Jaehyun prodded gently.

"I gave Code my old title. We got into a fight because he wouldn't tell me what he knew. I'm a nobody." I replied without thinking. Saying it out loud crushed me. I knew at some point I would have to cut those ties but doing it like that wasn't a part of the plan. I didn't have time to prepare myself for how empty it felt. It stung. I had lost a part of myself. My position defined me for years. It was all I could claim. I wasn't special. No power, no status. Nothing. I could have sworn, I heard my heart shatter into pieces once I realized it.

"You're not a nobody, Rose. This doesn't take anything away from you."

"I don't want to talk about it right now. Please. I'd like to get something to eat while we wait for the train, please."

"Okay. We can do that."

~Chapter 38~

I leaned against the counter in Remi's kitchen waiting for her to get back from running documents for Code. It was surreal standing in her house again. The last time I was here, I was admonishing her for another assignment that she screwed up and almost got me killed on. It got ugly. Even though she tried to patch up the holes in the walls and tried to paint over them, they were still noticeable. The paint didn't match completely. In some areas, the glass shards from the vase I threw at her were still embedded in the wall. Jaehyun came in from the living room and he took a deep breath. "I saw a car coming down the road. I'm about to call my dad. Please be calm. No rash decisions. We ask if she has the money. If not, we see what's next." he coached as he rubbed my shoulders. I nodded wordlessly.

To say I was on edge was an understatement. I was getting more and more frustrated and anxious by the hour. The knowledge of the situation constantly ran through my mind and the guilt I felt got worse. I had been trying to push myself to push it out of my mind so I could focus on the assignment. This part of my life was over and I couldn't do anything to change it. It happened. The lights of a car provided the only light into the house. Once it was turned off, we were shrouded in darkness again. I pushed him away to hide behind the eastern wall. The car turned off and I held my breath and waited for the door to open. My hand twitched as I fought the urge to pull my gun. She wasn't a threat. She wasn't dangerous. I didn't need my gun. However, it was the only thing that made sense when the emotions and nerves were starting to feel physically heavy.

The young girl walked around the corner and turned the light on. Her terrified squeal sounded the same. "Oh my god! Oh, you scared me, boss. How are you? When'd you get back? Code didn't tell me you were home!" Remi bounced excitedly. She bowed in respect and her smile was still bright. That hadn't changed about her. Her round brown eyes looked up at me and the sparkle in her eye infuriated me. How was she still so damn happy! How had she kept her innocence after everything she had been through? It made no sense. Her high cheekbones made her eyes disappear into crescent moon shapes. She had her father's laugh lines. Her black hair was in a high bun. No pigtails. She looked more like her mother. It was different.

"I'm here because I need information." I told her coldly. Her smile dropped and she put down her items and slowly stepped into the kitchen.

"W-What's wrong, Miss Rose?"

"Where is the money that your family owes?" She stared at me wide eyed and confusion crossed her face.

"H-H… What money?" she stammered. I groaned loudly and rolled my eyes.

"Look Remi. I don't have time for bullshit today. I need the money or this will get ugly." She shrunk back at that and chewed on her nail. "I was trying to help, I swear. My mom got sick and the doctor's said that the cancer would likely spread. I ran away to try and go make money. In March last year, some people from the Aizukotetsu-kai came and found me at a restaurant. They said they had a better job for me. More money. It would help allow me to pay more money for the bills for my mom. I was a glorified maid, but the money really was good. I was saving it." she said. I listened silently for her to continue.

"It wasn't happening fast enough though. The little bit I could save didn't make a dent in the debt. I was introduced to Han in May and he said I could make more money by joining the Yakuza officially and training with you. But mom died in July of this year. The money I was getting went to hospital bills." Remi explained as she looked down.

Sato Kiyo was dead? What? That didn't make sense. None of it made sense and it didn't answer the question. Kiyo was dead. Where was Haruto? Did Omega know that? What was the point of all of this if she was dead? I could feel a migraine beginning to form. I looked over at Remi and she had started to cry. It made my chest tighten with guilt and it pissed me off even more. My thoughts were racing a mile a moment and they were jumbled up and confused. The room felt way too hot. The twitching in my hand got worse and I just grabbed my gun, aimed it and clicked the safety off. "I just want the money, Remi! I don't care how!" I screamed. I want to go back to Korea, why was she making this so hard? Why was she putting up such a fight? She jumped back and raised her hands and started to cry harder. Jaehyun emerged from his hiding place and quickly ran beside me.

"Wait a minute, Rose! That's not part of the plan. She's a kid." he reminded me calmly. My gaze fixated on her was unwavering. The fear was evident on her face as she trembled. I've thrown knives at her, beaten her, punched her but I've never pulled a gun on her and aimed it at her before. The level of fear she was experiencing was something different. It was different for me too. I felt more volatile than ever before. Less in control. One wrong move from anyone could make a tense situation worse. "I want out of Japan. I want this to be over." I hissed. I fought back tears of frustration. The emotions were starting to bubble over.

"Calm down. Yua, I need you to hear me clearly. And answer yes or no only. The money that your family borrowed. Are you able to pay it back?" Jaehyun said softly to her as he snapped his fingers. She shook her head quickly. More tears fell down her face and I growled in irritation as my finger twitched.

"Rose! Easy! Please! I'm calling!" Jaehyun ordered as he put his phone on speaker and the ringing broke the tense silence.

"Hello?" Omega's voice came over the phone. He sounded tired.

"We found Sato Yua. Sato Kiyo is dead. She can't pay the money. What do you want us to do?" Jaehyun explained quickly. It was silent for a while.

"Good work. Let her go. It's taken care of." Omega said nonchalantly.

"What!?" I yelled incredulously.

"I-I don't understand… What's going on? This makes no sense." Jaehyun stuttered confused.

"We'll talk about it. Have a good night you all." Omega sang as he hung up without anything else. It was silent again. It was deafening. The confusion stunned Jaehyun and I into silence and we stared at each other. What did Omega mean by it had been taken care of?

"M-Miss Rose... Are you working for the Jopok? How did you know about the money my family owed?" Remi inquired. Shit. I looked back at her and Jaehyun's hand rested on my arm. He already knew what I was thinking.

"Rose... No. Don't do it." he pleaded.

"She talks too much." I informed him dryly as I recentered the gun.

"She's a kid. You don't kill kids, remember?"

"She's sixteen, she's lived enough. She'll ruin everything."

Remi talked too much. She would run her mouth and tell Code. After the fight with Code, he'd tell Han. I'd have all of the Yamaguchi on my back before I could do anything. I couldn't risk it. Jaehyun would be in danger and there was no guarantee that Omega would jump to my defense. It wasn't worth it. No matter how much sympathy or guilt I was starting to feel for her, I cared more about Jaehyun and myself. I aimed the gun to her forehead as she sobbed pathetically and begged for her life. "Rose, she just lost her mom. Come on. Think about it." Jaehyun pleaded as he tried to lower my hand.

"She can go be with her. Makes perfect sense to me. It'll be fine." I said coldly.

"I-I won't say anything! Please! Whatever's going on here, I won't say a word. My loyalty's with you! I promise! Please!" Remi begged as she tried to catch her breath from crying so hard. I wanted to pull the trigger so badly, but it was as if I couldn't move.

"We can go home, Rose. It's over. Don't you want to go home? We can do that now. Our assignment is done. Besides, she could be useful in the future. You never know what could happen. Just put the gun down, princess." Jaehyun reached for the gun slowly and tried to loosen my grip. I was conflicted. I was running through every possibility and scenario. The recurring nightmare I had. The guilt for the way I treated Remi. Everything she went through. She had a dad and siblings… A family who loved her and she wanted to help that was all… She was a kid, she wasn't used to this. She wasn't built for this. The pounding in my head got worse, the longer I thought about it. I screamed in frustration and let Jae take the gun from me. The sigh of relief he let out was audible. I never looked away from Remi as she grabbed her chest and bent over to catch her breath. I folded my arms across my chest and glared at her. I walked up to her and leaned down to stare into her eyes.

"Remember this kindness. It's not something that will happen again. You remain silent about seeing me and this conversation. It never happened. If I hear that you've said anything about this, I *will* kill you and whoever else is left in your fucking family." I growled as I met her nose to nose.

"Yes ma'am. I understand." Remi agreed unblinking. I pushed past her and made my way out of the house without another word. It was a strange feeling knowing that in two interactions with people, it had not ended in bloodshed. Especially this one. I didn't fully trust that Remi would keep the secret, in fact I was terrified that she wouldn't. I walked down the street to where the car was parked. I jumped into the passenger seat and leaned my head against the dashboard. I was nauseous and my head was pounding. I felt uncomfortable and anxious. I felt like throwing up. I didn't bother to look up when my door opened, knowing it was Jaehyun.

"Princess… I'm here… Do you want to talk about it?" Jaehyun asked as he leaned his head on my shoulder.

"I'm ready to go. Please. I don't want anything else. I don't want to talk. I just want out of here. I'm exhausted." I answered. I was emotionally and physically exhausted. My emotions had taken me on enough of a rollercoaster ride for the week that we had been here. The wave of emotions I had been on left me physically weaker because I wasn't sleeping. I just wanted to be… okay. I wanted a sense of normalcy and stability again. Tears of frustration spilled from my eyes, and I found myself sobbing in Jaehyun's arms as he held me together again. It was becoming way too frequent for my liking, but I felt like I wasn't in control of my emotions anymore. I had reached a point where everything felt out of my control, and I didn't know what was happening. Just when I thought I had found security, it took a week for it all to go up in flames. Jaehyun was the remaining constant.

~Chapter 39~

Jaehyun and I walked down the hall to the conference room. We landed in Seoul three days ago and he had convinced Omega to let us rest for a few days before we did our debrief. I was so exhausted that when I got back to my penthouse, I slept through the days. I felt more at ease being back in Korea, but I was still a mess emotionally and mentally. I could control it and hide it better though. I wasn't ready to address anything that happened in Japan and I don't think I ever would be. Any time Jaehyun brought it up, I shrugged it off. I just needed to get back into the swing of things. Once we had the debrief today, Omega would tell us what happened next. I still had so many questions. They were burned into my mind and no matter what I did to try to piece together the timeline it didn't make sense. I needed answers so badly, it felt like I would explode if I didn't get them. Jaehyun made me promise that I would hold them. An explanation would come eventually. I didn't believe him honestly.

We entered the conference room and Omega sat at the head of the large U shaped table like he did all those weeks ago. He was alone, which I thought was odd. He usually had the family with him. He looked up over the rim of his glasses when he noticed us. I shivered slightly at how much he looked like Jaehyun at that moment. It was scary. We bowed in respect, and he motioned for us to take a seat at his right and left side. He took the right, and I took the left. We sat in silence for what felt like an entirety before he spoke. "I want to congratulate you both on a job well done. A week isn't a bad time for completing an assignment, especially one as… *complex* as this." Omega chuckled slightly as he looked at us individually. My jaw clenched at the statement, and I looked down as I toyed with my fingers. I promised that I would relax, but the questions were gnawing at me. Was this a test? Was it to see where my loyalty would be? What was the reason for this, if it had already been handled? Was it to fuck with me mentally and emotionally?

"I know you all have some questions as to what happened and why I responded the way that I had." We nodded in response.

"In January of 2021, we were told that Sato Yua went missing. We agreed to stop the payments. Whatever happened during that year was none of our concern. That's true. We heard from Sato Haruto in January of this year. I lied there. He told us his wife's health was declining and it would likely deteriorate in the coming months. Haruto had been battling heart problems and things from the stress of everything. We agreed that when Kiyo died, the hospital and the doctors' offices would be sold to us. That happened in July of this year. The debt was settled." Omega explained as he folded his arms on the table. Remi ran away and didn't tell anyone. She probably made things worse for her parents by doing so, which led to the Satos reaching out to the Azi Kotetsu-kai to look for her. That depleted the money quickly. It was starting to make sense.

"Then why did you send us on this assignment? What was the reason? Was it to test Rose?" Jaehyun asked as he looked at me.

"It was for both of you really. I wanted to see how you two worked together under stressful situations. This required some thinking and research on your part, son. It was a test to see if Rose was ready and willing to cut old ties to her life. I'm certain that it caused you a lot of internal turmoil, but you survived it. This is only the beginning. It will get harder. The pruning and refining process is always the hardest. It's the messiest part. Consider this a win for you both. It's the first step into a promising future." Omega answered as he looked over at me. I felt lightheaded and on edge. What needed to be pruned and refined in me? How much did he know about me? Where was he getting this information from? Jaehyun's words echoed in my head. Be patient, the answer will come eventually. I tried to calm myself down and take solace in that.

"So, what's next? We did the initiation. Where do we go from here?" Jaehyun inquired.

"I'm going to set up your training program. Much has changed over the years, son. You'll need to catch up. Rose is new so she will need to learn as well. You'll be training with the family though. That's the best way, so we can find where you both fit in. I know you two wouldn't be able to stand being apart. So, I have to figure it out."

A training program? I groaned internally at that. I had enough training over my life. I was sick of it already. I tried to listen in on the conversation between Jaehyun and his father, but my mind kept wandering back to the statement he made about pruning and refining me. What the hell was he going to do with me? What did it mean? I felt my stomach twist uncomfortably and I felt nauseous. I could feel my control start to slip away again and I took deep breaths to center myself. Their conversation had become background noise. When I tuned back in, Jaehyun was shaking his father's hand and bowing in respect. I couldn't hold it anymore. I need answers. "Why was Remi sent to me? Did you have something to do with that?" I blurted out as I stood up quickly. Jaehyun gasped audibly and he stared at me blankly and then back at his father. Omega sighed and looked up at me.

"I guess we should talk before we officially begin our new business relationship," he suggested. He waved Jaehyun away and I saw the hesitation in his body. I needed this private conversation with Omega. I nodded that it was okay and Jaehyun bowed as he left the room.

"Did you send Remi to me? Did you send her to the Yakuza?" I repeated. He shook his head. "She found her own way there. Call it fate, destiny, the work of a higher power. She ended up under your leadership. A girl with no other choice." he replied as he watched me carefully.

"How much do you know about me?"

"Your reputation precedes you. Everyone in the underground world knows of the great Rose. You're a legend at a young age. It is well deserved, but it came as a great cost to you, I'm sure. I've known Han for a very long time. At one point long ago, we could have been what you called acquaintances. I watched power and rage consume him until it festered into what you know today."

"From my mother's death? Be honest with me. Jaehyun isn't here. Did you have my mother killed or did you send out the order? Did you do it yourself? You don't have to lie to save face." I asked him as my voice cracked slightly. I didn't know if I was really ready for the answer, but I braced myself for whatever would come. He looked at me with an unreadable expression. I couldn't tell if it was from my voice or something else. There was a fire in his eyes when I asked him about my mother. I couldn't decipher it. It was almost like he was defensive when I asked him.

"I did not. I had nothing to do with it at all. I wouldn't lie to you about that. You have my word. I have children of my own. I couldn't imagine someone taking their mother away. And if it was to happen, I'd want revenge. I can assure you that Han was the reason for your mother's death. I feel it. I meant when I said that I would help you figure out what happened to her." Omega pledged. I searched his eyes and body language to find something that would indicate he was lying. I saw nothing. Either he was telling the truth or he was a proficient liar and he learned how to control involuntary responses. I sighed in relief and nodded. I had no choice but to believe him for this to work. I remained quiet for a while as I thought about how to phrase the next question.

"Why did you offer Jaehyun a spot? Aren't you happy with where he is in life? Why did you let him uproot it?" I asked.

"Of course. He's my son. I will always be proud of him. I was always proud of him in everything that he did. He's done amazingly for himself. Whether he joined the ranks or not. But I know my son. I've had conversations with him about you. He was not going to let you join the ranks and he just sit on the sidelines. He's persistent. I just saved myself the headache, that's all." Omega chuckled as he shook his head. He had a point.

"Is that why you accepted me so quickly? Did you know?"

"Arsyn was the first one to suspect something. I heard her out and sent Iseul to meet you. Granted Iseul was already dying to meet you. She had to know who the woman was that made her youngest son so happy and think about a future other than school and owning businesses. She reads people well. That's why we match so well." Omega's eyes drifted to his wedding band as he smiled softly at the mention of her name.

It was actually endearing. He was human under all of the mystery and the bravado of being the strict Jopok head. "You know the one thing in life that I will never regret, Ms. Rose?" Omega said as he looked up at me and gave me a half smirk. I tilted my head in curiosity.

"Choosing to make the best out of a bad situation. Opening myself up to everything life could be despite what happened in the past. You'll be surprised by how much you grow."

"Why are you telling me that? What does that have to do with me?" I questioned.

"I told you. I read people well. It will probably make sense one day." Omega stood up slowly and I took a cautionary step back. He chuckled and stuck his hand out to me. I stared at it for a moment. It wasn't a threatening gesture, it seemed genuine but I couldn't be sure. At this point though, I had nothing else to lose. My title was gone, Japan wasn't good for me anymore and I felt lost in the world. What could go wrong? I shook his hand firmly and he smiled slightly. Before I left the room I remembered to ask one last question.

"What happened to Ace?" I inquired.

"Your partner? He's been sitting in a cell as a prisoner. I was content with keeping him there. What do you want to happen to him?" Omega answered as he looked down at some papers. I paused for a moment. If he was just going to be a prisoner then there was no need to worry him, right? I knew Ace though; he'd try to escape. That was a problem.

"Get rid of him. He'll try to escape eventually. He's been there long enough to have learned enough information to attempt. I don't want to risk it."

"We'll make it happen then." I nodded in thanks and turned to leave without another word.

I stepped out of the room and Jaehyun took a few steps away from the door. There was a slight grin on his face. "You and my dad are cool now?" He nudged me slightly.

"He's hard to read. I don't know how to take him. But I can see how him and Iseul are a perfect match. He has some of your qualities at

times. But I guess, it's a step in the right direction. We will see how it goes."
I smirked as I took his hand.

"A step in the right direction is sometimes all we need, you know?
It'll get harder from here on out with everything I have going on, but I
wouldn't want to do this with anyone else but you. And I really mean that."
I smiled at the confession and nodded in agreement.

"It's going to get harder for the both of us. Last minute vacation to
the Maldives again before shit gets serious?" I suggested.

"The Maldives? Of course, you'd choose something expensive.
Screw it, let's go. Work hard, play hard," Jaehyun smirked as he pulled me
into a surprise kiss before opening the doors for us.

Printed in the USA
CPSIA information can be obtained
at www.ICGtesting.com
CBHW072122120724
11509CB00025B/710